THE
FREEZER

DAVID A KERSTEN

To my good friend Terry

ISBN 1506181090
ISBN-13 978-1506181097

Dedicated to my mother.

CONTENTS

Part One

Darkness became light. He didn't comprehend it, it just was. Perhaps it hadn't been darkness, but rather a lack of anything at all. There was no understanding, no comprehension, no ability to ponder, and nothing but acknowledgement that where once there was nothing, now there was something. This went on for what could have been an eternity.

At some point, this acknowledgement of existence expanded, coalescing into thought. It started with one thought: *where*. This turned into other basic thoughts like why, how, what, and when. Slowly at first, then steadily building to a torrential pace, the questions flooded this newfound existence. Where am I? Who am I? Why am I here? Why can't I feel, or see, or smell? Did something bad happen? Am I dead? Is this Heaven? Is this hell? One after another the questions poured into his mind, increasing in complexity but none with any answers.

Each question didn't bring anxiety or stress, nor did it bring answers. Instead of the flood filling his mind, it created an expanse of emptiness that grew with each new question. As that emptiness grew, a vague sense of time began to form, just enough to bring a sense of urgency.

There was something there, just out of reach, perhaps a memory, but it was a phantom, a shadow, eluding his mental grasp, slipping away each time he tried to grab hold. He struggled to grab hold, hoping to fill the emptiness with something, anything other than another question.

He chased it for what could have been another eternity before the futility of the pursuit dawned on him and he gave up. The shadows were elusive, but the light was constant. His attention focused on the light, he reached toward it.

Chapter 1

Consciousness trickled into his mind, quickly at first, then rebounding softly to a place where dreams and reality were intermingled in a confusing mix of emotion, images, and even scents. The smell of her hair was replaced by the smell of warm, dry dust, the warmth of her presence by the chill of emptiness. The image of her face faded into the recesses of his memory, replaced by a soft pink glow. The tranquility of this memory was replaced with the cold knot of loss just below his heart. The reality of waking securely in his mind, he cracked open an eye.

Sunlight seared his retina, chasing away the last of the dream and snapping him to the present. He shut his eyes tightly and rolled over, his hand swinging up reflexively to ward off whatever had assaulted his eyes. Tentatively he opened them again to reveal his bedroom. The first rays of sunlight were peeking through the wood blinds, illuminating the dust swirling in the air from his attack and drawing lines of gold across the bed and up the opposite wall of the bedroom.

It was absolute now – he was in his bed, alone, and it was morning. The knot of anxiety eased as the memory of his dream faded, but it didn't go away completely. Part of him wasn't ready to start his day, and a part was simply unwilling. He lay there for another minute, searching his mind for a reason to just roll over and go back to sleep, but the bed, and his life, felt as empty as any excuse he could come up with. Worse, it was Monday.

The beginning of another week should hold the promise and potential of an unwritten life, but it was an empty promise these days. The bitterness of knowing the week would be filled with emptiness and loneliness created despair from optimism.

With a sigh, he threw the covers back, rolled off the bed, and planted his feet on the floor. The cold wood made him wince and hesitate once more. The bed might feel cold but it kept his feet warm. Scouting the floor with his toes, he searched for his slippers. He was as unsuccessful at locating them as he was at coming up with an excuse to stay in bed.

With resignation, he planted his bare feet on the cold floor and with a slight grimace, stood up. This wasn't a graceful move. Knees popped and his back groaned in protest, causing him to pause on his journey from horizontal to vertical. He spread his arms wide in an attempt to stretch his back, which nearly sat him back down as a sudden sharp pain caught him off guard. *Another night of sleeping on it wrong,* he thought to himself with a frown before making his way down the hall. There had been quite a few nights like that lately.

His morning ritual began in the kitchen with opening the electric percolator, pouring in a healthy scoop of coffee grounds, and filling it with water. Next was the bathroom, where he splashed cold water on his face in an effort to chase away the last remnants of sleep then ran the hot water to shave.

The mirror reflected a man who was at once both familiar and a stranger. His short dark hair was graying above his ears. The wrinkles between his eyes and around his lips certainly didn't help. He had been frowning a lot more lately, and it showed. Dark circles under his eyes betrayed his inability to get a solid night's sleep.

He examined the image in the glass as if trying to decide if it was a reflection or some kind of window to another room where another man stared back at him thinking the same things. The strong jaw, blue eyes, and slender (if slightly crooked) nose, were all features that hadn't changed much in the last two decades. The thin scar running from the corner of his right brow down the side of his face, where a series of smaller scars peppered his cheek and neck – compliments of a mortar round that had landed a little too close during his first tour in Korea – was a feature he had gotten used to over the years and felt familiar enough. The crooked nose brought back the memory of a fight at the age of fourteen. He decided, despite the signs of age, the man in the mirror was indeed himself.

Jenny used to say he was ruggedly handsome. He didn't exactly know what that meant, but he never seemed to have problems attracting women when he was younger. *Younger.* He wet a comb in the running water and ran it through his hair, frowning as the comb passed too easily through a thin spot on the top of his head. *I'll be forty before long,* he thought with a sigh. Scratching at his day old whiskers, he splashed the now hot water on his face and shaved.

For over twenty years, Jack would start each day with some pushups and sit ups, followed by a five mile run. He still ran occasionally, mostly out of habit and sometimes just to try to run away from the pain that lingered, but the rest of the exercises seemed pointless anymore. His interest in remaining fit was fleeting at best. The lack of exercise occasionally showed itself when he was buttoning his pants, but a lack of appetite and a job that didn't allow him to sit very often kept him pretty much within ten pounds of one-ninety.

After dressing, he made his way back to the kitchen, poured a hot cup of coffee and unplugged the percolator. The thought of his appointment this morning put a knot in his stomach just below the knot of anxiety in his chest, and the normally comforting beverage wasn't helping. After a few sips, he looked at his watch and poured the remaining coffee in the sink. If there was one thing he retained from all those years in the military, it was his dedication to being on time.

The beautiful, sunny morning was lost on him as he speculated on the upcoming appointment. With a grunt, he bent down to open the garage door. Most mornings he would pause at this point to admire the car sitting in the garage, maybe even brushing an imaginary speck of dust off the gleaming red paint. Today it was just a mode of transportation to get him to somewhere he didn't really want to go. Without hesitation, he slid behind the wheel.

A moment to get settled in the seat, two quick pumps of the gas pedal, and a quick flick of the key was all it took to get the well-tuned small block engine to fire to life. The deep rumble of the exhaust was a normally pleasing sound that, once again, went unnoticed. Pausing to let the engine warm up, he rested his forehead on the steering wheel and let his mind wander to the prior day's events.

~~~~

A small transistor radio was playing something new from the Beatles, the music rattling like tin from the small speaker. Jack didn't care much for the 'hippie rock-n-roll' but it was the only station the small radio would reliably pick up in the garage. He only knew the artists playing because the younger folk he worked around all had transistor radios either strapped to their equipment or hanging from a strap on their belt, and if they weren't talking about the girls they dated, they talked about the music. The only reason it played was to keep a rhythm going as he worked. With a sigh he rubbed the last of the dry wax off the cherry red paint. The August sun was out in full force promising another hot day, but it was early yet, only eleven a.m., and he was parked under the shade of a large tree. Despite the cool temperature and a nice breeze, he was still sweating. This kind of work wasn't all that strenuous, but there was a dull throbbing in his back, just above his belt. Stepping back from the car, he reached both arms out wide and with a groan arched his back to stretch. Not too many weeks past he could have waxed his car three times in a row without any pain at all. Either he was getting old or it was time to step up the morning exercises again.

He mopped at the sweat that beaded on his forehead like water on his freshly waxed paint. The pain subsided as he took a final deep breath then took a moment to admire the car. The 1965 Ford Mustang was the only thing he had really treated himself to since the accident. When he saw one sitting at the local Ford dealership, he impulsively pulled his 1958 four door Chevrolet, a gift he bought Jenny after the honeymoon, into the lot. After fifteen minutes of discussion with the salesman, he special ordered the car in cherry red with the race tuned V8 and three speed Cruise-o-Matic transmission. It took almost two months to arrive. To Jack, the car was a work of art; from the red paint to the white vinyl bucket seats. Every Sunday at ten a.m. he washed and waxed it in the driveway, unless it was raining or snowing, in which case he used a spray bottle and a cloth diaper to wipe it down in the garage. This was his ritual, his routine, the end result of twenty years of discipline in the army, and the neighbors could probably set their watch to it.

A sound worked its way into his conscience, interrupting his fascination with the freshly waxed thing of beauty in front of him. *Was that the phone ringing?* "Who the hell is calling on a Sunday?" he said out loud as he walked to the back door, which entered directly into the kitchen. "I'm coming, I'm coming," he mumbled impatiently to nobody in particular. He picked the phone up off its cradle and said, "Hello."

4

"Is this Jack Taggart?" A woman's voice.

Confusion best described his reaction – it was Sunday, and this didn't sound like a social call. "Uh, yes it is, how may I help you?"

"Please hold." There was a click and some music, like you would hear in an elevator. His heart rate elevated and his mind raced as he tried to figure out why someone's secretary was calling on a Sunday morning. *Military? Vietnam was heating up, and some retirees were being called back to duty. No, it couldn't be the military calling him, they wouldn't have hold music. That only left...*

"Jack, sorry to call you on a Sunday. I-" Bill Callun. His Doctor.

"Hi, Bill, how are you?" Jack interrupted, trying unsuccessfully to feign enthusiasm.

"Good, Jack, thanks for asking. Say, I got those blood test results and x-rays from your last visit, and," a small hesitation, "well, can you come in tomorrow morning first thing?" His already upset stomach gurgled, and his dry forehead started beading with sweat again.

More confusion, this time with a knot of anxiety forming in his chest. "Results? Bill, I... I don't understand." A little over two weeks ago, Jack had started suffering some indigestion and spasms in his lower back. Fearing it was maybe a kidney stone, he had gone to visit Bill. The doctor didn't find blood in his urine, a sure sign of a kidney stone, so he went ahead and gave him a full physical, took some blood and urine for some more tests, and even did a couple x-rays – just as a precaution of course. He was, after all, getting close to forty and it was a good idea to start paying a little closer attention to his health. Until now, he hadn't heard anything and figured it meant there was no problem. "Why are you calling on a Sunday for Christ's sake, and what is it you can't tell me over the phone?" Jack wasn't a particularly religious man, but he was irritated at the trend of businesses starting to remain open on Sundays. He could understand a grocery store being open on a Sunday afternoon, but certainly doctors weren't coming in to work on the day of rest.

"Look I'm sorry Jack, I was out of the office most of last week, and decided to come in to catch up on some work this morning, before hitting the golf course. The test results were waiting on my desk. I... well I didn't want to wait until tomorrow to call, you know how hard you are to reach at work, and I want to talk to you first thing in the morning about it." He *was* hard to reach at work, especially when he was on the job site.

"Uh... sure, I can be there." *Wait a second...* "Bill, why did your secretary call me? Don't tell me you dragged her in to work on a Sunday just to help you make a couple phone calls." Jack never missed a detail, and was pretty good at reading between the lines. It had helped him to be a good officer, being able to quickly read a situation, whether on the battlefield or when dealing with the bureaucratic bullshit the army is built on.

"Uh... I..." Bill stuttered for a moment, then went silent, then tried again. "She uh, knew I was going to come in to work, and um... needed the overtime." Jack didn't buy it for a second. There were rumors that Bill was nailing his secretary on the side, but nevertheless it still came as a shock. He was a doctor, and he had so much to lose – Kathy, and the kids... *Wow, what an asshole.*

"OK Bill, when do you want me to come by?" He said it like he no longer wanted to be on the phone.

Bill picked up on it, and hastily said, "Can you be here at nine?"

"I'll be there." Short again.

"Listen Jack, can we keep-" *Click.* He hung up before the doctor could finish. Bill's personal problems were none of his concern, and there were other things occupying his mind at the moment. *This can't be good,* he thought as he stood there staring at the phone on the wall. The sun had cleared the tree in the back yard and was now hitting the kitchen window full force. He opened a couple windows and the back door. Cool air breezed in and dried the sweat that had beaded back up on his forehead while he stood there pondering the nature of the call.

Still a bit bewildered, he stumbled to the refrigerator and pulled out a bottle of beer. Looking around for the bottle opener, he realized it was in the garage and headed that way. His stomach gurgled again, and he rubbed it even though he knew it wouldn't make the nausea go away. The alcohol wouldn't help either, but at least it could do something about this knot of anxiety. The bottle popped open with a hiss and he tossed the cap into a can he kept next to the bench. He took a swallow, and sat down on a stool.

Trying to make sense of it, he ran the conversation through his head a few more times. *It's gotta be bad if he won't tell me on the phone.* While he pondered the implications, his thoughts wandered, as they often did, to his wife. If that excavator hadn't broken down and cost him an afternoon wading through the mountain of forms to get another machine allocated to his crew, he may very well have never even met her. In fact, the more the thought about it, it seemed like everything good that happened in his life came about after some misfortune or other.

He finished the beer and tossed it in the bin with the other bottles he would return to the grocery store for deposit then set about cleaning the interior of the mustang. Anything to keep his mind off that phone call. He reflected on other unfortunate circumstances that brought the various good fortunes in his life. His first broken nose resulted in his first girlfriend. His opportunity to become an officer came from one very inept colonel calling in mortar fire on his position. The list went on and on, if he looked at things in the right light. In fact, the only bad thing that never seemed to bring about good fortune had been his wife and daughter's passing. In fact, he couldn't think of a single good thing that had happened in his life since that tragic day. He had to admit though, he hadn't been very open to enjoying life either, so perhaps he was just using that as an excuse to withdraw from the world and avoid anything that could lead to something good. Regardless, he hoped that whatever the bad news was this time, it would bring about something good in his life. He figured he was due.

Once the car was spotless, he started the engine and let it warm up. Just before putting the car in gear for his ritualistic post cleaning drive, he changed his mind and shut the engine off again. He had hoped that keeping busy would be a nice distraction, but it was no use. Every thought seemed to either lead back to the conversation with Bill or to his dead wife and daughter, and he couldn't get away from the feeling that Monday would once again bring bad news.

Chapter 2

Jack snapped out of his reverie and looked at the gauges. Everything looked good, so he put the car in reverse and backed out of the driveway. Bill's office wasn't far, and morning traffic in the small city of Great Falls, Montana was pretty much nonexistent. He didn't bother to turn on the radio. *They'll probably just be playing more of that hippie music,* he thought as he turned into the parking lot. He pulled up next to the doctor's car, a 1959 Chevy Bel Air four door with sea-foam green and white paint. It was very similar to the one he had traded in the year before. There was only one other car in the small lot, a 1963 Dodge Polara that looked like it hadn't been washed in a month. That was Bill's secretary. *The secretary.* "Dammit Bill, what the hell are you thinking," he mumbled to himself. As if his own problems weren't enough, it seemed the rest of the world was going to hell in a hand basket. If the Commies didn't attack, the hippies would end up turning this country into a socialist mess anyway. Even though he knew from experience that war was not a good thing, he couldn't help but think that maybe if some of these "new age" hippie type kids got a taste of the real world, they might see how great of a country we have, and stop trying so hard to change it. Pushing the thought from his mind, he opened the door to the small office building.

Music was playing softly in the background, but rather than the typical music one would hear in a waiting room, it was rock and roll. Not real rock and roll like Elvis or Buddy Holly, but more of this new stuff the hippies liked. It sounded like something from the Doors. *Figures,* he thought.

"Good morning Jack." The secretary stood up when he walked in, a nervous looking smile on her face. She was around twenty five years old, busty, blond, and, remembering the last time he was here, had a pretty nice ass too. Her dress was a yellow and orange flower print that was cut just low enough to show about two inches of cleavage and just high enough to expose a few inches of her thighs. Her bouffant hair was done up to perfection and her attractive face didn't need makeup, although like most girls her age she was wearing lipstick and a little too much eye shadow.

"Good morning." He put a fake smile on his face to match her nervous one. What he wanted to say was, "How are Bill's wife and kids?" That would be rude, though, and it really wasn't his business.

"I'll tell Bi... er... Dr. Callun that you're here." She blushed a little as she turned around. Jack watched her sway down the hall and thought to himself, *I can see the temptation, but damn, you've got three kids you stupid asshole.*

Jack loved his wife dearly, but she had been gone for almost two years now. Little things constantly reminded him of her, and every thought brought a little pain along with it. But the pain got a little less each day, and sometimes the memories contained joy instead of anxiety. For the past couple months he had been thinking it was time to get his life back on track. He figured the first step was finding a nice girl, preferably one he could settle down with. He was young and healthy, made damn good money, and was, as he had recalled that morning in front of the mirror, ruggedly handsome. *What's not to like?*

"Jack, you can go in now." He snapped back to reality, and when he regained focus, his eyes were pointing directly at her cleavage making it look like he was ogling her. He quickly looked away, probably making him appear even guiltier than he felt. Now it was his turn to blush. He stepped away from her without another word.

As he walked down the hall his mind went back to figuring out where he could meet a decent woman. These days there were plenty of young, loose women running around talking about 'free love', even here in the middle of Montana, but Jack wasn't interested in a roll in the hay with a hippie chick. *Well, a roll in the hay with that receptionist wouldn't be that bad,* he thought, but immediately chastised himself over it and unconsciously said a little word of apology to his wife who was probably listening in on his thoughts from above. *It's bad enough that Bill is diddling her.* His shame at the thought was also a little comforting on some level… At least he was still young enough to be attracted to the opposite sex. It had been two years since he had been with a woman, and he was still a man with all the natural urges a man has. The problem was, he seldom socialized, and he wasn't enough of a hypocrite to go to church *just* to try to meet a 'nice girl' either. He surmised it was probably a good thing he wasn't in a position to meet anyone, the guilt he felt for even thinking about it was still strong enough to keep him from actively looking.

As he entered Bill's office, his stomach gurgled again and his bowels felt a little loose. Normally confident under the most stressful of circumstances, he was facing the unknown, and courage wasn't about not being afraid, it was about taking the next step despite that fear. He recalled his earlier thought about being healthy. *God I hope so.*

Bill was sitting in his high backed office chair looking out the window. He spun the chair toward Jack, and gestured to a seat opposite him, across the desk. Before the doctor could get a word out, Jack, in the tone he used to address enlisted men, said, "Okay, Bill, I'm here. Now tell me *why.*"

"Please Jack, have a seat, this is… not going to be easy." Jack's stomach sank further, any hopes of this just being a visit that the doc is using to pad his bill going out the window. His military discipline kept him looking composed as he sat down. "I have the blood tests back from your last visit, and the x-rays too." Bill took out an x-ray and laid it in on the desk in front of Jack. He pointed to the middle of the film and said, "You see this white spot right here?" Jack looked down but was hesitant to focus on the dark film lying on the desk. He just stared at Bill, waiting for the bad news. Bill looked down at the file in front of him, then back up at Jack. "The indigestion isn't… well, I'm not going to bullshit you Jack, it looks like cancer."

A wave of shock followed by numbness washed through him from head to toe, leaving him feeling like he was in another room looking back at himself from a distance. He'd faced death dozens of times in Korea and lived to tell about it. He'd lost his wife and child, and survived long enough to try to put his life back together. He was a tough man, but those words sent fear and despair coursing through him. He was nearly paralyzed by the declaration, and he wasn't sure how long it was before he spoke. "Is it treatable?" he asked, practically holding his breath.

The doctor hesitated as if trying to decide what to say. "There are some things that Oncologists are trying with radiation and chemical therapy in Minnesota, but..." Bill shrugged. "Jesus Jack, of all the people this should happen to... Man, I am so sorry."

Jack started to speak, stopped, then started again. This time he couldn't keep the emotion out of his voice. "How... Are you... Are you sure this is cancer Bill?" The doctor just looked at him for a moment, then turned away and looked back out the window.

"I'm not a cancer doctor, so I'm sending the x-rays to a specialist in Rochester, Minnesota. The Mayo clinic has some good Oncologists. I'll know more in a few days."

Anger flared in Jack, and the words came out a little louder than he intended. "Come on Bill, you drag me in here to tell me in person and you can't even be sure it's cancer?!" He knew it wasn't the right response, but he couldn't help himself. He stood up and now he *was* yelling, "This is bullshit doc! What the hell kind of crap are you pulling here?"

Bill leaned back a little in his chair almost flinching, but it was obvious he expected Jack to get emotional and he held his composure. "Jack, I know this is hard, please calm down." His hands came up almost in a pleading gesture. "Look, I will tell you what I can but you need to calm down! Please!"

Jack sat down heavily. His mind wasn't working right. His reaction to the fear was to fight, but there was no enemy here. His heart was pounding and heat had flooded his face. Then all of a sudden, the numbness slammed back into him and he withered in his chair.

"Aww shit! I'm... Geez I'm sorry doc... It's just... SHIT!" He was looking down at his hands as if some answer might be there. He could feel the weight of depression and despair starting to push down on him again. He opened his mouth, but nothing came out, so he just sat there, staring at his hands.

"Look, Jack, I'll tell you what I know, but we'll have to wait until I hear back from the Mayo Clinic before I can give you a definite answer. I want to do a biopsy and send them a sample so we can be sure. Let's schedule it for Wednesday." Bill jotted something on the calendar that lay flat on his desk, then looked Jack in the eye. "Jack, if I wasn't damn sure, I wouldn't have dragged you in here like this." Jack studied Bill and something told him the man was right. "Like I said, they're doing some things with radiation and chemicals now. It's no picnic, but at least you can fight it. If you just decide to give up I don't think you'll last six months." Bill attempted to look encouraging, then, knowing it wasn't working, slumped down in his chair. "I'm really sorry Jack."

Jack looked up at him, but the only words he could find were, "What time on Wednesday?"

Chapter 3

He was back to the void and nothingness. If he had a body, he would be gasping for breath and sweating, but if he had a body, he couldn't feel it. There was only the knowledge of existence and now a memory. And that memory had been so vivid it was as if he was there again. At the same time though, it felt foreign and detached, more like he had been a puppet in a play.

As he pondered what it meant, he realized that the re-living of that day brought back a lot of the background memories leading up to it. Before, he was just aware of *being*; now he was aware of his *life*. Did this mean he was dead? Maybe he was sick from the cancer and this was all just a side effect. Or maybe it had killed him. Perhaps the answer was in the memory. He focused again, and after a time, his consciousness shifted back to that day.

~~~~

The rest of the day, Jack went back and forth from his garage to his living room, drank a few beers, listened to the radio a bit, and even went for a cruise in his car, but his mind and heart were elsewhere. He went to bed early that night, after attempting to eat a little dinner. Sleep was as far away as his appetite, and mostly he lay there thinking about Jenny and Ally. It would be two years in January...

~~~~

Jack had hit the twenty year mark back in July, and with the war brewing in Vietnam, he decided to get out while he still could. He had joined the army at age 16 using a forged birth certificate he bought from a guy he worked with at a local garage. He did it to get away from his foster family, and just like any teenage kid he was hoping to get a chance to fight the Germans or Japanese before the war ended. By the time he got out of training, the war was pretty much over. He made it to Germany in time to help liberate some death camps, but he never saw any real action in Europe. He re-enlisted after his first four years, and a year later, he went to Korea. Jack was good at being a soldier, his bravery earned him a reputation as a fearless soldier and a nickname "Mad Dawg" which befit his ferocity when things got intense. It turned out he was a good leader as well.

During that second tour, the commanding officer of his battalion, a fairly young lieutenant colonel, made a series of mistakes that killed half of Jack's platoon, including the platoon's officer, and nearly cost Jack his life. Injured from the friendly mortar fire, he somehow managed to take charge of the situation, not only completing his platoon's mission objective, but also thwarting a flanking maneuver by the enemy that would have trapped the lieutenant colonel and his staff, and quite possibly result in his capture or death. Almost two hundred men lost their lives in that one battle, and another hundred were injured. Naturally, there had been an inquiry, and Jack "Mad Dawg" Taggart was awarded a silver star for his actions that day. Knowing the commanding officer's career could hinge on how Jack responded to the inquiry, he played his cards right and squeezed the young colonel for a nomination to OCS, Officer Candidate School. He returned to Korea as an officer, leading a platoon in several successful missions before the war ended. He reached the rank of Captain before retiring, which gave him a decent retirement check.

His last post was Fort Carson in Colorado, where he met his wife, Jennifer Williams. After High School, Jenny had moved to Denver to get away from the family farm. She ended up landing a job as a secretary on the military base in Colorado Springs, shuffling documents all day. She hated it more than farming and after six years, was about to give up and move back home when she met Jack. Some equipment had broken down on the job site Jack had been managing, and he was trying to get some requisition paperwork pushed through to keep the job on track. Jenny was the one who ended up helping him. There was no question in Jack's mind that she would be his wife one day, and after two months, they were engaged to be married. Eleven months after they said their vows, she gave birth to Allissa Mae Taggart.

His last seven years in the military were mostly spent overseeing construction of a secret fallout shelter near Fort Carson, and that gave him the experience to get a job as a consultant to a civil engineering and contracting firm after retirement. Jenny was from Montana, near the city of Great Falls, and the new job allowed for them to move up there and be closer to her mother. With the combined income from the army and the consulting job, they were easily able to buy a house right away.

Christmas 1964 was as idyllic as it could be. The fireplace was crackling with flaming pine logs, the Christmas tree was dazzling with ornaments and tinsel, and three stockings were hanging from the mantel, one for Jack, one for Jenny, and one for Ally. It was a prosperous year for them, and the Christmas gifts reflected it. Jenny got a stunning pair of diamond earrings, and Ally got more toys than any child should have.

The next few days were picturesque. The sun was shining, the trees and ground blanketed with a few inches of snow, and with a few days off, Jack got to enjoy some lazy mornings in bed with his wife while Ally played upstairs with her new toys. His job often meant he was out of town, and he cherished this time with both his wife and his daughter. Life simply could not be better.

The following Monday, they headed out of town to visit Jenny's mother, Mabel. Jenny was younger than Jack by about five years, she would be thirty years old that summer, and Mabel was still a young woman when Jenny was born. Mabel's husband had died in a farming accident when Jenny was nine years old, and despite still being very young, she never remarried. Most of her time was spent running the farm, which she was good at, but occasionally she had tried to date other men over the years. Usually, the men she dated were only after her farm, and the rest were deadbeats. She was smart enough to recognize this, so for the last ten years she had avoided relationships altogether. There were some rumors that one of the farmhands warmed her bed once in a while, but otherwise she seemed content to be alone.

Jack, Jenny, and Ally spent the week at her farm house, and on Friday afternoon, Jack headed back to town to go to work. There was a new project near the airbase that his firm was working on, and Saturday was the only time the engineers could get out there to survey the site with Jack. Jenny was going to catch a ride back to town with one of Mabel's farm hands on Sunday.

The night she and Ally returned it was bitterly cold, as it can get when the January wind is blowing hard in Montana. The temperature was easily ten degrees below zero, and flurries of snow were swirling around in the wind. The snow on the roads that had been soft in the recent sunny days turned to rock hard ice. The accident was nobody's fault really, it just happened. The car slid off the road and dropped into an embankment, and it was the next day before anyone found them. The driver was killed on impact, Jenny and Allissa probably died from exposure before their injuries had a chance to claim them.

Monday after work, Jack returned to his house to find a patrol car out front. He didn't think it unusual when he pulled up, as the officer, Frank, was an old school friend of Jenny's who used to help out on her family's farm. Jack figured he was just there to visit his wife. Frank was a good man with a wife and two kids of his own, and Jack never felt threatened by their friendship. When he pulled into the driveway, Frank got out of his car and walked up to him. "Jack," he said, "I have some terrible news."

~~~~

Sometime in the early hours of dawn he finally found sleep, but it didn't last long. At seven a.m. he was up and showered. He had so many things to do, and he felt as if he were now racing against a clock. In Korea, there had been times when he was sure he would be dead before the sun rose again, but even in those cases, there were always things that needed to be done. The military had taught him to work through the fear, and that discipline drove him this morning. The first order of business was to contact Mabel.

He hadn't talked to her in almost a year. It wasn't anything she had done or said to him, he was just trying to put that part of his life behind him. It was an attempt to ease the pain that was there all the time, and while it gave him little reprieve, he stuck to it, not wanting to add to the pain by opening that door again. There wasn't really any other family in his life, and he needed someone to take care of whatever was left after he was gone. His parents died when he was in Middle School, and not long after that he joined the military. There were no brothers or sisters, and both his parent's families were small; a couple distant cousins and uncles but nobody he had kept in contact with over the years. In the military, he'd had buddies, but many died, and after getting his commission, he just didn't quite fit in with either the enlisted men or the traditional officers. Furthermore, the secret nature of the projects he worked on the last few years forced him to be somewhat of a loner. The phone rang seven times before there was an answer. "Where the hell are you Dick!" Mabel didn't get too many calls at the farm, and obviously she wasn't expecting any calls out of the ordinary.

"Mae, it's Jack, how are you?"

Mabel paused for a second, recognizing that it was not Dick on the other end of the phone. "Jack! My goodness! Sorry about the way I answered, my field hand was supposed to be here over an hour ago with the winter seed and... anyway, it's good to hear from you, I was worried, it's been a while." Mabel and Jack had always gotten along very well, and just hearing her voice was comforting. However, it also amplified his sense of loss, and emotions started welling up.

He swallowed hard, trying to wash down the emotion and keep his voice steady. "Not so good Mae, that's why I'm calling. Look, I uh, I went to the doctor a couple weeks ago, and it turns out I'm – well, I'm sick."

He could almost hear her heart drop into her stomach. Her next words were quiet and cautious. "Oh my God! Jack! What is it?"

"Mae, it's..." As hard as he was trying not to, his voice caught. He swallowed again, paused, and finally said, "they *think* it's cancer."

There was a long pause, and Jack wished he had just driven out to the farm to break the news face to face. "Oh Jesus! Oh Christ, no... no Jack... That's... That's just awful." More silence as neither of them quite knew what to say.

"Mae look, I don't know everything, yet. I have to go in for a surgery tomorrow to see how bad it is. I... I don't have any family that matters to me Mae, Jenny and Ally were all I had, and with them gone-"

In a very motherly tone, Mabel interrupted, "Jack, you don't even have to ask, I will come up to see you to the hospital, you know that."

He didn't expect that and quickly said, "No, uh... that's not why I was calling. You see, I don't have anyone else to uh... to pass on my belongings to and..."

"Oh hogwash! You quit talking that way! It's not over until you die, and you're a fighter. Always have been, Mad Dawg, so don't give up until you draw your last breath." Despite the circumstances, Jack smiled at her use of his nick name. Mae was indeed a tough woman and knew how to push his buttons as well. He blinked away what might have been the start of a tear, feeling new resolve.

"I know, Mabel. But I'm just being honest with you: if this is it, I want to be prepared. Look, I make a decent living, and I have a little money. Since Jenny... Well, I – aside from a car, I haven't spent much money, and it seems a waste just to give it to some charity or worse, some doctors."

Her voice softened, "Tell me straight, Jack, are you giving up here or are you going to try treatment?"

"I don't know what my options are yet Mae, and from what I do know so far, it doesn't look pleasant. This is difficult. I still feel fine. I only went in to see the doc because I was getting a little indigestion and my back was hurting."

15

"Jack, let's just wait until the doctors tell you exactly what your options are." Mabel was now taking charge of the situation, something she had done all her life. Jack was a military officer, used to being in charge, but it dawned on him that maybe he had called her because he needed someone else to take the reins for a little while. "When do you go in for your surgery? Tomorrow? I'll come in to town and drive you there." It was settled, and Jack knew it, but he wasn't giving up control quite yet.

"Mae, that isn't necessary, I can handle it myself,"

"Bullshit Jack, you'll need a ride home anyway, and there's no reason you have to try to do this alone. I'll be there in a couple hours." *Well so much for keeping control.*

With feigned resignation, Jack said, "Okay Mae, I'll have the guest room ready for you."

~~~~

The next call was to his boss, Phil Norland. Jack had been working for Phil since retiring from the military. His official title was "Coordination Consultant", but really he was more like a general contractor, and unofficially, second in command to Phil. When it came to work, their relationship was professional. Before Jennifer's death, Phil and his wife were frequent guests at Jack's home, but these days there was just the occasional beer after work. If Jack could call someone his friend, it would be Phil, but like Mabel, he had neglected to spend much time with him outside of work.

After explaining the situation, it took Phil a minute to speak.

"Oh Christ, Jack, this is just awful news." He sighed heavily, "I can't even tell you how sorry I am to hear this. You take all the time you need and keep me up to date on what the doctors have to say. If you need anything, don't even hesitate to call. Theresa and I will be there for you." The sincerity in his voice made Jack feel guilty for not being a better friend lately.

"Thanks Phil, I appreciate it. I'll let you know as soon as *I* know something." Jack was about to hang up, but he sensed Phil was going to say something more.

"Uh, Jack..." There was a long pause. "Uh... never mind, we can talk about that later. Call me if you need anything."

Jack hung up, curious what that last exchange was about. He worked in an odd business, and a lot of what went on was not supposed to be talked about. The latest job was, like most of their projects, for the military. Technically it was for some big corporation, but no corporation in the U.S. had a need for a multi-billion dollar underground bunker. Jack had a high security clearance within the army the last few years before retirement which was sort of a prerequisite for building secret bunkers and it played into the importance of his role with the firm. Still, they never knew exactly what they were building, or at least Jack wasn't privy to it. The current project started the weekend his wife and daughter died, and the progress in the last twenty months had been good. Whatever the purpose of the project, it required a lot of room underground. For all he knew though, they were just making another big bomb shelter. With the nuclear threat from the Communists, bomb shelters and underground bunkers were good business these days. For many, it was just a matter of time before the "cold war" turned into a real war.

After getting the guest room ready for Mae, he spent some time thinking about all the projects he had either worked on personally, consulted on, or knew about during his time both in the military and working for Phil. He was confident that if the missiles ever did fly, humanity would survive, but God help us if it ever happens. It was a morbid thought, but anything was better than thinking about the cancer.

Chapter 4

The memory was as vivid this time as the last, down to what he had felt and what he had been thinking deep in his mind at the time. There was still a sense of disconnection there, but it was no longer quite as strong. He still didn't feel much, and that extended to emotions. The constant light source betrayed nothing. He was beginning to think he was indeed dead, and this was the afterlife. There was still a vague sense of time, but deprived of all senses, it had little meaning. With nothing else to do and a lot of emptiness still left to fill, he focused on the memory once again.

~~~~

Wednesday morning, Mae drove Jack to the hospital. The surgery was going to require he be put under for about an hour, and because of the anesthesia, it needed to be performed in the hospital as opposed to Bill Callun's office. They drove Mae's car instead of the mustang. She thought the mustang was too fancy to drive, and too loud. "If I wanted to drive a race car I would go to the race track," she said. Jack really didn't care either way. His mind was focused on the next few hours.

"Mae listen, I know this is just a formality and all, but here is a power of attorney for my belongings, just in case..." He handed her an envelope.

"In case of what? They're gonna knock you out, go inside you, cut off a piece of your liver, stomach, and kidneys, and put it in a bottle, then wake you up... You aren't going to the gallows or nothing like that Jack."

He smiled and said, "I know, Mae, but you never can tell with these things. I've seen my share of surgery gone wrong. I'm sure everything will be okay, but like I said, *'Just In Case'.*"

Mae shook her head and took the envelope and muttered something about "always prepared". Jack just smiled and sat back. She really was a good woman, and obviously she cared about him. Jenny and Jack were married for over six years before the accident, and during that time, Mae was the closest thing Jack had to a mother. "Mabel, I feel bad that I haven't stayed in touch. I guess I thought that seeing you would be too hard, but I was wrong. Thanks for being here for me." She just nodded and started looking for a parking spot.

~~~~

"Okay Jack, I'm going to put you under now, and when you wake up you might have a headache and feel groggy. That'll be normal. It might also take you a little while to remember where you are. Once you are coherent again, we will tell you how things went. You will probably be able to go home after a few hours, but you will need to take it easy for a couple days. Just relax and don't worry, this will be over quickly. See you in a couple hours." Jack nodded to Bill as the anesthesiologist injected him with the anesthetic.

"I thought you used ether to knock him out?" Mae asked the doctor.

"Not these days, now you have all sorts of intravenous anesthetics available. Ether was too volatile. It blew up too many patients, so they developed better stuff." Bill said it with a smile.

"Wow, the technology these days, it's amazing isn't it?" Mae shook her head in wonder.

"Indeed it is, Mae, indeed it is." It was the last thing Jack heard as he drifted off.

~~~~

The memory faded out one last time. It no longer felt distant and disconnected. It actually felt like he was beginning to wake from a dream. He blinked and the world flashed dark. This was new. He closed his eyes, and darkness settled in. Perhaps he wasn't dead. For the first time since awareness came to him, he began to *feel*. The realization that he was still in a body was a relief, and he settled back into sleep.

~~~~

"Can you hear me?"

"He's starting to come around, Doc. You really performed a miracle this time."

"Only time will tell."

~~~~

The veil of unconsciousness slowly lifted and Jack opened his eyes. He blinked a few times in an attempt to clear away the foggy haze that not only covered his mind, but also seemed to surround everything in his line of sight. As his mind cleared, the confusion built. He became aware of somebody next to his bed. "Jenny, is that you?"

"Just relax; your vision will take time to start working right. How do you feel?" A man's voice. *Why did I think it was Jenny?* He tried to will himself to think clearly. The sharp memory of Jenny's death came back to him and faded just as quickly.

"Where am I? Who... where am I?" The disorientation would not go away any more than the blurry vision. Even his own voice didn't sound right to his ears, and not just because he was slurring his words, it just felt... off. "What the hell is going on?" Memories threaded their way into his consciousness, and he tried to grab hold of one that would explain where he was. The cancer, the biopsy, the surgery... *Surgery!* "Bill?? I can't see shit here." He tried to sit up but his arms didn't seem to respond to his commands.

"It will take some time for your eyes to work properly. Your muscles too. Just relax and try to get some sleep." A hand patted his shoulder.

19

He started to relax and sink back into slumber but something plucked at his brain and he tensed up again. "Wait... what do you mean, my eyes – what are you talking about? Bill, you said I might be groggy and disoriented, not that I wouldn't be able to move or see!"

"He thinks he's just had surgery. Do you think the freezer burn was too great?" A woman's voice.

The figure next to him moved away and in a fading whisper, "No, I think we are safe. Now let's let ..." The voices were gone.

What the hell is going on? "Wait, come back!" But the voices didn't return. He tried to focus, to use his senses to gain an understanding of where he was and why he was here, but nothing seemed to work quite right. He couldn't move, couldn't see, and the air tasted horrible, musty and old. Something nagged at him, but he couldn't put his finger on it. He felt like he had just been dreaming about being dead but like all dreams, he had already lost most of the memory of it. He looking around again but it felt like gauze was covering his eyes.

He focused on feeling, as if that was something new to him. He could feel the weight of gravity holding him down, and even felt a little chilly. But something wasn't right. Primarily, there was a distinct absence of pain. *Am I paralyzed?* he asked himself. *No, I feel cold in my feet, and the weight of the blanket on me, and the tubes attached to my arms. I even feel a little hungry, but no pain, no nausea.*

It was unexplainable and incredibly different from how his mind was telling him he should feel. *It's the anesthesia, it has to be. I am still loopy from the stuff they gave me. Just go to sleep, it will all be clear when the drugs are out of my system.* With that, he finally relaxed and sank into a deep slumber.

Chapter 5

Consciousness came slowly. Jack looked around and blinked a few times. Everything around him had a haze like he was looking through a foggy glass window. He tried to wipe at his eyes but his arm just flopped up and smacked him in the forehead. "Ouch." Closing his eyes and focusing his thoughts, he tried to will his memories to the surface. *Hospital. Cancer. Biopsy. Okay, I'm in a hospital, after a surgery.* He remembered waking up and being confused; something about a doctor saying vague things about his eyes, something about some really weird dreams. "Man those must have been some crazy drugs they gave me." He was talking out loud but he didn't realize it.

He went through sort of a mental checklist of his body parts. *Toes? Check. Fingers? Check. Legs? Check. Arms? Check. Body? Check.* He wiggled his toes, or at least he thought he did... it felt right. He wiggled his fingers and felt something on his forehead. His hand was still there from when he tried to rub his eyes, and his fingers were wiggling. "Okay, that's a little odd." He said it to himself, out loud again. He tried to move his arm, and it flopped off his head back to his side, feeling numb as if he had been laying on it all night, but without the pins and needles. He could control individual joints like his fingers or his elbow but when he tried to coordinate more than one thing he felt... disconnected.

What is the problem here? Did something go wrong with the surgery and put me in a coma for a while? He had read an article in Life magazine about a lady coming out of a coma after ten years and not being able to move. Something about muscle atrophy. That would explain a lot.

But then he noticed how... *good* he felt. There was no other word to describe it. He felt good. There was no pain, no upset stomach. It wasn't until that moment that he realized how much pain he had suffered the last few months. The sore back, the indigestion, the sudden spasms of pain during normal tasks – all were symptoms of the cancer eating away at him, but they had come on so gradually that he hadn't even noticed when the symptoms started. Only in the absence of the pain did he realize how much he had been suffering. *Why was the pain gone?*

"Well, I see you are awake." The voice startled him. His eyes were closed and he had been concentrating so hard on what was going on with the inside of his body that he hadn't even heard the man walk in. The voice sounded familiar, perhaps it was the same one he had heard the first time he woke up.

He opened his eyes again and tried to focus on the speaker. It was indeed a person, and the size and shape of the body confirmed that it was a man, if the voice hadn't already given that away. He could tell the man had dark hair, but his face was still a blur. He blinked a few more times ineffectively.

"Do not be concerned about your vision, it will come in time." *Who was this guy?* He talked... different.

"Where am I? Who are you? Why can't I move?" The questions just fell out of his mouth before he even realized he was talking, and without effort, he was already getting frustrated. He wanted to know where he was and what had happened to get him here.

"Relax, I will answer all your questions in time, but for now I would like to ask you a few things. Let's start with your name. Do you remember your name?"

Jack was now convinced that he had been in a coma. Something had gone wrong during the biopsy, or maybe he was in an accident later and had some amnesia. "Of course I remember my name, the question is, why don't you know it? Where am I?"

"Please, I am trying to... judge your mental condition."

"Hell, I'm starting to question my mental condition myself. My name is Jack. Now can you *please* tell me where I am?" The frustration was turning to anger.

"If I told you where you are you would only be more confused. My name is Teague. Do you have a surname?"

Surname? Oh, last name. "Uh, yeah, Taggart, Jack Taggart. What do you mean I'll only be more confused? Am I still at Deaconess Hospital, or was I moved?"

"Jack, there is much to explain and some of it will be... difficult to grasp. If you can let me get my questions out of the way, I can maybe start to shed some light on the, um, situation."

Jack thought about this for a moment. What was the harm in answering a few questions, maybe then they will tell me where the hell I am and how I got here. "Okay, ask away, but at least tell me if the surgery went bad or something."

"Surgery... right. Tell me, Jack, What is the last thing you remember, besides waking up here?" During his twenty years in the military, Jack had met many different doctors, from field medics and surgeons that fixed people's bodies to the psychologists and psychiatrists that worked on their minds. This guy felt more like a head shrink than a medical doctor. Jack didn't care much for the head doctors, and the fact that he was ignoring Jack's questions did not help.

"Uh, well, I remember my doctor telling me that I would feel disoriented when I woke up, and that I might have a headache. Then I woke up here and you told me I would be confused if you answered my questions, and you must be right because by not telling me anything, you cleared everything up just perfectly, Doc." Jack tended to get a little sarcastic when he got frustrated. "Tell me, Teague, *are* you a doctor?"

If Teague heard the sarcasm, he either didn't recognize it, or he ignored it. "Yes, Jack, I *am* what a Doctor of sorts. My specialty is more along the lines of working on people's brains though." *Bingo!* "Can you go back a little further and tell me more about what you remember? I don't need details, just generalities."

Jack suddenly got the feeling this was an interrogation. The whole situation was so alien, all of his internal alarms were worthless – *everything* was ringing alarms in his mind. *Well, if this is an interrogation, I'm fucked anyway, I don't know shit.* He sighed. "I was going in for a biopsy. My mother-in-law drove me to the hospital, and they put me in bed and then gave me the anesthesia. Now please answer my question, did something go wrong with the surgery?"

Teague appeared to be writing in a notebook, as far as Jack could see. And without looking up, he said, "The first biopsy? No, you lived through that surgery."

"That surgery? Doc, you aren't making any sense, does that mean I've been through more than one? Did something happen that gave me amnesia? I feel like some time passed since then, because the last thing I remember..." Confusion, frustration, and adrenaline caused him to try to sit up, which was not entirely successful. Actually, all he managed to do was flop his arms around a little.

"Jack, take it easy!" Teague placed a palm on his chest and held him down, although it was not really necessary. "You are in no condition to try to get up!"

Jack took a deep breath to calm down. He was angry again and he knew that anger would not help him to get the answers he wanted. He needed to have his wits about him. After a few more deep breaths he said, "Okay doc, I won't try that again, but you have to start being honest with me. What in HELL is going on?"

"Jack, I need to tell you some things that will be difficult to hear, and your first reaction will be disbelief, but bear with me please. Once I have told you these things, hopefully I will be able to answer some of the questions you have. In the meantime, I want you to spend some time trying to move your fingers and toes. You need to teach your brain how to move again. Now before I get started, are you hungry?"

Chapter 6

After a meal of something that resembled sawdust mixed with Jello, washed down with water that tasted somewhat of dead fish and old motor oil, Jack started to feel human again. Despite the sensation of his body suspended in thick grease, he felt better than he had since, well, since before he could remember. His mind was incredibly clear, and his vision was clearing up every minute. Most things were still out of focus, but he felt like he was picking up details that he never would have noticed before.

"Well Jack, how are you feeling?" Teague walked into the room, holding what Jack had thought was a notepad but now was looking... well, not as much like a notepad. It appeared to be piece of mirrored glass a little less than a quarter inch thick.

"Better Doc. Say, what is that thing you are writing on? It doesn't look like paper."

Teague looked down at the object and after seeming to ponder the question for a moment, said "It's just a fancy clipboard," and sat down in a chair near the bed, crossed his legs, and placed the clipboard on his lap which obscured it from Jack's vision. "Your vision seems to be improving, that is great."

Jack just gave him a flat look and shrugged. He knew an evasive answer when he heard one, and obviously there were things this man was going to hide from him.

Teague continued, "Okay, I have done this more than a few times, but I suspect it will be more difficult with you. Let me start with what I know about you. You are Jack Taggart, born April 23rd 1928 in Bakersfield, California. Joined the military July, 1944. Married Jennifer Williams in July, 1958. Gave birth to a daughter, Allissa Taggart in 1959, Retired from the military July 1964. Diagnosed with Cancer August 1966. You are six feet, two inches tall, black hair, blue eyes, Caucasian. Is all that correct?"

"You left out 'ruggedly handsome'." He meant it sarcastically, he felt a dangerous mood coming on, and was ready to start being just as evasive in his answers. If he could have seen clearly, he would have caught the look of amusement on the doctor's face. "Can you sit the bed up so I can see you better?"

Teague reached across and worked some unseen controls, moving the bed up to a sitting position. "Thank you. Now, tell me where the hell you got that information. Aside from my mother-in-law, there is nobody alive, other than me, who knows all that." Most of that information would be pretty easy to find, but one small detail revealed something that even the military didn't know about him. "Did you hire a private investigator to find all that information? Or do you work for the military?"

Teague smiled a little. "Jack, come on, I told you I would answer all your questions as we go. If it helps, then you could say that I am involved in the military in some capacity. That is where I got your records."

That explained a lot, but he still didn't feel like he could trust this guy, there was still something he was hiding. Jack filed it away for later. "Does all this have to do with the project I was working on for the military?"

Teague looked down at his 'clipboard' and appeared to be drawing circles on it. After a moment he looked up and said, "Jack you are a very perceptive person. That's a good thing. Your mind is functioning very well, which tells me a lot. Once again, to answer your question in a way you can understand, I would say, yes, this does indeed have something to do with the project you were working on for the military, but it is not relevant to the current situation, nor is it relevant to the information I am about to give you. Shall I continue?"

His frustration was building, this man was being evasive and not completely honest, and Jack didn't know why. But it was clear that he wasn't going to be able to control the conversation, and so far nobody else had shown up with any answers. He sighed in resignation. *Best to let the man just speak his piece.* "Okay doc, let's have it."

Teague stood up nervously, looking as if he were struggling to find the words, which was another irritation as the man had been beating around the bush for so long already. He paced back and forth from one end of the bed to the other. "Okay, what I am about to tell you will be a shock, and might be hard to take."

Jack's chest bounced once as he laughed derisively, "Doc, two days ago I was told I have cancer, and it was pretty obvious that I wasn't going to survive it for very long. My wife and kids are dead, I am dying, and I just woke up in a room that smells like a basement, I can't move, I can barely see, and I haven't seen anyone I know or trust yet. I can't think of a situation that could be any worse than this, and you think that you can say something that will be hard for me to take?" He hadn't intended to just explode like this but the frustration had peaked very quickly.

Teague took it all in and if anything, it seemed to bring him to a conclusion. "Okay, you want it straight, here it is. In 1967, you died as a result of the Cancer that spread through your body."

Chapter 7

Time seemed to stand still for perhaps ten seconds. Then, like a blast from a shotgun, the irritation exploded into anger. "Oh Christ! What kind of bullshit are you talking about now! Dammit, you said you were going to give me answers, and all I am getting from you is evasive responses and now some kind of cockamamie joke!" He nearly fell out of the bed trying to reach out and grab the man and throttle some sense into him, which only served to frustrate him more. With a roar he shouted out, "Goddammit! Is someone out there who can tell me what the hell is going on!"

Teague stood at the end of the bed, passively watching Jack lose control. He didn't react to the outburst, and even looked like he expected it. He resumed pacing. "Jack, please, I understand your frustration, and given your circumstances I can see that you are going to have an incredibly difficult time coming to grips with this."

This fueled his anger even more. "Bullshit doc! Look, I wake up in a room I have never been in, surrounded by people I have never met, I can't see, I can't move, and now you're trying to tell me I'm dead! Tell me that I was in an accident and I was in a coma, tell me something went wrong with my biopsy and I didn't wake up for a few months, but don't sit here and tell me that I'm dead... how can I even talk to you if I'm dead?!" He shouted out again, "Hey! I need some GODDAMN ANSWERS IN HERE!"

Teague sighed heavily, and stopped pacing for a moment. "Please Jack, calm down. If you don't calm down I will have to sedate you and let you rest for a bit. I can explain this to you if you want to listen."

From the doorway to the room, just out of Jack's line of sight, a woman's voice said "Doc, do you want me to bring a sedative?"

"No, that won't be necessary, will it Jack?"

The voice was like ice water on his rage, cooling it instantly and allowing a chance to get himself under control. He sat there panting from the tirade, shaking from the adrenaline, and started counting slowly to ten in his head. By the time he reached ten, he had not only taken control of his emotions once again, but also started analyzing the situation. He really had little choice here. He was practically an invalid, and aside from the woman outside the room, there was only one person he could get answers from. But despite the anger cooling, he wasn't ready to start believing this man. "Am I in a loony bin? Is that it? I went nuts and you are just another kook trying to mess with my mind?"

"Jack I can assure you that you are not crazy, even though it might very well seem that way. If you let me explain, it will start to make sense." Teague was incredibly calm this entire time. *Either he's had a lot of practice laying this lame prank on other people or he thinks he's telling the truth.*

The adrenaline spent, he suddenly felt the weight of the situation on his shoulders. It pushed him down into the bed as if it was a physical weight. He realized he was acting like a hot-headed kid, and that thought sobered him up a little. He sternly said to himself, *you're a military officer, Taggart, start acting like one!* This guy obviously wasn't going to go away, so he might as well humor him. He took a few long slow breaths, and said in his 'officer' voice, "Okay, continue."

"Tell me Jack, do you know what DNA is?"

Jack shrugged, thought for a moment, then said, "Yeah, I read an article in Life about it." The outburst of anger had somehow relieved the pressure of the frustration and anxiety he had felt just minutes before, and with that gone he was starting to feel like he could put up with this guy's BS long enough to maybe get some answers.

Teague's brow wrinkled as he looked down at his clipboard, scribbled something, then said, "Ah... Life magazine, Okay. Well, DNA is the biological 'blueprint' that all life is based on. It contains all the information about how your body is built, from the way the cells form for your heart, to the color of your eyes. Are you following me so far?"

Jack rolled his eyes and said, "Yes, I follow. Like I said, I read an article on it. Scientists said that it will prove that Darwin was right and that all living things evolved." Jack rolled his finger signaling for him to continue.

"Yes. Well, in the – um, let's just say that at some point in time, scientists figured out that by using DNA, they could re-create an organism that was already alive. Make an exact duplicate. They called it 'cloning' and they had some success in proving that it worked. However, for many years, it was considered immoral to try to recreate God's work –"

Jack blurted out, "They were right, scientists playing God are what brought about the nuclear bomb." Jack was not a particularly religious man, but he believed in God, and had seen enough war to know that God was nowhere to be found when man started taking God's work into his own hands. "I've seen first-hand the destruction something like that can cause doc, trust me, people were not meant to meddle with those kinds of power." Jack watched the expression on Teague's face change. It was the first time he had truly seen some emotion out of this man. *Is that guilt? Fear? Both?* Perhaps the man was just irritated at being interrupted, but Jack didn't care about that; if he was going to have to listen to this quack's spiel, he was doing it on his terms.

Jack was hardly a scientist, but he had an analytical side that always served him very well both in the field an when dealing with politics. "What you are talking about is only theory, though. Unless the military was dabbling in it..." This thought created a sudden flood of insight. "Wait a minute, is that what I am building out by the air..." He cut himself off. Teague had said he was involved in the military, but he had never shown any credentials, never proven anything. Sure, this whole situation screamed military – the evasiveness, the vague answers, the windowless room. But Jack had to tread carefully here, for all he knew someone had set this whole thing up to get information out of him, information that required some very top secret clearances to even discuss. But the train of thought was not stopping. Perhaps the underground facility he was building was some experimental lab that the military will use to conduct experiments with DNA and 'cloning'. If it was possible, the military would go to any length to take the best soldiers and make an army of exact duplicates. It was a chilling thought. Jack had seen first-hand what some Nazi "scientists" had been doing when he was helping to liberate the death camps only reinforced that there wasn't too many things governments would not attempt to do to gain the upper hand in military force.

Teague recovered from whatever had come over him and smiled. "I think I see where your line of thought is headed Jack. The military probably *was* working on cloning in secret, somewhere, but what I am talking about was very public, and a lot of people were not happy about it."

"Doc, you're talking like a quack again. I would have heard if these experiments were going on, and I never heard anything about it, except for maybe in a sci-fi book." Annoyance was building again and he struggled to keep it in check. This guy is clearly deranged but something about this whole conversation rang true and until the real doctors showed up, he wanted to get as much as he could out of it.

"Jack, cloning experiments started hitting the mainstream in about the year 1980, and moved on until – well until about the year 2012." Jack blinked a couple times. The statement took him by surprise, but he quickly recovered. *Does it ever end with this guy?*

He let out a short laugh, shook his head, and sat there for a few moments trying to figure out how to start getting some truth out of this conversation. "Look, I can't help but think that what you are telling me is pure bullshit. You're just messing with my head. Come on, you're sitting here trying to convince me that I died and was remade in an experiment years later. Next thing you will try to tell me that it is the year 2020 and Martians took over the planet."

Teague smiled. "No Jack, as far as we know, there are no Martians, or any other 'alien' life, although this world might seem very alien to you now." Teague's smile went away, and he said, "And it is not the year 2020, more like the year 2320, near as we can tell."

Chapter 8

Jack leaned back and closed his eyes. He wanted to start laughing hysterically. "So what is this, some kind of time travel thing? I have read some science fiction in my time doc, and you sir, could author a bestseller. Now let's go back to the beginning and you can tell me the *real* truth." Jack opened his eyes and fixed him with a stare.

Teague's shoulders dropped as if he was finally giving up trying to pull of this practical joke, and for the next minute he wouldn't meet Jack's eyes as he appeared to be lost in thought. Suddenly his eyes lit up and he said, "Do you want to see what I have been writing? Has your vision cleared to the point that you can see it clearly?"

Jack had been so preoccupied with this crazy conversation, he hadn't noticed at what point his vision had cleared. Now, not only was he seeing things without the haze, he realized he could see much more clearly than ever before. He had always been a little near-sighted in his left eye, but every detail was sharp and clear now. As he looked around the room, testing his vision, he saw some things that only added to the confusion. There was a square sheet of glass on a stand next to his bed that had what looked like colored text and symbols written on it, but they were moving! Like a television screen only a quarter inch thick! Furthermore there were no wires going to it! On one side of the room there were some devices that looked to be machined from all sorts of different metals, but it kind of resembled a chemistry set with all sorts of tubes and pipes twisting around in a seeming random fashion. The room had a 'medical' feel to it, but the walls were raw concrete, and the lighting had a slight bluish tint to it. Jack looked back at Teague, completely befuddled by what he was seeing and nodded.

"Are you okay to hold something in your hand yet?" Teague said motioning to his hands. After having to be fed at dinner, or breakfast, or whatever meal it was, Jack had been wiggling his fingers and making fists. He lifted his hand to see how it was working. He could lift his arm fairly well, and could turn his hand around at the wrist, open and close his hand, pretty much at will.

"I think so, give me something to lift". Teague set the 'clipboard' in his lap, and Jack immediately noticed it weighed a lot less than he expected, even though it appeared to be made of glass and should have weighed at least a couple pounds. He was able to lift it without much difficulty and he picked it up with both hands, examined it front and back. It did indeed look like square sheet of glass that was mirrored on one side, or maybe was shiny metal, reflective but the reflections were dull and blurry. On the other side however, it was like a two way mirror and he could see through it to the blanket beneath. That wasn't the confusing part though, seeming to be printed directly on the surface of the glass was some typed text, laid out similar to a newspaper. He started to read.

> **Life Magazine** - a publication that started as a humor and general interest magazine in 1883 and was purchased by another publication company in 1936, at which time it became a weekly magazine with a strong emphasis on photojournalism. In 1972 it became a special publication that was only occasionally released, and in 1978 it became a monthly publication until 2000. From 2000 on it was an occasional special publication that appeared in Time magazine and in some newspapers until 2012.

Teague tapped the glass, which then changed before his eyes to be a document containing all of Jack's biological information, history, and even a color photo. The photo was from Jack's retirement, and looked faded, like a very old photo that had been well preserved. That, like everything else, didn't make sense because he had never seen an 'old' color photo. Teague then reached down with the pen and tapped again. This time, a detailed history of Jack's cancer appeared, from August of 1966 to June of 1967, when according to the document, he passed away as a result of the cancer.

Chapter 9

He just stared at the notepad for a few minutes while Teague patiently waited. "I think I need some time alone to... absorb this." He felt like he was going to puke.

Teague didn't even hesitate. "Most certainly," he said, "I will give you some time to rest. Let me show you how to adjust your bed." He showed Jack how to manipulate the bed so he could lay it flat or sit it up. "When you are ready, just touch the box on the bottom left of the monitor next to your bed and I, or someone else, will be in here shortly to assist you. I will have more answers for you later." Jack looked over at the square sheet of glass on the stand next to his bed and just nodded, still speechless.

Upon close examination he saw that it had all sorts of what appeared to be medical information on it, like blood pressure and heart rate.

Teague went on without prompting, "This screen is monitoring all your body functions. It is a touch screen like the one on my datapad here. Just touch that square on the bottom left corner if you need anything. Can I get you some water before I leave? I realize it's not the best tasting stuff but you won't get sick from it, and your body could probably use the hydration." Jack nodded again.

After bringing in a glass of water, Teague left the room for the 'evening.' There were no windows in this room so it was impossible to say whether it was night or day. The conversation had not lasted more than an hour, but he felt tired and was as mentally drained as he would be if he had spent the whole day filing requisition papers for the military. He lowered the bed and stared at the monitor for a while, watching the lights bounce around in an almost hypnotizing pattern. Finally he drifted off to sleep, dreaming about Jenny and Ally, and crazy Dr. Jekyll type doctors creating people in little glass beakers.

~~~~

"So tell me, Teague, how is he coming?"

"Very well. Very well indeed considering the age of the material we had to work with. His mind is working very well, and despite the potential errors in his memory it is accepting his biology perfectly. I can already tell he is an exceptionally intelligent man with a gift for being very perceptive. At first I thought his technology background would be a roadblock on his path to accepting his situation, but it appears it worked in my favor. As soon as he saw technology that couldn't possibly exist in his time he was convinced. I think we have a very viable candidate here."

"Good. Do you think he will be able to do what we need? And if so will he be ready in time?"

"God willing, yes."

"Good, good. Carry on."

Chapter 10

Consciousness came quickly for the first time in years. Sleep didn't linger and try to draw him back in – he simply went from a deep, dreamless slumber he hadn't thought possible a few hours before to not just being awake, but alert as well. And it wasn't just the rapid transition to consciousness that surprised him, it was the fact that he was at complete peace when it happened. By all rights he should be a mess right now. He was in a foreign place, with only an impossible explanation for why he was here. But the cancer, the grief, the stress from work all felt distant and disconnected, as if they were someone else's problems and not his own. Even reflecting on his wife's passing did not stir the pain in his heart he should expect.

In this state of relaxation, thoughts, memories, and reasoning flowed effortlessly through his mind. There wasn't much to distract him, the only source of light was the dim glow from the medical monitor that cast a slight blue aura on barely half the room. The rest of the room was as much as mystery as how he got here. It was irrelevant, there was no desire to explore. He closed his eyes and just let the thoughts and feelings flow.

He started at the beginning, his first thoughts upon waking the previous day. Pain, or rather its absence, was the first thing he recalled. Why was that? At first he decided he hadn't felt this good in years. Then he decided he hadn't felt this good *ever*. As he pondered it, he came to the realization that he didn't really remember how he felt when he was younger. It was like the difference between two friends, one you see every day and one only every couple of years. They may have aged equally over time, but you don't notice it on the one you see every day, only on the one you haven't seen for a long time. One day you wake up and feel miserable but you don't know if it's because you are getting sick or if it's just normal since you felt almost as miserable the day before. Your frame of reference is only the day before, or maybe the week before; you can't really compare how you feel now to how you felt a year ago. In fact, the stark difference in how he felt when he first went to the hospital with Mabel and when he first woke up here the day before was already starting to fade. He was getting used to it and couldn't frame a reference point to when he had felt this good.

Thinking about Mabel and the hospital shifted his focus. This was a troubling train of thought. The trip to the hospital, the preparation for whatever might come of his surgery, and even the few hours he had spent reconnecting with Mabel were all fresh in his mind. For him they happened yesterday, or perhaps a couple days ago. It was clear, however, that some amount of time had passed. The technology alone was proof positive that it wasn't 1966 anymore. It was surprisingly easy to accept that. The rest, not so much. He wasn't sure what to believe. The simple biopsy could have gone awry, and he could have slipped into a coma for a number of years. He recalled the article he had read about the woman waking from her coma after nearly twenty years. It took her months of extensive physical therapy before she was able to perform the simplest of physical tasks. She couldn't even talk for weeks, and walking again was probably unlikely. They had called it muscular atrophy in the article. But he felt like he could get out of the bed and dance a jig right now.

He supposed if the technology to make a television the thickness of a sheet of glass existed, then medical advances could explain his physical condition. However, if thirty years had passed while he played sleeping beauty, he would be well into his sixties, or even seventies. He felt like he was a new man, even younger than his nearly forty year old body should feel. There was no way he was in his seventies, and what he had seen of his body so far in no way suggested he was any older. Despite how good he felt, he found it hard to believe that medical science would ever have the cure for aging, and certainly not within the span of his life. Try as he could though, he wasn't ready to accept that hundreds of years had passed or that he had died. It was far beyond his capability to reason and even outside the scope of his imagination. This train of thought led to a pile of questions that he could barely form into coherent thoughts let alone try to reason out. The sheer volume of unanswered questions shattered his feeling of utter relaxation and the tension, frustration, and anxiety began to build at an uncontrollable pace. He suddenly felt an uncompromising need to learn more about his situation.

In effort to regain the sense of serenity he had held only moments before, he shifted his thoughts again, this time to what had just happened. When he was younger, he was a bit of a hothead, quick to lose his temper. It had led to some bad decisions and more than one fight. Simply growing up, along with twenty years of military discipline, had burned out that youthful spirit. It was confusing that he had been hot tempered in his earlier conversation with Teague. Every time the doc said something he didn't like or didn't comprehend, he got seriously angry. That was simply not like him. He was "battle hardened" and even devastating news like the death of his wife and child or learning he had cancer had not gotten him too riled up. Ironically though, just thinking about this uncontrolled temper triggered another jolt of anxiety over his situation and his tension grew. The last bit of clarity and peacefulness was now gone, replaced by the overwhelming need to *know*.

Perhaps it was his sudden desire to explore his surroundings, or maybe he heard the faintest sound. Whatever triggered it, he was abruptly aware of another presence in the room. He stopped breathing, held perfectly still, and even tried to will his heart, which had started beating harder when the wave of anxiety washed over him, to be still. A second passed, two, then three. Another sound – the slightest rustle of fabric or maybe the intake of a quiet breath.

"Is someone there? Teague is that you?"

There was a hesitation and then, softly, a female voice spoke up. "No." It came out a little choked, like she hadn't expected to suddenly have to talk. She cleared her throat and said, "Would you like me to wake the doctor for you?"

"Uh… no, I… Who are you?" Jack had been half convinced his mind had been playing tricks on him so the response startled him. He wasn't prepared to reply. "What are… were you watching me sleep?"

There was a long pause, as if the person were contemplating whether or not to answer the question. "Um… Yes actually, I was." Jack could hear guilt and embarrassment in the voice, and it almost felt like he could feel her blushing. "I'm sorry if I woke you, I was just…" She was obviously uncomfortable trying to explain, probably not expecting to have been caught.

Her voice sounded vaguely familiar, but he couldn't place it. She hadn't offered any more, and he got the feeling she couldn't come up with a good excuse for being here. He broke the uncomfortable pause with, "Who are you?"

Her voice became more confident. "Um, my name is Wendy. I'm a technician here, among other things." Again, she left it hanging like there was much more to say but wasn't sure quite how to proceed.

As she spoke, he probed the dark room with his senses, trying to focus in on her voice. He located the source behind him, probably in the corner of the room. As much as his vision had improved she was completely hidden in the dark. "Can you come over here so I can see you? I don't like talking to people when I can't see them." Actually he didn't really mind it, he was just curious to see her and it sounded like a good excuse.

There was the sound of wheels running on a smooth floor, and Wendy materialized out of the darkness pushing an office type chair. As she stepped into the pale blue light of the monitor, Jack felt the hair on the back of his neck stand up. She moved like someone who was very in tune with their body, no wasted movement and every step filled with confidence that it would land exactly where it was supposed to. Her five foot six inch frame was noticeably athletic, even in the dim light. The attraction he felt was electric.

She rolled the chair next to the bed, near the foot, facing him, and sat down gracefully. He had only caught a glimpse of her face when the first jolt hit him, and now that she was sitting here facing him, it was a good thing he was already lying down. She was stunningly attractive. Her straight dark hair was cut fairly short, almost like a woman's military cut, and framed her face perfectly. Her cheekbones were just high enough to anchor her strong jaw line without making her face look masculine. Full lips, a short slender nose, and eyebrows angled just right completed a look that made it difficult for Jack to speak. He put her at twenty-something years old, a little young for someone like him. Nevertheless, he felt the need to say something witty, something impressive. "So, can I ask why you're in my room watching me sleep?" *Wow, impressive.* To cover up his underwhelming attempt to dazzle her, he manipulated the bed controls to sit up then fixed her with what he hoped was a smoldering gaze.

She looked down at her knees in embarrassment, not seeming to notice the effect she had on him. This time Jack could literally feel the heat radiating from her body. "I, uh, guess I wanted to meet you. You know, like without Doc or anyone around."

The sound of her voice was electricity running up his spine. He didn't recall having this kind of attraction to anyone, ever. Not even seeing Jenny for the first time had triggered a reaction like this. It sent his mind ablaze and made it hard to even form a coherent thought. He was starting to get a grip on it though, and he chastised himself for his lack of ability to control his attraction. He fumbled on through the conversation, trying to regain his composure. There were questions still burning in his mind and he wanted to keep her talking. "Are you... um... not supposed to meet me or something?"

"Oh no, nothing like that," she answered quickly. "It would be... difficult to explain." She looked like she wanted to say more but left it at that. Her answer was frustrating, but she was now staring at him. He felt another rush from the attention. It had been a long time since such an attractive woman, *okay, any woman at all*, had shown him this kind of attention, and he felt himself getting a bit aroused. He shifted in the bed a bit, surprised to find that he could move a lot better than before he slept. "Am I making you uncomfortable?" she asked.

"No. Well, not really. I uh... well I... you see, I think you are very attractive, and uh... well..." Now he was the one blushing, not only because he was aroused by this complete stranger, but because he was finding himself blubbering like a teenager who was trying to ask his dream girl to the prom.

She was smiling at him, seeming to almost enjoy his discomfort. "Relax. I'm not so attractive that you should be uncomfortable around me, and besides, you have nothing to be worried about; you're not so ugly yourself." She was trying to put him at ease, but once again Jack was having a hard time controlling his emotions. He couldn't seem to get comfortable in his bed, and it felt like the temperature in the room had gone up about twenty degrees. In his mind he was struggling to come to terms with his behavior, but it was getting more and more difficult to think clearly.

He had never been a smooth talker around women, relying mostly on decent looks and a steady confidence to help him score points with the ladies. Even that confidence seemed to have failed at the moment. "Thanks," he said "but I don't know what's gotten into me lately. Oh, and by the way, you *are* that attractive." He smiled nervously.

She still hadn't stopped staring at him, but now her confidence seemed to slip a little. She didn't look quite as relaxed as she had a moment ago. "The... uh... reason you are feeling so out of sorts is a side effect of the whole growth process you have gone through the last seven weeks. Your body went through puberty just recently, and the hormones that triggered the changes are still raging in your system. You have this young body, and your mind and memories don't quite match. Being," she seemed to search for a word "emotional, is a perfectly normal response to the situation."

The words took a moment to settle past the chemistry he was feeling. Despite the maelstrom of emotion, anxiety, arousal, and confusion, his curiosity grabbed hold of her words and the gears started turning at a furious pace. "I'm not quite following you." His mind raced, running back over his earlier conversation. "You make it sound like I'm a teenager instead of a forty year old man." He had not seen himself in a mirror since, well, since before he went in for surgery. Despite his earlier conviction that reversing the aging process was simply not possible, he had to suppress the urge to look under the covers at his body or even to just touch his face. Just a simple statement from this complete stranger about hormones and puberty rang true and brought a thread of doubt into his mind regarding what he knew couldn't be possible.

Wendy sort of giggled, and in automatic reaction Jack grinned like an infatuated schoolboy then caught himself and straightened out his face, somewhat embarrassed both by his reaction and to his lack of understanding. He tentatively asked, "You aren't suggesting that what Teague told me earlier about dying and being remade is really true, are you?"

She frowned, "I'm sorry, I was under the impression that you understood. Perhaps I should go and leave this to Doc. I don't want to cause you problems and he is much better than me at explaining it…"

"NO! Um, I mean, please, don't go."

Wendy had tensed like she was going to stand up, but at his quick outburst she paused and then settled back into the chair. The look of concern on her face was more sincere than warranted. She seemed to struggle with something in her mind before speaking next. "Look, I'm not a doctor, and I sure as hell am no scientist. I can, however, tell you that I watched you grow from a few chemicals in a jar to a full grown man. Whether you understand it or not, Doc wasn't lying to you."

They sat in silence as minutes passed. The chemistry he felt at first sight of her was still there but now it was mixed with the tension of disbelief warring with his desire to believe that she would not be dishonest. He wasn't ready to accept or dismiss what she had said. Some part of his mind knew that if didn't put this issue aside for the moment it might all start to come apart. He had reached his limit in understanding and accepting, at least for the moment. He tried to just clear his mind, filing away the issue for another time. The tension eased and he visibly settled back into his bed, unsure of whether he wanted to continue talking to Wendy or if he should just go back to sleep.

By the time he let his eyes meet hers again, she tensed as if to get up. She was clearly distraught over his reaction to her words. He decided quickly that he didn't want her to go quite yet. "Wait, it isn't that I don't believe you, I just don't understand it. My emotions are all over the place, and it doesn't let me think clearly enough to process something like this. I… I can't think about this right now but…" He paused to consider what he might say to keep her here a little longer, and decided to just keep it simple. "Please stay."

She smiled and settled back into the chair, sending another wave of warmth through him, flushing away any thoughts or concerns about how, why, or where he is. "I understand how hard it can be to come to terms with this. I… It took me a lot of time to understand, to believe. I don't want to rush you here; I know you'll understand soon enough. Whether you understand or believe, the fact is you have the body of a twenty five year old, and the accelerated growth… uh… the process that got you here has left your body filled with all the side effects of puberty."

He simply had to take her word for it. He was no longer processing the 'how' of coming to be here, but he *was* filing away the information on some level. Words that stuck out, like 'grown' went somewhere in his brain for later consideration.

Despite his inability to comprehend what she was saying, he was aroused by such an attractive woman talking to him about science that he could barely understand. Whether or not she even understood what she was talking about, she sounded incredibly intelligent to him at that moment, and again he felt the sudden need to woo her with his quick wits and strong intellect. "So my body is young, and full of hormones, so… what, you came in here to take advantage of me?" He closed his mouth quickly, not having intended to say it exactly that way. Or at all.

Wendy looked surprised for a moment, then embarrassed again. She bit her bottom lip like she was trying to decide something important. Like everything else, he found it attractive, almost sensual. She then looked him straight in the face. "I… have to admit that some of the reason I am here is…" she paused as if looking for the right words, then started again. "I knew that you would be, well, as horny as a sixteen year old, and I *was* curious to see how you would react around me." She sort of nodded at her own statement, looked first down at her knees then again directly at him, and said, "If you are uncomfortable and want me to leave, I will."

"No!" Jack exclaimed too loudly and perhaps too quickly. *Good God what is wrong with me!* he thought to himself. "I mean, no please, I am… enjoying our conversation." She smiled again. "What an incredible smile." *Oh Shit I just said that out loud!* "Uh…" was all he could manage as his face flushed again.

"Nothing to be embarrassed about. I do admit I'm enjoying this at your expense." She sat up in the chair a little, and a mischievous grin crept onto her face. "I'm actually very nervous myself. I am not normally this forward with anyone." While she talked she placed a few fingers on his leg, and was running them up and down his thigh. The whole time she did this her gaze never left Jack's eyes. This of course was getting the natural response she was looking for, and he shifted again in the bed.

The conflicting forces in his mind shifted. Up until now, he was torn between the anxiety of not understanding his situation, the overwhelming curiosity it brought on, and the incredible attraction he felt for this woman. The confusing yet perfectly clear signals he was getting from Wendy turned the hormonal maelstrom from a distant but raging desire into a possible conclusion. With the real possibility of something happening between them, his guard went up and he considered that he had not been with a woman since

37

Jenny died nearly two years ago. His body was practically screaming at him to make a move, but his mind was not sure he was ready for it. On the one hand it was a little disheartening that she knew he was in a vulnerable state right now, but on the other hand she was damned beautiful and she was touching his leg! He closed his eyes, swallowed hard, and then looked at her, "Listen Wendy, I am almost 40 years old, and I am – er – was, married. I'm way too old for you, and, well, I haven't been with anyone since my wife passed two years ago." It all sounded reasonable to him. *What the hell are you doing Jack?*

"Jack, your body is about the same age as mine, and it has *never* 'been with a woman'. Furthermore, while your memories tell you it's been two years since your wife passed, it's actually been more like three hundred and fifty years." *Damn, can't argue with that.* "You sound like you're not attracted to me Jack." She put a little bit of a pout on her lips, which melted any resolve he had left.

He practically snorted, forcing himself to look away from her eyes. There was no need for him to answer, the truth was standing on its own by this point. He wracked his brain for some logical reason that he should ask her to leave. Nothing came to mind. Their eyes met again and she seemed to be looking for something in his gaze.

She seemed to find what she was looking for, and stood up from the chair in a fluid movement stepping closer to the bed. "Last chance to send me away, Jack." Her hand went to the buttons on her shirt and she began to unbutton it, starting at the top. He just lay there rapidly losing the ability to reason as blood flowed to other parts of his body. Wendy finished the first button, and was working on the next. Jack's heart rate was climbing rapidly, and his breathing became shorter. She finished the second button, and Jack caught a glimpse of her cleavage. He practically shivered with excitement and nervousness.

Trying to break the tension he said "Wendy, if I didn't know better, I would think that you were trying to seduce me." He put a dumb looking grin on his face, and she laughed. Her hands now worked the fourth and final button and the shirt opened up, revealing an incredibly flat stomach. The blouse slipped off her shoulders, framing her breasts before falling to the ground. He took in every aching detail as she slowly started working her pants loose. He had never seen a body quite like this. She was fit and toned but not skinny like a magazine model. Her firm looking breasts were not large, not small, and fit her frame perfectly. The pale glow of the monitor contrasted against her smooth and light flesh, highlighting the smallest changes in texture. Her nipples, just a shade darker than the rest of her skin, were standing erect, the areolas dimpled with goose bumps. She pushed her pants and underwear down to her ankles and stepped out of them. Standing straight up, she looked at him, her chest rising and falling to her rapid, excited breath. It was as if she was giving him a chance to admire her statuesque figure. He took advantage of the brief pose, confirming to memory every detail. Her legs were long and flawless, transitioning smoothly from her thighs to her hips to her waist. The shadow cast by the pale light drew a tall 'V' starting where her inner thighs touched moving up around her delta to the top of her hips.

He looked into her eyes for a moment, seeing a hunger there that was unmistakable; it was obvious she wanted this as much as he did, although for what reason, he had no idea. Perhaps later he would wonder if the doc had sent her to him as part of this whole... thing, but right now he was only thinking about what was about to happen. He scooted over in the bed and lifted up the covers. For the first time, he realized that he was not wearing anything under the blanket. He had not thought to check. "Holy shit I'm naked!" he exclaimed as he dropped the covers back down.

Wendy giggled and simply said, "Perfect," as she climbed in next to him.

Her body was like a furnace, and his hands instinctively found their way to her various parts very quickly. One hand landed on a firm breast, and one on her equally firm ass. As they embraced fully, his heart was beating so hard he felt like his chest would explode. Staring into her eyes, he used his hands to feel what he had already seen; a confirmation that he wasn't just hallucinating. If this was a dream, this would be the part where he woke up.

He leaned into her and they kissed, softly at first as if both were a little nervous to bring their lips together despite the fact that they had already had intimate contact with each other's body parts.

The kiss turned passionate and they frantically explored each other under the covers. After what could have been a minute or an hour, she climbed on top, reached down, and slid him into her. She was very wet, and somewhere in the back of his mind he registered that it was further proof that she was a willing partner. She pressed her breasts to his chest as they slowly started rocking back and forth, getting a rhythm going. He kissed her deeply then put his lips to her neck, then shoulder, then down to her breasts as the rhythm gained speed. A soft moan escaped her lips and their breathing became heavier as the passion built. The pace quickened until finally, with an explosive groan, he came, triggering the same reaction in her.

As the mutual orgasm subsided they held on to one another as if one of them would be ripped away from the other if they loosened their grip. Over the next few minutes, they relaxed, and finally she moved so that he slipped out of her. She lay on her side, breasts pressed against him and one leg draped over his, for quite a while.

Chapter 11

It was hard to tell how much time the whole thing had taken, but Jack didn't think it could have been too long. He was a bit out of practice, and as aroused as he had been he would be surprised if the whole experience had lasted two minutes. Normally he would have drifted off to sleep afterward, but now that his body had had a shot of endorphins and the hormones had subsided, he couldn't keep his mind from churning.

Three days ago I was waxing my mustang all alone, and here I am, like some kind of crazy dream, he thought. Looking at Wendy, he expanded on that thought. *Make that some kind of wet dream.*

More time passed, as they lay there intertwined. Finally, Jack said, "That was... incredible. I hope it wasn't too – uh – quick for you."

They locked eyes and she smiled. "Trust me Jack, you satisfied my every desire." She kissed him long and tenderly, then snuggled her head against his chest and drifted off to sleep.

He lay there for quite some time, reflecting on the details of what he had learned just since waking up. While he still wasn't ready to decide if he believed he was dead and reincarnated somehow, her words made some sense. It rationalized everything he was feeling. His quick temper, uncontrolled emotions, the raw chemical need to be with this stranger in such an intimate way, and his inability to filter his thoughts before speaking all would make sense if he had the hormones of a teenager.

Then there was the consideration of what had just happened. For the last two years of his life he had not been able to think about other women without thinking about his wife. There was more to his desire to be with this woman in his arms than just chemistry. He felt somehow disconnected from the love he knew he felt for his wife. There was no other way to describe it. A few days ago he still couldn't think about his future without a feeling of anxiety and a sense of loss. The death of his wife had shattered his identity and he didn't know his own role in his future. People had told him that it was normal, that the death of a spouse would turn your world upside down and only time could heal things. After two years he hadn't made enough progress to do much more than think about introducing another woman into his life. He had been starting to feel like it was necessary for him to move forward but it always stopped there. As soon as he thought about another woman in the same way he had seen his wife, the anxiety of losing her would take over. Yet here he was, pressed up against the warm naked body of a woman he just met. There was no guilt. There was no sense of wrongness to it. If anything, he felt a connection to this stranger that he hadn't felt since the day he met Jenny. What had changed in him that allowed him to feel this way again?

He explored the emotion, wondering if it was real or just a result of having shared such an intimate moment with her. He knew the next few days would tell him the answer. Thinking about it and feeling the woman sleeping in his arms began to arouse his desire again. He held her just a little tighter, pressed against her just a little more, and savored the feeling. As thoughts of waking her for more of what they had done earlier formed in his mind, exhaustion swept through him and he settled into a deep sleep.

~~~~

Jack woke again, maybe three hours later, and discovered himself alone in bed. He was disappointed, but not surprised. She had come to him in the middle of the night, and while she hadn't explained her motives, obviously she chose to do it at a time when there would be no possibility of being seen. He thought again about whether the doc, or whoever was in charge, had sent Wendy to be with him. Unless he had completely lost his ability to read people, she was there for her own reasons. He smiled at the thought of the previous night, not really wanting to think about the motives behind it.

Unfortunately, the train of thought brought him right back to the original situation. He had to face this head on. They had told him he was 'cloned', that he had died and been reborn three and a half centuries later. It was such a departure from reality that he was more inclined to believe he was in a mental institution. However, everything Teague had told him rang true. The woman in his room last night had backed it up with information that made perfect sense, if he could just make the leap from insanity to reality. Could it possibly be true?

He took a different track. If he assumed what he had been told was in fact true, then he was in a world where things were completely different. What happened last night was not just unusual to him, it was downright impossible, in his world. Incredibly attractive women didn't come to you in the middle of the night while you were in a hospital and have sex with you for no understandable reason. It just simply didn't happen. Unless they were crazy and this was indeed a mental hospital.

That didn't feel right though. He admitted to himself that he didn't have a single bit of experience with the clinically insane, but aside from the explanations coming out of their mouths and the actions they were taking, they seemed completely normal. This couldn't have happened in 1966, because people didn't act this way. A different time, a different world, made sense to him though. He recalled the social changes just from after the war to the mid 60's. So many things had changed in such a short time, imagine what would change in hundreds of years. It was not a big leap to think that perhaps in this world, it was perfectly normal for a woman to come into a man's room at night and seduce him then slip away while he sleeps.

The questions were piling up. He was not fully convinced that they were telling him the truth, but he was ready to learn more and decide for himself. It was time to ask some of these questions to the doctor.

He reached over and pressed the button on the monitor. There was a faint 'ding' in the background, but he couldn't tell if it came from the monitor or from outside the room. Furthermore, when he rolled over to press the button, he became aware of another sensation. He had to pee – bad.

Within two minutes, Teague walked into the room. He was wearing green scrubs like you would find on a surgeon. *Is that what he was wearing yesterday?* So much happened yesterday, during most of which he had been practically blind, he never noticed. "How are you doing this morning?" Teague asked him.

"Is it morning? I wasn't sure. I have to pee." Jack was not sure if he could stand, but he didn't want to pee in a bottle. Then he realized he didn't even have clothes. Then he started wondering if they have bathrooms in the future... so many questions!

"Of course! Yes, it is morning, about 8 a.m. Here are some clothes, do you think you need help getting them on?" Teague asked as if reading his mind.

"Um... Let's see." Jack pushed himself into a sitting position. He was a little dizzy for a second but it passed. He swung his feet over the edge of the bed, prepared to lay back if he swung too far. He found that he was exactly where he wanted to be, sitting on the edge of the bed. "Doc, I think I can handle it." He started getting dressed. Twenty years in the military took away any notions of embarrassment when it came to dressing or even using the toilet next to other men. However, Teague left the room to give him privacy. The shirt was actually pretty simple, and Jack was surprised at how well he could work his hands and arms. Yesterday he could barely move, and today he felt like there wasn't anything he couldn't do. The pants were also simple, with just a fly in front and a cord to tighten the waist. He realized, however, he would not be able to pull them up without standing. After a moment's hesitation he decided it was worth a shot and slowly put his weight on his feet.

He let go of the bed to see if he could balance. It took a second and he wobbled a little, but he steadied out pretty easily. His first thought was how cold the floor was. He pulled up the pants and fastened them, then took a step forward. "It's like riding a bike I guess," he said out loud as he took a few steps and turned around to walk back to his bed. The bed rushed up to meet his face as he completed the turn. His head bounced off the mattress before he could regain his footing and catch himself with his hands. "Okay, maybe not." The fall had not hurt very much but he was seeing stars. He stood there holding the edge of the bed until the urgency to pee started to overwhelm him again. He decided to try the walking thing again. As long as he didn't turn too quickly, he seemed OK. He called to the doc. "Teague, I'm ready to use a bathroom, where is it?"

Teague entered the room again and said, "Right over here." They left the room, and entered a hallway, dimly lit by what looked like miniature fluorescent lights that cast everything in a slightly bluish tint. The walls, floor, and ceiling were all concrete. They walked a dozen feet down the hall to a small door.

Teague pointed and said, "You can go in here. Holler if you need help."

Jack smiled and said confidently, "I think I can figure it out." As he stepped into the small room the light automatically came on and the door closed behind him. "That's convenient." He looked around. There was a sink, a small mirror, and what looked like a toilet in the corner. He rushed over to the toilet, lifted the lid, and saw there was no water in the bowl. "Hey Doc! There's no water in the toilet!"

Through the door, he heard Teague's muffled voice say, "The bowl is made of a frictionless material, no water necessary, just go, you'll see."

Jack shrugged, opened the fly on his newly acquired pants, and started peeing. It was quite an amazing thing to watch the first droplets hit the bowl and rapidly swirl around before dropping into the drain. He watched in awe as the steady line of urine swirled three times around the bowl and disappeared without a trace down the hole. He was actually disappointed when he was done. He reached down and swiped a finger in the bowl to check for himself that there was no residue that needed to be rinsed away. His finger glided across the bowl surface as if it were warm, wet ice, yet came away totally dry. "Amazing."

Jack moved to the sink to wash his hands, but the water spout was only about a quarter inch in diameter and there was no lever. Embarrassed to call again for help he put his hands under the small tube, and to his surprise a glop of jelly like liquid dropped onto his hands. He shrugged, rubbed his hands together as if washing them, and as the jelly sloughed off his hands, it swirled around the sink in the same manner as his urine in the toilet. He shook his hands in the sink and a few remaining jelly beads danced around the sink as they spiraled into the small black hole of a drain. It reminded him of watching water dance on a hot griddle. When he finished, he looked for a way to dry his hands, before realizing they were already dry. "Amazing." he repeated.

As he began to exit the room, he caught a glimpse of the mirror. It must have been a window, not a mirror, because the man on the other side of the glass was not him. A rush of adrenaline and amazement raced through his body leaving goose bumps over his whole body and the hair on the back of his next standing straight. Knees weak, he turned and stared into the glass. There was no way to describe what he felt when looking at the man staring back at him. It wasn't him. But it was. As a matter of fact, he had seen this man before, in pictures from his youth. That wasn't right though. He had never seen this man. This man wasn't just younger, he was *flawless*. Since he was fourteen his nose had been slightly crooked, but this man's nose was perfectly straight. There were no war scars on his face, no pock marks from acne, and his two day beard was a perfect shadow. Although he didn't have much hair, in fact nearly bald as if freshly shaved with an electric clipper, his hair was uniformly growing everywhere it should be. Jack moved again, to confirm that it wasn't a window. The movements reflected his own. There was no question this was a mirror. The man in the glass was him: a roughly twenty five year old version of him, only better, with none of the history of his life written on his face.

For the first time, he began to truly believe that they had been telling him the truth. The realization was overwhelming. He spent a few more minutes studying his face, exploring it with his hands. He touched the various parts, making sure they were real flesh and bone. He smiled and admired his perfectly straight teeth, looking for the silver scars of cavities filled over the years. It was no longer a surprise to discover there was only white enamel, no silver.

When he exited the restroom, Teague saw the look of wonder on his face, and smiled. "It is quite cool the first time you see it, isn't it?" Jack didn't know if he was referring to the frictionless bowl and sink, or the face. He simply answered with, "Yeah." Everything that had happened since he woke up yesterday was about as overwhelming as it could be, but oddly enough, all he could think to say was, "I'm no longer ruggedly handsome... does that mean I'm just handsome?" Jack laughed at his own statement mostly because he felt giddy with the discovery and the acceptance that seeing his own face had given him. Teague laughed along mostly because he found the remark amusing.

Teague led him to another room, one with a table and about a dozen chairs. Nobody else occupied the room at that moment, but it was obvious it was a small mess hall or kitchen of some kind. They took seats at the table, and Teague asked if he was hungry. "Ravenous," he replied. He was fed the same sawdust Jello that he had the previous night, but this time it tasted like apples. Once again, it left him very satisfied, and he reserved any questions about the food until a later date.

~~~~

"So," Teague started off, "shall I continue where I left off last night?"

"Please," Jack said. There was little question in his mind that everything he had been told so far was true. Up until seeing his face in the mirror, he had doubts, reservations, and a desire to look for some other answer that made more sense, something that would put him back in the world he came from. So despite the fact that he had not had the time to process how he really felt about everything, he found himself eager to learn more.

"Okay, I will jump right in then." Teague stood up and started pacing again. "We left off talking about cloning." He paused long enough to see Jack nod in acknowledgement. "So, up until about the year 2012, there were scientists around the world who had no reservations about attempting all sorts of cloning experiments with humans."

Jack shifted uncomfortably in his seat, not sure if the sudden anxiety brought on by the subject was because of his hunger for more information or if it had to do with the sketchy nature of human testing. Teague went on, "At first they created test tube zygotes, er... fertilized eggs that had split a few times," another pause to confirm he wasn't talking too far above Jack's understanding, "and genetically altered them, planted them in the womb, and waited to see the results. Some experiments were a success, and some, well some were not. After a few years, one group was successful in cloning a human. They were able to remove the DNA from the zygote, replace it with complete DNA from a living person, and after nine months, a baby was born."

"Is that what you did? Grow me inside a test tube then inject me into a woman? Then where have I been growing for the past twenty five years?" Jack interrupted. He knew from Wendy that somehow they sped this up, but he wanted details. It was his nature, probably from his teenage years in the orphanage where the nuns would always tell him that the Devil was in the details. Of course they were referring to his confessions, not experimenting on cloning, but ever since that part of his life he'd figured out that the details were usually where the most important information resided.

Teague didn't hesitate long. "I'm guessing you had a visitor last night?" The room felt suddenly warmer. The doctor stopped pacing, waiting for an answer.

Jack was a little embarrassed, and a little hesitant to explain the previous night. "I uh… I don't want to get anyone in trouble, but a woman came into my room last night. She um… enlightened me to the age of my body." He was not sure how much he should say. If there was some kind of social protocol she had broken, he didn't want to be party to any trouble it might cause her, particularly given the circumstances.

Amusement was plain on Teague's face. "Oh don't look so embarrassed Jack. It is practically a custom these days that one of the women 'enlightens' the men on the first night." Teague started chuckling then shook his head thoughtfully. "Some of the men have even tried it on the women but the results are… less predictable." This was clearly an inside joke and Jack wasn't exactly sure what to make of it, and he was more concerned about the nature of last night's visit to really consider what that meant. "Did you get a name by chance?"

Jack's hesitation was not lost on the doctor. "Oh, don't worry, whatever happened last night is very acceptable, even encouraged around here. If you don't want to say, you don't have to, we will figure it out soon enough."

Another hesitation and Jack spilled it. "Wendy, her name is Wendy." He picked up his glass of water as if signaling that it was time to move on to another conversation, but kept a close eye on Teague's reaction, hoping he hadn't really screwed up.

The look of surprise was not what he was expecting. "Really." It was not a question, more like a statement. "Hmph." The doctor seemed to be putting something together in his head. He shook it and shrugged, then in explanation said, "She is very… reserved. And shy."

Jack was taking a sip of water when he said that and almost choked as it went down the wrong tube. He started coughing. Teague looked at him to see if he was all right, and Jack looked away. "I will do my best to explain the women's behavior as we go here. I think I owe you that one. I hope it was not too embarrassing?"

Still coughing and turning a little red, although whether it was from the cough or from embarrassment he wasn't sure, Jack exclaimed, "Oh, no! I mean, not in the least. It uh… It was… well, can we talk about something else?"

"Oh certainly, I don't mean to… well anyway, where was I?" Looking down at his notepad he said, "Oh yes, so they successfully cloned a human." He started pacing again. "But, it was just another baby. Genetically it was the same as the host, but it was really just a twin, the only real difference was it was younger than its counterpart. Just because it would grow up to look identical to the parent didn't mean much, at least financially."

The doctor didn't give Jack a chance to ask what he meant. "There was no financial gain in creating a twin of someone, and back then there was only one reason to research anything – money." The way he said it made it sound like something about the concept was somewhat foreign to him. "For a while it was popular, among the wealthy, to have a child that was an identical twin to one of the parents. But it was never enough to keep the research funded."

"I'm not quite following you here, Doc, what financial gain did these scientists hope to capitalize on?"

"Well, organ replacement was one of the goals. If you could create a perfect replica of a person, that replica would have organs that were identical to the host. With perfect replicas, transplant was a nearly guaranteed success. If someone's heart was failing, you could grow a new heart and replace it."

Jack thought about that for a moment, then said, "I read about heart transplants and how doctors couldn't do it successfully because the body rejects it as something foreign. I guess if the body thought it was an original part, it wouldn't reject it." This was all incredibly interesting, and he was enthralled.

"Not to split hairs, but eventually they were able to use drugs to keep the body from rejecting the new organs, but it was crude and didn't always work right, so yes, the idea was that if it was already genetically the same as what you had, it would not be rejected." Teague was on a roll now. "So organ replacement became the driving force behind cloning, but you can't exactly have a baby just to kill it and take its heart. And even if you could, it would take too long – nine months to give birth, then you would have to grow the child for at least five years before the heart is mature enough to put in another person. Most times, if an organ failed, the person would die relatively quickly. The research did eventually lead to advances in organ replacement, but the moral and scientific boundaries were an insurmountable barrier toward any kind of cloning for parts.

"There was a better reason to research cloning, however. It was perceived as a potential fountain of youth. There were many people in the world who would pay any price for immortality."

"Immortality? Like living forever? How could cloning make someone live forever?"

"Well, it isn't like the historical fountain of youth, or the biblical Holy Grail, but think about it. If you had a dictator who didn't want to give up his power, and he had the means to clone himself, with all his memories, he could rule his domain forever. The same thing goes for super wealthy people. They either wanted to live forever, or if they lost someone, they wanted them back. People with wealth and power assumed they had the right to try their hand at wielding the power of God."

Jack thought about his wife and daughter for a moment. *If I could have them back, memories intact, would I? Even knowing that it was not really them?* Now Jack started thinking about philosophy, and another truth struck him. If he died, and was cloned, he is not really the same person, just a copy with all that person's memories. That is all good and well for the clone, since, as Jack himself could testify, for all intents and purposes that clone thinks he is the original, but the original has to die at some point. "Religion," Jack said. "What happens to the soul?"

"You are a sharp one Jack. That is exactly the moral dilemma. If the original person dies, and is cloned, did his soul go to Heaven or Hell, or did it come back to inhabit the body? Furthermore, if that clone has the memories of the original, but not the soul, is it a soulless creature or does it get a new soul? These were questions that the religious authorities had to answer, and they couldn't. They were lucky though, because they never had to answer. The cloning never got further than making babies with the same genetic material."

"Wait a minute, then how am I here? What do you mean that it never got further?" Jack was suddenly angry. It had taken him a lot to get to the point where he believed what he was being told. Now the doctor was telling him something different. The idea that this was an elaborate hoax set up by some mentally unstable patients came back to him. This was frustrating and he was about to give Teague a piece of his mind about it. A grim look from Teague stopped the emotional outburst in its tracks and he waited for an answer.

"War. In 2012, war broke out, and for the next hundred years, nobody was worried about cloning humans." Teague stopped pacing and sat down.

Chapter 12

The news stopped him cold. He knew all about war. He had fought on the front lines in Korea for over two years. He had watched his friends die, and then later, after becoming an officer, he watched soldiers under his command die. Korea wasn't even a real war. Not on the scale of WWII anyway. Jack served with enlisted men who had fought in the big war. He was just a kid back then, barely sixteen years old and full of piss and vinegar, but he remembered the stories they told. He also remembered the concentration camps. Worst of all, he served a two year tour in Japan, just before going to Korea. He saw first-hand the power of the atom bomb, and the horror of radioactive fallout. In a way, seeing the damage in Japan had helped to make up his mind to re-enlist after his first four years. He figured as long as there were people willing to give up their lives then the leaders of the military wouldn't have to drop those horrible bombs. Looking back now it was probably very ideological, but he was young, and young people follow their heart.

"Was it nuclear?" It was a simple question, but Jack was holding his breath waiting for an answer. He had lived the last 20 years of his life in a "cold war" with Soviet Russia. A few years ago he had feared, along with the rest of his country, that Russia's moves to put missiles in Cuba would result in the mutual destruction of both countries, and subsequently the world. Everyone knew that the next big war would be the end of life on earth if nuclear bombs got involved. The idea that people he knew might have been in a nuclear blast was making him sick to his stomach.

"Not at first, but, eventually, yes, bombs were dropped." Teague stared off into the distance, as if remembering it. That was crazy though, from what he had said this would have taken place some three hundred years ago. Jack knew that there was a lot more to this, but he wasn't sure he wanted to hear more about it.

"Look Jack, I could spend hours telling you what I know about the war, and later I will, if you want me to, but I need to finish explaining how you came to be here, and we might be a little short on time." Jack wondered what he meant by that, but he looked up at him and just nodded. Teague got up and started pacing again. He opened his mouth to talk, and just then, two people walked into the room.

~~~~

The first one to walk in was a man, about six feet tall with dark, weathered skin and black and gray peppered hair cut pretty short. He looked to be about thirty years old, and he appeared to be in excellent shape, evident by his lean stomach, broad shoulders, and sinewy neck and arms. Jack imagined that if the only diet around here was the odd slop he had been eating, that just about everyone would be lean. The man had a weariness about him that suggested he had already had a long, hard day, despite the early hour. As he walked in to the room, he smiled at Teague, and seeing Jack, he nodded and said, "Well, doc, you haven't lost your touch. Hi, I'm Charlie, you can call me Chuck. Your name is Jack right?" He had a gravelly voice and his eyes were compassionate, but Jack also saw in them something he had only seen in people that had been in hard battle. He didn't appear to be focusing on anything in particular, but Jack didn't think for a second that there wasn't a detail in the room Chuck hadn't noticed.

"Yes, nice to meet you Chuck." He was wearing what could be called military fatigues, and they were rumpled as if he had been in them for a while. Jack was still taking in the new face when he saw the second person coming in behind Chuck. The person was not nearly as big, and was wearing greasy coveralls. As she walked into the room, Jack did a double take. The red hair and freckles threw him off, but it was Wendy! The night before he only saw her in the dim bluish light of the monitor next to his bed, and the tint of the light camouflaged the red, so he never saw the freckles and assumed her hair was black or brown. Wendy was not making eye contact but headed right over to sit down next to him. "Uh, Hi." was all he managed to say to her.

He wasn't sure she was going to respond at first, she seemed intent about not meeting his eyes. Finally she glanced at him, and smirked. "Hi, Jack, did you sleep well?" Their eyes held for another moment, and then his attention was pulled away when Chuck, opening what must have been a refrigerator and burying his face in it, said, "Jack, care for a brewski?"

Jack looked over and said, "Isn't it a bit early for that?"

Chuck popped his head out and grinned at him. "Not for me it ain't." He pulled out what looked like an old fashioned root beer bottle, with a rubber cap and a wire lever to hold it on. He popped the lever and the bottle made a small pop sound, and a little mist wafted out of the mouth. Chuck took a deep pull, winced a little, and let out a little belch. "Ahhh, nothing like a refreshing drink after a long night of work." Before Jack could ask any questions, Chuck sat down, looked over at Teague, and said, "So doc, you done playing teacher yet? I'm anxious for some company out there."

Teague rolled his eyes in irritation and said, "Fuck you, Chuck. For your information Jack here accepted his situation in less than three hours. It took you a damn week!" Jack was surprised at the comment and looked at Chuck both watching for a reaction and wanting to ask him a lot of questions.

Chuck just smiled at Teague and said, "Bah, it isn't like you haven't had the practice. I figured you would've taught him how to pilot a flyer by now." The smirk on his face made it clear that he took no offense to anything the doc said to him. "Jack, it's been a pleasure meeting you, but I need to hit the rack. We can chat later this afternoon or tomorrow, after I've caught a few hours." He got up from the table, set the now empty bottle on the counter, and headed toward the door. As he passed Teague he slugged him on the shoulder and said, "Don't fill his head with too much of your bullshit doc, he seems

49

like a decent guy." Teague just shook his head as Chuck left the room, letting out a decent belch that echoed sharply down the hallway.

Jack was kind of dazed by the whirlwind encounter with the man. He had about a hundred questions, but he hadn't been able to get a word in edgewise. He looked at Wendy, half expecting her to get up and follow Chuck out of the room, but she gave him a look that said she wasn't leaving just yet. "I suppose you told Doc here all about last night?" she said a little tentatively, in a not *too* accusing tone of voice. Teague was taking the bottle that Chuck had emptied and putting it in a stainless steel looking cabinet that had a few other bottles and a couple dishes from breakfast in it. He closed the door and pressed a button on the top of the door, and a whooshing sound was faintly heard coming from within the cabinet.

He looked at Wendy and said, "No! I mean, I told him that you visited last night but not..." He stopped mid-sentence because he realized that even though he hadn't shared any more than that, Teague pretty much knew what went on. He blushed a little, feeling embarrassed that he had let the cat out of the bag. "I mean, he sort of figured it out and I..." once again he stopped because there was no good way to say it.

She gave him a look as if she was offended and Jack sort of withered in his chair, but then she smiled and said, "Don't worry about it; I knew Doc would get it out of you, I just wanted to make you squirm a little." Jack was relieved that he hadn't made some social misstep and relaxed in his chair a little. Wendy leaned in and gave him a peck on his cheek and whispered in his ear, "I had a good time last night, maybe I'll visit you again later." And with that she got up and walked out, not meeting either man's eyes.

He looked up at Teague as if to ask if the last few minutes in the room was normal around here. Teague just smiled and said, "People here are always a bit odd around the new guy. Nobody is sure what to say yet."

Jack had picked up on a lot in the last few minutes. The first thing he noticed was that the two new strangers' speech – *well, Wendy wasn't quite a stranger* – was a little different than Teague's. He couldn't exactly put his finger on specifically what was different, except maybe Teague spoke a little more 'formally', with much less slang. Jack was never good at picking out accents or dialects, so maybe there was a subtle difference in accent he could only sense when comparing the two side by side. Whatever it was, he filed that piece of information away in his head for future use. *Just another piece of the puzzle.*

Next, it was obvious he was not the first one to be here under these 'circumstances', and it was also obvious he was not here because someone felt charitable or wanted his company. He was here for a reason, and now on top of figuring out where he was and how he came to be here, he wanted to know why he was here. *That might be the most important question,* he thought to himself.

Perhaps sensing that Jack was working some details out in his mind, Teague let the silence linger for a few more moments. Finally, he broke the silence, "Well, now that you have tasted a bit of the local culture, shall we continue?" He didn't wait for an answer. "So as I was saying, the war put research into cloning on hold for about a hundred years. As a matter of fact, the only research going on in that time was either on how to kill people, or how to save them."

Jack wasn't ready to get back into the story yet, so he asked, "Doc, why am I here? I mean, it's obvious I'm not just a hobby for you, there has to be a good reason you went through the effort you did to..." He searched for the right words. Saying they 'cloned' or 'grew' him felt kind of weird. "You know what I mean. Can you just cut to the chase and tell me why I'm here?"

Teague hesitated. "I don't want to drop too much on your brain and make you process it all at once Jack. I'm not saying you will, but people have snapped by hitting them with too much at once. I feel like you have accepted that you are not in 1966 anymore, even though your memory tells you that less than twenty four hours ago you were heading into surgery. Until you know how you came to be here though, you probably won't understand the why." Teague was pacing again, and again Jack had the impression that he was more of a psychologist than a medical doctor. He was phrasing his words carefully. "Okay, I will tell you this much. You *are* here for a reason Jack. We need help, and we think you are – *qualified* – to do what we need, in more ways than one."

Jack accepted the answer, not really expecting to hear anything different. Nearly all his life he had been ordered to do things, and he was used to doing what was required of him, even when it meant his life was on the line. He was a square peg and if there was a square hole, he could fit in it. There were still a million questions however, and one in particular had been burning in his mind for a while now. "Do I still have cancer?" It was simple question, but the implications of any answer weighed heavily on him. Three days ago he was told that his life was coming to an end, and now it appeared he had some kind of second chance. The idea of being told that was not the case was a bit frightening.

"No, Jack, I can happily say that not only do you not have cancer, it is extremely unlikely you ever will. Not only that, but any other genetic defects you might have had were cleansed from your system before you were reconstructed. As things sit right now, you could very well live to be a hundred years old."

A weight lifted from Jack's mind and emotion gripped his heart. He didn't realize how tense he was in waiting for that answer, and the relief came so quickly that he actually teared up for a second. He looked away from Teague and closed his eyes.

Not sure if he could trust his voice, and not wanting to look so damned vulnerable, he cleared his voice and simply said, "That's good to hear doc, thanks!" There was a pause as he struggled to change the subject. "Was that really beer that Chuck was drinking?"

"In a manner of speaking, yes. I imagine you would not think it tastes like beer any more than you would think that our water tastes like a Pepsi." Teague chuckled at his own attempt at humor. Jack got it – there probably hadn't been a human alive who had tasted Pepsi in hundreds of years. Teague was a bit of a nerd. "Some of the guys set up what they call a 'microbrewery' a few years ago. The ingredient we use in our food is combined with some specific bacteria and some vegetable matter and allowed to ferment. Once processed, the resulting beverage is said to taste something like 'root beer'. It has a ten percent alcohol content. It is a popular drink around here, especially considering the alternative beverages, but it is in pretty short supply. I would prefer you wait until later today to try one, we have a lot to go over today and I need you staying sharp."

Jack smiled and said, "I was just curious doc, I was serious when I told Chuck it was too early for a beer. Speaking of Chuck, there seemed to be a little tension between you two. Care to tell me why?"

"Bah. Chuck and I get along fine, he is just a soldier through to his core, and doesn't really respect the more... educated people. I guess you could say he is sort of a bully." Teague seemed to think about the word bully and nodded. "He is a good man though, and I can honestly say he would lay down his life for me. Even so, I don't take his crap, and I give it back just the same."

Jack knew the type, and easily accepted the explanation. He could tell that the doc was anxious to get on with his story though, so he finally relented with the questions and said, "Okay Doc, continue."

~~~~

Teague looked at his notepad to find where he left off. "Without getting into too much detail about the war, society had degraded to what you might think of as the Dark Ages. There was no ruling government, and people had about run out of reasons to fight. To make this worse, the population of the world was probably less than ten million." He paused to watch the reaction on Jack's face.

"Oh, my Christ in Heaven." Jack whispered to himself. The thought was sobering. He tried to imagine a world where billions of people had died fighting for who knows what. "How could so many people have been killed? There were what, four billion people before the war?"

"Closer to eight billion. At first you could number the dead in millions, but when the bombs dropped, the gloves were off. Biological warfare was the weapon of choice after the nukes, and in the process, entire continents were nearly wiped out. To this day there are entire cities filled with dust and bones lying where they dropped as invisible plagues swept through, killing nearly everyone in their path. Some of these plagues killed instantly, and some left people dying a horrible agonizing death, but they all accomplished the same thing in the end." Teague fell silent for a full minute, and Jack took the opportunity to say a silent prayer. He knew it would take a long time for him to really appreciate that nearly the whole world was dead. Right now, he could only do what he could to understand his own situation.

Teague finally broke the silence by clearing his throat. "When things settled out, there were many small communities, but nothing much larger than a few hundred people, only a few that numbered in the thousands. Most of the world was a wasteland filled with radiation or worse, completely uninhabitable by anything living. There was little food, few animals had survived the devastation, and those that did were usually tainted in some form, either radiation or biologically. People lived by scavenging what they could, but it was not easy. Although there was little reason to fight, it was truly a matter of only the strong surviving. If you were stronger than the next man, you could take what he had for yourself. The communities had rules, but it really came down to using everything you had to survive.

"Then something changed. About the year 2100, give or take thirty years, a new type of community appeared. They called themselves 'Enclaves of Science' or EoS for short, and they were all led by groups of scientists and engineers. Nobody was really sure how these groups were related, or where all the scientists came from. Some people theorized that they were a network of people who had survived by living underground in old military bunkers for a few generations, and once they determined that the fighting was over, the educated descendants emerged to try to recreate civilization.

"The fact was, they had some real talent in their numbers, and they had some real technology. It did not take long for their communities to grow. After all, if you had been living day by day, foraging for food and safe water, freezing in the wintertime, and fighting off people that would just as soon take everything you have and leave your body to rot as to help you, and someone said 'come live with us, we have fresh water and electricity to heat our homes', you would probably drop what you were doing and go have a look for yourself. All you had to do to live with these people was follow the rules, and rule number one was: everyone contributes. If you couldn't or wouldn't contribute, they showed you the door, and if you didn't accept that, they killed you and hung your body at the gates of their cities to remind everyone that their rules had consequences.

"It might sound harsh but given the conditions people had survived, it was like a paradise, and the EoS flourished. Soon they were powerful cities, and they sent out expeditionary groups to search out old technologies that had been thought lost in the war. Within a handful of years they had ascended to the level of technology that existed before the war, and soon after, they far exceeded it."

Jack was captivated with the history. He had questions, but he didn't want to interrupt the doc to ask. Teague continued on. "In the cities, they had running water, electricity, and all the amenities of a modern civilization. Crime was almost non-existent, as punishment for committing a crime was either death or banishment. Banishment was the worse of the two. Inside the cities it was safe, and populations grew to tens of thousands. There were about a dozen cities in total, and each one shared their technology with the others, trading it as if it were currency. It was a completely open society, where wealth and status was measured by your contribution to the collective population.

53

"However, as with anything on this world, life in the EoS was far from perfect. First off, there was no moral guidance. The entire population had come from poverty so overwhelming that human life itself had no value beyond a person's ability to contribute. When life is not sacred, you have no moral ground to stand on. There were laws, like don't murder, don't steal, et cetera, but those were not in place because it was wrong to do so, they were in place because murdering your neighbor takes away his contribution to society and stealing creates tension and lowers productivity."

"What about religion? Surely there were religious folks who believed in an afterlife and the consequences of living an amoral life."

Teague was quick to answer, as if he had spent a lot of time considering this very point. "Have you read the Holy Bible Jack?"

"More or less, I was in a Catholic orphanage for part of my life."

"Are you familiar with Revelations?"

"The Apocalypse, yes…" Jack was seeing where this was headed.

"Anyone who survived the devastation and still believed in God pretty much believed that they were the ones left behind, unworthy of Heaven, destined to live a life of Hell on earth. Few people were inclined to pass that on to their children. Why teach a child about Heaven when you know they can never reach it? In their minds, God had abandoned humanity. So they abandoned God."

Jack shivered. His faith was never strong, and his taste of religion in the orphanage kept him from spending too much time even thinking about religion or God. But despite his weak faith, he couldn't imagine a world where nobody believed in a higher power.

Teague let that sink in for a moment before continuing then said, "With this lack of a moral base, science had no restraint. Technology grew at a rate that was almost uncontrollable. When computer processing was elevated beyond that of the human brain, things really heated up."

Jack interrupted again, "Computer? The last computer I saw was the size of a room but it could do math faster than any person I knew. What made these new machines so special?" When Jack was first in the army, a 'computer' was a man or woman who was really good at doing math, and he or she sat around all day computing things. Soon after the war, electronic computers came into existence and the last couple years had seen huge advances in that field. "I mean, I don't know much about computers, but if it can multiply two numbers faster than me, isn't it already smarter than me?"

Teague tried to explain. "A lot of people confused the ability to crunch numbers with intelligence, but the fact is, a biological brain is an incredibly powerful processor. Are you familiar with math Jack?"

Jack nodded. "I know a little bit, enough to do a little engineering on a job site."

"So you know what pi is? For finding the circumference of a circle?" Jack nodded again. "Well, pi is an infinitely long constant, and a human can spend weeks crunching numbers to get to a hundred decimal places, where a computer can figure pi to a million decimal places in a very short amount of time. On the other hand, a human brain can *discover* pi in the first place and then apply it to other mathematical equations to learn even more. A computer just couldn't do that. By 2012 that computer you saw that took up a whole room could be put on a piece of silicon the size of a tip of a needle. The first IBM computers had transistors that numbered in the thousands; by 2012 they were making processors that had billions of transistors, but they were still just glorified calculators, and a simple rat's brain could out think a computer. The scientists in the EoS studied biological brains and used that knowledge to create computers that could think like humans, and soon they could learn like humans. It paved the way for some incredible discoveries."

The subject went way over Jack's head, so he took the doc's word for it. "So when did they figure out how to clone a person?" Jack was interested in the history, but he really wanted to get back to the point: How did he get here.

"I'm getting there Jack, just have a little patience." Teague said it with a smile, and Jack nodded, knowing that if he jumped ahead there would only be more questions. Better to answer those questions now.

"Well, now they had computers that could think and learn faster than the smartest scientists, and hence the development of technology was accelerated a great deal. The biggest boundaries in science at the beginning of the twenty first century were breached and it seemed like there was no end to how advanced things could get. Medical science in particular leapt forward to imaginary heights. Cancer was cured. Disease all but eliminated, limbs and organs could be recreated with mechanical devices that were far better than what God himself had created. They did hit a limit however. They could keep a person alive by keeping his organs working, but they couldn't stop the aging process, nor could they reverse it. Eventually the brain would age to a point where it no longer functioned, and you can't replace the brain with a machine. And of course, they couldn't create life in the first place.

"They figured that if they were ever going to discover a way to do these things, that cloning was the technology that will lead to it. So they started playing with cloning again. The first approach was to see if they could make a perfect copy of someone, memories and all. They found the same thing that scientists from before the war found. You can make a perfect twin easily enough, but it's the environment that makes a person what he is, not biology. Since you cannot recreate the experiences of a person, you cannot recreate that person.

"So they turned their attention to the other organs they could not replace by mechanical means, such as ovaries. No mechanical device can create eggs, it requires a biological device. They took the research they had done on aging, and while that research never lead to the discovery of reversing age, it did lead to the discovery of accelerating age. With the ability to accelerate age they could clone a person, grow them to puberty in a matter of weeks, and then harvest the parts they wanted, and discard the body."

"Oh my GOD! That's disgusting!" Just hearing something like that made Jack sick. To create a human being just to harvest the parts! "How could anyone do that and live with themselves? It's unthinkable!"

Teague grimly nodded in agreement. "I agree with you, but you have to understand, these people did not have the same moral ideas that you and I have. They were raised in an environment where the value of human life was measured by its contribution to society." He stopped pacing, went to a cabinet, took out a cup, and filled it from a pitcher he got from the refrigerator. "Would you like some water?" Jack nodded and he poured a second cup. Putting the two cups on the table, he sat down and took a sip. "In the EoS, a ten year old child would not hesitate to put a gun to his father's head and pull the trigger if the man could no longer work. These were a people raised in an environment completely alien to the world you grew up in, Jack. It wasn't that people were cruel to each other, they were just raised to believe that contribution is sacred, not life." He took another sip to let this sink in.

"But wouldn't a child have love for a parent? That alone should prevent someone from killing a loved one."

"That is a good point, and you are correct. Even a lack of religious morals doesn't prevent people from caring about one another. But it is that caring that leads to the willingness to sever a connection even as deep as the one between a father and his child. You see, this is a culture built on contribution. A child is taught from the beginning that life is only as valuable as the contribution it can provide. A man might be able to work hard enough to provide for himself and his family, and a ten year old child might be able to work hard enough to contribute his own share. But that ten year old could not provide for himself and his father, let alone the rest of the family. Perhaps though, a ten year old could provide for his siblings, and they still had potential to contribute and provide for themselves, where the father who was unable to contribute was simply dead weight at this point. What use is love if it doesn't lead to sacrifice for those you love? A loving father would not only insist that his child do what is best for the family, but teach him from a young age that it is the right choice. Hence it was practically an honor to end the life of a crippled or elderly parent."

This was so foreign to Jack that he wasn't sure he would ever understand it. So he just nodded and said, "So there was no religion or morality to prevent someone from suggesting that it was bad to grow a human being solely to kill it and harvest the parts, because it served the highest purpose they believed in: contribution to society."

"More or less, Jack. You are very quick to understand." Jack again simply nodded. "But there was more to it than just what they could get out of the harvesting.

"See, the bodies they grew had been alive for four to eight weeks. Their brains were growing but there was no input to make them develop. Humans have very few native instincts and rely on the parents to teach them how to survive, and that takes years. Nobody was willing to sacrifice time and resources to "raise" a full grown human body that consumed as much as an adult. It could take years before it could contribute on its own, and the sacrifice was too much, at least when you look at it in raw terms of contribution versus consumption."

"Without the morality that religion brings, people looked at it in the simplest of views. A human body that cannot think on its own and survive without the aid of others is simply not human, it is just a mass of biological organs, an animal that can provide something for humans."

Jack had to take a drink of water just to keep from vomiting. "This is making me ill, Doc. What about a newborn baby? A baby can't survive on its own, what is the difference?"

"Don't forget that at the core, we are biologically programmed to procreate and care for our offspring. Nobody gave birth to these bodies. And if you looked at it from the purely mathematical perspective, a baby does not require many resources to raise, at least compared to what a full grown person requires, and while it requires sacrifice to raise a child, it is a worthy investment that will return far more than the sacrifice."

Jack understood this part, but it still left a nauseating feeling in his gut. "Do they still do this?"

"Oh no, the EoS no longer exists. It was ironic, but the policies that they put in place to become so successful were their ultimate downfall. Regardless of the medical advances, the original founders of the EoS realized that they would soon be unable to contribute to society themselves, and be turned away from the very cities they built. They had to come up with a way to change a lot of people's minds in a hurry if they were going to remain in power.

Teague paused here, almost as if remembering the events himself but perhaps as if this was a turning point of some kind and needed a dramatic pause. "The history they had learned from the spoils of the technology hunters showed them that the fastest way to change a culture was with religion. The tool they chose was Christianity."

Jack frowned. "You say that like it is a bad thing."

"Jack, don't get me wrong, but if you look at history you will see that some of the worst atrocities were done in the name of God. Religion is a powerful force."

"I don't disagree with that, but religion can also prevent a lot of atrocities. The world you have described is sickening to me, truly a Hell on earth. Surely if people hadn't given up their faith things would have turned out different."

"Perhaps, but to use a phrase you might be familiar with, that is neither here nor there. Things happened the way they did."

"Okay, go on." He wasn't happy with this, but it made sense.

Teague moved on quickly, "First, they brought forth a new discovery. They declared that their inability to create life from nothing was irrefutable proof that there was a God, a being that created life on earth, and then created man. They used scripture from the bible to convince people that the Great

War that decimated humanity was in fact the Armageddon. The End Times had come and gone, and all the people who deserved to spend eternity in Heaven were taken and the rest left to rot on earth until they perish and spend eternity rotting in Hell. They taught that they were all the descendants of these damned, and they themselves were damned to an eternity in Hell as well. But then they offered redemption, a way to cleanse their tainted souls and gain a shot at getting into Heaven. All they had to do was follow the rules set forth by God, given unto them, the scientists, to spread to the forsaken. They wrote their own book of the bible, a new age warranted new rules.

"The general population had not been raised with religious morals, but after a couple dozen years of living in the prosperity and comfort of the cities, the idea of having an all-powerful God to watch over them and protect them and give them eternal life was appealing. Nobody wanted to go back to the way it was before the EoS came along. The most appealing aspect of religion, however, was that God had created life, and therefore only God had the right to end life. This meant society could not turn people out when they were no longer able to contribute to society. Contribution was written into the new book of the Holy Bible as an unbreakable rule, but once you were no longer able to contribute, you could retire to enjoy the fruits of your labor. The popularity of this concept grew very rapidly.

"Again, however, the creators of the EoS had stepped on their own foot. The power shifted from the people who controlled the technology to the people who controlled the church. At first these were the same people, but the personalities best suited for scientific work were not necessarily suited for religious leaders. Those previously in power formed and funded their own churches, each with slight variations, but in most cases they lost control of their creations when someone would come along who had the right personality to rally people to their beliefs. The more people who joined their church, the more power that church had. Lines were drawn, and tensions began to build. Each new church had more lenient rules and better rewards in Heaven. The struggle for power eventually led to the same result most struggles end in: religious war. Only, this time the technology was much further advanced than in 2012. Within another decade, all that technology had been focused on eliminating each other from the face of the planet. The EoS lasted about forty years in total before they were completely destroyed."

There was a minute or two of silence as this sunk in. All this information made sense, but it still didn't explain how he came to be. "So the EoS died off, where does that leave me?" He took a drink of water and tried to relax.

"Oh, I'm sorry Jack, you had asked if the EoS was still around and... oh never mind, I just got side tracked. Okay, in a way, the most important discovery *ever* came from the formation of these churches within the EoS. Every so often, someone comes along that just looks at things in a different way than anyone else. There was one scientist, we know him as Christopher, who had quietly worked for years on studying the development of the human brain. His research focused on teaching computers to be creative. He figured that the key was in the way a person views things, or more simply put, his upbringing. To learn how various events in one's life lead to being more or less creative, he studied how the brain stores memory. His goal was to give computers a history, or a set of memories, so they would develop goals for themselves rather than be slaves to the creativity of the person programming the computer. In the process, he figured out not only how the brain creates memories and personality, but also how to duplicate the cells that have memory stored in them, and cause those cells to develop in another brain. Unfortunately the only way to 'read' the memories was to destroy those cells, which would kill the person whose memories you were reading. Because of this he could only use freshly dead people in his experiments, or people who were about to die. In his first successful experiment, he took the memories from a person who had just died, and grew them into another person's brain so that person now had the memories of the dead person. It was something of a success, and that person now had some memories from the one who was dead. However, the conflicting memories drove the person insane in a relatively short period of time.

"With the success and the knowledge that two personalities in one brain is a bad idea, Christopher wanted to take that technology and apply it to a brain that was a blank slate. The only blank brains he knew of were the clones that were being grown to replace people's organs. They were perfect candidates, but if he grew a full set of memories into them, then they were no longer just meat, now they were people who could contribute to society, and of more value than just an organ. Keep in mind that wealth and power were gained from the contribution that your technology gave to the society, and the scientists who were making cloned body parts were enjoying a very high status in the EoS. Because of this, they did not allow Christopher to experiment with their cloned bodies for fear they would lose that status. His research on creating memories came to a halt and he started to look back to applying the memories to the thinking computers.

"Then along comes the religious folks, saying that God gave us the gift of life, and we need to treat human life as the most important thing on earth. In other words: no more making humans just for spare parts, even if they couldn't think for themselves. The power shifted away from the scientists who cloned and the door was open for Christopher to grow a person and copy a brain from a freshly dead person into the newly growing brain.

"Again, Success! And again, a failure. The first time they did it, the person woke up, remembered that he was dying, and that triggered his body to die again. That was an issue."

Teague paused and took a drink of water. "So he spent some time figuring out how to determine the new memories from the old memories. Once he got that down, he transplanted all but the last few days from a dead man's brain into a new brain in one of the clones. Another success, and another failure. The successful part was that the clone didn't have memory of dying, so he didn't die right away. For all intents and purposes, he functioned normally. It took a few hours for his brain to reconnect with the rest of the body, something to do with the way the body was grown at such an accelerated pace, kind of how it takes a baby time to really see things, and to move and figure out how to use its body. Like the accelerated growth of his body, his brain learned quickly and soon the person was up and moving, even walking and talking."

Jack understood that this was why it took him time to see and move the previous day. "You said it was another failure though. What happened?"

"It was quite simple, actually. The man's memories did not match his body. They put his memories in someone else's body. In the first experiments, Christopher was able to put some memories into someone else's brain, but that person had already established his identity. His brain knew exactly how his heart worked, how all his organs worked, and most importantly, who he was physically. He didn't die, he just went insane from the conflicting memories. In this latest experiment, he put an incompatible set of memories in a body, and within hours, the man's heartbeat was irregular, his breathing was out of sync, his liver and kidneys started to fail, and eventually, he died. The subconscious memory was too unfamiliar with the body and it caused him to shut down. Like I said earlier, the mind is an incredible computer. It knew those things weren't right and rejected them."

Teague took a final drink of water, then got up and put the cup on the counter. He started pacing again as he finished the story. "So it was obvious at that point you had to put the memories into an exact clone to get it to work, and when he tried it, it worked! He cloned a freshly dead man, accelerated his growth, implanted the memories, and he had the first successful true clone of another human being.

"Christopher had done what nobody had ever been able to do, and he never would have been able to do it if it hadn't been for the religious groups that outlawed the harvesting of the cloned bodies. In a manner of speaking, God had been the catalyst that led to the success."

Jack looked at him in silence for a full minute, taking in the whole sequence of events that led up to the ability to re-create a human with all his memories, then finally asked a question. "So how come you said it's the most important discovery ever?"

Teague stopped pacing, sat down across from Jack, looked him in the eye and said, "Quite simply because it will save humanity from extinction."

Chapter 13

"Come on doc, isn't that a little melodramatic? How is it that cloning will save humanity?" Jack was skeptical of the idea. Humans had been on earth for hundreds of thousands of years without the need to clone; he found it hard to believe that it was now that important. The story behind it all was logical enough that he could buy into it, and he was pretty much convinced that Teague was telling him the truth here. How else could he explain where he was? This would have to be the most elaborate hoax ever, if it were not true. There was only one thing he could think of that didn't make sense. Teague was about to try to answer his question when Jack blurted out another question. "You said that Christopher had to use a freshly dead brain to clone, how is it that you used mine after three hundred and fifty years?" Jack leaned back, convinced that he had knocked a big hole in Teague's story.

"That's a good question, and it ties in with your first question." Teague said it like he was proud to have gotten this far. "First let me go back to the EoS. I told you that they used their technology to try to wipe each other out. Well, they pretty much succeeded. One religious group in particular was sort of hell bent on wiping out humanity. They figured that God had meant for humanity to become extinct in the first big war that started in 2012. They genetically engineered a virus that took out the gene in male DNA that allows for reproduction. It was a time bomb virus that only affected male babies that were conceived by men and women who were exposed to the virus. So it took over fifteen years before anyone knew that it had happened, and by then there wasn't a human on the planet that hadn't been exposed to the virus. There was about a one in six thousand immunity rate, but it was so incredibly small that humanity didn't stand a chance. The next generation was nearly the last to be born naturally. On top of this, all the biological warfare still going on was killing people by the thousands."

"Are you saying that it wiped out everyone? Then what about you and the people here? Are you the last people on earth?" This had taken Jack by surprise. He hadn't seen this one coming. He could deal with a world torn apart by nuclear fallout because even radiation had a half-life and eventually it would be gone, and humans could once again rebuild. But infertility, how do you overcome that?

"Remember when I told you that the EoS shared its knowledge?" Jack nodded. "Well, once Christopher was successful in a complete clone, he published his work and traded it for status and wealth. The power may have shifted away from the scientists, but this was a pretty big deal and while it didn't give him much political status in the EoS, it afforded him better facilities to work in and a better lifestyle. By the time the information got to everyone, however, the power struggles had already begun, and most of the scientists were either creating new ways to kill people, or finding cures for the stuff the others were making. When the fighting was over, and only a handful of people were left in each city, it was clear that the only way to survive was to use that technology to clone each person as they died. I and a handful of people that live in this bunker are cloned descendants of those few survivors."

Jack thought about that for a second. "That would mean that you have all the memories from all the copies of yourself since..."

"Yes," Teague said, "according to my memories, I have been alive for one hundred and eighty years. I am the third clone of my original." Teague got up and excused himself to use the restroom, and to let Jack think for a few minutes.

~~~~

Jack was deep in thought when Teague returned. In a very short time a huge amount of information had been delivered, but it was still just information, it didn't feel like a history, and certainly not a history of the world Jack had lived in. Many events in his life had changed his perspective of people, his country, and the world in general, but nothing like this. Billions of people dead from unnatural causes. The near extinction of humanity and the destruction of most life on earth. These were not things that were easy to accept. He needed a break, time to come to terms with it, but there were still questions that needed answers before he could take a break.

Teague refilled their water glasses and took a seat across from Jack. He didn't speak for several minutes, perhaps waiting for a cue from Jack, or maybe because he was collecting his thoughts. Jack finally ended the silence, picking up as if they hadn't paused the conversation. "Well, that explains how you know so much of the history. But that still doesn't explain how I got to be here. How did you clone me without a fresh body?" That term still bothered Jack, but he just wasn't ready to process it yet.

Teague nodded and said, "Let me go back to some history from your time." Teague settled in the chair across from Jack again, and began. "Sometimes, the creativity of a story teller can spur a scientific discovery. Someone comes up with an idea that is out of this world, and years later someone else decides that it isn't too far-fetched, and figures out how to do it. You got to see a lot of the race to get into space between the Russians and the Americans. You missed the moon landing by only a couple years."

Jack smiled at this. "We made it huh? And we beat the Russians?"

"Yes. You did. My point is, there were stories for decades about traveling to the moon. Eventually, it happened. Another popular science fiction story line was where someone is frozen, maybe in an avalanche, and is discovered and brought back to life in the future. In 1967, a company in the United States opened its doors based on this premise. They were selling immortality. They figured that in the future there would be a way to cure all illnesses, and if perfectly preserved, a person could be brought back to life when the cure for whatever killed them was discovered. It was quite popular among the wealthy, and the company thrived.

"Unfortunately for them, the facility was destroyed in the war. Furthermore, nobody had ever figured out how to revive someone who had been dead for more than a few minutes." Teague looked at Jack and said, "Jack, do you recall that last project you were working on, not too far from the city of Great Falls, Montana?"

A tingle went up Jack's spine. He *knew* that had something to do with him being here. "Yeah, is that what that place was? They froze people?"

"The facility you were building before your last memory was completed in February 1967. It was designed to house a cryogenic storage unit for experimentation. The military was freezing soldiers who died in battle and some who died of incurable diseases like cancer, in order to try reviving them when medical technology improved. The cryogenic capsules required very little power, and originally a small hydroelectric power plant was built a few miles away to power it. In 2010 the facility was made to be self-sufficient and a small, automated nuclear power source was placed in the lower levels with enough fuel to last hundreds of years, as long as nothing went wrong. They sealed up the complex with the plan to go back in a few generations when medical science progressed further."

~~~~

Jack didn't know what to say. It all made sense now. Somehow Phil had gotten him in as a candidate, and here he was three hundred plus years later, exactly as planned. But the revelation didn't quench his curiosity, at least not quite yet. "So you found me and cloned me, and with a frozen brain you were able to recreate my memories?"

"Yes, it was a stroke of luck, or fate, or whatever you want to call it. We were all that was left of humanity, basically waiting until enough accidents happened where there were not enough of us left to keep cloning or when the equipment we use to clone ourselves irreparably breaks down. I told you I have been around for a long time, and for many decades we have built machines to scour the earth looking for other survivors. It is a bleak task that yielded very low results, and in the past two decades we have not found a single undocumented survivor."

"If people were unable to bear children, how are there any survivors at all?"

"Women are carriers of the virus but are never infected, they don't have the gene that the virus attacks. Only the men born of these women are infected and end up infertile. If a man was immune to the disease, he could father children, but since all women are carriers, every baby is a carrier as well. This leads to an exponential infertility rate across the generations."

"Exponential?"

"Yes, the chance of a male child never exposed to the virus to be immune to it is about one in six thousand. The chance of that man to father an immune child is about one in twenty. Before this virus, it was estimated that nearly six million people existed on this continent. With the ascendancy of the

EoS, birth rates were up and for each person alive, at least one new child was born before that person died. After the virus infected the entire population, around 10,000 men of the next generation were fertile. Between the wars going on and the still relatively high rate of infection, fewer than a thousand fertile men were estimated to exist after the cities began to fall.

"Hundreds of communities across the continent, mostly small in population, were formed by survivors. By the time we had the technology in place to start looking for survivors, the total number of fertile men were estimated to number in the hundreds if not less."

"Doc, I am no mathematician but you make it sound like humanity doesn't have a chance, even with those few hundred fertile men."

"In a way you are exactly right. But that doesn't mean humanity hasn't tried to find a way." Teague said this with a hint of a smile.

"What exactly does that mean?" He suspected he knew, but wanted to be sure before he gave his initial suspicion any merit.

"Basically, it means that once they knew that most babies born would be infertile, they started having a LOT more babies. In the communities we found, it wasn't unusual for fertile men to father dozens of children, sometimes hundreds, and from dozens of different women. The culture changed very dramatically mostly because of the instinctive need to preserve the species. People could no longer afford to hold any taboo or conservatism toward sex, and monogamy was out the window as well. The only insurance of continuation of the species was to copulate far more frequently and to spread the virile seeds as far and wide as possible. Most communities didn't have the knowledge or equipment to check for fertility, so as soon as a boy reached an age where he was fertile, he was expected to attempt to get as many women as possible pregnant. In many cases this started as young as eleven years old, and until it was determined that they were infertile, they were encouraged to continue trying at least until about twenty years old. Because of the immediate necessity to keep the population alive, recordkeeping was seldom accurate as females were often encouraged to have sex with many different males during each of their cycles. So, successful fertilization was not always a sign of a man's fertility. Sex became a regular part of life in a way no other human culture has ever seen."

"Do you find this as disturbing as I do? Holy shit, Doc, you are telling me that for the last hundred and fifty years humanity has whiled away its days in one big orgy?" On the surface, it sounded like a dream for any man, but his conservative Catholic background still made it seem incredibly immoral, unclean, and unsavory.

"That would be a crude way to put it, but yes, sexual relations became as common as a handshake. And I can understand why this is disturbing to you. However, I grew up in a completely different time than you, where certain things were necessary for the survival of our species. I was never exposed directly to this sort of culture, I was born infertile so there has never been any pressure on me to impregnate women, at least not to the degree that many of the communities since the fall of the EoS have had to endure."

"So how many of these communities are still out there?"

"Well, despite the low rate of potency in the population, the efforts of the community to keep the fertility rate up led to sizeable populations, at least compared to what would have been if they had stuck to a monogamous culture. But even so, each generation held fewer and fewer fertile men. Plus, the lack of control over this cultural change led to some pretty major issues. Inbreeding and disease were two of the larger issues. After a couple generations, it was extremely likely that the man who is getting her pregnant is a half-brother or cousin."

"That is just wrong Teague, any way you explain it."

"I agree, and from my viewpoint, one of science, it disturbs me to think that this sort of activity, while having the right intentions, was executed so poorly. Some decent records would have gone a long way toward keeping inbreeding to a minimum. Many of these communities have failed over the years as a direct result."

Obviously Teague's sense of morality was far different from Jack's. This was neither the time nor place to point that out, however, this line of conversation was both interesting and disturbing and it was time to get back on track. "So you have made an effort to find these communities and rescue them?"

"Yes, with a little success. Over the years we managed to find about a hundred survivors and bring fifteen of them in. Not everyone was interested in living with us or the other communities like ours. We represent, to some, the EoS, or at least the remnants of it. Our groups are mostly made up of cloned infertiles. Like I said, in the past two decades we have failed to locate any more undocumented survivors. We try to get along with the other communities, but each group is very protective, and for good reason. We don't know exactly how many fertile men each community has. We have done our best to keep inbreeding to a minimum, and part of this effort involves arranging virile men to impregnate women from other groups, in exchange for the same from them. Even so, of the breeding population here, most are related at least as second or third cousins. After over a hundred years, we have expanded our group to about fifty people; about eleven of them are virile men, able to father children. Despite careful selection of mate combinations, there just wasn't enough diversity in the gene pool, and things have slowed down."

"Wait, if you knew that only one in twenty children born were going to be virile, why don't you have hundreds of people in your group?" Jack felt like he didn't really want the answer to this, but he had to ask.

"Good question, Jack, I have to say I am amazed by your ability to pick up on the details." Jack didn't even blink; he didn't want this conversation derailed until he had the details he needed to process it all. Teague continued, "First off, when those of us who founded this community escaped the cities during the wars, we didn't leave empty handed. We brought along some tech, and between us we had some decent medical expertise. We had several women but only one fertile man, and it didn't take long before he had fathered several children, none of which were fertile themselves. Our resources were very limited at first, and we just couldn't support too many children. So we worked on the problem in the way we knew how. We attacked it from two angles: first was finding more fertile men, and second was ensuring that the children they had were all fertile. The first required us building machines to search for signs of human life, the second involved developing a method to detect infertile children before the pregnancy was too far along, and terminate any that weren't going to give us the results we needed."

"Good Lord, is there no end to the immorality?" Jack felt ill again, a feeling he was growing used to during this conversation.

"Jack, you have to understand that the survival of humanity was at stake here, this was not a decision we took lightly."

"Doc, you don't have to defend your actions with me."

"I know, Jack, I know." Jack could see the pain on his face so he let it go. "Anyway, even after we found a few fertile men in the survivors, it was rare to have a birth around here. We could have had more, but it would have resulted in inbreeding, so the population only grew with the discovery of more fertile men. We have had a few successful births through the exchange program, but overall things were not developing as fast as we would have liked. At the rate we were going, there was little hope of humanity surviving in the long run.

"We estimate that there are about forty eight hundred people that we know of out there, less than five percent of the males are virile. There are more on other continents, but our best guess puts the world population of humanity below ten thousand people."

This was staggering. Jack had traveled a good portion of the world in his life and had a very good idea for how big this planet was. To spread ten thousand people out over that kind of expanse was almost certainly going to lead to extinction, even if they could reproduce, which they pretty much couldn't, at least not at a rate that was ever going to support any real growth of population.

"Doc, this is a grim story and I would love to learn more about it later. For now, I would like to know how this leads back to me."

Teague had stood up to refill his glass and offered to refill Jack's. After this conversation Jack was ready to try one of those beers but it was still too early. "Four years ago the nuclear reactor in that facility started to malfunction. The electromagnetic noise from the faulty generator was detected by one of our probes while searching for signs of life. We sent a party to the area formerly known as Montana to find out if it was another group of survivors, and instead we found that facility. Only about half the bodies are in good enough shape to clone. Mostly the early ones are in bad shape because the chemicals used to prevent cell damage when they froze the bodies, was insufficient. The last body was added in 2010 when they closed the facility, and that was the first one we were able to bring back. We have since recovered about fifty more people, mostly men, but some women too. You are the oldest successful recovery to date. We now have over thirty children in our population, and, over seventy percent of the men are virile." With that, Teague sat back and fell silent, waiting for Jack to absorb it all.

~~~~

It was beyond overwhelming. He felt exhausted even though he had just been sitting here the whole time listening and thinking. He knew it would take time for him to really absorb it all and be able to think things through. He excused himself to use the restroom. His mind was too occupied to pay attention to the amazing technology in the bathroom.

Foremost in his mind was that he had been given another chance at life. In the short time since waking up he hadn't once thought of this situation as bad for him, after all if he weren't here he would be dead. But what did that really mean?

What happened when he died? Did he go to Heaven? Did Heaven exist? The thing is, he didn't know because he isn't really the Jack Taggart who died in 1967 from cancer. If he died again without losing his brain, there is a chance that they will bring him back again. But it won't be *him*, it will be a copy of him that thinks it's him. *If there is a Heaven, I will still get a chance to meet Peter at the Pearly Gates*, he thought.

Next he thought about the reason he was here. *Hell, I am one of the last men on earth capable of fathering a child.* At first that made him grin. Then a cold realization hit him. *Is this why Wendy came to his room last night?* That would be a huge disappointment, despite the briefness of the encounter, he felt a chemistry with her he hadn't felt since he met Jenny. As he got back to the kitchen, he was brimming with questions.

"So when you talked about the cultural changes in the communities after the virus, how does that affect *this* community? Do the virile men spend their time having sex with the women?"

Teague looked like he had expected the question. "It is true that there are some expectations here, and I can assure you that the culture will require some getting used to, but we will get into those details later. Frankly I am surprised with you Jack, most of the men we have brought back were extremely happy about this part, but you have shown reservation from the first time I mentioned it. Your generation is obviously far different from the others." This was no surprise to Jack, he saw where things were headed long before he even learned about the cancer. "I suspect you are looking for a second answer as well, perhaps regarding last evening?" Jack didn't need to answer, it was probably written all over his face. "I can't tell you Wendy's motive, but what she did is not only acceptable to us, but encouraged. I *can* tell you that she was under a lot of pressure to get pregnant, and until you have impregnated more women, she will have a unique child that can spread the gene pool. In our community that will elevate her standing as well as help the community greatly. In many ways it is perhaps the most key aspect of our society right now. As I said, it's all about the survival of humanity.."

"You sound pretty sure that our... *tryst* will lead to a child being born. Isn't there a high probability that even if she gets pregnant from me that you'll abort her... *our* baby?" There was a dangerous tone to his voice. Regardless of the situation, Jack would risk anything and everything to prevent anyone here from harming a child of his, born or not.

Teague seemed to pick up on this and chose his words carefully, "There was a third element in our effort to ensure the survival of humanity: looking for a cure for the virus. We have not found a cure, but we have found something of equal value, at least now that we found the facility in Montana. We have an immunization. You were immunized when you were brought back, and you can be assured that any child you father will be immune to the virus and able to have children of its own."

~~~~

At least one weight was lifted from his shoulders. He needed to be alone, to think about everything, to process and figure out how he felt about it all. Before he did that though, he needed to answer one more question.

"Doc, tell me one more thing. Is this the only reason you brought me back? To have babies and spread my seed?"

It was a legitimate question; one that Teague obviously wasn't sure whether to answer. After a few moments, he said, "I won't lie to you Jack. We are hoping that you are a solution to a problem, maybe even to a lot of problems. We select people to bring back based on both their potential worth to the community and the chance that recovery will be successful. We are trying to rebuild humanity, but in order to do that we have to survive first. Rest assured, Jack, you will have a lot of value to this community and quite possibly the whole world, but let's just start out by worrying about tomorrow."

It was a vague answer, but good enough for Jack, at least for now.

In some ways, he was disappointed. Even if he fell in love with one woman, it would be expected, *hell, his duty*, to be unfaithful to her. At some point he would need to consider the fate of his friends and family and mourn his loss, even though they lost him, not the other way around. And the memory of his wife and child were still very vivid and a part of his personality.

However, there was some excitement brimming in the back of his mind at the thought of fathering another child, or even more children. Any fear of having to relive the horror of losing a child was surpassed by the hope of another chance to experience what he once lost. In fact, despite the potential challenges, he had a chance to experience love again, and that alone made it all worth it.

For the first time in nearly two years, Jack was truly excited about his future.

Part Two

Chapter 14

The past few days had been a whirlwind. He hadn't even come to terms with having cancer, let alone everything since waking up in this strange environment. Before leaving him alone with his thoughts, Teague gave him one of the 'clipboards' he had been using. "I will show you more of how to use it later, but for now, if you want to make notes on any questions that you come up with, just write them on here as if it's a piece of paper." He showed him by writing a few words. As he wrote them on the surface of the pad, they appeared at the top of the page, neatly typed and even formatted properly.

"Jesus Teague, make this thing answer the phone and you could eliminate secretaries altogether." He said it offhand, but two things hit him as the words left his mouth. The first was that this was no longer 1966 and he would no longer be able to use that time frame as a reference for pretty much anything he thought he knew. Second, it dawned on him that he could probably not even comprehend the way society changed in the years immediately following his death, let alone the changes since the war. He voiced his concerns

It was obvious Teague didn't want to get into it right now. "Look Jack, you've been bombarded with information, and it will take some time for your brain to process it all. Just write down any questions that come up and we can talk about them later." Teague then walked him down the hall to another room. It was a bedroom, about ten foot square, with a small bed, a table and chair, a small set of drawers, and a sink and mirror like the one in the restroom, only this one had regular water faucet. The mirror opened to reveal a small cabinet built into the wall. It was filled with toiletries. He showed Jack how to use the light switch, and how to control the temperature in the room. "Feel free to explore the complex, or just go back to your room and lie down. This is a small community, and for all intents and purposes, everyone knows everyone else. Most people like to meet the latest reborn, so don't be surprised if those you meet are interested in getting to know you. Just carry your datapad with you; with it we can locate you if something happens or contact you if we need to talk. I would probably recommend just getting some rest if you can, however. It is amazing what the brain can do subconsciously to process stuff like this, especially when you are resting. If you need me for anything, just tap the icon I put at the bottom left of your datapad." He pointed to a little symbol that looked like a stethoscope wrapped around a red cross.

"Is that what you call people like me? Reborn? And this is called a datapad? And the symbol here is called an icon?" The terminology was completely new to Jack. "I can see that I'm going to be learning a new language." He said it in a lighthearted fashion, but he knew it would be tough for the first few weeks.

"Jack, I know it will be difficult, and the learning curve will be high, but I can assure you that not only will you pick it all up fairly quickly, but you will be a great asset to us. Is there anything else before I leave you? I have some work to attend to – saving humanity is a busy business." Teague chuckled at his own grim humor but Jack's attention was elsewhere. His mind was already wandering back to the many subjects they had discussed.

"No, no, I think I can handle it. Thanks Teague." He didn't even notice the man leave.

Jack sat heavily in the chair and jumped back up with a yelp when it started moving. A little freaked out, he stared at the chair as if it was possessed. Looking around the room as if he were making sure nobody was watching, he tentatively touched chair. It didn't move this time. He set the datapad on the desk and slowly backed into the chair. The moment his weight was in the seat he felt the bottom and back begin to move. His curiosity kept him from leaping out this time, and after a few seconds the movement stopped. He was sitting rigidly, waiting for something more to happen. The foolishness of his actions sank in, and he relaxed back into the chair. It began to move again and he tensed, then forced himself to relax again. When the chair stopped moving, he was amazed. This was perhaps the most comfortable chair he had ever sat in. He tested it by leaning back, slouching, leaning forward, and then sitting back again, and each time he shifted position the chair adjusted itself to be just as comfortable. "Damn I could get used to this."

He leaned back and started mentally reviewing the last twenty four hours, beginning with the latest information and working his way back. He jotted notes as he went, and soon, all the questions he wanted to address were written down. The list was substantial, and he knew getting answers would only lead to more questions.

He settled back in the chair a little further and, while pondering his fate, drifted off to sleep.

~~~~

Jack woke a few hours later, slowly easing himself out of the chair, fully expecting to be stiff and sore. Somehow, he wasn't all that surprised to find he felt no different than if he had slept on the bed. His internal clock told him it was dinner time, and the sound of his stomach rumbling confirmed it.

He found the kitchen empty. He didn't even know if people here ate meals in the same intervals as in 1966, so he wasn't really surprised. It also dawned on him that maybe the rest of the residents didn't eat in a community kitchen or even live on this level. He didn't even venture to guess. There was a bowl in the cabinet, and he used the food dispenser as he had seen Teague do it earlier today. This time it tasted of meat loaf – in an odd sort of way. He was about to fill his cup with water when he remembered the 'beer' in the refrigerator. There were fifteen bottles in there, and he felt a little guilty as he took one, remembering how Teague had said it was in short supply. "Bah, screw it. I need a drink after all this anyway." He said it to nobody, as nobody was in the room, but it alleviated his guilt just enough for him to open the bottle and take a sip. He grunted as it hit his mouth. It was far from beer, there was no doubt of that. It was heavily carbonated and almost went out his nose. He sputtered and coughed after swallowing, and said, once again to nobody in particular, "Smooth."

"You know, drinking that stuff can decrease your sex drive." The voice startled him and he almost dropped the bottle. He turned around to see Wendy standing there, wearing the typical casual attire, which looked like surgeon's 'scrubs'. She walked into the room, took the bottle from him and took a long pull.

"Christ Wendy you scared the shit outta me." He took the bottle back and sat down to eat. She sat across from him, watching him eat. He decided you didn't so much 'eat' this food as you 'gummed' it. He looked at her after swallowing and asked, "Are you stalking me?"

"Not at all," she said, "I was just out looking for a good lay, and came across you." Jack choked on his food at that comment, coughed a few times, and took another drink to clear his throat. Wendy laughed, and he realized that she was just pulling his leg. "Actually I was sort of waiting for you to come in and eat. I didn't want to interrupt your rest, I figured you needed it. The first couple days can be a lot to take in and can really wear you out. I mostly slept my first week."

Jack was happy she had come to visit with him. He was not entirely comfortable with the idea that she wanted to have his baby or that other women would be wanting, even expecting, the same thing, but there was a familiarity about her that he did find comforting. On top of this there was that feeling that he hadn't felt since the day he had met his former wife, or since the day she had died. He wanted that feeling to last. Jack was a bit old fashioned, and although he never had a hard time getting women, he had never abused that ability and slept around. In fact, he had only 'been' with a half dozen women in his life. There was his wife Jenny, Wendy of course, a girlfriend when he was sixteen that he had convinced to take his virginity before he went off to die in the war, a couple flings in the military before he met Jen, and one young Japanese woman that he had hired to do his housework when stationed in Japan before Korea. He had been pleasantly surprised that housework was not the only thing she did for the monthly pay. He felt a little odd at first with that one, but it wasn't like she was a prostitute off the streets that he had picked up one night, so he didn't feel too bad about it. When he was a young enlisted man, he saw too many of his buddies come back from leave with diseases brought on by their need to satiate their pent up lust. He never felt the risk was worth the embarrassment of having to face a military nurse with a sore penis, not to mention the possibility of having to live with some disease for the rest of his life. He'd had a handful of girlfriends with whom he had *not* slept with throughout that time, but he was never really good at the relationship part, so without the sex, those didn't last too long, at least not until Jenny.

"So you're one of us Wendy? A 'reborn'?" He didn't know anything about her, aside from the carnal knowledge he had acquired the night before.

"Yes. I was brought back four months ago." She opened her mouth to continue, but stopped, her brow scrunching up. Hesitantly, she said, "I still feel awkward referring to my death as a point of reference in my life, and it's even worse in conversation."

He understood. "So how did you die?" He wasn't sure if it was appropriate to ask, as it might be a very personal thing for some people.

"Well, according to my records, I went down in an Apache." She saw the confusion on his face and explained, "It's a helicopter. I was a helicopter mechanic in the Army, and I liked to go out with the pilot after fixing the aircraft to make sure things were working correctly. The first time I went up, the pilot had been raising a ruckus after learning that a female mechanic had been the last one turning a wrench on his bird. I confronted him, and in an effort to get him to trust my work, offered to go up with him on the first flight. Once we were in the air and he had done some maneuvers to assure himself that everything was as good as new, he decided to show off. He did some light aerobatics, put us into a couple dives, and finally put us back on the tarmac as gently as laying a baby in a crib. I fell in love with flying that day, and used the whole 'test flight' idea to get up in the air as often as I could. It wasn't hard to get what I wanted from the pilots, and soon I had them teaching me to fly. I took some ground school courses, and eventually got my pilots license." Wendy stopped suddenly, as if she hadn't meant to open up like that. Jack was engrossed in the story and motioned for her to continue.

"Being a female, the male pilots were keen to show off their piloting skills when I went on flights with them. Although the details in my record were a bit vague, I figure it was most likely that one of these pilots was trying to impress me and got us all killed. Of course, anything could have happened. For all I know, I may have been sneaking some stick time, and made a mistake. The military saw fit to just call it a mechanical failure, with no further detail. The pilot survived, I made it to the hospital but died from severe internal injuries."

The concept of female enlisted mixing with the male enlisted in typical military roles was foreign to Jack. There were women in the military when he was around, but mostly as nurses or secretarial staff. He didn't want to offend her by asking the wrong question, but he really wanted to know how that worked. "It must have been hard, being a woman in the Army. During my time the only women that were enlisted were basically secretaries and nurses, and they had it rough enough. I can't even imagine one being in the common ranks with other men." He hoped he didn't sound too chauvinistic with that comment. The women's liberation movement had just gone mainstream in '66, and Jack was sympathetic to their cause. He knew there were plenty of women qualified to do more than type and look pretty, and they should have their fair shake. He wondered if they were allowed to be regular soldiers too.

She smiled, and Jack got the sense she recognized his consideration in choosing his words carefully. Despite his interest in the conversation, it was hard work paying attention when she smiled like that. He felt like he could spend the rest of his life just watching her smile. "It wasn't too bad by the time I joined. There were seven women in my platoon. Women were allowed most jobs, but not overseas combat soldiers. They always thought the enemy would use us against the men, either by targeting the women or by capturing and using us as bait. I joined to get money for college, and found myself on my third re-enlistment getting prepared to go to Iraq as a behind the lines support mechanic, but I guess I never made it there."

The only woman Jack had ever met who aspired to be a mechanic was a beefy, butch dike. Granted, in his time if a woman was interested in that sort of thing, she was ridiculed. Learning that Wendy was passionate about roles which, in his time, were exclusive to men, fascinated him. On some level, he probably suspected this was just an infatuation brought about by his recent hormonal changes combined with the need to latch on to someone emotionally after all the trauma he had been through in recent days, but right now, he wanted nothing more than to continue this conversation. "So how old were you when you... uh –"

"Died? I was twenty seven. I liked the military and decided to stick with it. It was a much more peaceful time than when you were in the military. I never expected I would have to go to war. When I was told I would be going, it seemed unreal to me. I knew the chances of seeing any real action were slim, but it definitely made me see my military career in a whole new light. I went through the same combat training everyone else did, and I was pretty sure if it ever came down to a fight I could handle it, but even at the time I never thought it would happen."

"What year was it?" Jack had no sense of the time line after 1966. Teague had mostly breezed over the years before 2012.

"2009, March. I was born in 1982." She was watching for his reaction, and despite trying to make light of it, he felt himself pale a little.

"My god I robbed the cradle. You might have been friends with my *grandchildren!*" He was trying to tease her a little, but his words reminded him of his daughter. *If only Ally'd had a chance to live that long.* He had spent so many nights thinking about the what-ifs, but now that he knew what her future would have held, he wasn't so sure that he would have wanted her to live through it all.

Wendy saw the change on his face and asked, "What is it Jack? Did that really upset you? I wasn't trying to – I mean I was just giving you some crap."

Jack hastily said, "No, I just... I was thinking about my daughter, that's all. She would have been almost fifty when you died. I'm beginning to think maybe her death was a blessing. She didn't have to watch me die of cancer, and she didn't have to suffer the war, potentially losing her own children – or grandchildren."

"I don't believe that, Jack, and I don't think you do either." Wendy put her hand over his. "I think, despite what hardships her future might have brought, getting the chance to live would have been a wonderful gift. I am truly sorry for you *and* your daughter – that she didn't get to experience life. It does, however, make me even more grateful that I – we – were given a second chance at life." She had teared up a little, and Jack squeezed her hand.

"Thank you, Wendy. It's good to know you care. Let's change the subject shall we?" Jack was getting a little emotional, and while her empathy towards his daughter made him feel good, he didn't want her to see him blubbering like an idiot. "Tell me everything about the time from 1966 to 2009."

Wendy laughed. "Everything? Trust me, you don't want to know everything. How 'bout I give you the highlights, and if you really want to know about the bad stuff you can talk to someone else about it." He sat back to listen to her talk, enjoying every minute of it.

~~~~

"So a black man was elected president?" Jack was stunned, although he wasn't sure how, after all the things he learned tonight, something like this still amazed him. He had grown up in a poor neighborhood in California, and was not a racist by any measure. A good percentage of the men he had served with, and even some of his closest buddies, were black. He didn't see their color as making them any different than him. He had, however, witnessed how hard of a time they had, compared to the white men, and that must be what made it difficult to see how a country whose majority population was made up of white men would elect a black man as their leader. It really put the differences between 2009 and 1966 into perspective. *To think I might have lived to see that, if the cancer hadn't gotten me...* Of all the amazing things Wendy had told him tonight, that ranked high on the list of those he regretted missing.

"Yup. Two million people showed up for his inauguration. Of course, it wasn't long after that I went down in the chopper, so that's about all I have for you." She had covered it all like a pro, from Vietnam and Nixon, to Iran and Disco, to Ronald Reagan and John Lennon, to Bill Clinton and non-sexual oral sex, to George W. and 9/11, and finally to Iraq and the crashing economy.

"Incredible. That's all I can really say... just... incredible. To think I was in my garage less than a week ago, waxing my mustang, listening to some hippie music on the radio, and here I am, having missed such amazing things as the end of the Cold War, cellular telephones, and iced mochaccinos." Wendy laughed, but it ended in a yawn.

"Crap, do you believe it's four in the morning? I have to get up soon to finish fixing that damn heat exchanger on level four." She yawned again and stood up.

Jack said, "Wendy, I've had an absolutely great time talking with you. I haven't had this much fun in months. Thank You." He was being sincere.

Wendy laughed at that and said, "Ha! If this is the most fun you've had in months, you must have been pretty damn bored!" She walked around the table as she said it. Jack stood up, looking a little sheepish. She was dead on, even if she was just joking with him. She walked right up to him, put her arms around his neck, pressed her bosom to his chest, and looked into his eyes. "You know, if you are looking for some real fun, I bet I can accommodate you." She leaned in even closer and kissed him. Jack was instantly aroused and returned the kiss with passion.

He broke off the kiss, and said, "Isn't this the part where I walk you to your room and give you a kiss goodnight?"

She pulled away, took his arm and said, "Let's go see your room instead."

Chapter 15

This time, when Jack woke up, Wendy was still in the bed, snuggled up against him. He smiled, and carefully stretched, trying not to wake her. He didn't have a clock or a watch, but figured he had slept a little late. He lay there, enjoying the warmth of Wendy's body and thinking about the night before. *What an incredible night!* He wasn't just thinking about the sex, *well, that was incredible too,* he thought with a smile, but the whole evening just talking with Wendy, learning about her life and the history that he had missed. *Is that the right word? History?* He considered the question and decided if it had happened before now, so it was indeed history.

Back in the present he was sensing his bladder was full. Knowing the consequences of failing to reach a bathroom soon was barely enough to convince him to move. He carefully extracted himself from the bed and stood up. Just before he made it to the door, he realized the hallway was public. Even though he had not seen anyone other than Teague around here, he didn't think it would be appropriate to run into someone while in his birthday suit. He sort of hopped his way into his pants as he made his way to the door, and they were about halfway up when the door opened automatically. Jack stopped hopping and looked up to see two women standing in the hall, mouths open, staring at him. He quickly finished pulling up his pants, flushing a deep red that covered most of his naked chest.

"Well good morning!" one if the women said. They both laughed in a giggly sort of way but neither turned to leave. One of the two women looked past Jack and then glanced at her friend, an almost disappointed look on her face. Something passed between them and they turned and started walking down the hall. They both glanced over their shoulders after a few steps and the one who hadn't spoken said, "Nice to meet you, Jack. Very nice!" More giggles.

Jack leaned against the door frame, feeling like an idiot. "Smooth move, Mad Dawg," he said out loud to himself.

"Jack what the hell are you doing?" He turned around. The voices of the women had woken Wendy up and she was leaning on an elbow in bed with an amused look on her face. The sheet had slipped down and exposed her breasts and his eyes wandered down to admire them before answering.

"I uh... I was going to use the bathroom and the damn door opened before I had my pants on all the way! There were two women standing there. I don't know who was more startled, me or them." Jack was still embarrassed but as he said it he chuckled. "Is there a way to make it so the door doesn't automatically open like that?"

Wendy burst out laughing, laying back down on her back. "God I wish I could have seen the looks on their faces when the door opened. Did they get a good look?"

"Are you kidding? I had my pants at about my knees and was hopping on one foot trying to pull them up! I didn't even notice the door opening, I just looked up and there they were with open mouths." He was laughing now too.

"Good," Wendy said, "gives them something to be jealous about. By the way, the switch next to the door is set to auto – change it to manual and you will have to press the button below it to make the door open." He pressed the button and the door closed, then he changed the switch. By the time he turned back around Wendy was already out of bed walking towards him. She was stark naked and the sight took his breath away. She put her arms around his neck, and gave him a big kiss. "You know I have a little time before I need to get to work..."

Jack said, "Hold that thought, if I don't hit the bathroom soon, we're gonna need a mop."

"Ewww," she said as he turned, hit the button, and ran down the hall.

~~~~

They were lying in bed, sweaty limbs all entwined. The blankets were on the floor and the sheets pushed off to the side. "So I have one question Wendy, and I want you to be honest with me." He looked over at her, and she adjusted her head on the pillow to look him in the eyes.

"What is it?" she asked, looking serious now. He could feel her body tense just a little in anticipation of a tough question.

"How do you shower around here?" She smacked him in the chest, but smiled.

"There's a shower unit in the room next to the restroom. It's too small for two people, so I will have to let you learn how to use it on your own." She leaned over and kissed him, and then said, "I'm going to get dirty working on that exchanger anyway, so I'm going to skip a shower. Besides, I have your scent on me right now, and I rather like it. I better get going too, it isn't going to fix itself." She hopped out of bed and started to get dressed. He watched her until she was done, and then got up himself.

"Do I need a towel?" He was remembering the sink in the bathroom where the goop he washed his hands with dried itself. He really hoped that the shower didn't spray that slime on his body.

She walked to the dresser, took out a robe and a towel, and handed it to him. "Thankfully, some things never change."

~~~~

After a rather refreshing shower, Jack returned to his room. He looked through the drawers and found a clean change of clothes (more scrubs), some boxer style underwear, and a device that looked like a small electric shaver without a cord. He thumbed the switch on it and it kind of felt like it was vibrating but not making noise like he was used to. He put the end that looked like the shaver head on his arm to confirm that it was indeed a shaver. It tickled a little and left his skin as smooth as a baby's butt. He walked over to his mirror and ran the device over his cheeks. He was impressed, it was better than a good barbershop shave. He finished getting dressed, grabbed the datapad and pushed the icon the doc had shown him. He nearly dropped it when a voice came from the pad.

"Morning Jack, how about some breakfast?" He was staring at Teague through the pad, and judging by his smile, he was enjoying a laugh at Jack's expense.

"Christ Teague I nearly pissed myself!" He felt weird talking to the pad, but Teague continued on like he heard him perfectly.

"Meet me in the kitchen on your level." As quickly as he had appeared on the pad, he was gone.

Jack headed to the kitchen and was greeted by some new faces. They were all looking at him, and Jack, a little surprised, scanned each of them. There was a huge black man, easily six feet six and as wide as a car. A white man, about five nine, maybe one-sixty, blond hair, brown eyes, and a beard that partially covered a scar that ran from his ear to his chin on the left side. He looked to be in his late forties or early fifties, with just a touch of gray in his hair and a splattering of gray in his beard. A white woman, one of the women from the hall, about medium height and build, short-ish blond hair, fairly attractive, and smiling like a cat that had seen where the mouse lived. There was Teague, seated at the table looking a little weary as if he had been up late. Finally there was one more man, Caucasian but weathered skin that looked dark, especially in contrast to Teague's pale skin. He had light brown hair worn a little long, looked to be about six foot tall, although he was seated and Jack couldn't quite tell, and had bright blue eyes and a sharp face. "Uh, hello," Jack said to everyone.

The man sitting next to Teague spoke first. "Hi Jack, nice to meet you, welcome to our little slice of Heaven." He had a smooth voice, and Jack's first impression was that he was a ladies man. "I'm Gabriel. Most people just call me Gabe."

"The rest of us call him Slick." That came from the woman, and when she said it everyone laughed. It seemed Jack's first impression was right on. Gabe smiled too and shot her a glance that made it obvious he had... spent some time with her.

The woman spoke up again. "I'm Cathy, Jack, you can call me Cat like everyone else. We met earlier, in the hall, but I didn't get a good look at your face." There were some chuckles in the room, and Jack suspected she had been talking about their meeting earlier that morning. Jack colored a little.

Trying to roll with the punches, he said "I hope I didn't startle you too bad, you looked a little scared for a second when that door opened." Now the laughter was at her expense. Cat rolled her eyes, but smiled. He knew she could be trouble.

"Jack, it's nice to meet you." The voice was so deep he almost jumped. The large black man was the source, and his voice lived up to his appearance. This guy was BIG. "I'm Ezekiel, but please, call me Tiny." Jack nodded at

Tiny, not really surprised at his nickname. It seemed like every time he met someone really large they were either named Tank or Tiny. "This here fella next to me is Chin. His real name is Frances."

"Goddammit Tiny!" the rather small man exclaimed. "It's Frank, not Frances. Don't let his cuddly teddy bear looks fool you Jack, Tiny is really just an asshole." Tiny wrapped his massive arms around Chin, which all but engulfed the small man.

"Aww, there, there Frances, we all love you." He said in his deep voice. Laughter all around at this.

Chin pushed Tiny off him and said, "Boy you better watch it or I will knock you on your ass!" He said it with a grin and everyone laughed again. "So you're the latest corpsicle huh?" When he talked his jaw sort of moved a little to the side, apparently from the same injury that gave him the scar. It gave him a little bit of an old Chicago gangster accent.

"Oh Christ Chin, do you have to use that term? You ever stop to think that someone might be offended by it?" Jack got the impression that Cat was not very fond of Chin.

Before he could ask, Teague gave Jack an uncomfortable glance and said, "That's what some of the residents here call those who… came from the same place you did. Some people find it a bit offensive."

Jack wasn't offended in the least, he had been called far worse in his life. In the army, everyone had a label of some kind, whether it was had to do with your race, your size, your personality, or your rank. "I guess I am, Chin." Looking around the room he said, "Is everyone a … corpsicle here?" More laughter. Either these people were all very friendly or there was some underlying tension that had everyone a little slaphappy.

Teague spoke up quickly, "No, Cat here is a refugee, we found her about 70 years ago." Jack did a double take before remembering they could clone people and make them young again. "Chin is her grandson." That one caught Jack completely off guard and all he could do was blink a few times.

Chin laughed and said, "Yeah, it's kind of spooky knowing your grandma as a hot chick ten years younger than you are."

"That's enough Frances!" Cat yelled at him. She was a little red, both from anger and embarrassment. "And I'm about twenty years younger than you, thank you very much!" Jack tried to work out some of the logic with all the cloning and such, and was immediately confused. It would be very awkward to meet someone you are attracted to only find out they are the clone of your Aunt or something. At least now he understood the animosity between Chin and Cat.

Teague continued on. "Tiny here just about broke the incubator when we grew him." Chin chuckled. "And Slick has been around for about two years. As most of the new reborn, they were both military. Tiny was a Gunnery Sergeant in the marines and Slick a Corporal in the Army. Gentlemen, Jack here retired as a Captain, so don't forget that not only does he outrank you both, he has probably seen more conflict than either of you combined."

Slick kicked in, "Hell Doc, before coming here the closest I had seen to conflict was on TV." Jack was intrigued by this statement.

"I don't understand Teague, are you at war with anyone?"

Teague didn't really avoid the question, but he didn't really answer it either. "The remnants of the EoS are not all on friendly terms," was all he said. "Jack why don't we take a little tour and you can ask me some questions along the way." It was not a request. "Besides, these folks probably have things to get done." That seemed to put a bit of weight on the mood.

"I look forward to getting a chance to learn more about each of you," he said to the other people in the room. He made brief eye contact with everyone but Cat, hoping to send the hint that he was not really interested. He was enjoying his relationship with Wendy and didn't want to mess it up.

Cat was undeterred however and said, "I look forward to getting to know you better as well, Jack." The meaning was not even thinly veiled, but nobody in the room even seemed to notice. That part probably disturbed him even more than the thought of women like Cat trying to… what would be the right word? Seduce? How long before he just accepted that every woman not already pregnant would be after his seed? He hoped he could retain at least some of his values and morals.

Dismissing that train of thought he asked, "Can I get a quick bite to eat first? I'm ravenous." Teague nodded and Jack went to the cabinet and got a bowl, went to the dispenser and poured him a nice glob of slime. He got some water and sat down. Chin had wandered out and Cat was over by the doorway talking to Slick. Tiny sat down across from him, his huge hand gripping what looked like a small cup, but it was the same size cup that Jack had in front of him. He had seldom seen anyone that size before. "Damn you are not a little boy are you Gunny?"

"No sir, I guess I'm not. So you were an officer? Are you a ring knocker or..?" Tiny was obviously used to being called Gunny being as it was a common nickname for his rank.

"Nope, I was a mustang; enlisted for almost ten years. I took advantage of a light bird that was in a tough situation and got nominated to OCS. I made it back to Korea in time to lead a few good men to their death, and after that I spent almost ten years digging really big holes."

Tiny was impressed, but he was confused about the last part. Officers didn't dig holes, even really big ones. "What do you mean by holes, Captain?"

Jack absently rubbed his face, where the scars used to be, and smiled. "I had some experience in Korea with mortar fire, and when the war was over I had a few words with some higher ranking officers about the ineffectiveness of our bunkers. As a result, I was put in charge of a crew and sent to a few newer bases to build some better bunkers. I took the job seriously and when working with the engineers we were able to improve the designs of the bunkers we built. It got noticed, and I got put in charge of building some really big bunkers." By nature, Jack wasn't inclined to talk much about the details of the projects he worked on. He supposed it didn't really matter now but it was habit.

Tiny mulled that over and then said, "Any chance you had anything to do with the Freezer?" He had no idea what that meant, and it must have showed. "The Freezer, you know, the 'cryogenic facility' we all came from."

"Oh, yeah… I guess I built it, just didn't know what I was building." Jack liked Tiny. Gunnery sergeants were good at getting things done. "So what about you Tiny, how long were you in?"

"I was at eighteen years when I had my accident. I saw a little action in Iraq the first time we went in, but mostly we were chasing the front line, and the Air Force was doing most of the work for us. I led a recon platoon, and we did work wherever things were hot. Panama, Afghanistan, Kuwait, places like that. I was working a joint task force with the air base up in Great Falls, trying to figure out if we could help them set up a forward air base inside enemy territory without the enemy knowing. We were doing a live training mission where we moved in, painted the enemy with lasers, then the air support bombed the hell out of the target and we secured the runway for them to bring in troops and supplies. We had it down to a science and it was the last training mission before taking it live to the desert, to try to get ahead of the insurgents in Iraq. According to the records, there was an accident, something about a laser guided bomb malfunctioning. I guess it killed about half my team, and I was the only one to survive long enough to be a candidate for the Freezer. My last memories were from just before we called in the strike."

Jack reflected on that in silence. He wasn't sure what a laser guided bomb was, but it wasn't really important, he understood the gist of Tiny's fate… What he was interested in was how many people, or rather frozen bodies, were in the 'Freezer'. The place was huge, but he had no point of reference for how many dead people you could store in a facility that large. Was the whole thing one big freezer or did they add rooms where the bodies were stored? *Just another question to add to the rapidly growing list.*

Teague interrupted his thoughts and said, "Jack, you look like you are done with breakfast, let's go on that tour shall we?" Jack nodded.

As they were walking out, he turned back to Tiny and said "Good to meet you Gunny. Or would you prefer I call you Tiny?"

"Gunny is fine, whichever suits you really, I respond to either. What about you? You prefer Jack? Or maybe Sir?" The last part was said with a little bit of a grin.

"My newest troops called me Sir, my friends called me Jack. You can call me Jack, or if you prefer, some of my men called me Mad Dawg back in Korea." He chuckled and left the room before Tiny could respond to that.

~~~~

They started the tour in the hallway. "Okay 'Mad Dawg', we are going to talk about your new home."

Jack shook his head, Teague seemed like a smart guy, but socially he was a bit of a nerd. "This facility is geographically located somewhere in what was once eastern Nevada. I can show you on a map later if you want. I've found that some reborn are more comfortable knowing exactly where they are."

"Eastern Nevada? I don't recall anything military around that area of the state."

"What makes you think this was a military complex?"

"Obviously we are underground, and who else other than the military had the kind of money to build something underground?"

Teague nodded and considered this. "It was built after the war started, before the nukes were used. From what we learned, it was relatively secret, most of the government, or what was left of the government at the time, didn't even know about it."

Jack filed that one away for later, he didn't really feel up to talking about the war yet.

"The facility is made up of six levels, all underground, with level one starting forty feet from the surface. The EoS city that we came from discovered it before things got really bad there, and a few members of higher standing used their resources to retrofit the facility with some more advanced equipment, like the frictionless plumbing and a power supply that will likely last another thousand years before needing to be replaced or even fed with more fuel. Some of the equipment, like the air filtration system and the heating and cooling systems are old, and require constant maintenance."

He took Jack's datapad and tapped a few buttons, bringing up a wireframe schematic of the bunker. He showed Jack how to use his finger to spin the schematic so he could examine it from any level, and then how to zoom in and zoom out so he could see the inner workings of the place, as well as all the key points. When looking at a side view of the entire complex fully zoomed out, it resembled a stack of pancakes. Each level was an individual pancake, a large thin disc, with six discs in the stack. When he turned his viewpoint axis so he was looking down at it at an angle, the pancakes revealed themselves to be more like spoked wheels. Zooming in revealed the outer ring of the wheel to be a corridor with rooms coming off both sides, and the spokes to be passageways that converged on a central shaft. The shaft was like a big axel, centered on all the wheels. The spokes were not symmetrical though, some were spaced further apart, and between the spokes were larger rooms. Level four only had two spokes with long rooms on each side of the central shaft. Levels two and three had one large shared open space that occupied an entire half and even extended up to the top level. There were rooms that looked like full apartments surrounding this common area.

"We are here now, on level five." He pointed to a section on the fifth disc down from the top. This is mostly a medical level, with some small apartments like the one you are in now. We use this level for the newly reborn before easing them into regular living quarters. Those are up on levels two and three, along with some family housing. Level four is armament and training, and level six is mostly utility and control. Level one is primarily an activity level, with some very large rooms for simulation training as well as entertainment. There is even an underground park with a fake sun that rises and sets." He pointed to the huge open space on levels two and three. "That park alone covers an acre of area. There are some community facilities on level one as well, and on top of all that it is built to be a first line of defense for if any enemy should breach the actual bunker." As he talked about it, he manipulated the schematic on Jack's pad to show what area's he was referring to.

Jack pointed to what looked like a long tunnel coming off of level one. "What is that?"

Teague zoomed the schematic out and pointed to the other end of the tunnel. "This is a railway that connects to our flight deck. It is about five miles long. Externally, the bunker is built near some natural rock formations, with well camouflaged ventilation and access points." He brought up some exterior drawings and even some photos of the area.

Jack was struck by the scale of the place. *An acre? And that is only one half of the diameter of this place?* This was larger than anything he had ever even thought about building. He was no engineer, but even he wasn't sure how they could construct a building like this. "Any ideas on how they built this place?"

Teague shrugged, "Not really my area of expertise, but we think maybe they drilled it out then reinforced the walls with concrete. Look at the corridors, they are all tubular on the outside, and square on the inside."

Jack wanted to study this for a while, but there was much to see yet. He asked how to get back to this on the pad before they moved on.

"Let's head to the medical facility on this level. It's down this main corridor, and past it is one of the two lifts that you can use to access different levels. As we walk, you can start asking questions. We have most of the day, and then we have some work to talk about."

Jack didn't waste any time. He pulled up his notes, took a moment to review them, then said, "Okay Doc, first question. You said an engineered virus wiped out the ability for the scientist's children to reproduce. Why is it you can't just reverse engineer it and cure the problem in yourself? You said you cured Cancer, and even for me you said my DNA was altered so I would never get it. Seems after all that a little problem like infertility would be a walk in the park."

"Well, you just jump right to the tough questions, don't you! To answer this, I will need to summarize a few technical details." Teague mulled it over for a moment before starting. "When cloning a person, you take a fertilized egg, remove the DNA, and replace it with the DNA of the person you want to clone. From there, nature more or less takes over, with the exception of the acceleration process and the part where we write in your memories." He paused to make sure Jack was following.

"DNA is made up of millions of pieces, and certain sequences of those pieces make up your 'genes'. We can modify genes to a certain extent, but it is a very limited science. Usually it just means looking for certain genes and rendering them ineffective. To change a gene from one sequence to another is far more difficult. Usually we use a modified virus if we need to change something, but the research to get to that point took many years and required very specialized equipment to create. What we have here is a fairly basic setup of predefined modifications we can use to fix things like your cancer. We also have modifications that can make you more healthy, allow you to live longer, and even give you better vision and better motor control. We no longer have access to the computers and equipment that allowed us to create new fixes and cures. But even if we did, it isn't as simple as making a cure."

They stopped at a doorway marked with the same symbol he had put on Jack's datapad to get in touch. "Before we go in I will finish the explanation, so that we don't get sidetracked.

"The reason we did not know of the virus's effect for so many years was because it took out a chunk of DNA in the next born child, yet everything else remained the same. The child grew up healthy and normal, and our screening processes only looked at a few thousand genes for known problems and defects. However, at puberty, the part of the DNA that tells the body to start making sperm was there, but it was being suppressed by another gene. There are still many genes we have never identified because instead of being responsible for something developing in the body, they are responsible for suppressing something from developing in the body. Remove the right combination of these genes from our DNA and we might grow wings, for all we know. Our current level of technology just isn't sufficient to experiment on this level. Some scientists have tried, and the results were, well, we can talk about that later.

"The last research done that I know of suggested that the virus caused a series of genes to change, on top of removing a key piece of the DNA. Technically it's possible to splice the missing gene back into the DNA strand, but if those researchers were right, it would also require manipulating some other combination of genes. Given enough time and an incredibly powerful computer, it might be possible to figure out how to restore the proper sequence of genes and cure someone like me, but it is so incredibly complex that nobody has bothered to try. Even if they found a way to do it, the only reliable way to introduce the cure would be by cloning, and if you haven't figured it out by now, that wouldn't do anything for me, just for the next copy of me. If we hadn't found some fertile men and an immunization for the virus, we might have continued on that path, but for the few of us left, it is a waste of effort. There is one more reason as well – risk. When splicing genes, you can't be completely sure of the results. We only get one shot when transferring memories from a dead body to the clone. If we tried it, and it failed, we would be permanently damaged, or worse. As old as I am in my head, I am not ready to die willingly, even if it gave me a shot at having a child of my own."

The explanation was a little over his head (and he imagined it was dumbed down for him already), but it made enough sense to him to satisfy his curiosity. He did get the feeling that Teague wasn't telling him the whole story, but it seemed irrelevant. He scratched the question off his list and moved on. "Okay, so yesterday you told me how they used to make twins of living people, just with their DNA. Why aren't there a dozen little Teagues running around?"

"That one is really simple. What would be the point? Another version of me without my knowledge would just be a waste of resources for another infertile man."

"Sure, but it would be one more person who could be working on the problem. After all, you are obviously intelligent, and that isn't a learned trait, even I know that."

Teague looked a little uncomfortable, and Jack wasn't sure if it was the subject, the compliment he just paid, or something else. He decided not to press the issue and shifted the question slightly. "So what about making twins of the fertile men you found? If the issue with making twins of yourself is that they are infertile like you, what about those men who aren't? Seems like having thirty or forty of them would be better than only having eleven."

Teague shook his head, "Same problem, you see, the issue we have isn't in each fertile man being able to spread his seed, it is in the variety of DNA. Multiplying one fertile man doesn't add to the gene pool, so again his value to the community would be nullified, and hence a waste of resources."

He let that hang in the air for a few heartbeats, then said, "Now, shall we go see where you were born?"

Chapter 16

The room was substantially larger than Jack had expected. He had to blink a few times before his eyes adjusted to the brighter, more natural light. The walls, ceiling, and floor in this room were all painted white in stark contrast to the raw concrete on the rest of the level. Large machines made it difficult to judge the scale of the room, which at first glance appeared to be about fifty feet square. Teague walked over to one of the machines, looked at a glowing panel, tapped a few buttons, and then headed closer to the center of the room.

The room layout was simple, really. There were four massive machines, one in each corner, and in the middle was two large desks, a few pieces of unidentifiable equipment, and some workbenches. On one of the workbenches was an apparatus that Jack could only assume was a complicated chemistry set. The four large machines reminded him of a large distillery he once visited; wide upright cylinders with pipes and other bits of equipment attached around the sides in a seemingly random fashion. As he walked past the two flanking the door, he realized that they were far larger than he first thought. Easily over ten feet tall and twenty or twenty-five feet across, his earlier estimate of the size of the room was way off. With ten feet of empty space around each machine, and the large desks, workbenches, and other equipment taking even more room between them, the room had to be at least one hundred feet long in each direction and not a single supporting column anywhere. Jack's experience in building underground bunkers told him this just wasn't possible, at least not with the technology he had available in 1966

Teague stopped in the middle of the room, spread his arms and said "This is it. Four artificial wombs. We call them tanks, and that one over there," he said pointing to the machine to Jack's right, "was yours." Teague paused for effect, then continued, "It took about eight weeks to get you to the age you are now. Currently we have four buns in the oven, three men and a woman. The next will be ready in a week. Do you want to see him?" Jack nodded. They walked over to the far left hand tank and he pushed some buttons on the panel. A window, about two feet square, went from black to clear, showing a red tinted liquid behind it. Teague pressed a few more buttons and the water began to glow, brighter and brighter until Jack could see a body about the size of a nine year old child in the murky water. There was a tube running from the edge of the tank wall that ended in the child's mouth. The body twitched a couple times and Jack jumped back, the hair on his neck standing up.

"Jesus Doc, that is creepy. I didn't expect him to move." Teague smiled and pressed a few more buttons. The light dimmed and the window went back to flat black. "Why is there a tube in his mouth and not his belly?" Jack was no doctor, and his only point of reference here was remembering his baby girl coming into the world, the doctor handing him a scissor and telling him to cut the umbilical cord.

"After he grew to the equivalent of nine months old, his body told him it was time to start breathing, so we had to disengage the umbilical cord and put a tube in his throat that would provide him with air and food. The tube also delivers chemicals that essentially force the memories we scanned from his old brain to grow in the new one. The murky water he is floating in is a catalyst that uses careful mixtures of hormones, steroids, vitamins, minerals, and some special types of bacteria to force his body to age. The accelerated aging process causes his body to generate a lot of heat, and the water temperature is about ten degrees below normal to keep him from overheating and expiring."

Jack just nodded slowly, feigning understanding. "That's, um, pretty cool, doc." He tried to sound enthusiastic, but Teague seemed to sense both his disinterest and discomfort and steered them toward the door.

They exited the room and took another turn down the hall to a similar door. "Behind this door is an identical chamber to the last one. We are working on building four more tanks, so we can increase the rebirth rate of the subjects in the cryogenic facility. There are a few key components that we need, however, and they have been difficult to acquire." He didn't go into more detail but Jack made a mental note to expand on that at a later date.

As they headed further down the hall, Jack looked at the list of questions on his pad and said, "So when I talked to Tiny earlier, he remembered events just hours before he died. How come is it I lost nearly a whole year of my memory?" Knowing he had lived another year beyond his memory was like a thorn in his side. Even amidst the chaos of questions in his head, the need to learn what happened was difficult to ignore.

"Well, you remember when I told you that you were the oldest one there that we had revived?" Jack nodded. "In the sixties and seventies, when they went to freeze a body, they simply replaced the blood with some alcohols and then put it in the freezer. Every so often, over the next couple decades, they would try to revive one of the corpses, and in their failures, they learned it was harder to freeze a cell without damaging it than they had originally anticipated. Did you ever have a pipe burst from freezing?" Jack lived in Montana; it seemed like a rhetorical question, so he didn't answer. "Your cells are filled with water just as a pipe, and when frozen, they tend to explode. The stuff they put in the bodies back then helped but if the body were put in too cold of an environment it would completely destroy the cells.

"By the nineties, they had come up with some chemicals that were really good at keeping that from happening. We attempted to save a couple of the older bodies we found, but it was no use. Their brains were just too badly damaged to get any memories, and the results were not desirable. You were the first one from your generation we were able to recover. It was a stroke of luck, really, or fate, if you believe that."

"What made me different from the others?"

"I think it was the chemicals your doctors used when trying to fight the cancer. Chemotherapy was pretty new when you were at the Mayo Clinic, and something they pumped into you toward the end really ended up helping to preserve your cells. It is surprising that it didn't kill you, to be honest."

The irony of it was not lost on Jack, and he knew he would have to come to terms with this information in time. He didn't ponder this long, however, simply because he also now had a hint of what might have happened in his last year. "So I ended up going to Minnesota to try treatment? Mae must have done a good job convincing me." Jack couldn't see himself voluntarily going through experimental treatment, especially if he knew if would just make him sick. Mae was probably the only one he would have listened to, and he hoped he had thanked her for it, especially now that he was here as a result.

"According to your death records, yes, you spent the last few months in the cancer ward, and when the results were not quite what they had hoped for, you checked out and left for home. It was not long after that you, uh, passed." Teague said it as if he didn't want to get into the details, but this was exactly the kind of information Jack was after.

"Come on, Teague this is important to me, what else do you know of my last year?"

Teague spread his hands, shrugging. "Not much. Most of the information I had was medical history. You were the first subject at the facility, and apparently they didn't have a computer for storing the records yet, so they stored your paper file with your body. There might be something more personal left behind, but I never got anything other than the medical records."

"So what's the chance I will get to go back there and have a look for myself?" The idea that there might be something left behind that could fill in the blanks sent a small measure of relief through him.

"About one hundred percent, actually." Jack was caught off guard by the response. He had expected some spiel about the dangers of the wasteland, or maybe that he wasn't physically prepared yet to venture out. "You are already scheduled to go out with a small crew tomorrow. Uh, if you feel up to it that is."

"Of course!" He felt like a school kid that was just handed the keys to a new motorcycle and told to have fun. The thought of getting outside to see what had become of the area he once called home was exciting. An alarm went off in his head, though, and he pulled up his guard quickly. In a more cautious voice, he asked, "Why were you planning to send me there? What haven't you told me?"

They had reached a large door, and Teague pressed a button next to it. There was a faint ding and the doors opened. It was an elevator, a really large one too. As they stepped on, Teague said, "I figured you would want to get out, and we really want to evaluate your ability in the field." As he pressed a button on his datapad, the doors closed and Teague put on a half-smile. "Did you really think you were going to wander around here all day wearing casual clothes and fornicating with the women?"

Jack spotted the misdirection but decided now was not the time to get into an argument. He smiled and said, "No, of course not, but I figured you would ease me into some responsibilities. It sounds like you already decided I was going to be a soldier for you." It was not a question and Jack didn't expect an answer. He didn't get one.

Changing back to the original subject, Teague said, "So your brain was in decent shape, enough to bring you back anyway, but there was some damage to your memory areas. The older memories tend to be planted deeper in the brain, with the newer memories closer to the surface. The deeper parts of your brain didn't suffer as much damage as the outsides. Thankfully we only cared about the memories – there were a couple parts of your brain that were in pretty bad shape. The problem we had was that the cancer therapy, combined with the cell damage from freezing, made it difficult to tell exactly when you died, from a standpoint of the memory center of your brain. So we sort of guessed."

"You guessed?" That surprised Jack, and even made him a bit angry. "What would have happened if you guessed wrong?"

"If we guessed in the wrong direction, you would not have survived the awakening. If we guessed in the other direction, you would simply remember less than you do." At least he was being honest about it.

"Did I lose anything else? Were there other parts of my memory that were damaged?" He hadn't thought about this before, but suddenly it was a question that had deep implications.

Teague looked uncomfortable. "Jack I wish I could tell you that everything was fine, but the fact is there was some damage to all parts of your brain. I can't answer this completely at this point because there is simply no way to know what affect, if any, this had on your memories. It is not a perfect science. Each brain is a little different, and while we can make educated guesses at what part of your life is stored where, the fact is your brain is way more complex than you can imagine. It is possible you are missing vast parts of your memory, and possible that your brain has filled in the holes based on information surrounding it as well as other memories. You might not remember meeting a particular person, but you still know them from other memories and can recall their name. You know you met them because you knew them, so your brain has filled in the missing parts that can be derived from other memories. What affect this has had on your personality is impossible to say. I didn't know you before, so I can't tell you how different of a person you are then you were before you died."

This may not be what Jack wanted to hear, but at least it sounded like Teague was being honest about it and not hiding anything. "So, I might be missing memories but I won't really know it?"

"Not any more than if you simply forgot something, or are even blocking it to avoid dealing with it. A particular battle in the war you fought in, for example. You might remember fighting in it, but maybe not the details. It doesn't change who you are by not remembering."

It made sense, although Jack was far from an expert. He sometimes forgot people's names, but it never meant that he didn't know them or couldn't remember why he knew them. At the same time it made him wonder what he had forgotten, or if it was the reason he felt different than he remembered. "Doc, I have to ask this: I have felt a little... disconnected from my former self. In particular, certain feelings I remember having before I died, I don't really have any more. It is a bit distressing. Is this a result of the damaged parts?"

Teague thought it over before answering, "It is difficult to say. I have gone through the process and have never felt the kind of disconnection with my former self that you are talking about, but then I have never been in the same situation you have been in. The people you remember are long past gone, so knowing they have been dead for centuries could create a disconnect from them. On top of this, you lost roughly a year of your life, and just as it is possible to remember something differently than it really happened, your brain could have edited those memories in that last year of your life. You don't have the new memories to back up the changes though, so it could cause some of the disconnection you are talking about as well. It could also be that you are missing some key memories that gave you the feelings you remember, but now that you don't have them you don't feel the same way. On top of all of this, feelings, emotions, and love are not things that are only fueled by memories, there are pathways and receptors that are created during the hormonal and chemical reactions when we interact with other people, and those don't get recreated when we inject the memories. I wish I had a more definitive answer for you, but there are so many variables at play. I just don't know."

Jack shrugged. It was food for thought but there was nothing to be done about it now. He figured there was nothing more to learn from Teague about his past, but there was still one thing that had been bothering him, and now seemed as good of a time as any to bring it up. "How do you know what year I was born?"

Teague looked at him in confusion. "Well, from your medical records I suppose."

Jack shook his head, "No, I don't think that is it. See, when I joined the military, I had a new I.D. forged. To get this, I paid a guy I worked with who was dating a girl who worked for the county, and she filed a revised birth certificate for me that showed I was eighteen years old instead of sixteen, then I used that to get a new driver's license and with that I was able to join the military. Ever since then, legally I was two years older."

Jack was watching closely as he revealed this information, but Teague was either really good at hiding things or he simply didn't know what Jack was referring to. "Jack, I don't follow."

"The birth date you gave me when I woke up was my real birth date, not the one that would have been in my medical or military history."

The two men stared at each other, each looking for an answer to a different question. "I will pull the images later and compare it to our records. I am sure that whatever the medical records showed, that is what we entered. Perhaps you revealed your true age to the doctors during an exam. Or maybe this is an example of the damaged memories we were talking about."

Jack nodded slowly. "Maybe." But he wasn't buying it. Teague didn't look like he knew anything about it, so he let it drop for now. Plenty of time to get back around to it.

The elevator doors opened back up, and a small child ran past followed a moment later by a middle aged woman. "Welcome to the family level."

~~~~

Jack was disappointed, they had skipped to level three and he had hoped to check out level four, the armament level. Looking at the next question on the list he said, "So if most of the world is a wasteland filled with radiation, how do we get to Montana? That's a long way to walk, and I imagine the roads are in pretty rough shape by now."

Teague stepped off the elevator and Jack followed. The hallways on this level were wide with higher ceilings, and, similar to the cloning room, the light was brighter and much more natural. Unlike the cloning room, the walls were painted in warm tones, not sterile white. Up ahead looked to be a courtyard of some kind, and they were headed that way. As they walked, Teague said, "The world up above us is not like you are used to, of that you can be assured. But it isn't quite the wasteland you might be thinking. We are in a desert of course, so it's pretty barren immediately outside the bunker, but there are all sorts of climates out there, just as there were before. Much of the radioactive areas have settled out, and there is very little of the radiation and other contamination in the air, as there once was. Perhaps twenty percent of the land is inhabitable, but the problem isn't finding safe land, its finding safe land that isn't broken up by radioactive zones. Sometimes the 'safe zones' are as narrow as fifty feet. Navigating from place to place is difficult, and downright dangerous without the right equipment."

They approached the courtyard and Jack was impressed. They were at the lower of two living levels, and the courtyard extended up three levels. It was about a square acre, and the ceiling was as bright as a noonday sun. As they came out of the hall into the courtyard, the 'sun' washed over Jack's face. He felt his spirits rise instantly. Most of the courtyard was covered in green grass, and air was incredibly fresh here, a big change from the air a couple levels down. "This is amazing! To have an open area of this size..." Jack had been impressed with the size of the cloning room, but he was in awe when he saw the courtyard. Seeing more than one level from a "cross section" like this allowed him to get an idea of how they had constructed the bunker. In his day, they dug a big hole, built a strong building, and buried it. If structures built in the decades after his death were all like this one, he questioned again what value he could have in a world like this. So much had changed.

There was a bench next to a walkway and they wandered over to it and sat down, enjoying the warmth of the fake sunlight. "So there aren't many large radiation free zones? I mean, with enough room for farms and cities and such?" He was interested in what resources humanity had left to work with.

"Actually, there are hundreds of areas, maybe thousands, where people could start a good sized community, set up some decent sized farms, and live in relative comfort. Some of those areas are more than a thousand square miles, and could probably support a hundred thousand people. The problem is, they are not interconnected. You can fly small amounts of people or equipment in, but anything bigger than a bus you would have to build there. It is not impossible, just impractical. Think of Hawaii. Plenty of land to live on, but imagine if you couldn't get a boat there. You could fly a plane over for anything you absolutely needed, but if you wanted housing or transportation, you would have to make it with the resources available.

"After the big war, almost all the 'safe zones' were populated with the survivors. Some of those areas included entire cities from before the war, and a handful had it pretty good, particularly in the grain belt area where farms were plentiful and cities could generate electricity. Regardless of the resources available to them, none of the communities ever got much larger than a few thousand people. Life was hard everywhere, and even where they had it good, things broke down fairly quickly. The problem was they were isolated, cut off from the rest of the world, and with no government to enforce the laws, natural selection took over. The strong ruled and the weak were oppressed."

"You said they *were* inhabited. What happened?" Jack wasn't sure he wanted to know.

"Disease, famine, inbreeding, conflict… you name it. The ones that survived without some natural or man-made disaster killing them off ended up trading or working with the EoS when they rose to power. There were resources in some of these safe zones, and it was easier to trade a little technology for them than it was to take it by force. The EoS wasn't interested in ruling anyone but themselves, but when the fighting broke out, no place on earth was safe. Traders inadvertently brought man-made plagues to these places and now they are, with a few small exceptions, all wiped out. If we had more people and more resources, we could give those areas a try again but it will take many more decades before we are ready for that." He looked like he wanted to say more but he left it at that.

"So with so much land broken up, finding paths through from one safe zone to another is tricky, and of course sometimes downright impossible. Since the air is pretty well cleansed of radioactive particles, air travel is pretty safe. During the height of the EoS, flying machines were commonplace, and luckily we got away with a few." Jack made a mental note to ask about space flight and if it ever played a role in the EoS. But right now he was more interested in the flying machines they had available here.

"How many is a few?" You can't lead men without knowing your exact strength, so it was almost pure instinct to ask that question.

"We have two heavy freight haulers, four medium transports, Two four man flyers, and a half dozen two man flyers. There is also a very large hauler stored on the surface a few miles from here, but it requires a runway to take off and land. We keep it maintained but it almost never sees use because it is difficult to find a place to land, and we have not had need of that kind of capacity. We were recently blessed with an aircraft mechanic though, and soon she will be up to speed and will be able to maintain the larger craft. She is already proficient with the small craft, and I understand she has become quite the pilot as well." He was talking about Wendy of course.

Jack wondered if air was the only means of transportation. "Do you have any ground based vehicles?"

"We have a couple transports, and a dozen smaller vehicles made for two or four people. They do okay out there, but some of the terrain is challenging, and while their theoretical range is almost unlimited with the power source they have, realistically they are only good for about two hundred miles."

Jack was satisfied, so he looked over his list of questions. He was able to cross off the ones about where they were and how big the place was they were in, those were all but answered already. He spotted one question and chuckled. "What exactly is the food? And where does it come from?"

Teague smiled and said, "Do you really want to know?" Jack nodded although Teague's smile made him feel a little uncomfortable. "Okay, but don't tell me I didn't warn you. Level six is the utility level, everything happens there. Power is generated, air is filtered and exchanged with outside air, water is brought in from some rain catchments up on the surface, and the water we use is recycled. This includes water recovered from the air with condensers, from the human waste, and gray water from the showers and cleaning machines. We retain almost one hundred percent of the water in this facility and we get the rest of what we need from catchment. The rain water is not radioactive but it is dirty from all the debris still in the atmosphere from the nukes. Water is filtered, then purified and stored. Everything else that is waste goes into some large vats, where some very handy bacteria go to work on it. They eat anything you give them except the lining in the vats, and they excrete some very nutritious stuff." Jack had gone a little green at the thought, but Teague wasn't finished yet. "The excreted goop rises to the top and is scraped off and some of it is made into the sawdust like stuff in the food. It is processed and cooked to kill off any biologicals, so it is totally safe. It is basically like a super multi-vitamin, containing just about everything a human needs to survive, with the exception of protein. The rest of the goop is fed to another organism, this one is more like a worm. It feeds on the goop and grows rapidly, and then splits, like a bacteria would, and continues on as long as there is nutrition to eat. The worms are processed into a protein paste, and a powder is made from that. When mixed with water, it's something of a gelatin. The machines mix that with some artificial flavors and the sawdust-like nutrients, and it comes out of the dispensers in the mess halls or in the kitchens of the apartments." Jack felt positively ill now, and Teague just grinned and said, "I warned you."

"So basically bacterial poop and worms. I ate some crazy stuff in Korea and Japan, from fried bugs to dog stew, and most of it tasted worse than the food here, so I guess it isn't all that bad. Far better than C-Rations too." Trying to take his mind off the food, he looked at his list once more. *Cross that one off and never bring it up again,* he thought. He didn't see any more questions he wanted to ask right at the moment, but then he remembered the question that came up when he was talking to Tiny. "By the way, Doc, how many frozen bodies are at the site in Montana? You have revived about fifty, right?"

Teague nodded, "Yeah, about that many. Like I said earlier, our success rate is now about half, but that includes all the ones we have to weed out due to condition and reason for death. If they died from massive head trauma, the chance of cloning is lower, and if they had a brain disease like Alzheimer's, we have to take a shot in the dark on where to cut off their memories, or we end up with complications. We had one unfortunate case..." He stopped, obviously not wanting to talk about failures. "Anyway, the facility was built to hold three thousand, and was about eighty percent occupied at the start of the war. We estimate that we can save perhaps twelve hundred more, give or take."

That many? "How many people can this facility handle?" This place was large but that's a lot of people to feed, clothe, and take care of, not to mention how quickly that many people could make babies. Given that men will spread the gene pool around and be encouraged to have more than two or three kids each, within twenty years the population could easily hit six or seven thousand, and then the next generation will be having babies.

"About two hundred families of five. If we are successful in this, we will outgrow this facility within the next four or five years."

"So what are you planning on doing then? Are you going to move everyone above ground? Try to make a go on the surface?"

"We aren't sure, but a lot of it depends on you."

"Me!?" Jack exclaimed. "What do I have to do with this?"

"We were hoping that you could build us a new home, actually."

Chapter 17

Wendy was working on the cooling system for the armament level, but her mind was not on her work, and it was going slow. It was unlike her to not be able to focus like this, but she knew the reason why. She was almost in a manic state now, compared to the depression she had felt pretty much since she woke up four months ago and found out she had died. If her family or friends had ever had to describe her normal emotional state in as few words as possible, it would probably have been 'mellow'. That wasn't to say that she didn't have the typical mood swings that any woman is prone to having, but extreme highs and extreme lows were not a normal part of her life.

When she woke up four months ago, and the situation was explained to her, she sank into a deep depression. She was good at covering up her feelings, something that made life in the military much easier. It was okay for a man to get drunk and whine to his buddies when he got dumped by a girlfriend or missed a promotion, but one Goddamn tear from a female soldier and it was all about how women are too emotional to be in the Army.

Outwardly, she hid her depression by appearing introverted and shy, which also served to keep the men at bay, at least most of them. The men here were typically not at all inconsiderate about the situation. In fact it was quite the opposite. The woman was expected to approach the man whose seed she was interested in, and if anything, the other women were the ones pressuring her to get pregnant. Aside from the women in the community, Teague was the only one who had even brought it up. He reminded her on multiple occasions that the reason they went through the trouble of bringing her back was to expand their population, and she understood that. She just wasn't okay with the idea of sleeping around trying to get knocked up. He had talked to her about other methods of getting pregnant like insemination, but the thought of them squirting sperm into her with a syringe was almost as bad as having sex with the men in the first place. The best option so far was IVF, where they harvest her egg, fertilize it in the lab, and then plant it in her womb. Anything that avoided having sex with someone she didn't know was a good option. Her history of sexual encounters had left her somewhat jaded about sex in general, and not very trusting of either men or women.

Wendy knew she was attractive, and she learned early in life that while she could use that as a tool to get what she wanted, it was a double edged sword. Her first boyfriend in high school had been very persistent about getting into her pants one night, and although he had come to his senses before it turned into rape, she came to the realization that she needed to be able to defend herself. She enrolled in a kick boxing class, but it was geared more toward getting in shape than self-defense. Luckily, one of the students knew of a small school where they taught Jujitsu, and for the next four years before joining the Army, she spent four nights a week learning the martial art, and two nights a week practicing kick boxing. The combination kept her in perfect physical condition, and gave her the confidence to be around men without fear.

During basic training in the Army, her beauty was a huge liability. One moonless evening while returning to her barracks from dinner, a man jumped out from some shadows and struck her in the head. She was dazed long enough for him to get her on the ground and get her pants unbuckled, but she recovered and put a knee in his groin, punched him in the nose, and nearly broke one of his fingers getting out of his grasp. In the scuffle she caught an elbow just below her right eye, and by morning it had turned into a nasty looking black eye. That pissed her off almost as much as the man's intentions had. She went to report it, but her superiors made it clear that if she chose to file a report and try to pursue finding the man, they would make life very difficult for her. Most of the men in the Army were against women in the common ranks, and as far as they were concerned, rape was just one of the many problems associated with mixing a lot of sex starved men with a few women. They figured it was what the women deserved for wanting to join a 'men's club'.

That was not acceptable to her, so rather than go through official channels, she decided to take the matter into her own hands. It had not been hard to find the man, after all she had injured his finger and bruised up his nose pretty good. She waited until the sergeant was getting his platoon ready for PT, then confronted him in front of everyone. She didn't say much, just walked up to him, looked at everyone around him and said, "The next guy that thinks he can try to fuck me without my permission is going to end up like this piece of shit." She paused a second to make sure everyone's attention was on the private in front of her, then took him totally off guard with a shot straight into his nose, this time breaking it. He had tried to fight back, but he didn't stand a chance. Normally something like that would have landed her in jail, and possibly discharged from the military. In this case, however, the sergeant figured out right away that one of his men had tried to force himself on a female soldier, and if he put her in jail, he would have to put the man in jail too which would not look good for either himself or the Army. So he had let her finish, sent the man to the infirmary, and filed the whole thing as a training accident. Nothing ever came of the incident, and nobody ever tried to force himself on her again.

That's not to say that they still didn't try to get in her pants, they just tried to use their charms to do so. She had dated a little, but on the few occasions that she went to bed with them, not only was she disappointed in their performance, but inevitably they would brag about it, and sooner or later it always got back to her.

It wasn't just the men either. Not at all surprising, some of the women in the military liked women more than men, and seldom were they shy about it. They usually tried to start a relationship after she had dumped the latest asshole, but in the end they were after the same thing. It had been tempting, occasionally, and although she wished she could forget about it, she had found herself in bed with a fellow female enlisted after a late night drinking binge. Not to say that it wasn't sort of fun, but the woman just didn't have what it took to satisfy her, and in retrospect she wished she had not even opened that door at all. Just like with the men, it got around pretty quickly and she had to deal with those types of women even more often, not to mention the men who heard the rumors automatically assumed that she 'swung both ways' and hence would be willing to get into a threesome.

It didn't take long for her to come to the conclusion it was unlikely she would find someone in the military she could fall in love with. Wendy wanted what most young women wanted, a real relationship with a man that truly cared about her. One afternoon, while test flying an apache, the pilot started telling her about this program he had joined where they would freeze his body and try to revive him in the future when they could fix anything wrong with him. It had sounded romantic, being brought back in the future to start over, so she made some inquiries and discovered they were always looking for volunteers, but didn't make it public knowledge. She had just broken up with yet another man and was so frustrated in trying to find a decent relationship, she signed her death away. Then, while visiting her grandparents on a weekend leave, she had met Gene.

She was hardly a religious woman, having been the by-product of 'free love'. Her grandparents had lived in a commune in California, and her mother was born there. By sixteen her mother was pregnant, due to her loose morals and even looser knees. Wendy had loved her mother (still did), but they never got along too well, and the only father figure she ever had was the 'man of the month' her mother brought home. She got to spend the summers with her grandparents though, and over the years they slipped further away from their hippie heritage and closer to God and religion. Wendy respected this and when she visited the last few years, she even went to church with them.

She met him at a church function, and he was about as far from the typical military type as she could ever expect to meet. They dated a few times during her leave, and the most he had ever tried to do was kiss her. She had returned to base the next week, and for the next two months, they corresponded through phone and email. He visited her once, despite being three hundred miles away, and still he had not expected her to have sex with him. She asked about it, fearing that maybe he was gay and she was misreading the situation, and he simply told her that when the time was right it would happen.

The night before her accident, she had talked to him on the phone. The following weekend kicked off a one week leave, and they had booked a room at a romantic resort in Colorado. She had every intention of taking the relationship to the next level, and hoped that things went even further than that. Then she had to go and die. When she woke up to learn that not only was there very few men left in the world, but they were going to be expected to impregnate a number of women, her hopes and dreams of finding the perfect man and having a monogamous relationship with him were about as dead as she had been for the last three centuries.

The thought of her grandparents and mother living to see her die combined with missing out on what she was certain would be the one true love in her life had really weighed heavily on her heart. Adding the idea of willfully having sex with exactly the type of men she avoided her entire life had put her into a depressive state that she could not escape.

There wasn't much sympathy to be found here either. Most of the women were from this era, not hers, and they took for granted that they would have sex with any man that was convenient, in effort to expand their family. There were eight other Reborn women who did not see things the same way as the natives, but neither did they see things the way Wendy did. Usually when someone volunteers to have their dead body experimented on after they die, it's because they don't have anyone in their life that would care what happened to them after death. Wendy had a family, a man she thought she was in love with, and a life in the military that she enjoyed. Teague could sympathize, but that sympathy always carried the caveat that despite her dislike at the situation, she still needed to have a baby. Try as hard as she could, she simply couldn't shake the depression.

Then a couple months after her rebirth, she flew with a recovery team to the cryogenics facility, and while she had waited for them to get what they came for, she started exploring the facility. Way in the back she came across Jack's cryo-tube. The tube itself was unique. It was similar to the other old tubes, but it had more gadgets connected to it. Also, there was a lockbox attached to the end of the tube. None of the other tubes she had seen had a lockbox like this, and it had piqued her curiosity. She got some tools from her pack and managed to pick the lock on the box. It had been vacuum sealed, and in it were several well preserved documents and a diary with a worn black leather cover. She had looked around to make sure nobody had seen her, then stuffed the diary and papers in her pack.

They brought back two more heads to try to clone that day. She found it a little morbid that they only took the heads, but that was all that was needed and there was not a huge amount of room on the transports. She never looked for her tube, and had no interest in seeing her three hundred year old frozen headless corpse.

Back at her apartment, she took out the diary and documents. She didn't know what had prompted her to take them in the first place, and once she had them in front of her, she felt a little guilty about it. At the same time, however, she had felt a tingle of excitement at the prospect of reading something that was not intended for her eyes. Being depressed all the time had really been a burden, and this sudden change in the normal day to day boredom had already lifted her spirits a little, and it even got her mind off of having a baby.

All the medical records for the inhabitants of the cryogenics facility had been stored on the central computer, and when the place was first discovered, it hadn't taken long for their advanced computers to hack the ancient systems and get all the information translated into a format they could use. The leaders of the community reviewed the information in the files and selected the candidates based not only on being male, but also on their job before dying, their psychological reports, and their medical history. Wendy had been selected because she was a mechanic and an amateur pilot, or at least that was what they had told her. They needed someone to fix their aircraft and even to fly them, and aside from some massive body trauma, she was in great shape. The man whose body was in that tube was different. He predated the computer system, and had never been added to the database. The documents Wendy had found were all the information on this guy that existed.

Most of the documents were medical reports detailing his illness, the treatments, and the time line. Cancer. *Man what a crappy way to go,* she had thought. *Much better to go down in flames.* Of course she had no idea what it was like to go down in flames, or to crash at all, as she had no memory of it.

There was a personal letter in the documents, and Wendy had felt like a voyeur reading it. It was from a woman named Mabel, addressed to this man as if she was sure he would be revived one day and would want to read it. It talked about how they had spent some time together the last year and she was very happy that he had reconnected with her, then wished him a long and fruitful life. *Was this his girlfriend?* Wendy was intrigued, and next she had taken out the diary.

The first entry was dated September 1, 1966. The penmanship was obviously that of a man's, and the content was not very eloquent.

> Today I got the results from Dr. Bill Callun. There is no question that it is cancer. I don't know how to feel about it yet, but there is little doubt that I won't live through it. Mae suggested I write in this diary, as a way to come to terms with my feelings. I feel a little silly doing it, but the truth is, I have never been so mixed up inside. If it doesn't help, I can always stop. She is a very convincing woman. She convinced me to fight this cancer. I suspect I will be leaning on her for support in the coming months.

> So far, the only thing I have found comfort in is the hope that when this is over, I might get to see my wife and daughter again. With death now a certainty, I don't think it is worth spending what time I have left trying to find a woman, just so I can break her heart. I got my chance at love already, and despite the fact that she was taken away from me, I feel like I was blessed.

So Mae must be a relative or old friend, and his wife and daughter must have died. How awful, she had thought as she read it. She had put down the diary, intending to savor it for a while, like a good book from an author who only writes a new one every few years. She then looked more thoroughly through the rest of the documents. When she came across his military history, and the notes on what he had done, particularly involving the very facility that was his final resting place, Wendy knew that this had to be brought to Teague's attention. Despite trying to appear withdrawn to the rest of the community, she was well aware of the challenges they faced. If he could be brought back, he could help to solve a lot of problems.

Before taking the documents to Teague, however, she hid the diary and the letter in her dresser. They weren't going to need it, and chances were, as old as the body was, it would be far too freezer burnt to have any chance at cloning.

~~~~

The wrench slipped off the nut and she banged her knuckle hard enough to make it bleed. "Dammit!" she exclaimed and grabbed a rag to wipe the blood away. She needed to concentrate on the job at hand, but she was like a schoolgirl anxious to meet her new boyfriend under the bleachers to make out. Thinking about the diary sobered her up a little. She knew she had to come clean about it sooner or later, or the guilt would tear her apart. What she needed was a way to bring it up and explain why she had read the diary, without making her seem like some kind of stalking freak. It really didn't look good on the surface, and even when she rationalized it in her own head it looked pretty bad.

She had read a little bit more of the diary each day, learning more about Jack, his illness, his dead family, his mother-in-law who was damned near a saint to him, and even about how he found out the facility he was building was the ultimate irony in his life – a place to be stored until someone could come along and fix the cancer and bring him back to life. The more she read, the more she wished she could meet this man in person, give him a hug, and maybe even ask him to marry her. At first the writing was pretty basic and to the point, but as he got closer to the inevitable death that would mark the end of his diary, he opened up and it was as if he was writing poetry. Even though he was dead, he had filled the void in Wendy, and it had given her a reason to continue on.

The diary had helped her come to terms with her own situation. She didn't like it, hated it in fact, but the bottom line was that she was given a second chance at life that most people would never get. Not only that, she was brought into a situation that, no matter how grim it was, she had a chance to be a part of saving humanity. There were literally only dozens of humans left on earth who could give birth to a new generation, and she was one of them. She was a daughter of Eve herself here, and would be the mother of a good percentage of human kind, if it could make it past the wars and the fighting. Reading Jack's story gave her the insight and the strength to look at things in a different light. She had decided that she would make the most of it, give it a shot, get pregnant and have a child and do her best to help restart the human race.

That's when things got really complicated. Teague had agreed with her that this could be the best find yet at the facility, and perhaps the solution to the second biggest problem they faced. They took the utmost care bringing him in, and were meticulous in mapping his memories. From what Wendy knew of the process, it was incredibly unlikely that they could bring this man into their world. It would take a miracle. It was a harsh world, and miracles were not in abundance these days.

It turned out that the some combination of the experimental Cancer treatments he had undergone actually aided in the freezing process, and they had their miracle. When Teague announced they had successfully started the first stage and he was already growing, she was beside herself. The feelings she developed when reading the diary were for someone that would never exist, so it was safe to fantasize about him being alive and falling in love with her. Now, however, it was going to be a reality. She didn't know if she was more frightened that he would turn out to be someone entirely different than she had imagined, or that he would end up being exactly the man she longed for.

Wendy did not have much respect for the women here, primarily because she felt that they didn't have enough respect for their womanhood. She tried not to judge them, knowing full well that they had been raised in an incredibly different and difficult environment, but she felt a person cannot unlearn a set of morals and values.

It had been discovered fairly early on that the freshly reborn men were like seventeen year olds that had been locked in the closet with a porn magazine and a flashlight. Wendy wasn't sure who had figured it out, but it had become something of a ritual to try to get the men alone on the first morning after regaining the ability to move. Even if the love she felt for this man was based on nothing more than whimsical fantasy, she didn't want Jack to fall *victim* to one of those women. She rationalized her hanging out as close to the medical ward as she could by telling herself she was just trying to protect him from something that would likely embarrass him. From what she read, she saw Jack as a fairly old fashioned guy with a strong sense of duty and incredible loyalty to those he loved.

When he first gained consciousness, she didn't wander more than a hundred feet from his room, and when he woke that night, she told herself that she was watching over him to make sure none of the predatory women tried to take him in the night. Before five sentences were out of his mouth, however, she had turned into the exact sort of predator she was supposedly protecting him from.

She was incredibly embarrassed by her own actions that first night, and laying here under the HVAC unit daydreaming about it, she colored a deep red at the memory of how she had seduced him like that. Regardless of her brazen actions, she was, in a word, happy. Last night had been positively wonderful, as had this morning.

So far he was turning out to be everything she had hoped. He seemed to enjoy the hours they spent talking, and he latched on to every word she said as if it were the most important thing he had ever heard. When she smiled at him he would pause as if his train of thought had been interrupted.

101

Despite the emotional high and the signs he was interested, deep down she knew that the chances of him having similar feelings for her were very slim. He was still driven more by his raging hormones than by any coherent thinking, and she had been for him what every man would desire. Soon he will meet many more women all just as attractive as she is who are willing to jump his bones at the first opportunity, and the special intimacy that they had shared will probably be viewed by him as the result of just another woman looking to get pregnant. From what she had read in the diary, his wife's memory had stopped him from not just looking for companionship from another woman in those last few years of his life, but kept him from even seeking a single night's reprieve from loneliness. She had feared that the first night they met he would decline her advances just based on that alone. Now she feared that her boldness would drive him away when he learned that every woman here would be doing what they could to get intimate with him.

On top of all this, as if that weren't enough, if – no, *when* – she gave him the diary, he would probably see her not only as a slut, but as a slut that used his personal information to help seduce him. The thought of losing him like that made her bowels feel loose, and she threw the wrench down in frustration and fear.

Chapter 18

In the past couple days, Jack had envisioned various motives for being brought back to life. None of them included building a massive underground city. He was a glorified contractor; his best asset on a project was his ability to see where there were potential problems and fix them. Not just with machinery, engineering, or structure, but also with people, material logistics, and political conflict. He was a wizard when cutting through a bureaucracy, but that was in a different world, with different people, different politics, different machinery, and different conditions. "Teague, I don't know what kind of help I could possibly be. I'm no engineer. So much has changed. I…"

Teague held up a hand, "Nobody is expecting you to design anything. We have a few people who are pretty smart, and some of the technology we have enhances that greatly. The problem we have is not whether we can conceive a project of this magnitude, it's finding someone to go out and do it. There isn't a man alive that has dug a hole bigger than a grave, let alone excavated enough earth to house a park like this," he gestured to the courtyard all around them, "eighty feet underground. We need someone who can lead men, not into battle, but in a project of awesome proportion."

This did relax Jack a little. He still didn't think Teague had any idea of what he was really asking though. "An operation like you are describing requires a lot of specialized machinery, a lot of skilled operators, and the resources Teague…" He let that hang while his mind processed the amount of steel and concrete alone it would take to build something just the size of this structure, let alone something larger.

"We understand it will be a monumental task, but there are two factors that we believe make all the difference here."

"Yeah, what are those?"

"First, we have done it before. The EoS built more than you can imagine, and they started with nothing. We might not have those resources at hand, but we have, for all intents and purposes, a detailed history on how those people were able to build magnificent cities from nothing but wasteland.

"Second, we have a need, and the fate of humanity may very well ride on it. We simply can't fail here or in another hundred years, humans might just be a part of the Earth's history, not a part of its future."

They sat in silence as the weight of that statement settled in. Jack finally spoke, "I don't know what to say. I need to learn a lot more about what we have to work with before I can wrap my mind around the idea of leading a project of this magnitude."

"If it helps, this is not the most immediate issue, so you will most likely have months to prepare. As long as this can be ready in five years –"

"Five years?!" He shook his head, "No no no, you don't know what you are asking here." Jack scoffed, "Impossible! Maybe twenty years with the right crew, but five? I truly hope you have a plan B because what you are saying simply can't be done."

Teague's confidence appeared to waver slightly, but he smiled anyway. "I know it sounds impossible, but in my life I have seen the impossible achieved countless times, and I have faith in you."

"Why? You barely know me, how could you possibly think that I am going to be able to pull off a miracle?"

"Because you are all we have, Jack, and it will have to be enough. Shall we finish the tour?"

~~~~

The tour continued but Jack was struggling to pay attention. He needed time to process again, to accept what they were asking of him, just as he had needed time to accept how he had come to be here. They spent some time touring the single and family apartments, and by the time they were finished he had pushed his thoughts aside so he could concentrate on the situation at hand. He would worry about things later. As they took the elevator to the top level, he asked about the families. "So do you just put the women and kids in the family apartments?"

In his usual fashion, Teague seemed to see right through the question, "What you are really asking is do the men and women practice your idea of relationships, am I right?" Jack had to give the man credit, he was really good at reading between the lines. That made him both a great asset as well as a dangerous man. He hoped he never had to play politics against him. Teague went on without waiting for an answer, "The men and women from the past dozen or so generations have lived under the pressure of rebuilding humanity. Relationships are not the same now as in your time, any more than they were the same from your time to say, Wendy's time." If there was supposed to be some kind of subtle message in that statement, Jack pretended he hadn't picked up on it. Even in the last decade of his life, he had seen the changes in the social structure, particularly toward sex and morality. He was well aware of the challenges that lay ahead if he tried to make a relationship with Wendy, or any of the women here for that matter. "Since the fall of the EoS, monogamy has taken on a different meaning than it had in your time. For the most part, people of today's world see sex as a function that is required to survive. It is not tied to emotion or intimacy for them, so sex is not exclusive to a relationship and copulation outside the relationship is not a threat. Also, there are no moral or religious ties to sex. It is not like the parents teach the kids that sex is something they should be ashamed of or kept hidden, so it is a natural part of everyone's life. The fact that it is enjoyable practically makes it a good form of entertainment. Oddly enough, one of the reborn put it into words that I particularly like. He said, 'The women here don't get out much, and it's not like they can watch TV or go shopping. They need something to do to relieve the monotony.'"

Jack chuckled. It all made perfect sense. However, he was raised to believe that being faithful to your partner meant not having a sexual relationship with anyone else. Just thinking about adultery was a sin in some people's eyes. This concept of sex not being tied to emotion or morality was foreign. "How do, the reborn handle this?"

"The men typically don't have a problem with this at first, as you can imagine. However, once they start having feelings toward a particular woman, things can get difficult. For the women, it's far worse. Overall, it is not the ideal situation for us, but we have established some ways around it. If a man and woman want to be exclusive, we allow it as long as they agree on two things. The first is that he either procreates with other women or at the least, donates sperm to continue diversifying the gene pool. The second is that the woman agrees to have children sired by other men, as long as it is necessary."

Jack was not sure he would be comfortable with his spouse having other men's babies. "Necessary? How often is it necessary?"

"As far as I am concerned, it is vital, but in the past few years there has been some debate as to how to approach gene pool diversification. Frankly, my area of expertise is not in genealogy, so I am not really qualified to quantify how necessary it is. We have only run into a few situations, and in those situations it was the men who were not completely comfortable with our form of monogamy, so we have let the women decide, and it has become an almost primal instinct to diversify our families."

He hadn't really answered the question, but it seemed like a sensitive subject, so he just nodded, "Fair enough. I suppose it's comforting to know that you aren't going to force me to have sex with other women."

Teague laughed. "You realize you are probably the first man in two hundred years to say that." Jack grinned and nodded, conceding that most guys' fantasy was to have dozens of women willing to have sex with absolutely no strings attached.

The elevator had opened and Teague said, "So let me show you some of the defensive designs on this level."

~~~~

After the tour they got lunch. Then Teague excused himself, citing some duties to attend to at the medical lab. He asked if Jack wanted to join him.

"If it's all the same to you I would rather wander around a bit. I still have more questions, and if I am going to be busy tomorrow I would like to get them answered sometime today. Right now I just want to collect my thoughts."

Teague approved and told him to either come find him later or page him with the datapad. Jack looked at his datapad again, marveling at the technology. *Imagine the Army having communication like this... the effectiveness of such a force would be astounding. That is of course, as long as the enemy didn't have the same or better communications.* The thought actually sent a chill up his spine.

He found the elevator again, and went back to the third floor, figuring out how to use his datapad to get the elevator to work. There were buttons of course, but he figured it was important to learn to use the technology. The fourth floor icon on the datapad was washed out in red, and when he pushed it, nothing happened. Whoever was in charge didn't want him on that level by himself, obviously. When the doors opened, he started walking through the halls, trying to get a feel for the layout. When he passed the same intersection of three hallways for the fourth time, he began to wonder if he was lost, or if it just all looked the same.

The fifth time he got to that intersection, he noticed a mark on the wall that had definitely been there before. *I'm walking in circles*, he thought to himself. He knew he could just press the button to call Teague, but he was a little embarrassed and the doctor was probably busy. Instead, he started knocking on doors. He hit almost twenty doors before one opened. Jack was somewhat taken aback when a little girl with long curly blond hair and rosy cheeks answered the door. Before he could think of something to say, she said, "Hello, my name is Jessica, what's yours?"

Jack found his voice and said, "Hi, Jessica, I'm Jack. I seem to be lost, is your mother here so I can get some directions?" He figured if her dad lived with her, he probably wasn't home, being as it was the middle of the day.

"Why don't you just use your pad?" Her innocent question didn't keep Jack from flushing in embarrassment. His ineptitude with the datapad was probably incomprehensible to someone who had been around one all their life.

"Well," Jack said, "I can't figure out how to use it." The little girl thought he was being funny and giggled.

Probably thinking it was some kind of game, the little girl stood up straight and put a look on her face that was remarkably reminiscent of a school teacher. "Would you like me to show you how to use your pad, Jack?" He reluctantly nodded, figuring it might be enlightening.

She reached up and took it from him, stepped out in the hall, and sat down cross-legged. When Jack didn't sit down right away, she said, "Come on Jack, you can't learn anything from way up there!" He quickly sat down, feeling like he had just been scolded by his grade school teacher. "Okay, this is the stylus," she said as she pulled a pen like object from the bottom corner of the pad. Teague had been holding one of those whenever he was working on the datapad, but Jack didn't know he even had one. "You can use your finger most of the time, but the stylus is more ack-arit." She stumbled on the word, obviously not knowing its real meaning, but he knew she was saying 'accurate.' "Tap here to get the main menu. From here you can do things like call your mom or your friends. If you press here you get video, if you don't it's just sound."

Jack was impressed, not just with the pad, but with this child. "You seem to know a lot about these. Does everyone have one?"

She shook her head. "Only the adults, but we get to use them when we go to school." She went on with her lesson. "You can also bring up a map of the city, or even of the outside, in case you ever find yourself out there. Of course you would be in bad trouble if you went outside, and the Mutes or Calis would probably steal you away, so you will never need to use the outside map." She showed him how to bring up and read the maps. The map of outside showed terrain, radioactive zones, and could even show old roads that probably no longer exist, but might come in handy if he ever needed to travel by ground transportation. Jack was particularly intrigued about the mention of dangers outside the complex, and he made a mental note to ask about it. He recalled how Chuck had just come back from an evening patrol. It would be good to know what he was patrolling and why.

"Here you can control the temperture of the 'partment, lights, and even see what you have in the fridge. There is video so you can spy on the kids in other rooms too! Once I got mom's pad and spied on my brothers and sisters for the whole day!" Jack was reminded again that these people grew up with this technology and it was an integral part of their life, even if he barely understood any of it.

"And if you ever want to learn stuff, you just click here, and then write what you want to know and the answer comes up. You can also press here and say what you want if you don't know how to write it! The teacher makes us write our questions because we have to practice our spelling and grammar." She demonstrated by clicking the button for voice search, and saying, "What is an apple?" The screen showed a picture of an apple followed by information about the species of the plant life, nutritional value, climates they are best suited for, and history of the apple including the biblical history in the Garden of Eden, and the story of Newton getting hit in the head with an apple, leading to the discovery of gravity.

Now Jack was impressed. He wondered where the information came from, and how much information was there. He intended to spend some time playing with it later. Before he could thank Jessica, she said, "Oh, and you can press here and it will take a pik-sure or video that you can save." She pressed the button and a picture of Jack's crossed legs appeared on the screen. He flipped the pad over and saw a small lens embedded in the top corner.

"Is there anything else this thing can do?" Jack was almost afraid to ask.

"Yeah, it can tell you who everyone's parents are. Mom says that is so they know who they can have babies with so they don't inbreed, whatever that means." She clicked a couple icons and got to a box. She clicked a picture of herself then dragged it with the stylus into the box, and a new display came up:

> Jessica Fironia, Age 7, sufficient DNA spread. Warning! Subject not able to conceive due to age. Approximate time until next ready to conceive, 5 years, 7 months, 13 days, plus or minus 80 days.

Jessica was proud of what she brought up on the screen, although she didn't have any real idea what it meant. Jack however, had answered one of the questions from the list. *I guess that's how you keep from sleeping with your cousin or aunt,* he thought.

"Jessica, thank you for teaching me how to use this. I have to go now." Jack wanted to get back to his room, freshen up, and then go track down Teague for some more questions. Also he was thinking about Wendy and wanted to find her and see if she would have dinner with him.

"Jack, can you come back later to play? I am sure my mommy would like to meet you, she likes meeting new people, 'specially men!'" It was innocent but Jack chuckled to himself.

"I would be delighted to see you again Jessica, I am sure we will see each other again another day." Jack got up, got the map of the complex on his pad and saw there was a small arrow representing him and what direction he was facing. He shook his head in awe. Jessie jumped up and went inside the apartment, shouting, "Mom! I met a new guy named Jack! He didn't even know how to use a pad! Can you believe that?" Jack smiled as he made his way to the elevator. He thought it best not to meet Jessie's mom right now... she might want to take advantage of him.

Chapter 19

Jack headed back to his room, washed up and used the restroom, then settled in at the desk to do some research using the newly discovered tools in his datapad. He clicked through the menu options attempting to find the search function Jessica had shown him. He came across a directory of people in the facility. Curious, he looked for Wendy and found her under Roberts, Wendy J. He didn't know her last name, but there wasn't another 'Wendy' in the list, so it had to be her. He pressed the button for video call, hoping he was doing this right. It took a moment, but her image appeared on the screen, looking annoyed. On seeing who was calling, her face, smudged with grease, dirt, and sweat, lit up. She was lying on her back, holding the pad above her, her other arm reaching up past the view of the screen. "Jack! I didn't expect to get a call from you; I guess you figured out how to use your pad?" She looked away from the screen, focusing wherever her other hand was.

He smiled. "Yeah, a little girl taught me. I hope I'm not interrupting anything." She looked back at the screen and appeared perplexed at the little girl comment, but she didn't pursue it.

"No, not at all. I'm just in an awkward position under this heating and cooling unit and a little *frustrated* with the progress of the repair." She emphasized the word with a little grunt while she pushed on whatever she was working on. She relaxed after that and smiled. "So, what's up?"

"I was just playing with my pad and figured I would give you a call and see if you wanted to have dinner with me later." He didn't know if Wendy was feeling the same way about him as he was about her and didn't want to take it for granted that she was going to be with him tonight.

"Are you asking me on a date Jack?" She was poking fun at him and he recognized it, so he just smiled. Seeing her attempt to goad him didn't work, answered his question. "I'll be done here in about two hours. Do you want to meet me up at my place? It's a single apartment on the second level."

Jack didn't miss the emphasis on 'single apartment', but he wasn't sure if it meant she was single and available or just single and not with child. He decided he would have to wait until the right time to start asking questions like that. "I can do that. It might be about three hours though, I have some research to do and I still have to get together with Teague again to talk about tomorrow. How do I find your place?"

She told him how to locate her apartment, then with a note of curiosity in her voice she asked, "What is it you're doing tomorrow that you have to talk to Teague about?"

"I guess they're taking me to the Freezer tomorrow. I'm excited because I want to see if I can find anything about the year leading up to my death." What looked like a wave of anxiety passed over her face, and he took it as concern for him going all the way up to Montana so soon after waking up.

"Don't worry," he said reassuringly, "I feel like I could run a hundred miles, and I'm sure that a quick trip like this will be plenty safe."

Her brow wrinkled for just a fraction of a second before she relaxed. With a hint of a grin, she said, "I've seen first-hand how good your health is, Jack, and I'm sure you'll be fine. We can talk about it tonight." Jack nodded. With a distant look on her face she said goodbye and clicked off.

Jack leaned back in the chair. *A date?* He felt a little flutter in his belly at the thought. *I haven't been on a date in seven years!* He turned his attention back to the datapad in an attempt to take his mind off of Wendy. There were some things he wanted to learn before he spoke to Teague again.

~~~~

He found the search function with little difficulty, getting the hang of navigating the datapad. He clicked the icon for voice search, and said, "What is a Mute?" There was a flash and information scrolled onto the screen. It read:

Mute

Pronunciation: myüt

Function: adjective

Definition:

1) unable to speak : lacking the power of speech

2) characterized by the absence of speech

3) remaining silent, undiscovered, or unrecognized

4) contributing nothing to the pronunciation of a word or contributing to the pronunciation but not representing the nucleus of a syllable (i.e. The 'e' in Bike is mute.)

He frowned when he read the information. This wasn't what he was after, and he wasn't sure exactly how to phrase the question to get the appropriate answer. He tried again, hoping the machine could understand. "Is there a definition for Mute that is only pertinent to recent history?" This time the screen came up with a picture of a man that looked to be horribly burned. Aside from the rough skin and lack of hair, the man's features were all slightly out of proportion to one another. He was, in a word, *ugly*. Jack read the description.

Mute

Definition:

Mute is a slang term for a group of people who call themselves "The Evolved".

History:

Approximately thirty five years before the communities referred to as the 'Enclaves of Science' formed, a small trading outpost in an area formerly known as 'Oregon' thrived. Within a decade of its conception, it had grown to a city of thousands of people. While their technology was not very advanced, the trading had brought them some pre-war technology, including a library of medical text books and some very advanced medical equipment. The local doctors studied the medical texts and publications as well as computer databases that had been recovered and traded off to the merchants. Within a few years they were very proficient doctors and some had picked up research on genetic engineering. Their philosophy was: since the earth had changed so dramatically, the only way humanity would survive in the long term was to adjust people to fit the environment. They began experimenting on "forced evolution". There were two methods of research. The first was to create engineered viruses that would bring about massive genetic mutations. This was not very successful, and resulted in hundreds of deaths and a short but violent outbreak of plague before it was given up. The second, more successful method was to modify a strand of complete human DNA by removing various sections and then inject the modified strand into a clean, fertilized human egg. When the child was born, the mutations were documented. When a desirable mutation was discovered, the resulting child's DNA was used for the next experiment. The final strain of DNA that was used was a result of over four thousand deaths, most of which were fetuses or stillborn babies. A process to recreate the strain of changes in each newborn was repeated over the next ten years, and resulted in a documented population of over three thousand mutated humans.

Characteristics:

"The Evolved" retained a majority of human DNA, but the changes gave them traits not commonly found on a normal human. The most noticeable was the harder skin, about the thickness and density of the hide of a cow. The texture of the skin resembled that of burned flesh, and the body was completely without hair. The tougher skin allowed them to withstand harsh weather conditions substantially more effectively than a normal human, despite the lack of hair, and also allowed them more tolerance to the type of radiation found frequently in the post-war world. The organs like the heart and lungs were larger, which gave them more endurance and stamina. These organs were also far less susceptible to disease or infection. Musculature was slightly enhanced, as was the ability to see better in darkness, and the ability to hear.

The downsides to the mutations were a decreased sense of smell, increased tendency towards violence, and decreased capacity for intelligence. The reproductive process was changed enough so that mating with a non-mutated human became impossible.

Current situation:

The "Mutes" as they are referred to by normal humans, are considered ugly in appearance, and are regarded as undesirables. As such, no community, including the one that created them, allowed them to live within their ranks. The Mutes have developed their own culture, and tend to be somewhat nomadic. The differences in their reproductive capabilities made them immune to the anti-fertility virus that was released during the infighting within the EoS. There are currently believed to be between ten and fifteen thousand Mutes in the continent of North America, with an unknown number living in Central and South America. It is also unknown if any have made it to other continents. They usually travel in groups of twenty to one hundred, and are considered hostile to anyone not of their mutated race. Very little is known of their culture as they have only been observed from the outside. Attempts to establish trade or treaty with them have always resulted in failure. When a 'clan' of Mutes comes across another community, they will harass that community, steal from them, kill any patrols they come across, and will not stop until either they take over the community or are killed off.

A chill ran up his spine. Perhaps this was reason they needed to build another underground city to live in. He wondered why Teague had not mentioned this yet. Surely they were a threat, just based on the fact they warned the children not to go outside alone. It was time to get some more answers.

~~~~

He found Teague in the cloning room, talking with another man. The man was about six feet tall, medium build, grayish hair, and had very distinguished looking facial features. He was dressed in an outfit that hinted at formality, but Jack hadn't really met anyone dressed in anything but work clothes or the scrubs he was wearing, so for all he knew, this was standard casual clothing.

"Oh, hello Jack." Teague said when he saw him. "I would like you to meet Marcus. He heads up the council that governs our community, and is, for all intents and purposes, our leader."

Jack walked up to them and held out his hand. "Nice to finally meet the boss, Marcus." They shook hands. Jack got the feeling Marcus was examining him as if he were admiring a sculpture or a painting.

"I am pleased to meet you, Jack. Ironically, I was just down here getting a status update on you. I trust you are learning a lot today?" Jack wasn't sure he liked this guy. It was the way he looked at Jack, more like an object than a person. Something about the man, perhaps the way he talked, suggested he was cloned like Teague, possessing hundreds of years of memories. Perhaps having lived that long gave one a sense of superiority. Then again, maybe Marcus had been leading this community for so long that he couldn't help but automatically assess each new member. Jack decided to give him the benefit of the doubt, and ignore his first impression. This guy, after all, had been responsible for bringing Jack back, and he *was* grateful for it.

"Probably more than I ever wanted to know." Jack said it with a grin on his face, trying to keep the conversation light. "Teague has been an incredible resource, and a fantastic teacher."

"Good, good." Turning to Teague he said, "Why don't you two come by my quarters after Jack returns from his reconnaissance tomorrow." He turned back to Jack, "Jack, it was a pleasure meeting you, and welcome to New Hope." He turned and walked out of the room.

Jack looked at Teague in confusion. "New Hope? What was that all about?"

"That is the name of our community. I hope you didn't get the wrong impression about Marcus. He probably seems a little stuffy to you, but he is a great leader, and a real visionary." Teague looked sincere as he said this.

"You're right, he kind of gave me the creeps, but I'll give him the benefit of the doubt." Jack didn't expand on that. "So let's talk about the mission tomorrow." This was one of the reasons he had come looking for Teague, and he wanted to get on with it.

"Well, it's less of a 'mission' and more of an 'outing'. You will be looked after and never in any kind of danger."

"If there is nothing to fear outside, why are we living underground?"

Teague didn't take the bait. "I didn't say there was nothing to fear outside, just that you will be safe."

Jack wasn't about to let this go, "I will feel a heck of a lot safer when I know what we might run into. What kind of horrors exist in a post nuclear wasteland?"

Teague hesitated a moment before shrugging. "I suppose someone told you about the Mutes?" Jack only nodded, wanting to get as much information as he could.

"Okay, why don't we head to the armory and we can talk on the way." Jack's eyes lit up at the suggestion and motioned for Teague to lead the way.

"The Mutes are by far the most dangerous living thing on the surface, but there are indeed other dangers. There are two larger communities similar to ours that are not exactly... in line with our philosophies. The closest is the Calis." He pronounced it like 'Kal-eeze'. "They call their community Cali, after an EoS city that was near the location they currently reside. As you can probably guess, they are located in what used to be California. They have many mineral resources available, and that has given them the luxury to trade heavily with other communities. Their population currently numbers around three hundred, and like us, only their ruling class are clones of the original survivors. Relations with Cali have been strained for the past five years."

"Strained? Is that a fancy way of saying we are at war with them?"

"War? Oh no, nothing like that. There have been some situations that turned violent, but it's more like we have restricted trade, and we are always extra careful when dealing with them. We used to trade men with them, sometimes for resources, sometimes for men to come here and fertilize our women. The agreement was always to send a man to mate with a prearranged number of women. However, they started forcing our men to be with more women than was agreed upon, so in more recent years, we have traded fertilized eggs that they can plant in their women or grow in their artificial wombs.

"Like I said, Cali is not exactly in line with our philosophies on expanding the human race, particularly where it comes to government."

Jack was intrigued. "What's their problem? I would think after all humanity has been through, everyone would be working toward the common goal of saving it."

"The problem goes all the way back to the first big war. When the war started, the majority of California residents did not want to participate. The U.S. was already in Iraq, Israel, Afghanistan, and Iran, and California was the most outspoken about pulling the U.S. troops out and letting those countries' governments handle their own problems. China had been taking over countries to the north and south of them, and the U.S. had not responded with force, so they figured they could take Taiwan and nobody would bother to stop them. The problem was, the United States had a treaty with Taiwan, and were bound by it to protect them. If they let China take over, it would tell the rest of the world that a treaty with the U.S. was worthless. The U.S.'s hand had been forced, and troops were sent. With the other wars going on, the military was stretched to its limit, so the government had to bring back the draft. That was the straw that broke the camel's back, and California seceded from the Union. Many members of the military were from California, and all of a sudden they had to choose between their country and their state. It got ugly.

"The war escalated over the next few years until there were three main alliances. China controlled much of Asia, the Islamic State had the Middle East and much of Eastern Europe, and the U.S. and Western Europe more or less controlled the rest. There had been a few isolated nuclear attacks, but it wasn't until China had opened up another war front on the Middle East that nuclear weapons threats became a reality. China was afraid they didn't have the resources to fight two wars, so they decided to make a last ditch effort and a full scale nuclear attack was the result. Once the nukes started flying and it was obvious the war was going to get worse before it got better, both China and the U.S. decided to eliminate any potential threat from California. You see, after the secession, the President of the United States had ordered federal military forces to be evacuated out of California. The now sovereign nation of California had no protection, and was left scrambling for militia. They managed to put together a sizable ground force, and even managed to keep a lot of the assets from the military bases on their soil. They did not, however, have codes to launch the nukes that they had kept, and certainly had no viable missile defense system. They were an easy target and they were hit hard, worse than any other place in the world. Today the land is mostly radioactive wasteland. Not only that, the pounding they took was so intense that the fault lines that criss-cross the state were... aggravated. Earthquakes tore up what the nukes didn't. Despite it all, there were still some small areas that were left inhabitable, and the survivors there were not happy. The world had turned their back on California, and you could say that even after over two hundred and fifty years, they still hold a grudge."

Jack took it all in, not entirely surprised. He was from California, and he could definitely see where they could self-destruct like that. "So there is limited trade. How do you balance that with them being hostile? Is there something else going on that I don't know about?" The elevator had reached the fourth floor and they had exited and walked down a hall. There were heavy doors on either side of the hallway for about a hundred feet, and at the end of the hall was a set of double doors. As they talked, they approached the doors.

Teague nodded as he went on. "They are very aggressive, and figure that none of the other communities, with the exception of the Yanks, pose any real threat to them. They don't bother to live below ground, and even the Mutes don't trouble them. The area they control is a maze of radioactive zones, and, unlike the day the bombs dropped, their air defense systems are as good as can be. They have regular patrols looking for people to add to their population, and they don't usually ask whether the people they find would like to be a part of their community. We lost a patrol about five years ago, and it was pretty clear that Cali was responsible, even though they denied it. If it weren't for the resources they have, New Hope and many other small communities like us would have long ago stopped trading with them. Unfortunately, we need what they have, and they know it." They reached the doors and Teague put his eye up to a lens next to the door. There was a beep and a click and they proceeded through the door.

"You said there were two large communities. Are the Yanks the other one?" Jack was starting to get a mental picture of how things really stood, and while New Hope was in an excellent position because of the discovery in Montana, the question was quickly becoming whether or not they could hold that advantage.

"Yes, the other group is the Yanks. They are the largest single community in the world that we are aware of. We estimate their numbers at over two thousand, but we have no idea how many of those are fertile and how many are clones of the originals. We do know they live above ground on the east coast and that there is a facility similar to this one below their city. It is only inhabited by their core government, which numbers in the dozens. They are located between two major radioactive sites: New York, and D.C."

"Two thousand? How did they get so big?" Jack was astonished at this. Until now it sounded like there wasn't a community bigger than a few hundred.

"They merged three large communities together, pretty much by force, and in the last forty years have increased in size by ten times. Their size is only limited by their resources right now, and they have their eyes on expanding to other communities. They are similar to Cali only much larger and much more aggressive. The only upside for us right now is the distance from us to them."

They entered a room that was set up like a classroom. Banks of tables were lined up, all facing what looked like a huge sheet of white glass. There was a short table in front of the glass that had some controls on it.

Jack mulled over the information, and then asked the question that he felt was most relevant. "So what keeps you and the other communities from joining the Calis or the Yanks? It seems that the best chance for humanity to survive would be to combine groups and work toward a common goal."

Teague gathered his thoughts before answering. "It comes down to a matter of philosophy. The Calis are driven by greed. They don't care who they hurt to get their way. They learned from the mistakes of the EoS, but they never learned the value of individual life. The Yanks, on the other hand, are driven by a government that is not much different than that of the EoS. The only real difference is they don't turn people away when they can no longer contribute to the community, they simply clone them. Their cloning facilities are rumored to have a capacity of over fifty people at a time."

"Wait; in order to clone them, they have to kill them first, right?" The thought sent a shiver up Jack's spine.

Teague nodded grimly. "The last we heard, the governing body is able to do this by convincing their people that they are 'reincarnated' in the cloning process, and the death of their old body just paves the way for them to enter their new body." Before Jack could react to this, Teague quickly shifted gears, "You see, the leaders of the EoS didn't have any fundamental respect for life, but it went beyond that. If you lived in an EoS city, you were evaluated for your strengths and weaknesses and given a job that suited your abilities. Despite being safe and living in relative comfort, nobody was truly free. In many cases, some people found themselves working harder than others, and dissatisfaction turned to contempt. The population was looking for change, regardless of the nature of the change. They didn't necessarily know what they wanted, but they knew they were unhappy. When the new religions formed, the general population flocked to them. The struggles for power that ensued were fueled by the follower's anger. Cali and the Yanks may have learned that war is not the answer to any dispute, but we don't see any signs that either have really learned that keeping their citizens' freedom and happiness are the key to preventing the situations that lead to war.

"New Hope is founded on the principle that not only is all human life valuable, but freedom of choice and freedom from oppression are just as important to the health of a community as survival. Why survive if only to live at the whim of your government?"

Jack felt he now had a full understanding of the situation. He was a firm believer in the Constitution of the United States, and had put his life on the line to prevent the spread of ideas like Communism, which he believed were a threat to personal freedom. He was aware that a capitalistic driven democracy was not perfect, but in his mind it was far better than having a government that looked at its people as a whole at the expense of the individual, or worse, looked at its people as a tool to increase their power and wealth. "Teague, my own personal beliefs are in alignment with New Hope, but I have to ask, how are the people here represented? Are your leaders elected?" He believed that in order to have a government that is truly a democracy, the majority population has to have the right to choose who will lead them.

"New Hope is run by a council; all of us in the council are clones of the original founders of New Hope. There was no need to elect anyone as there were only a handful of us. Marcus was a natural leader, so if there was ever conflict when a decision had to be made, he was the one who had the final say. As we grew, most decisions were made as a community, but only in the past few dozen years have we grown large enough to even consider a specific leader."

Teague looked at Jack and grinned. "You are, quite frankly, the first one to ask this question. The few people we have found over the years never questioned our leadership, and neither did their children. The fifty people we have brought back in four years have all taken for granted that Marcus was our leader, and so far they have followed without question. Sometimes things have not worked out and people left New Hope. This was usually because of a relationship gone bad, but there have been cases of people leaving because they believed we were not aggressive enough, or because we didn't take from others what we were capable of taking. Those of us who are still here all agree that only destruction lies down that path. Within the next few years, perhaps even sooner, we may very well find ourselves in a position to hold an election, but for the time being the council sets the rules."

Jack was a bit disappointed in the answer, but it made sense. When there were very few people, you put them where they could help the most. In this case, the ones with almost two hundred years of experience were probably best suited to lead. At least they were open to the idea of a democracy. Teague gestured to one of the chairs at a table in the front row. Jack took in the room before sitting down. It was a fairly large room set up like an auditorium or large classroom, perhaps fifty feet wide and just as deep. The multiple rows of tiered seating curved slightly so everyone who was seated could focus on the front of the room where a large flat glass wall about ten feet high and twenty feet wide stood. The front row had a table curved along the length of the seating, and in the center was what looked like a control station of some sort. Teague walked over to the controls and started pushing buttons.

"What about other communities? How many are there and where do they stand on Cali and the Yanks?" Jack recognized that New Hope was very small in relationship to the other communities and that made them vulnerable. He was thinking that perhaps there were other communities they could ally with to prevent the big dogs from walking all over them.

"There are six other communities that we trade with, all in North America. We know of one more in the far north, and one down in Central America, and we have confirmed at least a dozen more throughout South America, Africa, Asia, and Europe. They are too far away to be either a threat or a benefit however, so we have mutually avoided them. Occasionally we pass information back and forth, but contact is usually only a couple times per year with each.

"The six that we do work with are mostly similar to us." He pressed some buttons and the lights in the room dimmed before the big sheet of glass lit up with a map of North America. "There is New Phoenix, Swamp City, Wisner Camp, Sunnyside, Deering, and NewBury." As he named them, dots popped on to the screens with a flash, signifying their location. New Phoenix was actually in Texas, to Jack's surprise. "Populations range from fifty to two hundred. They all more or less share our philosophy. Most of those who choose to leave end up at one of these locations. We have been discussing an alliance for about twenty years now, and quite frankly we were on the verge of agreement back when we found the Montana site. Since then we have stalled, knowing that if we form the alliance, they will either figure out for themselves or we will have to tell them about the cryogenics facility. Just like with Cali or the Yanks, we worry that just the knowledge of this could cause trouble for us. Soon we will have to make a decision."

Jack wanted to talk more about the importance of keeping the cryogenics site secret, understanding that its value to any of these communities was high enough that it could easily start another war. First, however, he had a question burning in his mind for quite a while that he wanted to answer. "Teague, tell me more about the trade arrangements. How do the males feel about being traded off to other communities?"

"Well, as I was saying earlier today, the men and women understand what is necessary if we want humanity to continue, and sex, while pleasurable, is simply a tool to get the job done. The trade arrangements were usually a man for a man, and the details would be worked out as to how many conceptions, et cetera. Sometimes though, like in the case of Cali, there are resources or supplies that we need, and we do not always have enough to trade for them. Since genetic diversity is perhaps the most valuable thing in the world right now, it makes sense to trade a man's seed for other items of value."

"What about the reborn men? Do they have a problem trading their morals for resources?" Jack would be offended to be the one offered up for trade, but he was wondering how the other men like him felt about it.

"We have decided not to use the reborn in trades, for a few reasons, moral issues being one of them, but less of an issue than you think. The men born later in your century are far more flexible in that area than you." Jack shrugged at this, he wasn't really all that surprised. "The secrecy of the cryogenics facility, however, is of paramount importance. It is the ultimate irony though, we have the most valuable resource on earth but cannot use it for fear that others will discover we have it."

"So what do you do for trading?"

"We now trade only fertilized eggs. It accomplishes the same task, and although they have less value, as it takes time and resources to do artificially what otherwise comes naturally, it serves the purpose of keeping our secrets. It was easy to pass it off on Cali; after they broke some trade agreements we simply said we would no longer give them that opportunity. The other communities, though, have been asking questions, and currently think we are dying off and are afraid we will lose our men permanently if we trade them. For now this works for us."

"Does that happen a lot? People wanting to leave and go to another community?"

Teague started shaking his head, then reconsidered his answer. "As I said before, occasionally there are issues, almost always with relationships between men and women. The men and women of my generation may have a different philosophy about sex than you are used to, but they still form relationships. Any time you have a relationship between two people, you have the potential for that relationship to end. Sometimes when it ends, it does not end well." Jack grimaced knowingly. He'd been down that road once or twice.

"So how do you handle it? I imagine in such a small community the tension between two scorned lovers would be amplified." Jack could see something like this getting out of hand in a hurry.

"Well, in the past we would just arrange a permanent trade with another community. This worked well because the man had another set of women in which to find his personal happiness, and both communities gained more diversity in the gene pool. It has become a greater issue with the reborn though. Most of the women here are from *my* world, the post-war world, and only a handful are from *your* world. Our women simply do not develop feelings for the men that impregnate them. This has not gone over well with some of the reborn men, especially when the women are fornicating with another man weeks after giving birth to their child."

Jack thought about Wendy, and how he would feel if she started screwing another man next week. Or worse if she had his baby and then moved on to other men. "So what do you do in those situations? You can't send the reborn to other communities, especially under those circumstances – they would talk about the facility for sure." Jack knew the answer was not something he wanted to hear.

Teague probably sensed his tension and put the appropriate grim expression on his face when he responded. "It puts us in a difficult position, and we decided we cannot allow anyone to migrate to other communities for the time being. Instead, we do what we can to ease the tension. We rearrange work schedules to try to keep the men, or women, from being around the people causing their distress. We offer psychological counseling and medication where necessary. We also move their residence to other locations in the facility so that they are not seeing each other all the time."

"I have to admit Doc, this is a sore spot for me. It makes me feel like I'm a prisoner here. I understand the reasoning behind it, but it still doesn't sit well with me. I spent a good portion of my life defending my freedom to do with my life what I chose. Just answer one question. When you have revived all the people you can from the Montana facility, will you continue to hold people here against their will?"

Teague mulled that one over for a few moments, then answered, "Ideally, no. However, until we are in a position to assure that allowing people to migrate from here will not affect the security of other members of our community, we will have to take it on a case by case basis. Like I said, we will do anything we can to make life better, and we do not forget the individual when planning for the whole. But we will also not put the whole at risk for the betterment of the individual."

It made sense to Jack, and for now was a good enough answer.

~~~

In Jack's day, visualizing an overview of a battlefield or even of a large project site was difficult at best. Looking at this giant screen, he couldn't help but marvel at the tactical possibilities it presented. However, tactical overview was not on his mind, but radiation was. "Can you use this screen to show me more about how bad the fallout in California is?"

Teague pressed some buttons and a large amount of red shading covered the map. Most of California was covered in red, with some small dots and lines being the only places that were not red. Western Montana was all red, as was the most of the south central part. As Jack looked around at the map he saw that the areas representing about fifty to a hundred miles around every major city were covered in red. It was actually easier to look at the area that was *not* covered in red. There were a few dozen large areas, maybe forty to sixty miles in diameter, but most of the continent was just speckled in white, complex patterns swirling about the whole map. In general you could see great swaths of red, usually starting at a major city location, then sweeping off in some direction.

The visual was, in a word, stunning. Ever since he accepted his "rebirth", he had more or less taken for granted that everything he was being told was the truth. However, he had only really seen the truth in his immediate environment, and his environment was limited to a few rooms, a few people, and a mirror. The large screen in front of him was not exactly proof of the state of the world, but it was the first representation he had laid eyes on, and it took his breath away.

"The sweeping red areas are the result of weather patterns. The nukes kicked up huge amounts of radioactive debris and the winds scattered it across these paths." Teague was tracing his hand along some of the broader red areas. "As you can see, there are some large areas that are free of radiation but totally isolated and surrounded." He pressed more buttons and the display zoomed into what used to be California.

"The complex pattern of radioactive fallout does a good job of isolating and protecting them. It makes it difficult for them to do anything that doesn't involve air travel, however. This is good and bad for us. On the one hand, it makes it nearly impossible for them to launch any kind of large scale military strike if they decide to get more aggressive. On the other hand, it makes trading large amounts of natural resources difficult as well."

He pressed more buttons and the view zoomed out to just include Montana, New Hope, and the land in between. "Compared to California, most of the rest of the continent is not nearly as bad. But that doesn't mean you can just get in a ground based vehicle and drive to Montana from here. If you look closely, you can see there *is* a path, but it is far from direct and would require passing over a portion of the Rocky Mountains as well as the Grand Canyon."

Jack studied the map for a minute longer then said, "Speaking of the path to Montana, what is the plan tomorrow?"

Teague again manipulated the control panel and the display panned over to Montana. "Like I said, it isn't so much a mission as just a tour. As you know, the facility is near the old Malmstrom Air Force Base. We will fly you and two others in a four seat flyer up to here," he pointed to a location about seven miles south of the entrance, "and you will take a small transport vehicle to the entrance. This way, if anyone is tracking you by satellite, you won't lead them directly to the entrance, and it will appear you are just surveying the area."

Jack interrupted him, "Satellite? Like those things up in space?"

Teague looked embarrassed and said, "Sorry, I forget sometimes that you were dead before much of this technology came about." He took a moment to refer to his datapad then said, "In your time, satellites were pretty simple. They mostly relayed telecommunications around the curvature of the earth. Later during the Cold War, particularly in the 80's, technology heated up and satellites were used for everything from communications to weather to spying, and eventually, even to help find where you are."

"And these are still up there and working?"

"By the time the war started there were thousands up there. Mostly they were powered by fuel cells and solar panels, and eventually all but a handful of them either ran out of fuel and fell out of orbit or just simply broke down or fell victim to some kind of debris. See, back then people concerned with the environment didn't want nuclear powered satellites potentially crashing down and spewing nuclear waste all over the planet." Surprisingly, he said this without an ironic tone. "However, after the war started, the various military powers no longer cared or were held back by environmentalists, and their satellites were built to withstand a lot. Many of these are still active, and we have control of two of them. If we have control of two, chances are Cali and other communities also have control of some."

"How many do you think they have? And they can use them to keep track of what you are doing?"

"We have confirmed a total of a dozen satellites that are still in orbit and seem to be functioning on some level. One of those was sent up during the time of the EoS, to monitor radiation patterns. It simply broadcasts the information as it orbits the earth, and anyone with a radio receiver hooked to a computer can read it. That leaves nine that we don't control, and despite not being sure if Cali or anyone else controls them, we have to take precautions as if they do. We are fairly confident they have at least one of the old missile tracking satellites because of their superior air defense, and that gives them the ability to track any flights we make. Those can't track us once on the ground though. If they have control of any of the old spy satellites, they could potentially track us with long range video cameras. However, even if they have control of one, getting it into position to track anyone is not easy to do. Chances are, once you land they will not bother to get a satellite on you even if they could. It is not abnormal to send out exploration parties, and we doubt anyone has the resources to keep track of everyone else's exploration crews. Furthermore, from what we know of the spy satellites, if they happen to have one in the right place at the right time, the window they can use it is short, fifteen minutes at the outside. So to ensure they don't find the facility, we will land twenty minutes away. Absolute worst case scenario, they would track us within a couple miles of the entrance, but when we replaced the power source there, we were able to mask it enough that they would have to be within a few dozen feet of the door to detect the facility at all."

Jack nodded. He had become practically numb to the level of technology he was learning about, but when it came to tactical intelligence, he automatically pressed to learn as much as he could. This need to know probably stemmed from some of his near death experiences in Korea where bad intelligence meant dead GI's. "What kind of satellites do we control?"

Teague referred to his datapad again and said, "One communications satellite and one GPS, or Global Positioning System satellite. The communications satellite is above Texas in a geosynchronous orbit, and the GPS is a little north of that. We can bounce a laser off the communications satellite to get secure communication from just about anywhere in North America, but it takes a rather large device to do that. The flyer you will take will have one, but your own devices will be shorter range. They do have the capability of using the satellite to communicate back to here, but the range is limited and we will lose the signal about the time you hit Colorado. The GPS satellite will allow you to determine your position on a map, but since we only have one satellite, it is only accurate to about ten yards."

"You said that I will have a device for communication?"

Teague reached in his pocket and pulled out what looked like a datapad only smaller. He gave it to Jack and said, "This is your PDP, or Portable Data Pad. It has all the functions of your current datapad; a smaller screen and a powerful satellite communicator are the only real differences. It is tougher too, and can withstand a lot of abuse. It will automatically stay in constant communication with us as long as you are roughly south of where Denver used to be. Anything north of that latitude and you will have to be in range of an active laser link to the communication satellite. In an emergency, it has a beacon that is quite powerful, but there are downsides to using it. First, it takes an enormous amount of power to send out the signal, and during that time you will lose the use of its other functions for a short period of time, and second, the beacon uses the open airwaves, so anyone monitoring the emergency frequencies will know exactly where you are. Unless it's a last resort option, don't use it. This device is your lifeline if anything goes wrong, and I want to make sure you know how to use all the features before you go tomorrow."

Jack was playing with the PDP, and saw that it had all the same functionality of his datapad. "Uh, actually a little girl taught me how to use my datapad this afternoon, so I think I know most of the functions." Teague chuckled at this, the irony not lost on him.

"I will give you a rundown and explain anything she missed later." He pressed some buttons on his datapad and a wireframe model of the cryogenics facility came on the big screen. "Here you see the layout of the facility. I imagine it looks familiar."

Jack looked at it and nodded. It was definitely the site that he built. "What's the reason you are sending me there, Teague? I mean, I want to go and am happy you are letting me, but you have to have a reason in mind."

Teague smiled and said, "You're just tagging along. The two that will be with you are there to collect some new candidates. I wanted you to see the facility in person, partly to get you thinking about design and logistics, and partly to see if it stirs up any possibility that you made more of these for the military."

Jack hadn't thought about that. It was possible that other projects he worked on had been used for the same purpose, and finding another would be a good thing. "I could probably point out the other sites that I worked on right now, but I would still like to see this one first hand. The last thing I remember, it was just a big hole in the ground with only the lowest level in place. I want to see how we finished it and what it looks like now."

Chapter 20

After discussing the specifics of the trip and a short tutorial on features of the PDP, they headed to another door in the large classroom, this one opposite the one they came in. Once again, Teague put his eye near a lens in the wall and there was a beep and a click. The door led them to a long but somewhat narrow room, with lockers lining both all the walls. The center of the room was occupied by a series of tall, narrow tables that paralleled the lockers. The space just in front of the lockers was occupied by a long bench. About halfway down the wall to the right was a door. They headed in that direction.

As they entered the next room, Jack was surprised to find Chuck standing there, proudly wearing a big shit-eating grin. Next to him on a table was an object Jack could only believe was a futuristic weapon. It was nothing like he had ever seen or used, but there was little question that it was made for killing.

"Hello, Jack. How's life treating you?" Jack couldn't help but smile. Chuck's smug look told him what was coming next.

"It's been an interesting couple of days Chuck. I feel like it is about to get a whole lot more interesting." He looked down at the weapon on the table. The only thing about it that resembled a rifle was a barrel barely poking out one end and a trigger that he could spot near the middle of the weapon.

Teague spoke up, "Chuck will get you outfitted with the standard exploratory gear. Don't get excited, just because you will be well armed doesn't mean we are expecting any trouble. This is all just for safety sake." Jack just nodded, his attention solely on the gun.

Chuck got right down to business. "So I hear you were in WW2 and Korea. I am guessing you carried an M1 Garand?"

"I didn't see any action in the big war, but in Korea the M1 was my lifeline. Helluva rifle." He finally looked up from the weapon on the table and met Chuck's eyes, holding out his hand.

Chuck met his gaze and shook his hand without hesitation; his grip firm but not overbearing, a sign that he was both welcoming Jack as a friend and neither threatened nor intimidated by him. "Thirty aught six, one hell of a wallop. I would hate to be on the receiving end of one of those."

"You and me both. It was a heavy weapon to hump around but if you hit the enemy with it, they weren't getting back up. I have a feeling what you are about to show me is just as deadly and a hell of a lot more friendly to carry around."

"I think you will be impressed. But before we get to that I would like to hear more about your weapons experience."

"I mostly used the M1 and my 1911 sidearm in combat, but toward the end of my career I got some time on the M14. I would have to say of every rifle I have used, that would be my favorite."

Chuck was nodding, "Did you ever get to use the M16?"

"I heard about it, mixed opinions, but I never shot it myself."

"Well, this," he picked up the rifle from the table, "is no M16, and I can tell you right now that your opinion of it will not be mixed." The smug grin was back, and Jack could tell that he was very proud to have the privilege to present it.

"This is the M74 assault weapon. Developed during the war, in about 2025, near as we could tell, it is by far the most advanced infantry weapon ever made. The weapon itself is incredibly impressive, but it is the platform that really makes it incredible. It fires a .202 caliber round that has a small bundle of titanium flechettes imbedded in soft lead and jacketed in a copper alloy. While the caliber sounds small, the Muzzle velocity is fifty eight hundred feet per second, which gives it more kinetic energy than the rounds you fired with your M1." He handed Jack one of the rounds. It looked like just a bullet, not an entire round. "When the round hits a target, the lead mushrooms like the ammo you are used to, but the flechettes spread out and continue on, tearing through just about any kind of armor you can imagine. Soft targets just cause the flechettes to sprawl through the body and cause maximum damage. The ammunition magazine holds two hundred rounds and weighs less than the twenty round magazine of the M14. The casing is only three quarters of an inch long and the entire round is a little over an inch. It uses a chemical that burns eight times faster than gunpowder and expands over fifteen times more. The reason the round is so small is because the chemical propellant is solid and doesn't need a shell. It is completely consumed when firing, so nothing to eject. The gun uses a hybrid closed bolt system that completely contains the explosion, routing the excess energy to power the action, and even to help counter the recoil."

"Fifty eight hundred feet per second? Even a bullet that small needs a heck of a lot of energy to get moving that fast. This thing must kick like a mule."

"Actually, the action on the weapon uses a shock absorber filled with a magnetic fluid that changes viscosity depending on what the fire rate is set to. If you fire a single round, it softens up to make recoil almost nonexistent. If you go automatic, it stiffens up to increase the cyclic rate. The weapon itself is made of composite carbon fiber and titanium alloys, with a frictionless surface in the barrel and on all moving components. It's a bitch to clean because each piece is like wet ice, but it almost never needs cleaning because nothing will stick to any part that matters."

He paused, probably just to take a breath. "The rifle itself uses a bull-pup design to keep it perfectly balanced for maximum control while firing, and can be fired from any orientation, under water, covered in mud, or frozen solid in ice."

Jack was immediately skeptical of this by nature. Most automatic and even semi-automatic weapons were usually incredibly susceptible to dirt and debris, and to fire one that was muddy or dirty was almost certainly going to cause a jam. To fire a gun that had water in the barrel was a quick way to blow up the gun and cause yourself a really bad day. "I would really like to see that, from a distance of course."

Chuck just smiled, "I understand your reluctance to believe it Jack, but weapons have come a long way since your time. Even in my time you could build a fully automatic gun that could fire reliably in just about any condition. This thing takes that to the next level though."

Jack didn't have anything to say to that. He would just have to take Chuck's word for it. The man certainly seemed to know his way around guns.

"The barrel has a built in suppressor so it can't be heard more than a half mile away over the flattest land and doesn't need hearing protection to fire safely outdoors. The sight is a green laser that is invisible without the filter, so you look through the lens and you see the dot – wherever the dot is, that is where the bullet goes. The weapon has a computer processor on board that controls the recoil and adjusts the laser sight dependent on the range of the target in your sites as well as environmental variables like wind, humidity, and temperature. On the side of the weapon is a display you can flip up showing whatever the weapon is aimed at. You have a choice of regular, thermal, or night vision. The screen can also flip to the side so you can hold the weapon around a corner and still see what you are aiming at."

Jack was completely in awe. In the last few days, he had been shown technology that only existed in science fiction stories when he died, but this, by far, was the coolest thing he had ever seen. "Can I hold it? Is it loaded?"

Chuck nodded and said, "It has a full magazine but is not chambered. The safety is here, the fire selector is here, and the bolt is here." He pointed to them respectively and handed the weapon to Jack. He took it and his eyes got wide.

"It hardly weighs anything!" He held the weapon to his shoulder and thumbed the laser. It was the most comfortable weapon he had ever held. The bull-pup design meant the ammunition magazine was between his grip and his shoulder, and the receiver was just in front of that. In fact, the balance was so perfect that he needed almost no adjustment to his aim to put the green dot wherever he was pointing. It was as if he had been practicing with this weapon his whole life. "Where can I try it?" He was anxious to fire the weapon to see what it could do.

"This way." Chuck gestured toward a door on the opposite end of the room. The two men were like teens who had just purchased a bag of fireworks. When they got to the door, Chuck handed Jack a set of very small ear plugs. "Put these in, they are electronic and they cancel out the noise from the weapon but let everything else through. We could hold a whispering conversation while firing the weapon fully automatic." Jack felt like a kid on Christmas.

The room they entered was a firing range, about a hundred feet long by ten feet wide, with two lanes. There was a target set up fifty feet down range. "The target is paper in front, then a material about the density of bone, then a material the equivalent of half inch plate steel." Chuck said. They lined up on a lane and Jack put the ear plugs in, worked the bolt to chamber a round, selected single shot, then shouldered and fired his weapon. It had less kick than a .22 rifle, and with the ear plugs, he never even heard it fire. He looked at the weapon for a moment, then at Chuck.

"Did it misfire?" he asked. Chuck laughed and motioned for Jack to follow. Jack flipped the safety on and followed Chuck down the lane, keeping the weapon pointed away from both of them. His jaw dropped when he saw the backside of the target. The hole was about two inches in diameter with jagged chunks of metal-like material peeling around the edges.

"Pretty impressive, eh?" Chuck was beaming. "Now go try full auto. It's gonna kick harder the further you pull the trigger. The trigger is variable, so you get anywhere from thirty rounds per second to two hundred. If you pull it all the way and are not braced properly it will put you on your ass, so squeeze gently the first time."

They walked back to the lane and Jack reached in his ear and carefully extracted the ear plug. "I want to hear this without the protection first." He turned off the safety, shouldered the weapon, and fired a single round. He might as well have been lighting firecrackers instead of shooting a weapon that could punch a large hole in a half inch of metal. In the closed space it was just loud enough to make his ears ring. It was quiet enough, however, to hear the sound of the bullet passing the sound barrier and the 'thwapp' of it hitting the target. He put the ear plug back in, selected full auto, shouldered the weapon, leaned in and squeezed. The recoil gently but firmly pushed him back about a foot before he let off the trigger. The display just below the optics showed he had fired nearly a hundred rounds in just under a second. The target had a large hole in the middle that narrowed as it climbed up about seven inches, looking like a teardrop. Jack had fired quite a few fully automatic rifles in his time, and every one of them had climbed off a target twenty feet from him by the third round. Unless it was anchored by a bipod, it was only good for throwing a lot of lead out in a hurry. With this weapon, his grouping had remained relatively close at fifty feet while firing a hundred rounds per second!

Jack looked at the folded screen, which was tucked into the side of the weapon at the moment. He flipped it up so it sat on the top of the sights. The screen showed the area in front of him with a cross hair in the middle. Chuck reached behind them and pushed a button, turning out the lights. The screen took on a green tint and in it Jack could see everything in front of the weapon as if it were in bright daylight. He shouldered and fired a small burst again. The muzzle blast was about two feet long and the flame was light blue instead of the yellow Jack was expecting. He turned sideways, flipped the screen to the side, pointed the gun down the second lane, holding his arms out in front of him with the rifle perpendicular to his body. He thumbed the selector to single shot, lined up and fired three rounds. The weapon barely moved in his hands despite him having almost no leverage to hold it still. He had just shot around the corner while only exposing his hands to the wrist! Chuck turned the lights back on and Jack turned back to the target, thumbed the selector to auto, leaned in deep and squeezed all the way. The last eighty six rounds were out of the barrel in less than half a second. It felt like a horse had kicked him in the shoulder, but the spot on the target he was aiming at had a hole the size of a watermelon in it.

He thumbed the safety, worked the bolt to make sure it was clear, and handed the weapon back to Chuck. "I think I'll name her Charlene," was all he could say. Chuck laughed wholeheartedly at this. He hadn't lied; Jack had found a new best friend.

"Now let's go see to some body armor." After the long day of learning, Jack just followed. His brain could no longer process anything new.

They spent twenty minutes getting fit for chest, shoulder, arm, groin, hip, and leg armor. He was given a full body suit that fit skin tight and was very thin and flexible, much like a wetsuit for diving. "This is made of a material that is very resistant to small arms fire, although a direct hit from an M74 round will penetrate it. The armor segments will stop any light weapon's fire and most forms of shrapnel, but if something hits you between the pieces of armor, it will hurt like hell. You might break a bone but unless it hits dead on it will glance off." He was fitted with skin tight gloves and socks, lightweight boots that were surprisingly comfortable, and finally a helmet. The clear shield on the helmet had a heads up display that showed him a small view of what was behind him in the top right. There was an overlay display that showed night vision over the top of what he was looking at, and he could switch back and forth on the fly. There was a button on the M74 that fed the video and ammunition count to the helmet so he could see it without using the screen on the gun.

He was finally given a pack to hold the armor, the rifle, ten magazines of ammunition, a sidearm that fired the same ammunition, five magazines for the sidearm, a holster for the pistol, and some webbing that allowed him to have it all stored neatly on his body and within easy reach. There was a strap that allowed him to put his PDP on his wrist, and of course he could link the display from it to the helmet as well. Also in the pack was two weeks' worth of field rations, a water bottle, a medical kit, and packets of water purifier. Chuck showed him how he could fill the water bottle with the nastiest water he could find, put the packet of purifier in, and within five minutes he had the purest water you could imagine. The bad stuff that the purifying chemical took out of the water was flushed out a valve in the bottom of the bottle.

Chuck looked at Jack and said, "Any questions?"

"Yeah, does it only come in black?"

Chuck grinned. "The nature of the material does not allow us to paint it or stain it, so we are stuck with this color. While we can repair the material, creating a full set of this armor is very difficult with the resources we have. Our supply of armor came from the urban police force of an EoS city. It would be nice to have it in camouflage, but I'm just happy we have a good enough selection to outfit a couple hundred people."

Jack didn't have any more questions.

"You are all set. I will see you on level one at 0700."

Jack's eyebrows went up and he said, "You're going with?" He hadn't been told who the two other people would be.

"Hell, I'm flying the boat," he smiled and walked out of the room.

Teague had been hanging back in the locker room the whole time, letting Chuck do his thing. "Ready for some dinner?"

Oh crap! Dinner! "Actually, I have a date. Is there anything else you need from me tonight Teague?" By his internal clock, he was at least an hour late and felt bad that he had lost track of time like this.

"Just one thing. Make me a list tonight of what kind of talent you would need to get started with the project we were talking about earlier. Just skill sets you would want on your planning team. We will use it to determine who to harvest next." Jack was disappointed, he wanted to spend the whole evening with Wendy but now he had a 'homework' assignment.

"Will do. I'll get to it after dinner. Seeya Teague!" He was practically running toward the elevator, towing his pack, which despite being filled with all his new toys, only weighed about fourteen pounds.

Chapter 21

He found Wendy's apartment and knocked. The door slid open and he heard her in another room saying, "You're late! Is that any way to start a date?" Jack felt bad for being late and not calling to tell her.

He dropped the pack in the corner and said, "I'm sorry Wendy, I was tied up with training and lost track of time." The room was modest in size, had a couch and a chair facing each other off to the side with a coffee table between them. Two archways led into other parts of the apartment. It was warmly lit, the walls painted in earth tones, and the floor was cushioned like carpet although it looked like hardwood. As he finished surveilling the room, she walked in through one of the archways. Her dress took his breath away. It was a simple cut that rode on her shoulders and hugged her curves all the way to her knees. The front was cut low and showed about three inches of cleavage. She had on earrings and the slightest hint of makeup. She smiled, stopped in the middle of the room, and turned around once to show off the dress. He got just a glimpse of her incredible body before she closed the distance between them. His knees went weak as her soft lips brushed his just before she pulled back.

"Don't sweat it, I figured you would be there longer than you anticipated. I just had to give you a little crap first. I couldn't let you off the hook without making you feel a little guilty first."

"My God Wendy, you look fantastic!" Then with a feigned look of confusion, "What's the occasion?" She punched him in the chest and they both laughed.

"I wanted to do something special tonight. It *is* sort of our first date. I pulled out all the stops. Are you hungry?" Jack was ravenous, but he wouldn't mind standing there for a few more minutes admiring her.

He said, "Very, but for more than just food." He put his arms around her and kissed her deeply.

"Easy there buddy." She said as she squirmed out of his grasp. With a wink she said, "I'm not that easy on the first date," and headed back through the archway into the kitchen. Jack chuckled at the joke and followed, admiring her backside as he went.

"So, lemme guess, jello with sawdust? What flavor tonight?" When he saw the table his jaw dropped. There was a steaming stew in the middle of the table, and next to that, a plate with what appeared to be vegetables simmering in a sauce. There was a bottle of what could only be wine open and sitting next to the food. There were two place settings with wine glasses in front of them, and a candle burning right in the middle of it all. "Holy shit, is that real food!"

Wendy giggled. "Of course it is, do you think we eat that jello every day?" He moaned with pleasure as he inhaled the aroma of the stew.

"That smells fantastic! Where do you get the food? Is there meat in there?" He had not had meat since before his surgery. Despite his memory telling him that had only been two or three days, he truly felt like it had been centuries since he had a decent meal.

"It is. We trade with other communities and one called Deering in North Dakota has cattle. I had salvaged some old equipment on a patrol a few weeks back, and traded it for some steak and vegetables. I also scored this bottle of wine, but don't be too surprised if it doesn't taste like wine. It was made from some kind of fruit up in Washington at the Sunnyside community. I had been saving it for a special meal, but until now I didn't have anyone to share it with me. I'm not that good of a cook, so I hope it isn't too bad."

"Wow, I'm flattered. I can't tell you how much it means to me." Thoughts of his other hunger were forgotten for the time being. "Can we eat? I'm starving!"

~~~~

After dinner, they sat on the couch nursing their full stomachs and sipping at the wine. The food had been absolutely delicious, and the wine wasn't half bad either. Jack wanted to sit here for a while enjoying Wendy's company, but he had some work to do. "I need to make a list for Teague tonight. I would rather stay here and do it, but if you want I will go back to my room. It shouldn't take me more than an hour."

Wendy gazed into his eyes and smiled. "Of course you can stay here... and afterwards..." She left the thought hanging, sending a little electricity up Jack's spine. He got out his big datapad, and sat back down on the couch. Bringing up the notes screen, he saw that his questions from earlier were still there. He read through what was left, and scratched out all but one. The remaining question was, "tell me about the war". It was irrelevant but he wanted to know more, so it could wait until another day. He deleted the rest of the list and started a new list. He titled it 'Skills'. He then made a column titled 'required' and one titled 'requested'. He concentrated for a few minutes, then under required he wrote: Engineers, anyone from Army engineering corps, architects, pilots, heavy machine operators – crane operators specifically, carpenters, accountants, mechanics, electricians, plumbers, sheet metal workers, anyone with concrete experience. Under requested he wrote: Human Resources specialist, supply staff, interior designer, painters, cabinet makers, seamstress.

He looked over his list, wondering what else he would need or want. He didn't need a cook, just a machine to dispense the jello, and he didn't need any secretaries, since he had devices like the datapad he was working on right now. He remembered what Wendy had said about bartering for the meat and vegetables, so he added 'recruiters' to the list. A military recruiter was a good salesman, and who better to barter for materials down the road?

He decided it was good enough for now, so he hit the button to send it to Teague, then put the pad away and sat down next to Wendy. She'd been playing a game of solitaire on her datapad, which would have been amazing to him if he wasn't already numb from the barrage of new technology. "So you're heading to the Freezer tomorrow?" She was flushing a little and her breathing seemed to get shorter, as if she had just sprinted up a set of stairs. Jack knew the only strenuous activity she had done in the last hour was clearing the table, and was wondering why she appeared so out of breath. *Is it nerves?* She had been calm, even when undressing and climbing into bed minutes after having met him the other night, so he found it hard to believe that she was nervous about being intimate with him.

"Yeah, I report in at 0700. I should be back before the end of the day though. Do you want me to come over to see you after I get back, or are you tired of me yet?" He said it kind of like he was kidding but he was also probing for a hint at how she felt about him. Wendy looked lost in thought, and he misinterpreted the silence, thinking that maybe she was indeed getting tired of him. "Look if I am being too... clingy, just tell me and I will back off a little. I like you Wendy, and I was hoping you felt the same way."

She looked up at him as if hearing what he said for the first time. "I'm sorry, I was sort of... not really there when you asked. I absolutely want you to come over when you return. I do feel the same way, Jack, probably even more so, and I wish I could spend the next month just being with you. But..." Once again she was talking like she was out of breath.

But? That was a bad word when having a serious talk about feelings. Jack had heard that word a few times in his life in this manner and it now left him suddenly short of breath. "But... what? Is something wrong?" he tensed in anticipation of her next words, fearing it would be something about just wanting to get pregnant or something.

"Jack, I have a confession to make, and I am afraid you will hate me for it!" She suddenly looked like she was going to cry. A million thoughts ran through his head trying to divine what she was going to say, and how he was going to react. He pulled back from her a little, trying unsuccessfully to steel himself against the words that would surely mark a change in their relationship.

"A confession? Um, okay, let's hear it."

What she said came out in one long sentence, and was so far from what he expected, it didn't make sense right away. "I was the one who found your body at the facility. I read your records, and your personal documents, and you see, I never thought that you could be reborn because your tube was so old, but I was lonely and depressed and reading your diary made me feel so much better, and I didn't know it at the time but I fell in love with you before I even met you, and then when Teague said he was successful, I sort of freaked out and decided to protect you from all the whores around here, and then I saw you and just melted, and..." she paused to take a breath, "My God Jack I am so sorry, can you please forgive me? I really do love you, and I feel so bad about this." Wendy finally stopped talking, and when he didn't say anything right away, she looked like she was about to die from agony.

Jack blinked and his brow furrowed. "You found a diary?" He was still trying to make heads or tails of what she had just said.

"Jack, I swear I wouldn't have read it if I had thought that you would be brought back, but reading about your thoughts, emotions, and fear of the unknown really helped me with my own situation here. You have NO idea how much pressure they put on us to hook up with men, and it was just too much, and... and..." She rambled on as if she didn't know what to say. Jack was only half listening as he still sorted out her first words.

"You found me? And got Teague to bring me back?" Between the lethargy from the full meal, a couple glasses of wine, and a long day of overwhelming learning, sorting through this was like trying to swim in cold molasses. "And you're saying you love me?"

"Yes, Jack, I know it sounds silly but after reading all about your last year of life, I couldn't help but fall in love, at least with the idea of you, and when you were brought back, I just lost control. I made a total fool of myself, coming to you that first night like a tramp, seducing you like that. Oh my God I think I'm going to die of embarrassment! You must HATE me!" She buried her face in her hands, missing the look of pure pleasure on his face.

She actually flinched when he reached for her and exclaimed, "That is NOT what I was expecting you to say! Wendy, why would you think I would be mad about this? If anything, I'm flattered. You fell in love with me without even meeting me, and after meeting me, you felt even *more* certain of it? The last few days have been an incredible whirlwind of emotions, and you have been like a rock that I could focus on to make sense of it all! You have no idea how good that makes me feel! I thought my life was over a week ago, and now I have a whole life ahead of me! I think we have something good going here, and quite frankly I'm just happy that you don't want to run off with the next man that comes along." The look of surprise on her face melted off when he kissed her long and deep.

Before the passion could build, she broke off the kiss and looked at him. "So, you aren't mad that I stole your diary and kept it from you? And you aren't mad that I wasn't honest and was pretending to not know anything about you and just looking to take advantage of you?" She appeared flabbergasted that he was reacting this way.

"I'm furious, actually, but I wanted to get laid tonight." He said it deadpan and she had to do a double take. She punched him in the chest and he laughed. Then she kissed him passionately again.

When the kiss ended, Wendy looked into his eyes. "Jack, please tell me that this thing between us is not just a mixture of loneliness and raging hormones. I feel like this is all too good to be true. Too convenient. I was so lonely when I found your diary, and in reading it I fell in love with someone who didn't exist. How can I be sure that you are the man I fell in love with? How can I even trust my own feelings here? How do we know this isn't just a hot romance that will burn itself out in a few weeks?" She had worked herself into tears again.

"Wendy, I don't even remember writing in a diary, so I can't tell you much about the person that you read about. I'm a simple man. I was never one to sleep around, and I feel that I'm a pretty good judge of character. I have to be honest with you when I say that I haven't felt this way about anyone since my wife died, but at the same time, maybe I just forgot what it was like to just be with a woman. I've enjoyed my time with you, and not just the intimate time, the chemistry between us seems to extend way beyond that. I want to spend time with you, get to know you, and you can be assured that I won't run around behind your back and have sex with every woman I meet. Besides, I'm under the impression that there will be one more reason to be with you before long."

Wendy smiled. There was little doubt that a baby would be on the way soon, if not already. She put her head on his chest and sighed. "Jack, I'm sorry about being so emotional about this. I certainly don't want to put any pressure on you to have feelings for me. I appreciate your honesty, and I think you're right, we need to just spend some time and see where this is going. I'm sorry if this ruined our date. I just didn't want you to go all the way up to Montana and discover an empty lock box. What can I do to make it up to you?" She looked back up at him, this time with a mischievous grin on her face.

"This date was perfect. If I died tonight I would have to say that I went out happy. As far as making it up..." He leaned in and kissed her again.

Suddenly she broke off and said, "Oh, I almost forgot." She ran into the other room, then came walking back out. Music filled the room. He couldn't identify its source, but it sounded fantastic, as if just around the corner there was a piano player. It was a classical piano piece, but not one he recognized. His taste in music leaned toward orchestra and symphony. Country Western was enjoyable if the mood is right, and when he was younger he loved rock and roll from the likes of Elvis or Buddy Holly, but nothing beat a good piano solo.

The music was fairly slow, and perfect for some close, romantic dancing. Wendy's eyes were closed and her hips swayed to the music. He stepped up to her, took her hand in his and wrapped his other around her waist. They slowly danced around the room for at least a half hour, bodies moving in perfect unison.

Wendy was smiling, staring into Jack's eyes. "I wasn't sure how you would react to the music, or if you would even be interested in dancing. I always liked going out dancing on a date, and I figured this date wouldn't be complete without some. You make a fine partner Mister Taggart."

Jack put on his smoothest smile, spun her around slowly and then dipped her. "You're not so bad yourself, Miss Roberts." With that he kissed her deep, and she sort of sunk into him. They broke off the kiss and settled back down on the couch. He took the lead for a while, and they made out like a couple teenagers on the basement couch. Wendy finally stopped and stood up, holding Jack's hand, urging him to follow.

They made their way to her bedroom. He stopped at the end of the bed, and kissed her neck, then slid the shoulder of her dress down and kissed her shoulder. He slid the other shoulder off and kissed the nape of her neck. Working his way down her body he slowly peeled the dress off and kissed each inch of her body. He paused at her very erect nipples and gave them a little extra attention before continuing down her body. When he reached her hips, the dress slid the rest of the way to her ankles by itself. He kissed just below her navel, then slid back up her body, sliding his hands up her thighs, over her hips, landing finally on her breasts as he kissed her deeply again. A little moan escaped her throat and she backed up to pull his shirt off. She kissed his chest as she slid his pants and boxers off, then embraced him and kissed him deeply on the lips again. He picked her up, her legs wrapping around his waist, and carried her to the bed. He laid her down and went to work again with his lips and tongue, working his way all around her body. He brought her to orgasm with his tongue, and she screamed out his name. He then slid back up to kiss her on the lips, and finally entered her. He worked slowly and with perfect rhythm, until she was practically screaming, gripping at the sheets, wrapping her legs around him. He released when she peaked and they shared a long, intense orgasm.

They lay there for about five minutes, him on top of her, just gazing into each other's eyes as if communicating telepathically. Finally he slid off to the side, and lay on his back. She cuddled up to him, one leg draped over both of his, pressing her warm body to his. "My God, Jack, that was incredible." She was still a bit dazed, the remnants of the intense orgasm tickling her spine.

Jack didn't feel the need to say anything; he just held her tight and closed his eyes. They lay like that for about an hour, drifting in and out of sleep, totally at ease in each other's arms. Two more times that night they repeated the performance, taking the passion to new heights, and by midnight they were completely spent and both sound asleep.

~~~~

Wendy woke up in Jack's arms. The lights in the apartment had slowly gotten brighter, simulating a rising sun. The effect worked as intended and soon she was wide awake. Jack was still sound asleep, so she carefully extracted herself and climbed out of bed. The clock on her datapad showed just before six a.m. Standing up revealed a stiffness in her legs that was a little painful but completely welcome. It reminded her of the evening before, and a smile made its way onto her face.

She used the bathroom, and then went to the kitchen. While she dug out the diary, she thought about the night before. Ever since he called her earlier in the day, she had been nervous about that evening. She knew that at some point in the evening she would have to confess about the diary. Although she didn't feel good about the motives behind the meal and the dress, it did give her great satisfaction to make him happy.

135

At some point during preparations for the date, she came to the conclusion that she was being too hard on herself about the whole thing. There should be nothing wrong with a woman doing what she can to please her man, even if part of the reason is because she did something she feels bad about and doesn't want him to be mad about it. It had been a complete surprise when he reacted by grabbing her and kissing her. At that moment she would have done anything for him. In retrospect, she felt a little guilty about the date and dinner, but since she genuinely cared about him, it was all acceptable.

She got the diary out and headed back to the bedroom to watch him sleep for a little while before waking him. They nearly collided as she rounded the corner. "Oh shit! You scared the hell out of me Jack!" She smiled and kissed him. They were both buck naked standing in the middle of the doorway.

"Good morning. What time is it?" He looked worried that he had overslept.

"It's only 0600. Plenty of time. Here, I was digging this out for you. It is yours after all." She handed him the diary. He took it, looking at it in reverence as if it held all of the answers to life's greatest mysteries.

"Thank You. You have no idea what this means to me. I was hoping I could find something like this to give me some insight into how I died." He walked over to his pack and put the diary in it. Wendy figured he would read it on the flight this morning. He paused after he stood up, looking down at his pack. "Say, you didn't by chance change my computer file after reading that, did you?"

It was an oddball question, but the fact was, she had. There was an entry in the diary about how he had changed his birth certificate to get into the military, and she figured that having his correct age in the system might make a difference in bringing him back. Of course, she hadn't been able to just tell Teague without revealing the diary, so she snuck into his office and made the change. She blushed and said, "Yeah, actually, why?"

"Oh, just clearing up a mystery. Teague will get a kick out of that." He chuckled, shaking his head."

"Wait, you can't tell him, it might get me in trouble!"

Jack seemed to think about that for a second. "True. Don't sweat it, it isn't a big deal anyway. I need to use the bathroom, then take a shower." He patted her on the butt as he walked past. She admired the view as he walked into the bathroom. After using the toilet, he started the shower and said, "Any chance you want to wash my back?"

She smiled, went into the bathroom, and climbed into the small shower stall with him.

Chapter 22

Jack stepped off the elevator on level one and made his way down the hall to a small locker room that was next to a loading dock for the rail line that ran five miles away from the complex to an underground air field. He had called Chuck ahead of time to find out where on level one they would meet. Chuck was nowhere to be seen, but a new face was there putting on his combat gear. He was a fairly light skinned African American, just under six feet tall, lean body, and appeared to be about thirty years old. His hair was cut to the nap, and his features were sharp. When Jack walked in, he looked up from lacing his boots, and smiled. "You must be Jack. I'm Emmet Johnson, nice to meet you." His voice was about that of a tenor which seemed to fit his size and stature, and there was a hint of southern hillbilly accent. He held out his hand and Jack shook it. The grip was firm and his hands were well calloused.

"Pleased to meet you Emmet. I assume you are the third team member?" The question was rhetorical. Jack put the pack on a bench and pulled out his gear. He started getting undressed. "So tell me Emmet, are you a reborn or a native?"

"Reborn, actually. One of the first. I have been here for just about four years now. I was a staff sergeant in the Army when I died in '97 from lung cancer." Jack was pulling his under suit on, and the word Cancer had stopped him dead.

"I'm sorry to hear that, I know what it's like to learn you have cancer. Thankfully I don't remember the year that I spent getting treatment or having to deal with it..." Their eyes locked for a brief moment and it felt like a bond passed between them. Jack resumed getting dressed.

"I knew you were going to be short on memory, but damn, a whole year?" Emmet had a very expressive face, and his eyebrows did as much of the talking as his mouth did. He wrinkled his brow and said, "Of course, I was surprised that Teague was able to do anything at all, given how early you had been frozen." Now his eyebrows went up and he closed his eyes as he said, "It was a miracle, my man, God himself must've had a hand in it." He had finished securing his armor, and was putting his webbing on, making sure he had all his gear.

"I sure feel like I was blessed. A week ago I was told I had cancer and was going to die, and here I am, healthy as can be, younger than I was, a beautiful woman to keep me warm, and one hell of a rifle to keep me safe." They both laughed. "So I imagine you have kids, but are you married?" Jack was at ease with Emmet, he seemed to wear his heart on his shoulder.

Emmet pondered the question for a moment, his face visibly working as he thought. "The first couple years, I went from woman to woman, having the time of my life. But after a while it felt a little lonely. I dated one woman here steady for about a year, but Teague told her she had to have a baby with one of the new guys we brought back, and it kind of pissed me off when she jumped right in the sack with him. I told her I would rather she did the artificial thing, but she blew it off and told me not to be silly!" His eyebrows were all over the place as he told his story. "Can you believe that shit? Those women can be cold about sex, Jack. Just some friendly advice, have fun with the natives but don't get involved." The last sentence ended with his eyebrows in a flat line across his brow, signifying that he was dead serious. Jack was surprised that he had opened up like this. Most military types would keep this sort of thing to themselves, and just pose and posture when asked about women. He decided he liked Emmet. "You about ready?"

Jack was just securing his last piece of body armor and he nodded. He grabbed his pack and said, "Lead the way."

They stepped out of the room into the loading dock. There was a small rail car there, the shape of an egg if you stretched it to about twice its length. The door was open and inside were some benches. They climbed in and Emmet pressed a button next to the door. It slid shut and the car accelerated very quickly. Jack's ears popped as they rode along, and he figured they were not only moving away from the complex but also climbing in elevation. In about two and a half minutes they slowed down and the door opened.

They exited into a huge cavern-like room with natural rock walls and ceiling. The room was basically a large dome, perhaps four hundred feet by seven hundred feet, lit with an orange tinted light, reminding Jack of a warehouse lit with mercury lamps. On one wall there was a giant set of doors, easily eighty feet high.

Chuck was holding a datapad and a flashlight and was inspecting inside a panel on a small aircraft that looked like a sleek helicopter with short wings on either side and no blade on top. It was painted in desert camouflage, had a door on each side, and the cabin was surrounded with large windows. The short wings had small propeller blades inset in them, but Jack couldn't see any engine or turbine. Chuck closed the compartment he was looking in, and made a note on the datapad. He dropped the datapad and flashlight on a cart next to the aircraft and turned to the men walking toward him. "Good morning gentlemen, your ride is checked out and ready to go." He said it with a smirk on his face, and without waiting for a response, opened the door and climbed in the front seat.

Jack went around to the other side with Emmet and climbed into the back seat, stowing his gear next to him where Chuck's pack already rested. Emmet handed him his pack and climbed in the front. When the door closed, Jack felt his ears pop again. He asked why.

Not turning to look at Jack as he was busily flipping switches and getting ready to fly, Chuck said, "The cabin is pressurized. We will come out of those doors up ahead and shoot up to an altitude of about forty thousand feet. The ride will take about two hours, and according to my weather info, should be pretty smooth."

Jack was surprised when the aircraft suddenly lifted about ten feet off the ground. "Holy shit! I didn't even hear you fire up the engine!"

Concentrating on flying, Chuck said, "Yeah, it's driven with electric motors so it's quiet, but also the same technology that went into those ear plugs I gave you is used in the cabin here to keep it quiet. If you were outside right now it would be loud, but nothing like an old chopper or plane."

Jack nodded. Emmet was fiddling with his PDP up front, and Chuck was busy flying, so he sank back in the seat to enjoy the ride. The large windows to either side gave him a nearly three hundred sixty degree view. The giant doors opened up and the aircraft shot forward. He held his breath as they cleared the doors with about a foot to spare.

Sunlight filled the cabin and they were surrounded by red and brown desert, with little clumps of grayish green brush dotting the landscape. The sight was quite stunning, and as Jack took it in, he realized he could not even spot the camouflaged door they had exited. The morning sun was coming in from the east at a steep angle, suggesting that sunrise had only been in the last hour or so. That likely meant it was late fall or early spring. Jack had never asked what season it was, but now that he was outside, it all of a sudden felt relevant. "What time of year is it?"

Emmet turned around and said, "Early spring, about March I would say. It was a long cold winter, brother." He was smiling when he said it as if he was happy to have it behind him. His eyes narrowed slightly and his brow wrinkled just a bit as he said, "So tell me Jack, did you have a family back home? Any kids?"

A thread of sorrow made its way through Jack's heart, followed by a little guilt. He hadn't thought about his wife or daughter for two days, and with all that had happened, it felt like two months. He softly sighed and said, "I had a wife and daughter, but they died in an auto accident about two years before I, uh, passed." Jack still felt weird referring to his own death as a point of reference. "I was just getting over it and about to start trying to find a nice woman to date when I was told I had cancer."

Emmet nodded slowly and his brow and mouth both scrunched up. "Sorry to hear that Jack. A man should never have to bury his child." The way he said it suggested that he knew from experience what he was talking about. His expression changed as fast as his topic and he asked, "I know you haven't been here long, but tell me what you think so far of the whole female situation. You mentioned you had a warm body to keep you company?"

Under normal circumstances, Jack would hardly be discussing his sex life while making small talk with a stranger, but he felt a sort of camaraderie with these men. They were both military, and it was obvious to Jack that both had seen heavy combat at some point in their lives. He also understood that the community was small, and everyone would know most of the details of his life sooner or later. "Actually, I met someone that I think I could spend the rest of my life with." To his surprise the reaction from the two men was not at all what he expected.

Chuck glanced at him for the first time since leaving New Hope, and Emmet's brow shot up as his eyes seemed to catch fire with interest. "No shit!?" he exclaimed. Then more solemnly he said, "God I hope she ain't a local. They don't look at things the way we do." Emmet obviously had a chip on his shoulder regarding the local women.

"Nope, she's a reborn."

Chuck and Emmet exchanged a look that might have been envy then Emmet looked at Jack and said, "Consider yourself lucky. Now I myself wouldn't have wanted to settle down before having a few weeks of fun, but you *are* blessed if you already got yourself a main squeeze. Especially if she won't run off with the next swinging dick that comes along!" Emmet turned back to Chuck, and one eyebrow went way up and his eyes were wide as he exclaimed, "You hear that Chuck? He got himself a reborn in the first couple days!" He turned back to Jack and his brows once again furrowed, this time in concentration. "I know it isn't Elizabeth, Michelle, or Cynthia. They're all shacked up with someone already." He appeared to be going through a mental list of names trying to figure out who it was. Finally he shrugged and said "Damn, I can't figure out who it would be. There are only a few reborn ladies that aren't pregnant or involved at the moment, and I can't see any of them wanting to be in a relationship right now. It's not Heather is it?"

Jack chuckled to himself, thinking that he probably shouldn't have said anything, but now Emmet wasn't going to stop until he at least found out who it was. "No. I've only met three women since waking up, and I don't think one of them was a Heather. Just to put your mind at ease, Emmet, it's Wendy Roberts."

Chuck turned to look at him again, this time he didn't look back right away. Both he and Emmet couldn't have looked more surprised if Jack had said it was a man he was sleeping with. Chuck examined Jack for at least ten seconds, then turned back to the aircraft controls and said, "Bullshit."

Emmet continued to look at Jack, his brows hunkered down in concentration, and after another ten seconds the brows shot up and with a look of surprise he said, "Jesus Christ, Chuck I think he's telling the truth!" Jack considered this parlay, wondering why it was so unbelievable to them.

"I don't understand guys, what's the big deal?" He wondered what they knew that he didn't.

Chuck spoke first. "Jack I've been on over a dozen patrols with her. She's as cold as ice when it comes to men, and most of the guys around here think she is more interested in the women, if you know what I mean. About six weeks ago, a guy named Jeremy put his hand on her ass and she nearly broke his nose. I find it hard to believe that you're doing anything with Wendy. It's strictly business around that woman."

Jack just shrugged and sat back, trying to hide the smirk on his face. He figured there was no sense in arguing the fact, and quite frankly he didn't care if they believed him or not. Thinking about her, however, reminded him of the diary so he grabbed his pack to pull it out. He figured there was a good hour and a half before he had anything to do, and he was anxious to see what he had written in it.

Before he could open it, Emmet spoke up. "Jack, regardless of what Chuck here says, I believe you. Congratulations, Wendy may be a cold bitch but she seems like a good, solid person. She can tune up a flyer like nobody else too." Obviously that was the end of the subject, and he turned around to fiddle with his PDP some more.

Jack was not offended by the term 'cold bitch'. He felt like maybe he should be, but if Wendy had acted that way towards other men, it actually made him feel better. He smiled, filing away the term for later and settled back to read.

Emmet finished whatever he was doing with his PDP, and warm classical music softly filled the cabin. Jack had attended a few symphonies in his time and he now felt as if he were in the front row. He closed his eyes, and for a moment he was right there, just behind the conductor. "You don't mind if we listen to some relaxing music do you, Jack?"

It took him a moment to realize that Emmet had asked a question. "Uh, no not at all, but can you tell me where it's coming from? It sounds fantastic!" He had not questioned Wendy last night when she turned on the music, thinking at the time that there was some sort of player in the other room, but this was not a large cabin, and he did not see anything that resembled a playback device or radio.

"It's all in the PDP. Teague is sort of a connoisseur of classical music and he put some of his collection on my pad. I have some heavy rock and some alternative too if you're interested." Emmet took note of Jack's blank stare and tried to clarify. "The music is stored digitally on my PDP, and I am sending it to the sound system in the cabin here through the wireless interface."

Jack didn't understand the technology, but didn't want to appear stupid either. "So basically it's like a little eight track tape in there?" He knew it wasn't a tape player, but the technology was too foreign to have any idea how the music was stored on his PDP.

Emmet chuckled, his eyebrows bouncing in sync to his laugh. "Something like that Jack. The music's converted to ones and zeros with some complicated math, stored on this little computer, then transferred to the sound system in the flyer here and the ones and zeros are converted back to music using the same kind of math." Emmet was still talking over his head, but he didn't really mind. There was a lot he didn't understand in this world. He nodded at Emmet, feigning understanding, and settled back into his seat to enjoy the music.

Opening the diary revealed an old looking piece of paper. He carefully removed it from the book and read what was typed on the paper.

My Dear Jack,

If you are reading this letter, then by some miracle this hair-brained idea the military came up with has worked and you are once again alive. I found your diary and gave it, along with this letter, to Phil to lock away with your body.

I wanted to leave you with something, after all you did for me in the past year. I am ever so happy that you called that morning to ask for my help, even if you didn't think that was why you called. Reconnecting with you has made me feel like a whole person again. I have lost a lot over the years, and just figured it was the price one paid for remaining alive. You taught me to see things different, both through your pain as well as through your will to live.

In case nobody can tell you, you died on a lovely June morning. The funeral was very nice, and all your friends were there to pay respects. We buried a casket next to Jennifer and Allissa's grave, and never told anyone that your body was elsewhere. It was nice that your friends could honor you properly. Phil drove your race car in the procession, just as you had asked, and the Army gave a terrific performance with the military honors. Doctor Chambers drove out from Minnesota to attend, which I thought was very nice of him. He was such a kind man through the whole thing, and I was happy you two formed such a tight bond.

I never thanked you for leaving me your estate, and I wanted you to know that I gave half of the money after the sale of your house to the Mayo cancer research facility. I followed your wishes and paid off my farm debt with the rest, and even had some left to get that new tractor you told me I should get. The thing I needed to thank you for the most was for coming back into my life. When everything else is gone, the only thing left is the people you have touched.

One more thing. I followed your last wish, and set a date with John Parkerson. Thank you for opening my eyes to see that there was more to life than what we had already lost, and that sometimes what you needed most in life was right before your eyes the whole time.

Thank You, Jack, and good luck in your new life.

Love and Sincerity,

Mabel

Jack had to wipe a tear from the corner of his eye. He wasn't the type to show emotions, but he couldn't help but feel touched by the letter. He read the letter three more times, then carefully put it back in the back flap of the diary. The letter brought up more questions than it answered, but he was very happy she had left it and also that she had stuck around through the whole ordeal. He sincerely hoped that she had the chance to finish her life to the fullest.

~~~~

The first few entries in the diary only confirmed what he already knew: he indeed had cancer and it was going to kill him. If it hadn't been for Mabel's urging he knew he would never have taken a treatment option, and instead would have decided to live out his last months trying to make the most of whatever time he had left. He wanted to read more, but they seemed to be slowing down and descending, so he put the book away in his pack and waited to break through the clouds so he could get a look at the area.

As if sensing that someone was interested, Chuck announced, "We're about ten minutes from the landing zone. I will circle the area once to make sure it's all clear, then put her down." Emmet was dozing up front and the sudden announcement woke him up.

The aircraft cleared the clouds and Jack took in the scenery. Below them, the hills and gullies looked like giant wrinkled scars that rent the pale flesh of the earth. The winter snow cover was gone, leaving only the dry dusty ground dotted with brown clumps of brush. To the west, the overcast sky left the rocky landscape a dull, washed out gray canvas stained here and there with dark clumps of evergreens.

Within minutes, they had descended to about a thousand feet above the ground, and Jack started picking out the details, like trees and grass. He had flown over this area when surveying the land around the future cryogenic complex, and had been amazed at the patchwork patterns that the farms had painted on the land surrounding the city. Now there wasn't even the slightest hint of the farms that used to occupy this area. They crossed the Missouri river and Chuck turned a little to the north. Jack could make out the faint lines that marked where the railroad tracks and interstate used to be, but as they got closer he could see that the railroad bed and an occasional railroad tie were all that was left. He could see the path left by the interstate but there was no pavement left, just brown patches of overgrown brush.

He started looking for familiar landmarks as they flew over the former city of Great Falls. His heart sank as he observed what was left of the ruins of the city. In the residential areas, there was not much besides a few foundations and some remnants of rusted out cars. Ahead were shells of old buildings, some standing, and some collapsed to a pile of concrete and rusted metal. Other than that there was little evidence this area had once been home to nearly fifty thousand people. Chuck banked to the east, and a few miles ahead Jack noticed what looked like a pattern of long ridges crisscrossing the ground in front of them. As they got closer to the former site of the Air Force base, he realized they were edges of craters from what must have been some very

143

large bombs. The craters had long been filled in with dirt from the constant wind that blew out here, and only the gently curved ridge from the massive craters was visible now. He couldn't even make out the outlines of the old foundations. "Any idea what happened here during the war?" He doubted that either of the men knew what fate the city had suffered, but it didn't hurt to ask.

"The information in our computers is pretty sparse for this area. They didn't get nuked, we know that for sure. I read some of the history of the war, just to see how it progressed. There is not much to read from after the bombs dropped, probably because there wasn't anyone with the free time to record news and events. Most of what we have came from military databases that were recovered over the years. The Chinese landed ground troops in Alaska and Canada. They made a huge sweep along the U.S. Border, and most of the cities up in that region became strategic points, with the front lines cutting jagged edges back and forth across the border from Seattle to Lake Superior. Best we can tell, the Air Force base here was a key point for air attacks, and at some point, the Chinese threw everything they had at it, which, as you can see, wiped it off the face of the earth." Chuck stopped talking as he banked to the right, dropping to a few hundred feet above the ground. They circled around about a twenty square mile area, and seeing no signs of life, Chuck spiraled toward their landing zone: a coulee about twelve miles south of the former city.

A huge cloud of dust was kicked up as the aircraft came to rest. Before it cleared, Chuck worked some controls and the electric whir of hydraulic pumps could be heard. Emmet opened his door, and cool air rushed into the cabin. He hopped out and turned to Jack. "Hand me my pack, wouldja?"

Jack handed him the pack, then grabbed his own and climbed out. Emmet already had his rifle out and was making his way to the north bank of the coulee. Jack pulled his rifle out then shouldered his pack. He went around to the back side of the flyer where Chuck was pulling something out of the rear storage compartment. The ramp that extended from the large compartment to the ground was what Jack had heard opening when they landed. "Need a hand?"

"No, I got it," he said as he pulled out what looked like a dune buggy that had gone through a car crusher. It rolled down the ramp and Chuck hit a lever on the side of it and some motors started whirring. Before Jack's eyes, the vehicle started first extending the wheels out in each direction, then the sides of the vehicle unfolded to become the body. When it finally finished, it resembled a large wagon with a roll cage around the top half, four large knobby tires, and four seats. It was about nine feet long and four feet wide, and aside from a stick that looked like it belonged in an airplane, there were no controls visible. On the top of the roll cage was a box about three feet wide, two feet long, and six inches deep. Chuck climbed in, securing his rifle to a clip on the side of the roll cage.

Jack was wondering where the motor was when Chuck motioned for him to get in the back seat. He climbed in and before he was all the way settled the vehicle shot forward, all four tires kicking up dirt and dust. The vehicle made almost no sound, and the noise of the tires on the rough ground was all he heard. "Electric motors again?"

Chuck nodded. "The battery is below the chassis, about the size of a brief case, and will last about a year under light use before it needs to be charged. Technically the range is about four thousand miles, but I wouldn't want to have to travel more than twenty or thirty in this thing." Right then they hit a rock with the front tire and the roll cage shot up to clock Jack on the side of the head. He rubbed his head where he had been struck, feeling a knot already starting to form.

"I see what you mean," he said as he pulled the seat restraint over his shoulder and waist and fastened it. The vehicle bounced its way toward where Emmet had already started making his way up the side of the hill. Chuck expertly guided the vehicle up an imaginary path that zig-zagged up the side of the coulee By the time they reached the top, Emmet was already scouting the area using his helmet's built in binoculars.

"Well," he said, still scanning the area all around them, "if that cloud of dust you kicked up was noticed by anyone, they either aren't bothering to check it out, or they are hiding somewhere waiting for us." He pushed a button on the side of his helmet and turned to the vehicle. Jack could see a grin on his face as he climbed in the seat next to Chuck. Rather than stow his weapon, he kept it on his lap.

"Have you ever run into anyone up here?" Jack had been under the impression that there was nobody living anywhere near this area. He would have been at ease except for Emmet's reluctance to put his gun away. Chuck had put his helmet on, and Jack decided it was a good idea, especially after experiencing the joy of bouncing around in this vehicle.

"Nope, but you never can tell. Damn Mutes show up at the most inconvenient times." His eyebrows shot up and he turned to Chuck. "Hey, remember that time up in Colorado when we were trying to load that supply crate?"

Chuck nodded passively as if he had heard the story retold a hundred times and just wanted to focus on driving. Emmet turned to Jack, eyes filled with excitement. "So we had been scavenging some small factory in Colorado, and had three big crates full of supplies and machinery. The first two fit just fine on the transport, but the third was just a little too large, and we were trying to figure out how to squeeze it through the door and still be able to get it back out when we got home. The area was pretty badly overgrown with trees and brush so the only place to land was in a clearing down a hill from the factory. It wasn't the best tactical location, so we sent this guy, Jonas-" he interrupted himself and turned to Chuck, "You remember Jonas, that guy was as ugly as he was dumb!" he laughed, then picked up where he left off, "So we sent him up to the top of a hill to the south of us to keep an eye out. Just as we were trying to shoehorn the crate onto the loading ramp, we hear a shout." Emmet's eyebrows were hard a work as he narrated his story.

"Here comes Jonas, stumbling down the hill, barely keeping his feet under him, shouting 'Go! Go! We gotta go! Mutes! Mutes are right behind me! GO!'" Emmet was laughing as he told the story, trying to put a frightened look on his face to imitate what Jonas would have looked like. He was telling the story with such enthusiasm that Jack couldn't help but laugh along. Even Chuck seemed to be smiling and paying attention to the story, although it was hard to tell with his helmet on. "So me and Chuck look at each other like 'Oh shit!', we had this huge crate halfway loaded and the transport ain't goin nowhere!"

"So we just grab our rifles and get ready for a fight, when over the ridge rolls this huge cloud of dust and dried leaves. Jonas reaches the bottom of the hill and is running so hard he finally loses control, tumbles to the ground, rolls a couple times, and bounces back up like he planned it! Then he rushes to the transport and without missing a beat, dives over the crate to the inside of the transport and starts trying to push it off the ramp, all the while yelling and screaming "Go, Go, GO!"

Jack was riveted. "So by now the ground is rumbling, trees at the top of the hill are shaking, scaring flocks of birds from their nests, and this cloud of dust and debris is rolling over the top of the hill! I don't know about Chuck, but I was about to shit myself. You know that moment of sudden calm when shit is about to get real? When it is like everything pauses for just a second and then explodes into chaos?" Jack knew exactly what he was talking about. "Well that was exactly what happened. It was like everything stopped for just a fraction of a second and BOOM, out of this cloud of dirt explodes this huge herd of deer! There must have been over fifty of them! As they burst into our clearing they scattered every which way, and in seconds the clearing is filled with utter chaos. Then as if that weren't enough, two mountain lions crest the hill and come charging down into the clearing after them!

"Before we could really react, Jonas, who had climbed on top of the crate when he couldn't push it down off the ramp, opens fire, tearing these deer apart! He's yelling 'Goddamn! Goddamn! Fuckin Mutes!' as he blasts away!" Emmet was laughing so hard he could barely talk and Chuck's shoulders were shaking as he joined in. Getting his hysteria under control, he says, "We just looked at each other, and Chuck turns to Jonas, and says 'You Freezer burnt moron!' grabs his rifle, which was still slung around his shoulder, and yanks him clean off the crate! Then he grabs him by the collar and drags his ass over to one of the dead deer and says, 'does this look like a fuckin Mute to you?'." Emmet wiped a tear from his eye, still trying to keep his laughter in check. "So Jonas looks at the dead deer, then at Chuck, then the deer again, then back at Chuck and finally pushes himself off the ground, dusts himself off and says 'How the hell should I know, I'm from Miami!'." He burst out in laughter again and Chuck and Jack joined in.

Emmet calmed down and got a look of nostalgia on his face. "That dumb sonofabitch took down seven deer! We left that supply crate and crammed the hold full of deer. We ate venison for a month!"

~~~~

The entrance to the complex was an unassuming door. At least it would look like any old rusty and weathered door if it wasn't embedded in the side of a small hill in the middle of nowhere. Crusty dirt and rust covered the bottom half of the door, as if it had been buried for many years; the top was heavily weathered, and if anything had ever been painted on it, it had long since worn away. Despite the rust and other patina, it was obvious the door was still rock solid and sturdy. The entrance would not be visible from the sky, and even from the ground it was hard to spot. There was heavy brush all over the area. Someone had dug out the dirt that had drifted up to the door over the years, and a path had been stomped into the brush. As he looked around the area, Jack remarked at how different it looked. A week and a half ago he was in this very spot, but most of the hill to his left was an open pit almost a hundred feet deep, and the hill in front of him didn't exist. They had planned to use the soil and rock they had excavated to make natural looking hills to hide the entrance, and it looked like whoever finished did a damn fine job. Of course, three hundred years of weather helped to blend it into the surrounding landscape as well.

"How often do you guys come up here?"

A heavy steel bar that had obviously been installed fairly recently secured the door. Emmet went to unlock it while Chuck answered, "Every couple weeks, lately. We've gotten pretty good at picking candidates that will survive, and we have staggered the birthing chambers so that we can cycle a new one every two weeks. It's been almost six months since the doc had a failure. Before that we would collect six at a time and if we were lucky, two would make it. It was slow going at first, but in another year we'll have over a hundred reborn."

"What changed to get the failure rate so low?" Emmet had finished unlocking the door, and Chuck moved to it to help swing it open. A loud groan echoed between the hills as the heavy steel door swung on rusty hinges.

Chuck dusted off his gloved hands and said, "The selection process changed. We now have tools to examine the tissue before harvesting, and we leave the ones that we are not sure we can bring back. About one in three are no good to us because of injury or the nature of their disease. Another third are 'Freezer Burnt' leaving the rest as viable candidates. We harvested one that was questionable about two years ago and when he woke up he only had memories to the age of five." Jack shuddered at that thought. "We don't even try the questionable ones any more. Well, except you."

"Freezer burn? I caught that term in Emmet's story earlier, what exactly does that mean?"

"Ever eat a steak that was in the freezer too long? The meat isn't the same after that. Same kind of thing can happen to a corpse in deep freeze, and when it comes to recovering the memories from a frozen brain, that isn't good. Sometimes it results in some lost memories, sometimes far worse. Some of the native born started using it as a slur against the reborn, and it sort of caught on as a general insult whenever someone did something really stupid."

Chuck pulled out his PDP, and tapped a few times on the screen, then put it to his ear like a telephone. "We're at the entrance, shouldn't take more than an hour." He put the PDP away and looked at Jack. "They are in constant contact with our PDPs but once we go in there they will lose contact and we will not have communications with them. If we don't report back in an hour, they will send someone to investigate. We learned a long time ago that it's better to be safe than sorry."

"What happened?"

"One of our exploration parties stumbled on a Mute camp. They tried to retreat to their flyer but the Mutes pressed the attack and ended up damaging the flyer. The next day we sent out a search party and found one of them left, holed up in a small cave, down to just a sidearm and a handful of ammo. He and his group been cornered and made their last stand. They fought well, but Mutes are stubborn and mean, and once they start a fight, they don't let off until they win or die. By the time we got there, he was the lone survivor. The last few Mutes were just about to storm his shelter when the cavalry arrived." He paused, a distant look in his eyes, and Jack could sense he had a personal hand in the situation. "After that, we changed the rules to check in at predetermined intervals and to start the rescue process as soon as someone doesn't check in."

With that he grinned and marched through the door. Jack followed, and Emmet walked to the wall just inside the door and flipped a big lever. There was a thud and a whine and lights came on, illuminating the short hallway that ended at a large door. They approached the door, and Chuck typed a code in a keypad that looked out of place. The doors swung open to reveal a large elevator car.

Before Jack could ask, Chuck volunteered, "They installed this keypad and a security system when they figured out how valuable this place is. There are automatic turret mounted rifles above the ceiling there and there." He pointed to small holes in the ceiling in front of the elevator. "Our PDPs transmit a code that gives us a minute to get the system disarmed. If someone finds this place and gets through the first door, they won't make it past this spot."

Jack shivered at the brutality of such a security system. Chuck seemed to be reading his mind and said, "For a group of people who are on the verge of extinction, you would think they would take more precautions to NOT kill each other, but that isn't exactly the case. If I had my way, I would at least put some kind of deterrent or warning system in so anyone who came across this wouldn't end up dead before they knew what was going on. I'm sure Teague explained it to you, Jack, but if there is any question in your mind, put it to rest, humanity lost its respect for life a long time ago, and this is not the same world you and I grew up in."

They climbed aboard the elevator and Chuck pressed the second of five buttons. The complex was three levels deep, Jack recalled, the third level was where all the utilities and the power plant were located. When he was planning the construction, the drawings called for two large concrete reservoirs surrounding a massive platform on the third floor. The level also had plans for ventilation shafts that ran to the surface, and Jack had always assumed they were putting in some huge diesel generators and using the reservoirs for fuel storage. *They must have used the reservoirs for cooling the power plant.* Assuming level one and two were for the storage of the bodies, that left one button that didn't belong. It was red and like the keypad above, looked out of place. "What's the last button for?"

"Panic Button." Nobody said anything else, so Jack didn't ask further.

The doors opened to a small room with some old medical and research equipment stashed along the walls. The technology was Jack's era, and it was in poor shape. There was another door in front of them, and Emmet pushed through without a word, walking into a large chamber about five hundred feet long and seven hundred feet wide. There was a heavy concrete column every thirty feet spaced evenly over the whole level. In Jack's day, they couldn't make a room this big underground and not have the supports. It reminded him of the challenges ahead.

The room wasn't quite what Jack expected. After hearing the term 'Freezer', he sort of expected entire cold rooms filled with bodies. Instead it was just a really big room filled with what appeared to be large, cylindrical tubes, each about eight feet long and capped at both ends. They were wider than they were tall, so not exactly cylindrical, more of an oval shaped tube, like some kind of futuristic casket. There were hundreds, maybe thousands, evenly spaced in rows, as far as the eye could see. Jack shivered. *That's exactly what these are, caskets* he thought to himself.

There was a thick layer of dust on most of them, and most of the floor was covered in the dust as well. Even underground with very little air circulation, three hundred years is enough time for dust to collect. Footprints drew a big tree on the ground, starting heavy at the door, and branching out across the floor in all directions for hundreds of feet.

Jack walked up to the first tube and examined it. The tube was sitting on an elevated base. The oval tube was about four feet wide and about three feet tall. It was all black except for a short window on the side that ran for six feet of the length. There were tubes and boxes mounted to various parts of the cylinder, and a control panel with a screen at the end. The one Jack was looking at was no longer covered in dust, and he paled when he peered into the window at a naked, headless, blue corpse lying inside. "What the hell?"

He jumped as Emmet seemed to appear at his side and said, "We don't have room for the whole body, so we only take what we need. It's kind of gruesome work, but you get used to it." Jack shivered again, his stomach churning at the idea.

"How do you... remove them?" Jack only wanted to know out of morbid curiosity.

"There are two ways to do it. First way is to use a wide chisel and a hammer. The second way is to just grab them firmly and pull. They tend to break off pretty clean that way."

"Oh my God! You just snap them right off?" This made him retch a little, and he had to walk away to settle his stomach. Chuck walked to him and handed him a bottle.

"Take a drink, it will pass. These folks have been dead for over three hundred years, they don't feel a thing, and besides, they are usually pretty thankful when they wake up on a table back at New Hope." Jack took a swallow, forcing the bile back down his throat. He thought about that for a second, realizing that as gruesome as it seemed, it was done to give these people another chance, and to save humanity.

He handed the bottle back to Chuck. "Thanks. Look, you aren't going to make me break off someone's head as some sort of weird initiation are you?" There was no way Jack was going to 'harvest' anyone.

Chuck laughed. "No, we'll take care of that part. You just have yourself a look around. After we get what we need here we can go down below so you can see some of the inner workings and the modifications on that level." He pulled out his PDP and tapped a few things. "Hey Emmet, this way. We are looking for Mr. Henry Halstead and Miss Irene Russell."

Emmet's eyebrows shot up. "Another woman? God I hope she's hot and likes middle aged black men!" They both laughed and headed to the left back corner. Jack went the other way.

~~~~

He wandered the first level for about ten minutes, noticing that the further back he got, the tubes changed more and more. The ones at the front had control panels with screens like the one on his datapad. The ones he was looking at now had screens but they were more like the television screens he was used to. Most of the units had lights on them, even the ones that had been harvested. Jack figured that they left the units running when they harvested so that the decaying bodies didn't stink the place up. There were a few units where the light was off, and he surmised that those units had failed for some reason. Jack brushed the dust off one of the dead units and was shocked to see that the body was very well preserved in the tube. He would have thought that it would just be dust in there. He guessed that the tubes were vacuum sealed, and the extreme cold probably killed any bacteria that would have been around to consume the flesh. It was just a guess but it sounded good.

He reached the end of the room, and wandered along the wall for a while. There were few footprints back here, only a couple paths that led to a tube without any dust on it. He made his way back to the elevator, and waited for Chuck and Emmet. He could hear them in the distance talking, and even heard Emmet's laugh. Chuck was a no bullshit kind of guy, and Jack figured that he could trust him to have his back in any situation. Emmet was a character, and although Jack liked him, he wasn't sure if he would want to spend any serious time hanging around him. He was the kind of guy you loved to have drinks with but he didn't seem to have an 'off' switch. It would get exhausting spending too much time with him. Despite his exuberant personality, Jack could see him as a competent soldier; he was alert and knew he had a job to do.

As interesting as this place was, he didn't really have anything to do and his mind was on Wendy when the two men got back to the door. They were carrying what looked like two metal cases, each about the size of a bowling bag. They were flat black in color and had blinking lights on the side. Emmet looked at Jack and with a long face said, "She's kinda homely".

Jack shook his head, laughed, and said, "Maybe the doc can tweak her DNA a little and make her prettier." Emmet's expression suggested that he was giving it serious thought.

He looked at Chuck and said, "Do you think he can do that?" Chuck and Jack both laughed. "No, really, do you think he could make these women prettier? Think about it! If the women were hotter they could get laid more often and have more kids!"

Emmet was on a roll, but Chuck shut him up by saying, "I doubt it, I mean, just look at you! You think if he was gonna fix anything it would have been your ugly mug." They all laughed and got on the elevator.

Chuck pushed the third button. "We don't go down here much, there's a lot more freezer burn here, and most of the people here can't be recovered. This was where Wendy found your body. It's way in the back."

Jack was suddenly nervous. He wanted to see where he had been for the last few hundred years, but didn't know what he would feel when he saw it.

The elevator stopped and opened, this time directly into the storage area. It was identical to the one upstairs, only the units in front were older and a little bigger, like the units toward the back of the first level. As they walked toward the back, the units got larger and more ominous looking. In the far back corner, the dust had been cleared away from a tube that was fifteen feet long and eight feet in diameter. This one was not ovular in shape, it just looked like a big chunk of pipe with caps bolted on to each end. There was no screen or fancy controls, just a panel with a lot of buttons and lights, none of which were lit. Fixed to the cap at one end of the tube was a metal box, about fifteen inches square and six inches thick. The door was hanging open and the box empty. Chuck and Emmet were hanging back a little, allowing Jack to make his peace with this on his own.

Despite seeing his own final resting place, he really didn't feel anything. Morbid curiosity overwhelmed him again and he climbed up on a platform that was welded to the side of the tube and looked through the glass. The pale withered body did not look familiar in the least. Jack shook his head, thinking that he couldn't have weighed more than a hundred pounds when he died. "I'm glad I don't remember those last few months," he said out loud to nobody. He continued to stare at his body for a few more minutes then climbed down to leave. He took one last look around, but was satisfied there was nothing of importance here.

~~~~

They rode the elevator to the third floor in silence. Jack figured that both these men had seen their own bodies and knew that he would probably not be in a bright and shiny mood. They were right. Despite not feeling much when seeing his own dead body, it had seemed to drive home the idea that this whole facility was basically a cemetery.

The third floor was familiar to Jack. He had more or less completed it by the time he found out about the cancer. The massive reactor and its steam powered generator sat side by side on the platform he had helped pour. They were quiet and cold now, having been shut down four years ago when they were replaced by new technology. Chuck showed him the unit that now powered the facility, providing lights and running the compressors that kept the liquid nitrogen cold and pumped through all the tubes in the levels above. The unit was about six feet by six feet by four feet, and the four inch thick main power lines that had been cut from the nuclear generator now fed off that little black box. Jack marveled at it for a while, thinking of the possibilities of such a small and powerful source of energy.

"And this unit will power this plant for a thousand years?"

Chuck nodded. "Crazy, isn't it?"

They spent about twenty minutes poking around. Jack checked out the ventilation system, surprised it was still working. Nothing particularly useful was coming of this trip though, and he was disappointed. It was time to go.

On the way up, Emmet said, "So are you gonna build a new underground city for New Hope?"

He shrugged. "I don't know. I suppose I'm going to try." Jack was not optimistic. If anything, this trip had reminded him of how much trouble it is to build on this scale.

"Well, if you need a crew member, I wouldn't mind workin for ya Jack. I'm getting tired of comin here." His face was solemn; an expression Jack had not seen much from him.

"Emmet, I would be honored if you would be on my crew."

~~~~

The elevator stopped and the doors opened up. Emmet stepped off first, followed by Chuck and Jack. Two men appeared in the doorway, blocking the light coming in from outside. They had their rifles trained on Emmet. Nobody was expecting this, and Emmet had only one hand on his weapon, the other was carrying the frozen head. "Drop the weapons, hoppers."

152

The three men froze. Chuck eased in front of Jack, his rifle hanging at his side, the other frozen head in his hand. Jack's own rifle was hanging from his shoulder by the sling as well. Suddenly, Emmet threw the head toward the two men and pulled his rifle up, simultaneously squeezing the trigger down. The burst of bullets tracked from the ground at the men's feet and up toward their bodies, but it wasn't fast enough. The two men opened fire.

Emmet dropped to the ground. Jack was still reaching for his rifle when Chuck fell back into him, knocking him back into the elevator. Something kept punching him in the chest and helmet. He was on the ground and Chuck was on his back, lying on Jack's legs. Chuck had his rifle up, firing a long burst, and one of the two men screamed and went down to one knee. Jack reached out and got hold of Chuck's backpack, and in one movement kicked both feet out pulling them both back into the elevator. He reached up and punched the closest button. The doors closed and there was a very loud roar, followed by an even louder silence.

Chapter 23

The elevator was hazy with smoke. Both men lay on the floor of the elevator, Chuck was in Jack's lap, unmoving with a wisp of smoke coming from both his rifle and his body. It didn't take long for Jack to snap out of the confusion. The first thing he noticed was the smell of burning flesh accompanied by a faint sizzling sound. Not wasting any time, he pushed Chuck to a sitting position, which released a bigger puff of smoke from under his armor. He quickly got to his knees and examined the man. In front, there was a neat hole in the right shoulder, between the chest armor and the shoulder armor. He leaned Chuck's body forward and reached down his back between his under suit and his skin. His hand slid right in as if lubricated with oil, and he groped around, feeling something small and sharp. Carefully pulling it out revealed a heavily distorted but complete .202 caliber round, covered in blood and still sizzling. He tossed the bullet aside and realized that the lubrication that allowed his hand to slide in between the suit and Chuck's back was blood. "Oh shit, this isn't good." The elevator stopped at the first level and the doors opened, allowing the smoke to quickly clear. He judged that about twenty five seconds had passed since they stepped off the elevator into the maelstrom of gunfire.

Lying Chuck down, he stood up. Working quickly but trying to keep his nerves in check, he reached down and pulled off Chuck's backpack, chest armor, and shoulder armor. He then unzipped the front of the under suit and pulled it down. There was a small hole right above Chuck's armpit. Dark blood was steadily oozing out of the hole. Jack figured that the bullet went in, hit his shoulder joint, then diverted deeper down, and exited somewhere on his back. The hit was direct enough for the bullet to penetrate the material but upon exit was stopped by the back material and sat there burning another hole in his back.

Jack dropped his own pack from his shoulders, reached in and grabbed the medical kit. He opened it and took a quick inventory. Much of it he didn't recognize, but he saw what looked like big band aids and grabbed two of those, a roll of gauze, a tube that said antibacterial, and a tube that said coagulant. He glanced at the instructions on the tube of coagulant. It said 'squeeze liberal amount into wound, cover wound with skin patch.' Jack opened the tube and shoved the tube nozzle into the small hole and squeezed. He then took some gauze and wiped the blood away. By the time he got the first band aid looking thing out of its package the bleeding in front had stopped. He slapped the patch on and rolled him over. His back was a mess. There were three large burns where the bullet had come to rest against his skin each time they had stopped moving, and one hole about the size of a nickel that was bleeding profusely. It was just above his shoulder blade, and Jack hoped the bullet hadn't hit the lung. He shoved the nozzle in the hole and squeezed most of the bottle of coagulant in it. He wiped the area dry of blood, and waited for the bleeding to stop. It took about six seconds, and he wiped it dry again and slapped the patch on it. He then squeezed some antibacterial on the burns, which were easily third degree.

He then stripped the under suit down to Chuck's waist and looked for more holes. There was nothing on his back, so he rolled him over again. His chest looked like someone took a hammer to it. He had at least two dozen small bruises, and three large bruises that had already turned dark red. Obviously he had been hit by more than one bullet but the material had saved his life. Unfortunately his body had to absorb the impacts, and it looked like he probably had three or four broken ribs and possibly some internal bleeding, other than the obvious bullet wound of course. The fact that the bullet had been more or less complete meant that the armor had slowed it down enough so it didn't come apart inside the body. That was probably why Chuck was still alive, although there was no question he would need real medical attention soon.

He lay Chuck down again, using his pack for a pillow. He took a quick assessment of the situation, talking it through.

"Okay, there are bad men upstairs. They shot at us, probably killed Emmet, Chuck is hurt and unconscious. I think I hit the panic button when closing the elevator and judging by the sounds I heard, those turrets probably opened fire. I need to get up there and get to the flyer. Shit! I don't know how to disarm the turrets, or to fly the aircraft." Nodding as if confident he had everything straight, he checked Chuck's vitals. His heartbeat was strong and he was breathing. Jack went to the medical kit again, looking for some smelling salts. He found what he was looking for and cracked the tube under Chuck's nose. It took a second, but his nose wrinkled and he turned his head to the side. "Chuck, can you hear me?" He slapped his cheek a couple times trying to rouse him further.

Chuck moaned and quietly said, "What the fuck happened? Where are we?" He wasn't quite with it yet, but Jack needed help.

"Chuck, wake up. I need the code for the key pad so I can get us out of here. There were soldiers at the door when we got off and they shot you up pretty bad. I think Emmet is dead and I need that code!" Chuck opened his eyes and tried to look at Jack. He closed them again and winced.

"Holy shit... did I get shot? I can hardly breathe." Jack was worried he was going to slip out of consciousness again.

"Chuck, stay with me! You have some broken ribs, that's why you are having trouble breathing. Listen to me Chuck, I need that code!" he was about to get another tube of smelling salts out when Chuck opened his eyes again, this time he focused on Jack.

"Jack, what the fuck! Where are we?"

"Come on Chuck, we are in the elevator on level one. I need that code to disarm the turrets. Stay with me Chuck." Jack's mind was racing. Perhaps five minutes had passed now, and he knew if there was a chance he was going to make it out of here alive he had to act now. He was thinking maybe he could take the elevator back up to the ground level and call for help on the radio, then hole up here and wait for help to arrive.

"76362." Chuck's eyes were closed again but he repeated it. "76362. Those were Cali men, and they knew we were from New Hope." Jack felt relief that Chuck was thinking coherently. "If it's a patrol, there will be four of them, probably three on foot and one at the flyer. How did we get out of there?"

"I pulled you back into the elevator and punched the red button." Chuck actually smiled.

"Those two won't be home for dinner. Goddamn bastards deserved it though. You need to go up top and see if you can radio to base. If you run into any of them, aim for the throat, it's the most vulnerable point and a shot there is usually a kill. Be careful." He coughed once and then winced in pain. "Hand me the med kit, I need something for the pain."

He handed Chuck the med kit, and Chuck dug through it until he found a small tube. He broke end off of the tube which revealed a small needle, and he poked it into his waist and squeezed. Relief washed over his face within seconds and he settled back onto the pack he was laying on.

Jack had dropped his rifle and helmet next to his pack when he went for the medical supplies. He picked it up, and pulled the bolt to load a round in the chamber. After putting his pack back on, he pulled Chuck's under suit back up, zipped it, and carefully put the chest armor back on. He stuffed the various medical supplies in Chuck's pack, then scooted him to the side wall under the controls for the elevator and put his pack and his rifle next to him. Chuck was semi-conscious but wasn't moving.

He took a deep breath to clear his mind and pressed the top button for the ground level. He moved quickly to the other side of the elevator so he would have some cover if someone was ready for him up top. As the elevator headed to the surface, he put his helmet on and shouldered his rifle. The doors opened and he tensed up, ready for anything.

The room was full of smoke and Emmet's corpse lay face down in front of the elevator. Jack scanned the small room and stopped on what must be the remains of the two Cali men. Aside from their armor, nothing much was left. Bits and pieces of flesh and bone painted the walls and left a swath of red on the ground outside the door. He reached up to the panel just outside the elevator and punched in the code. There was a beep and a red light turned green. He put his pack in front of the elevator door so it wouldn't close when he left.

Hugging the wall, he made his way to the entrance, stepping over the remains of the two Cali men. He peeked around very quickly but didn't see anyone out there. He went back to Emmet's body and checked for a pulse. Nothing. *Dammit.* He looked him over and saw that there was a bullet hole in his throat and his left arm was nearly severed at the shoulder. He now examined the two men at the entrance. The heavy turret guns were large caliber with armor piercing rounds that had gone through their body armor as if it were cardboard. He turned his attention back to the door. *Are they hiding or are they back at the flyer or did they leave when the turrets armed?* He listened carefully for a few seconds, but didn't hear anything.

Remembering the camera in his rifle, he thumbed the switch to turn on the video. A small window popped up to the upper left of his field of vision showing what was in front of the rifle. He reached out with just the rifle and scanned the right then the left. He didn't see anyone. *Shit, I'm going to have to go out there and look.* The surrounding hills were great for hiding the entrance, but were just as good at keeping an ambush out of sight until it was too late.

Steeling himself for the run, he adjusted the butt of his rifle on his shoulder and took a quick breath. He sprinted out the door, and immediately juked to the right and spun around to look on the hill above the door. Just as he turned, about forty rounds landed right where he would have been if he hadn't broken right. He already had his rifle trained and he eased into the trigger. A small burst burped out of the gun and a cloud of dirt was kicked up in front of the person lying prone on the hill. Without stopping to see if he had hit him, Jack turned a quick one eighty, checking all his vulnerable points, then started running around the side of the door to get on top of the hill where his enemy was. He kept a hill to his left and kept checking his cover to the right while simultaneously watching the rear view feed in his helmet with his peripheral vision to make sure someone didn't try to come up from behind. He crested the hill that covered the door, took a quick look around before breaking cover, and went to the body. He had nearly taken the man's head clean off with his shot starting just above the chest armor and ending at the man's chin. Keeping a close eye on his surroundings, Jack dug in the man's pack to see if there was anything he could find that might help him. The man had pretty much the same gear as Jack had, so he grabbed the PDP and dropped it in his pocket.

Now that he was outside the complex, he grabbed his PDP to call for help. He found the icon that represented New Hope and pressed it. The message made his heart sink. 'Laser Link down.' *Shit, they must have gotten to the flyer. This is not good.*

From the top of the hill he was exposed to anyone watching, but he also had a line of sight for miles in every direction. He thought for a second about binoculars, then remembered his little training session with Chuck the previous day. He pressed a button on the side of his helmet and a screen popped up in the center of his vision, overlaying what he could see. He fiddled with the controls, working the zoom in and out until he had it set to '8x'. He scanned a full circle again, looking for anything out of the ordinary. Nothing. He pressed another button and the zoomed screen went away.

Back at the elevator, Chuck was still lying where he left him. When he approached, his eyes opened. "Well?"

"Emmet is gone. The two men were cut to pieces by the turrets. There was one waiting for me on top of the hill above the door. I took care of him." It had been a long time since Jack had killed a man, and he was trying not to think about it. Thankfully, there were more important things to worry about than his emotions right now. "I tried the radio but it says the link is down. What do you think we should do?"

Chuck tried to push himself into a sitting position, winced in pain, and stopped. Jack reached over and helped to pull him and scoot him against the wall. He took a few painful breaths and finally said, "We have two options. Either we can wait here and hope that a rescue team will be here in a couple hours, or we – I mean you, can go back out there and make your way to the flyer to see if you can find the other man and his transportation."

He weighed the options and then said, "How sure are you there is only one more Cali out there? Any chance there are more?"

Chuck shrugged, which made him wince again. "One of two things happened. Either this is a patrol that just happened to spot us, follow us here, and then wait until we came out to capture us, or Cali followed us with their satellite and sent a party to the landing site and then tracked us to here. If it's the first one then there is only one person left, they always have teams of four. If it's the second, then there could be more out there, and-"

"And they could be waiting for us to return to the flyer." Jack finished for him. "Worse, they could be waiting for our rescue party to come so they can capture them too." Jack cursed under his breath. He took a deep breath, again weighing the options. "Look, I don't want to risk losing a rescue team here, but even if I can make it to the flyer, I don't have a clue what to do from there. I can't fly it, and I don't even know how to re-establish the laser link."

Jack remembered the PDP he got from the dead man on the hill. "Is this of any value to us here?" He pulled it out of his pocket and handed it to Chuck. "I got it from the guy on the hill."

Chuck looked it over, a faint hint of a smile on his otherwise pained face. "Nice. This will be linked to whoever is left out there. Help me get over by the door so we can get a signal." Jack carefully helped him slide over to the door, careful not to drag him through the remains of the two men. Chuck tapped the little screen a couple times and a map came up of the area. There was an icon that looked like a side profile of a four man flyer. It was about seven miles south of their location, right where their own flyer was parked. There were no other icons on the screen.

Jack looked at Chuck and said, "Let's see if we can get them to come up here. Call them and tell them that you have two prisoners. I am going back up to move the body out of sight. I'll be right back."

"Wait. Check those bodies and see if you can get a name." He tapped some more on the PDP and said, "This guy's name was Larry. It will be easier to fool whoever is out there if I have some names." Jack carefully went through the dead men's pockets, but nothing was in them. Their PDP's had both been destroyed by the turret gun. He shook his head at Chuck.

"Okay, go get the body, I will call it in." Jack went to the door and checked all around, then sprinted out and to the right. He made his way to the hill again, and, making sure there was still no sign of movement around him, began to drag the body down the hill. He dragged it down to the bottom, and covered it with some of the low brush that was all around. He put a couple rocks on the brush to keep it from blowing off the body in the light wind. Satisfied it would be well camouflaged from the air, he went back to the entrance.

"Body is covered. Did you call in?"

Chuck nodded. "I told him we had secured two prisoners but there was a fire fight and we killed one of them. I also told him I was injured and we needed to get back home to get me stitched up. I think he bought it. He told me he'd be here in a minute or two."

Jack looked around, quickly forming a plan in his mind. He dragged Emmet and the two other men's remains into the elevator. He striped one of the men of his chest armor, which was orange and black, as opposed to just the plain black of their own. He looked at Chuck and said, "How about you wear this and as soon as I hear the flyer land I will go out and hide around the corner." He finished telling Chuck his plan and helped him get the armor strapped on. He sent the elevator with the corpses and the armor down to level one, and finally kicked some dirt over the pool of blood on the floor where the bodies were. From the door, most of the evidence left by the turrets was hidden. For good measure, he turned off the lights in the room.

By the time he had finished his preparations, the drone of the approaching flyer could be heard. He waited until the sound stopped, signifying the flyer landing, and quickly ran out the door and went around the hill to the left. He had placed his PDP behind a rock facing the entrance, with the camera on and linked it to his helmet. In the top left corner of the display was a perfect shot of the entrance, and he waited until he saw the pilot at the door to make his move.

The pilot had walked to the door with his rifle at the ready, but when he saw Chuck sitting against the wall in his orange and black armor, he dropped the rifle to his side. Jack made his move, crept in behind him, and placed his rifle barrel to the back of the pilot's neck. "Drop the weapon, NOW!"

Chuck raised his rifle to further convince the man to do the right thing. The man dropped the weapon and said, "Okay, okay! Don't shoot me. Please!" He put his hands up, and Jack took his sidearm.

"How did you find us?" Chuck demanded, still pointing his rifle at the man. Jack had started taking the man's armor off, searching his pockets as he went. He took the PDA from the man's wrist and tossed it to the side.

"We were patrolling near here and got a call from base. They told us to come see what you were up to. Look, you guys don't need to kill me. There will be another patrol here soon if they don't hear from me. Why don't you let me go and you guys can get the hell out of here before you get captured or killed?" The man was trying to reason his way out of this mess, but Jack already had other plans.

He finished stripping the man of his gear and sat him down against the wall opposite of Chuck. "What did you do to disable the laser radio on our flyer?" He punctuated his question by pointing his rifle about an inch from the man's left eye. It probably wasn't necessary – the man didn't hesitate to answer.

"I just unplugged it. There was no reason to destroy anything. We were going to get a hell of a bonus for salvaging a flyer like that in perfect condition." He said it like he was more disappointed in losing out on the reward than in being captured by the enemy or by knowing his companions were dead.

Jack turned back to Chuck, who took a painful breath and said, "We can't let this guy go. We have to secure the facility and cover our tracks. Chances are he didn't radio in to base about this exact location. More likely, they figured they could capture us and then loot anything they could haul out of here then keep it to themselves if they found anything of value." Jack had been watching the man's expression, and it was clear that things were exactly as Chuck had said. The Calis would likely only know about the landing site.

"So what do you want to do, kill him?" Jack was concerned that this was exactly what Chuck was thinking. The pilot visibly paled at this suggestion.

"No, I think we should bring him home. Let Marcus decide his fate." The pilot looked relieved, which reflected Jack's feelings as well. "As soon as the flyer had lost connection with New Hope, they would have mounted a rescue effort. I estimate it will arrive in about ninety minutes. I think we ought to just clean up here and wait. I can cover this guy if you want to get started."

Jack considered the plan and added, "I think we should re-establish connection with base first, tell them what's going on. Is there a way to do it from the Cali flyer?"

Chuck nodded "Yeah, they probably have a laser radio on board, and it would be easy to direct it at our satellite." He looked at the pilot for confirmation and the pilot nodded. He explained to Jack how to connect his PDP to the flyer's comm system and get it disconnected with the Cali satellite and connected to their satellite. "I got this guy covered. Go call it in. Use a call sign of 'Eagle' when you tell them who you are. That will tell them that they don't need to come in with guns blazing."

Jack went outside and made it to the flyer. He climbed in and followed the directions that Chuck had given him. "New Hope, this is Eagle, is anyone there?" He waited for a response.

"Mad Dawg, is that you?" The voice was deep.

"Tiny, it's good to hear your voice. Look, we ran into some trouble. A patrol came by and tried to capture us. We lost Emmet, and Chuck is hurt."

"Shit! I am en route to your location now, ETA about sixty minutes."

"Listen, I need you to land at the flyer and we will meet you there. We are going to clean up here and make our way back. The Calis know where we landed and they sent the patrol to find us. We don't think they know about the Freezer though, and we need to hide it from them. Chuck and I will be wearing orange and black armor in case they are watching with the satellite. I just disconnected their flyer's radio and they will probably be sending another patrol to find out what happened. We need to clear out ASAP when we get there. We will have two flyers, and no pilots." Jack figured that this flyer he was in was valuable, and there was no reason to leave it for the Calis to take back.

"No problem, Jack, we have two pilots in our party, one of them is looking mighty fine that you are okay." Jack smiled. It didn't surprise him that Wendy would have gone in the rescue group.

"Okay, we will see you in an hour. Eagle out." He got out and made his way back to the entrance.

Chapter 24

"Thank God you are okay!" Teague said, greeting Jack at the underground air field. "When we lost communication with the flyer we were very nervous."

Jack winced as he climbed out. His body armor had kept him alive, but it didn't do much to soften the blows. About the time he had been driving back to the flyer his adrenaline had worn off and the pain revealed just how hard those bullets hit. He would be sore for at least a few days.

"Good to see you too, Teague."

Wendy climbed out of the second flyer as it landed, came over to Jack, and helped him over to the rail car. She didn't say anything, but the look on her face told him she wasn't planning to leave his side. Men he had not yet met carried Chuck out of the transport on a stretcher and loaded him in the rail car. Tiny followed, escorting the Cali pilot whose hands were bound, not that he would try anything foolish with Tiny as his warden

When everyone was on board, the car made its way back into the complex. Along the way, Teague examined Chuck with some instruments, and said, "Nice work on patching him up Jack. I don't think he would have made it without the first aid you administered."

Jack only said, "I just did what had to be done. Besides, I never would have made it out of there without his help." Chuck was sleeping, having been given more pain killers on the transport.

When they arrived at the end of the rail line, Tiny took his prisoner to a lockup on the sixth floor. Teague arranged for Chuck to be brought down to the medical ward and told Jack to follow so he could give him a quick exam. On the way down the elevator, he said, "Don't worry about Chuck, he will be back on his feet by tomorrow."

"Tomorrow?! Teague, I thought you examined him back there. Didn't you notice the hole from the bullet? Or the broken ribs? He's going to be down for months."

Teague simply chuckled, "Medical technology has come a long way since your time. We will get his ribs set, repair a little damage, and then give him a shot of the same stuff we used on you the past few weeks. Trust me, in a few hours he will be feeling pretty normal, although quite exhausted. We will get you fixed up too. A good night's rest will have you feeling much better."

Jack just shook his head, not sure if he really believed the doctor, but not sure of much of anything these days. The elevator opened and they made their way to an exam room. Teague followed them in and told Jack to take off his armor and under suit. "Aren't you going to go take care of Chuck first?" Jack exclaimed.

"I'm not a surgeon. Someone else will handle that." Teague left the room while Jack undressed. Wendy seemed to relax a little as she helped him out of his body armor and under clothing, probably because there were no holes in him. She did wince when his shirt came off and revealed a pattern of bruises across his chest.

"Jesus, you could have been killed!" She was becoming distraught.

"Chuck and Emmet took the brunt of the attack." was all he said. Now that he felt completely safe, he began to brood over the fight. He had watched a fellow soldier die and then killed three men. During the conflict, he had held his emotions in check, but he was no longer the hardened soldier he once was, and he was a little shaken up. Wendy seemed to sense he was in distress and wrapped her arms around him.

It helped and he felt some of the trauma leave his body. Teague walked back in, and cleared his throat when he found the two in an embrace. "Wendy, can you help him lie down on the table?"

Wendy broke away, flushing a little, and helped him. Somewhat surprisingly, she said, "I'm going to go see to that new flyer we acquired and make sure it's in good shape. I'll be back in a few hours, after you are feeling better." She kissed Jack on the cheek and left.

Teague started to examine him with his instruments. "She's a fine woman Jack. It's a good thing you came along when you did. She was in pretty bad shape emotionally, and I was worried she would decide to end her life. She hid it well, but I knew what was going on. When she came to me with your file, she was adamant that we find a way to revive you. I couldn't figure out why she had latched on to you like that, before we had even considered trying to bring you back."

This was confusing as she had been an emotional anchor for him. Even Chuck and Emmet had all but called her a cold hearted bitch. Perhaps Teague had read her wrong, she seemed to him to be as tough as they come. "She's a wonderful woman, Doc, and whatever her motives, I'm happy she cares about me." She had revealed her motives to him and it was personal, so whatever information the doctor was fishing for here, he wasn't going to catch anything.

Teague finished the exam, gave him a couple shots, and said, "There you go. You bruised a couple ribs pretty bad, and those bullets tenderized your chest pretty well, but these shots will take care of it in no time. Why don't you get dressed and meet me in the council's chamber for a full debriefing." Jack nodded wearily, used to this sort of thing after an incident like this.

~~~~

Twenty minutes later, Jack entered the Council's chamber. The room was round with a circular table shaped like a large letter C in the center. The end facing the door was the opening of the C and the middle was about five feet in diameter. It was designed so everyone in the chairs would face each other, and a speaker could stand in the middle to address them all. As he entered, he glanced back to see a large screen like the one in the training room mounted above the door. The room was dim but lights in the ceiling illuminated the twenty or so seats so that each person at the table could be clearly seen. Only five of the seats were occupied. Marcus sat in the center, and Teague to the far right. He didn't recognize any of the others.

Teague said, "Jack, I would like you to meet Caleb, Theodore, and William. The five of us are the original founders of New Hope, and sit on this council together." As Jack moved to the center of the room, a light above came on. Although it was just so whoever was presenting in front of the council could be seen, Jack suddenly felt like he was the focus of an interrogation. He shook each man's hand before stepping back and assuming a parade rest stance.

Before they could ask the first question, he started talking. "Gentlemen, we have a problem. I believe it is only a matter of time before Cali discovers the cryogenic facility." Jack had spent many years addressing senior officers, often in debriefings similar to this one. Often they were inept and inexperienced, looking for intel from men in the field who had a far better understanding of the situation than they did.

Marcus spoke first. "Before we talk about that, let's discuss what happened today." Jack sensed that Marcus was trying to take control of the conversation, and he relaxed, knowing this had to happen. A few minutes of explaining was not going to make a difference in the long run.

He gave them a brief synopsis of everything leading up to when he re-established radio contact with New Hope. Teague interrupted him there and said to everyone, "The prisoner is in our holding cell. He has been cooperative. I spoke to him briefly before coming up here, and I think we can integrate him into our community. He was not happy with how things were in Cali, and can probably give us some insight into what has been going on there lately. Also, he's not a breeder and he is convinced they will execute him for losing a flyer to us." Jack studied each of the council member's faces as Teague said this, and wasn't particularly surprised to not see much compassion. Chuck seemed to be right, these men didn't show any signs of truly valuing human life, particularly those who couldn't contribute to rebuilding the human gene pool.

Jack continued his debriefing report. "After talking to Tiny on the radio, I went back in and we hauled the three Cali bodies into the complex. We stored them in the unoccupied tubes, that way the complex won't stink up with their rotting corpses. We brought Emmet's corpse back here with the hope of... I don't know the term. Recreating him?" He paused at this and looked at Teague.

Teague pondered it for a moment then said, "Emmet has struggled a little with relationships lately, but otherwise has been very useful. He is a good soldier, and is very loyal to our cause. And of course being reborn, he is fertile." Marcus and the others appeared to be weighing the information.

Jack spoke up and said, "If it weren't for Emmet we would have all been killed or captured. He could have surrendered, but he sacrificed himself so we could get away. He is a hero, plain and simple."

Marcus looked at his fellow councilmen, who each nodded to him, and he looked to Teague and said, "You have a subject coming out of the tank tomorrow, right?" Teague nodded. "Okay, get started on the process tonight then." Jack was relieved to hear that. They only knew each other for a few hours, so in all likelihood, Emmet wouldn't remember him. Jack was fine with that, but something was nagging at his conscience. Perhaps having the ability to bring someone back from the dead was pushing the boundaries of his morality.

Continuing on, Jack said, "Chuck went with the Cali pilot and held a gun on him while he flew back to the landing zone, and in case anyone decided to watch via satellite, I donned some Cali armor, loaded Emmet's corpse, and drove the ground vehicle back. I secured the entrance to the facility, and did my best to cover up the tracks in the area. We hauled all their gear back to the flyers. When the transport arrived, we threw our guns down as if surrendering then had Tiny and another man smash the Cali PDPs. They loaded us onto the transport, then Wendy and another pilot loaded up the ground vehicle and we all flew back here. If they were watching, it will look like their patrol captured some of us, then were captured themselves by our rescue party."

Marcus and the rest nodded, obviously impressed by the forethought put into everything.

Jack continued, "Look, I talked to the pilot we captured. The Calis have figured out there is something going on up there, and they believe it has something to do with why we will not trade our men with anyone any more. They have been running patrols in that area, just waiting for a chance to capture one of our groups. We need to do something now, before they find that facility."

Marcus and the others had paled slightly, and after a brief silence, Marcus said, "What would you propose doing?"

Jack had been thinking about this since they captured the pilot, and was ready to throw out some ideas. His real strength was in analyzing a situation, weighing his assets, and coming up with the best possible way to accomplish a task. This had served him well in his job building bunkers but didn't define him strictly as a contractor. If he had an understanding of the goal, reaching it was his specialty. "I have some ideas, but I don't know what assets we have. Much of what I will propose is built on assumptions from what I have learned in the short time I have been here."

Marcus gestured for him to continue. "I think we need to recover as many subjects as we can and store them here." Jack expected a reaction to this, and he was not disappointed.

Caleb spoke up first. "We don't have the capability to store that many bodies! Have you seen the size of that facility?"

Then William pitched in with, "Even if we could, it would take dozens of trips up and back, leaving ourselves way too exposed, and virtually showing our fellow communities exactly where we are going. Cali would not sit back and watch, and once they figured out exactly what we have up there, they will try to take it for themselves. It could easily escalate into a real war!"

Theodore was quiet, and Teague was observing as if he was not a part of the conversation at all, merely a student watching it all play out. Marcus spoke next. "Both these men are correct, we have neither the ability to transport, nor a place to store so many bodies – at least not without drawing unwanted attention from probably every other community in the western half of the continent. You said yourself that Cali was actively patrolling the area."

Jack waited until they were all finished. "I had surmised as much. I took the liberty of examining the schematics for this facility." He went to the table and collected his datapad, and punched a few times on the screen. The lights dimmed and the screen on the wall behind him lit up. Jack was becoming very proficient with his datapad, and loved using it when he had the opportunity. A schematic of level six showed up on the big screen. "I see seven rooms that are unoccupied. I am guessing these rooms could be turned into cold storage. Given that we do not need the entire body of the subjects, we could store at least fourteen hundred heads, by my estimation." He paused to let that sink in.

Caleb skeptically said, "How do you propose we turn them into cold storage rooms?"

Jack smiled and said, "I don't really know, I'm not an engineer, but I imagine that we have a few engineers in our population that could get us an answer pretty quickly." Marcus and Theodore nodded.

"How do you propose to transport them here? Fourteen hundred heads would require far more capacity than any of our transports can handle." That came from William.

Jack smiled again and said, "I had a great conversation with Tiny the day I met him. He had been training on how to set up landing strips behind enemy lines. Now I am not an expert on anything like that, but I bet if you put Tiny and a couple guys from Army engineering corps in a room together you could probably have a way to quickly go in and build a landing strip. Once you have a strip, I understand you have a very large transport plane you can land there?" He had posed this last question directly at William, since he seemed to be the man in charge of that aspect of New Hope.

William mulled it over for a moment then said, "Yes, if that transport had a place to land, we could probably do it."

Marcus leaned forward and said, "Jack, I am impressed. You are living up to and even exceeding my expectations." Jack suspected it was an empty compliment, designed to make a leader's underlings feel good about their accomplishments while subtly pointing out the underling's status *under* the leader. He was actually used to this sort of thing. He smiled despite this suspicion. "Teague, get him what he needs to get started on this. I expect a detailed report on it first thing in the morning." He looked at the rest of the people in the room and said "Let's meet in my chambers, we need to discuss the political fallout this operation will bring from both Cali and the other communities. Then we need to contact our friends to talk about today's actions."

Teague said, "I will join you when I am finished with Jack." Marcus, already on his way out, nodded without another word as if he expected it.

When the door closed, Teague turned to Jack and said, "Well played. I'm truly impressed. Just between you and me, Jack, I think they are more concerned with how you bowled them over so easily than the political ramifications of your ideas. And now I know how you got your nickname. When you set your mind to something, you get it."

Jack nodded, impressed himself that Teague had seen what he was doing. "I've been dealing with bureaucrats most of my life. I know how to satisfy them and get them to step aside so I can do what needs to be done." Jack's brow furrowed. "I don't understand you, Teague. You're supposed to be part of the council, but it seems you are more of a gopher than anything else. Why is that?"

Teague was uncomfortable with the question and actually seemed to wince at the gopher comment. "The others were research scientists when the final collapse of the EoS took place. In that society they were the upper class. The royalty if you will. I was just a lowly medical doctor, more of an assistant than anything else. The only reason I am on the council is because I helped them all to escape and kept them alive when they should have perished from the biological weapons, with the rest of the population. They say I am their equal, but they still cling to their old ways. Our friendship is old though, and even though they sometimes don't consider me quite their equal, they still respect me as much as I respect them. We have been through a lot, and they will never forget that it would not have been possible without me."

Jack accepted this, but suspected there was a little more to it. He let it drop. "Fair enough, now let's talk about our next move..."

Chapter 25

Jack was in his room, at his desk when the datapad beeped. He reached over and grabbed it, expecting the call from Teague. He pressed the button to answer. "Are they ready?"

"Yes, everyone is assembled at the training room. I hope you put on a good show, they are getting a bit restless." Jack pressed the button again and headed out.

When the elevator opened on the fourth floor, Wendy was standing there waiting. "Jack, how are you feeling?" She was obviously concerned, and Jack sensed that she wanted a heads up on what was going on in the meeting.

"I'm feeling perfect actually." He kissed her on the lips and then said, "I'm a little nervous to meet all these people though."

She relaxed a little and said, "So can you give me any hint as to what's going on? We haven't had too many meetings like this, and people are starting to wonder."

"I'm just about to explain it all, but don't worry, I have faith that everything will work out." He smiled confidently. "By the way, what's a Hopper?"

Her brow furrowed in confusion. "It's a nickname other communities use for those of us from New Hope – Sort of a slang term. Why?"

"Never mind, I was just curious."

The room was less than half full, but it was a big room and there were more than he had anticipated. He studied the crowd for a moment and judged there to be at least seventy people, maybe more. All eyes had turned to him and he looked for familiar faces before beginning. He spotted everyone he had met so far, with the only exceptions being the little girl and the council members. Teague was here, however, and he approached Jack. "Thanks for getting everyone together Teague, I appreciate it." Teague nodded and sat down off to the side.

"Good afternoon everyone. Thank you for being here. As most of you have probably heard, we had a little incident today at the Freezer. Emmet Johnson was killed in the fighting, and Chuck was wounded. In case anyone is wondering, Emmet gave his life to save mine and Chuck's, and quite possibly all of us." Jack lowered his head to give a moment of silence for Emmet. Most people in the room did the same, and Jack even heard someone towards the back row sniffle.

After a sufficient pause, he continued, "Thankfully, we believe we were successful in keeping the facility a secret, but it's clear that Cali, and possibly some other communities, are aware that something is going on up there. We need to act fast if we're going to secure our future."

Jack let that sink in for a moment, then shifted gears. "First, I would like everyone in this room who is an engineer or was in the engineering corps to stand up and move to the left side of the room." A few people stood, and some others got a confused look on their face, looked around at other people in the room, and hesitantly got up. Some people on the left got out of their chairs and moved to the right of the room to accommodate the engineers.

"Great, thank you. Now, whoever is not in the group that just moved who has had experience maintaining this facility, please move toward the middle of the room." More people got up, including Wendy, and moved to the middle of the room. Wendy shot Jack a confused look as she changed seats. He returned it with a wink and a smile. "Excellent. Now, anyone who has not been moved yet who has experience with salvaging patrols, please move to the right, and anyone that doesn't fit any of these groups, please move to the back row." More people moved and now Jack could get a clear picture of what assets he had available.

When everyone had been seated, Jack said, "Thank you, I appreciate your patience here. The musical chairs part is over, so you can get comfortable." There were a few chuckles. "Before I go any further, let me introduce myself to those of you I have not yet met. My name is Jack Taggart. I was reborn a few days ago, but I have learned a lot about what has happened since I died in 1966. I had a large hand in building the facility in Montana, although when I built it I didn't know what it was for. I don't remember anything about the last year before I died, but I was apparently the first resident of that facility. I was in the military for twenty years, I joined at the end of World War Two, and served in Korea, first as an enlisted man and then as an officer. When that was over, I ended up in charge of building underground bunkers at various military bases around the world. It started with some small command bunkers and eventually I was building underground facilities like the one we are in now." He had never built anything on this scale, but there was no need to talk about that right now.

"The reason we called you all in here is to come up with a plan to collect as many subjects as we can from the facility in Montana, and store them here until we can process them." Jack expected an outburst from some people, but was met with silence. He wondered if Marcus had ever come to the general population for advice on what to do, and guessed that he had not. That would certainly explain the silence.

He pressed a few buttons on his datapad and the screen behind him came on. It was the same schematic he had shown the council. An overhead view of level six was displayed, and he pressed another button that highlighted seven rooms. "First challenge we have here is to convert these rooms to be cold enough to keep the subjects frozen until we need them." He first turned to Teague and asked, "Teague, how cold do the subjects need to be to prevent damage?"

Teague was caught off guard, not expecting to be called on like that and took a moment to compose himself. "Uh... three hundred degrees below zero Fahrenheit give or take ten degrees."

Jack nodded. "Okay, engineers, can it be done and what do we need to do it?" There was silence in the room for about thirty seconds, and Jack was just about to ask if they understood when they all started talking amongst themselves at once. It lasted perhaps five minutes, and finally one stood up and said, "I think it can be done, but there are some things we will need that we do not have here."

Jack looked at Teague and said, "Can you write these down?" Teague nodded. He had been taking notes on the meeting already for the council, and started a list. Turning back to the engineer who was standing, he said, "What are you going to need?"

The engineer looked at his the people around him as if hoping to get an answer from them. Unfortunately, his taking the initiative to speak had sort of promoted him to be the representative for the engineers. "Uh... well, for starters we need liquid nitrogen. Lots of it. Then we need pumps and heat exchangers. We will need some heavy duty insulation. Power is not an issue, but we will need to drill some large holes in the concrete walls. Also, we will need to modify the entrance to the rooms so that we can get in and out without letting that cold air out. We will also need a cold suit – someone will have to go in and out to get bodies. Other than that I think we could do it." He looked around at the others looking for confirmation, and a few nodded.

Teague had been writing down what they needed, and Jack went to the controls for the monitor and pushed some buttons, switching the screen from his datapad to Teague's. "Okay, so this is what we need. Do we have any machinists here?" One man from the engineering group raised his hand and one member of the combat group in the back raised theirs. "Excellent. Let me ask you, could you machine the pumps or heat exchangers?"

The engineer spoke first. "Heat exchangers are easy, we just need lots of aluminum and copper tubing. The pumps are a little more difficult but we have the machinery to make them, we just need designs to follow.

Jack turned back to the man who was now representing the engineer group and asked, "Is this something you could design?" One female engineer said, "Yeah, no problem. As soon as we can get the math on the volume requirements, I can have a design whipped up in no time. We probably have the materials on hand to do it too." Jack nodded and looked at the list again.

"So we need Aluminum, copper tubing, insulation, and either the materials to make a cold suit or an actual working suit." He now turned to the salvagers. "Have any of you seen any of these materials on a scavenging run?"

They looked at each other, and a couple nodded. One spoke up. "I found a building in Iowa, I think, that had a huge cold storage room. I bet the insulation there would be good, and maybe there is some copper tubing and such as well. It was more of a freezer though, for food."

Another man said, "You damned idiot, that was in Idaho, not Iowa!" There was some laughter.

170

"Shut the hell up George, I said I thought it was in Iowa! Now that I think about it, it was in Idaho. It was probably a potato factory." He looked proud of himself for coming to that conclusion.

The other man, George, said, "They didn't make potatoes in a factory, they grew them. Idiot." More laughter. Before this escalated into a fight, Jack jumped in.

"Okay, good, good, we have a potential location for insulation, and maybe some copper tubing and aluminum. Anything else?" While this was going on, Teague continued writing notes.

Another man stood and said, "I might know where some aluminum can be found. It's a long shot though." He turned to the engineers and asked, "Would copper and aluminum wire be good? We can melt it and use it right?" He got some nods, and a Jack saw a few eyes light up in the salvaging group. Obviously more people knew where to find wire.

Jack now turned to the maintenance group. "Do you see any challenges in converting those rooms? Is the drilling going to be a problem? Hanging insulation? And we will need shelving, lots of shelving." The maintenance people all spoke at once. Jack gave it a minute then said, loudly, "Please, one at time, one at a time!" They went quiet, and an older man stood up.

"I have the most experience keeping this place running. I have been doing it for almost two hundred years. The modifications you want will be no problem at all. We can talk to the scavengers about materials for the doors you need, and should be able to do this fairly easily." There was some grumbling with the group, but many of them nodded in agreement.

"So the next question is how quickly can this be done?" Now the room was lively. Each group with the exception of the combat group was talking amongst themselves. Jack went and sat with Teague for a few minutes, letting them figure things out. This project was starting to take on a mind of its own, which was exactly what Jack had counted on.

After almost ten minutes, Jack stood up and asked for everyone to be quiet. "Engineering, how long do you think this will take?"

The spokesman stood up and said, "We need two days to get the plans down in the computer, but we can have a specific list of materials by tonight."

Jack looked to the maintenance group. "Maintenance?"

The old man stood again. "If we can get the drilling locations and requirements for the doors, we can start in the morning. I estimate that we could have all seven rooms ready in a week."

Jack turned to the salvagers. "How long to get the stuff we need?"

George stood this time and said, "It depends on how many flyers we can get out there. If we can get medium transports and have three groups I think we can have all materials in three days, barring any difficulties. We can hit that Idaho place tomorrow morning and have the insulation here by afternoon."

Jack finally turned to Teague and said, "Can we get three groups out there to scavenge?" Teague nodded.

"Okay, I want one volunteer from the combat group to go along on each scavenging missions, so that all scavengers can be focused on finding what they need instead of looking out for deer." There was laughter from many people in the room, confusion on some people's faces. Obviously Emmet had told his story to more than one person.

"Next order of business: Transportation. Tiny, you told me that you trained a group to go into hostile territory and set up a runway to get aircraft in. Can you do that here?"

Just like Teague, Tiny was not expecting the sudden attention, and he almost looked scared, which was an interesting sight to see considering his size and stature. "Jack, that was different. We don't have the equipment to do it. The enemy here is different too, we would need to approach this in a totally different way." He paused for about two beats, then asked, "What do you need an airstrip for?"

"The large transport plane." Tiny had known the answer, but needed time to think. Jack figured this and said, "Tiny, take your time. Think about it for a minute."

He turned to the rest of the group and said, "I imagine that we will need to be able to fly in a bulldozer. Does anyone happen to have one handy?" Laughs went all around.

Wendy spoke up now. "I know where there is one that we could have in working condition pretty easily." Jack turned to her and smiled.

"Go on."

"There's one at S.C." There were a couple gasps and groans, and the room went silent. Jack looked around in confusion.

Teague volunteered, "S.C. is Saber Cusp, the abandoned EoS city to the south."

Jack nodded his thanks. "Is there a problem with getting it?" The room erupted again, everyone talking at once. "Please people, one at a time!" It quieted down, and George stood up.

"Jack, that place is death. People left there for a reason! I think I speak for most people here, nobody wants to risk exposure to whatever latent biologicals left behind." He turned to Teague, "Doc, you know first-hand the nightmares that exist there." Jack looked at Teague, who stood up.

"It's true, there are dangers. Automated defenses left on, Mutes inhabiting the areas that are relatively safe, and of course the possibility of exposure to the now ancient weapons of mass destruction. However, the council has discussed it occasionally over the past few years, and I believe we can handle most of the problems that might come up. Frankly speaking, we have anticipated the need for heavier equipment in the near future, and our old home is the most likely place to salvage what we will need."

There were more murmurs of dissent, but for now Jack ignored them and turned to the combat group. "Who among you has the most experience leading people in combat, either here or before you were reborn?"

Three people stood in the group. One was Chin, the scarred man that Jack had met two days ago. The two others were a man around twenty six or twenty seven and a man who appeared to be in his late forties. "Chin, what experience do you have?"

"Well, I've been running patrols for twenty five years here, and have seen my share of skirmishes. I didn't get my nickname by cutting myself shaving." He pointed to his face and the scar.

He turned to the younger man, sizing him up. Aside from obviously being in excellent physical shape, there wasn't much to distinguish him from any other soldier Jack had met over the years. "What's your name, soldier?" he asked.

"Thomas Parker, sir. I died when I was almost sixty, and served for over thirty years. I was a Command Sergeant Major, assistant to a colonel who led my battalion in the first Iraq war."

"Your battalion was led by a full bird colonel?" Usually a battalion was led by a light colonel.

Thomas grinned and shrugged. "He was a career officer, perhaps had a couple bulbs out upstairs. His old man was a Medal of Honor winner, and quite frankly that's the only reason he ever got as far as he did. Let's just say that a lot of his tactical decisions were made by his assistant."

Jack knew from experience exactly what Thomas was talking about. He motioned for the man to continue.

"I was injured toward the end of the war, so I ended up riding a desk for most of the rest of my career. I finally retired in 2005. Since being reborn, I have spent the last three years running patrols." Jack nodded. Thomas could become a great asset.

He turned to the last man. He would have said this was a fair skinned black man at first, but as he studied him, he noticed characteristics of many races. The thought occurred to him that the past few hundred years would have finally seen the 'melting pot' that the forefathers of America had foreseen. There was now only the racial distinction of being a regular human, or a Mute... with the exception of the reborn, of course.

The man was older, which was further confirmation of being a native. "And you?"

"Just call me Red, I never had a formal name. I been leading patrols since I was found by New Hope bout twenty five years ago, never lost a man. Before that I spent my days fightin off Mutes or huntin for my nex meal."

Jack nodded. Although he hadn't really familiarized himself with the 'native' population, he assumed this man had no formal training of any kind, but probably knew how to survive and probably how to keep others alive. He wondered briefly if the mention of never losing a man was a jab at Jack's earlier encounter or just a bragging point. He didn't give it much thought beyond that, they would find out soon enough if he had what it took to lead men.

"Okay, Thomas, I would like you to get together with Teague and discuss what it would take to get into S.C. and acquire what we need. Red, I would like you to get with Tiny and help him plan the forward landing strip. Chin, I want you to organize a rescue squad, in case any of the patrols or scavenging teams run into trouble." Everyone nodded and sat back down.

"Engineering. Who among you was in the engineer corps in the military?"

Two men stood up. Both were young, as Jack expected. "I want you two with Tiny's group. You should be able to help with the building of the strip. If you come up with any materials that are required, I want you to liaise with George here and see if anyone knows where to scavenge it."

He looked at Tiny, who was still lost in thought. "Tiny, do you have any immediate concerns?"

In his incredibly deep voice he said, "Aside from getting a dozer on site, it should be pretty straightforward. I would also like to set up some kind of defensive measures, maybe a ground to air missile if we have it. You know, as a deterrent, just in case our friends from Cali decide they want a piece of what we are doing. Once on the ground, we are gonna be vulnerable. What kind of time frame are you asking for here?"

"I need you ready to go in a week. I think it will all hinge on the dozer. Does anyone know if we have the kind of defensive equipment he is asking for?"

Teague spoke up, and with a slight grin that suggested he knew of something that would work perfectly, he said, "I think we can accommodate him

Jack turned to the whole group and said, "There is one more task we need to discuss. We will need a way to harvest and transport about fifteen hundred human heads." The room went silent. Jack was not surprised, in fact he couldn't think of a better way to silence a room full of people.

"We need engineers to come up with some bins that can be kept frozen, enough to haul approximately fifteen hundred heads. We need anyone who is not needed on the other tasks to plan on being there to harvest the heads. It is not a pleasant task, but necessary. We will need to be able to get in there, collect and properly label each one, and store them on the plane. All this needs to be done in the shortest amount of time possible. The longer we are there, the more chance we will draw unwanted attention."

He turned back to Teague once more. "Teague, do any of our flyers have weapon systems?"

Teague nodded. "The small two and four man flyers have light air to ground arms, but are not much good in a dogfight. The medium transports have both air to air and air to ground systems, and the large transports have air to air systems."

"When we fly in, we need to defend the heavy transport with whatever we can. It's all for nothing if we can't get it back here safely." The room was once again more serious. "Does everyone here know what they need to do? Are there any questions?"

"Just one. Who put you in charge?" Jack turned to the voice and saw Chuck standing in the doorway to the room. The room erupted in laughter, and people started getting up, ready to go to work.

Chapter 26

"What the hell are you doing out of bed?" Jack was surprised to see him alive, let alone walking.

"Bah, I heard Mad Dawg was staging a coup up here and had to come see for myself." He turned to Teague, "And don't say a damn word Doc, I'll go back to bed in a few minutes." Teague just smiled and shook his head. "I just wanted to come up here and thank you for saving my ass, Jack."

Jack colored slightly at the compliment. "I just did what I needed to do, Chuck. Besides, I couldn't just let my human shield die." They both laughed while Teague and Wendy stood there looking confused. Jack filled them in the details of those first few seconds when they were caught in the entrance to the facility.

"Chuck, you're the one who needs to be thanked. I'm just glad we made it out of there in one piece. Besides, if it weren't for Emmet, we would probably be in Cali right now being interrogated." They looked at each other in silence for a moment, reflecting on Emmet's sacrifice.

Wendy broke the silence. "Chuck, I need to thank you too. I would have killed you myself if you had come back without Jack." His look of surprise was quickly followed by a sly smile.

"Damn, I really thought you were full of shit, Jack. Congratulations." Wendy's face clouded with anger and she shot Jack a look that said he would have to do a lot explaining. Jack pretended to not have seen her.

"Uh, thanks. Look, you'd better get some rest. The last time I saw you there was a large hole in your shoulder. That can't be healthy."

"Christ, you sound like Teague. Just make sure you include me in your plans here. After this morning, I don't want to see the Calis get a damn thing from the Freezer." That statement brought back the full weight of the situation at hand.

"If you're up for it, I want you to fly the big transport." Chuck just nodded. He suddenly looked weary.

"Looks like you're the boss, I'll do what I can. Right now, I think I'll take a nap, in my own room, not some medical ward." He turned to leave the room.

Wendy said, "Hang on, we can walk you up there together. Mad Dawg needs to get some sleep too... alone." Chuck shot a look of apology to Jack, fully aware that he shouldn't have said anything.

~~~~

Chuck had just settled in to bed and was already halfway towards unconsciousness when his door opened. He was instantly alert, but settled back down when he saw it was Wendy. He had halfway expected her to come back after walking Jack to his door, and wasn't particularly surprised to see her. The trip up the elevator with her and Jack had been somewhat icy, and not much was said. "What can I do for you, Wendy?"

"Sorry to interrupt your sleep, Chuck, I know you need the rest, but I have to ask you a question." He nodded, knowing what she was going to ask. "What exactly did Jack say about me today?"

Chuck tried to put on a little smile and said, "Relax, it wasn't his fault. You know Emmet just got burned pretty bad by a local?" Wendy nodded. "Well, Emmet was asking if he had, well, you know, been with any locals. Jack said he had found someone special, but it wasn't a local. Emmet couldn't let it go at that and grilled him for a name. Jack figured he wouldn't stop nagging, so he said it was you. To be quite honest, I thought he was full of shit. He didn't seem to care what I thought and sat back to read some old book he had."

As he talked, he could visibly see her deflate. This woman had a chip on her shoulder regarding men since the day he had met her, and she was always quick to anger when she suspected someone was objectifying her.

In fact, it was out of character for her to hook up with a man, particularly one she didn't know a thing about. Whether she felt something for Jack or just caved under the pressure this community had put on her, he figured this was her last hope of integrating herself into this new world. If she was putting herself in a situation like this, he knew it was tenuous at best and the slightest problem could push her over the edge. Although it was seldom mentioned, there had been a couple reborn that simply couldn't live in this world. Chuck only knew because he had been the first successful reborn. He had been there to clean up the mess when they decided they had been better off dead. The last thing he wanted was to be the catalyst that led her to an end like that.

She looked him square in the eye and said, "If you're just covering for him, I will kick your ass after I kick his." If she hadn't been dead serious, he would have laughed.

"Wendy, not all men are assholes. I may not know shit about Jack's personal life, but after today I think I can honestly say there isn't a man I have ever met who has a stronger character than Jack. I may be a little biased there, but I have never met anyone quite like him. Personally, I wouldn't hesitate to follow that man anywhere."

She dropped her gaze, looking a little ashamed and embarrassed now. "Shit, I'm sorry Chuck. I shouldn't have come in here like this." She looked like she was going to leave, but she turned back to face him. "One more question: why didn't you believe him?"

He felt his bowels loosen up a little. *You stepped in it now Chuck.* "Uh... Well, you know. You aren't exactly receptive to men Wendy. You sort of have a reputation here, you know..." He was sweating bullets now. This was not exactly the thing any woman wanted to hear, and this woman in particular was known for her quick temper. At least he was in bed and injured, so she wouldn't take a swing at him.

She blushed and looked away from him, which was not exactly the reaction he had expected. "Christ, have I really been that bad?" He didn't say anything, waiting to see what she would do next. "Look, I meant what I said earlier, Chuck. I can't thank you enough for making sure he got back safe. He means a lot to me. If you ever need anything, just ask." With that she gave him a quick but gentle hug and left the room.

For the second time that day, Chuck felt he had narrowly avoided death. Jack would have his hands full with that woman. She was incredibly attractive and incredibly volatile all at the same time. He thought about sharing his concerns with Jack but realized he trusted the man's character and knew he would do right by her.

The situation had been diffused, and he felt a little of the burden of debt toward Jack being eased off his conscience. Sometimes telling the truth was the best course of action. He sank back into the bed and was asleep in seconds.

~~~~

Wendy felt like an ass. Why had she jumped so quickly to the conclusion that Jack had been running around bragging to the first men he met about scoring with her? He was not like that and she knew it. It made her realize how vulnerable her emotions really were, and she didn't like that at all.

Furthermore, she had really kept herself closed off from everyone here in her effort to stay away from a relationship with men. Most people here were just trying to survive and ensure that humanity would outlast the hell that their ancestors had created here on earth. True, there were a few, like that asshole Jeremy, who deserved what she gave them, but most of these people hadn't done anything but help her. They deserved better, and she intended to start delivering.

She exited the elevator and turned toward Jack's room. Jack would be sleeping by now, after all the stress and excitement he had endured today, and he really needed the rest. She slowed as she got closer to his apartment, torn between apologizing right away and letting the man get some sleep. A couple seconds of hesitation turned into a minute, and she decided it was best to let him sleep and apologize in the morning. Despite this decision, she rounded the last corner, just in time to see Cat leaving his room. She quickly ducked back, wondering if the woman had seen her. Anger flared anew.

Indecision paralyzed her. Should she go confront him? Surely nothing had happened between them, she had only dropped him at the door ten or fifteen minutes ago. Had it been longer than that? The questions piled higher and higher, and her anger and anxiety grew with each one.

In retrospect, she had been rather cold toward him when dropping him at his door. She simply told him to get some sleep, and let him know they would have some things to talk about in the morning. How well did she really know the man? Despite her conversation with Chuck, she had too many doubts about her own judgment of his character. There had been so many times in life she had trusted her instincts about a man and been proven wrong just when she thought she had it all figured out. Why should this be any different?

The weight of depression slipped over her, and suddenly she was tired. She no longer had the energy to deal with this. In the morning, she decided, they would have a talk, and she would get the answers she needed, if she had to beat them out of him.

Wiping a tear from her cheek, she turned back to the elevator.

~~~~

Marcus leaned back in his chair. He was seated in his living quarters with the three other councilmen, and they had been discussing the attack earlier today. There had been other skirmishes with Cali in the past, but this was very disconcerting. If New Hope had a chance of surviving the next ten years, they would need the metal ore they were getting from Cali. He had hoped, for the last twenty or so years, that they could patch things up without any incident, but those years had shown that it was more and more unlikely. The reaction to today's attack would likely determine the future of relations between the two communities.

War was out of the question. The reason humanity was on the verge of extinction was because of situations just like this one. Marcus had no intention of starting another war. They had worked way too hard the last hundred and fifty years and he was not about to let that all fall apart. The problem was, if they had any chance of recovering the precious genetic material in the cryogenic facility, they couldn't even contact Cali and try to smooth the situation over. Joshua would want to know what they were doing up in Montana before he would ever try to make reparations for his people's actions today, and if they knew, the place would be empty before they could get up there again.

However, if he didn't contact Joshua and Cali attacked while they were working to recover what they could from the facility, he feared it would permanently kill any hope of reconciliation. It seemed to be an impossible situation. He had to make a decision, and it appeared the decision was between risking the precious lives of his people and the future of New Hope. He was unwilling to sacrifice either.

Theodore sighed and said, "Look, I just don't see any other options here. We have to either cut a deal with Cali, or push forward with joining the other communities. Either way we are going to have to share the facility with the others. We will still get at least four or five hundred more for the gene pool, and it's more than enough to ensure humanity's survival."

Caleb shook his head. "We have the chance to build a population that nobody can match. If we had a thousand fertile men and women, we would not have to worry about Cali or even the Yanks, let alone the other communities. They would be forced to join us and live under our rules. If we share that with other communities we would not be exclusively in power, and you know how I feel about that." Caleb had the opinion that every war starts when you have two factions of equal strength vying for ultimate power.

179

Everyone in the room more or less agreed with him, but not everyone shared his opinion of keeping New Hope isolated from the rest of the world.

William leaned back in his chair and said, "I stand by my opinion. We have an opportunity here to go out and secure that which belongs to us. If it means permanently severing diplomatic ties to Cali, then I say we are better off. They are in no better position to attack us directly than we are to attack them. We can find more ways to acquire the resources we will need. Don't think for a second that Cali will happily increase the resource trade with us by a hundred times when we start to build a new home. Joshua is not that stupid."

Marcus agreed with William. Joshua would not allow them to expand that easily, regardless of what they offered in trade. And if he knew why they needed to expand that quickly, he would make sure it took them twenty years to build a new home, leaving New Hope with no choice but to take their chances living out in the open while they were at their most vulnerable point. In twenty years, they might have the population to be able to live on the surface without fear of anyone, but until then they needed the shelter – and the secrecy – if they were to survive.

The door chimed and Teague walked in and took a seat. Marcus turned to his friend and asked, "How did it go?" Teague was a good man and a loyal friend, even though he was not much of a leader. He only had a seat on the council because of what he had done for them, sacrificing everything he had to protect them and get both the council members and the technology safely out of Saber Cusp. New Hope would not exist if it weren't for his actions, and it was only fair that he have a hand in governing the community. The others were grateful as well, but didn't quite feel the way Marcus did. In particular, Theodore didn't think he should be on the council at all. Of course, Theodore wanted Marcus' chair on the council, and Marcus knew it.

"Jack is a natural. He put together teams that should be able to execute this operation without too much difficulty. There are risks here, but I think it's necessary. The hardest part will be going into S.C. to procure the equipment we will need." Marcus had already figured out that they would have to send some people in to get the machinery they needed. He knew the risks but was still apprehensive about the operation. Losing people was a high price to pay, even with the potential rewards that lie ahead.

"That will be a dangerous task. Can we control who will go so we can minimize the loss to New Hope?" It was horrible to put it in those terms, but sometimes as a leader you have to prioritize your assets. Everyone in the room paled at the thought of choosing who could potentially be sent to their death. Despite their history, all the men in this room valued human life, at least more than they had before the fall of the EoS.

"I am in charge of that part of the operation, and I will decide who goes. The problem is, the mission is critical, not only for this operation but for our success in building a new home. If I send the wrong people, our chances of success go down. I will have to find the balance between acceptable loss of life and skill required to do the job." Marcus nodded, and the room was silent for a few minutes.

Teague broke the silence with a question. "So what have you come up with regarding Cali? Are you going to contact Joshua now or wait until after the operation?"

Marcus shrugged. "I am not sure yet. We have been weighing the pros and cons all afternoon. This is a tough situation, any way you look at it. I am leaning towards waiting until after we have secured the facility. I believe we need to think of our own community and that of humanity before considering how it will affect the others. My main concern is whether it will spawn open hostility between us and Cali, or worse, the other communities. I will have to sleep on this, and hopefully the answer that comes will be the right one."

The statement marked the end of the meeting, and everyone got up to leave. "Teague can you please stick around for a minute, I need to ask you a question." Teague sat back down and waited for the other men to leave. Marcus noted a look of discontent on Theodore's face, and made a mental note that he would have to deal with him pretty soon. The coming events could very well unsettle everything, and the last thing he needed was Theodore making a play for his job in the middle of it all. Up until now everything they had done together had been about survival, not just their own survival, but that of the entire human race. But the wealth contained in that bunker up north was a tempting prize for anyone, and it clouded what was so clear before.

When the other council members gone, Marcus looked at his friend and said, "Teague, I trust you more than the rest of the council." Teague knew this and nodded. "Tell me honestly, do you think that Jack is a threat to New Hope?"

"Jack shares much of your own philosophy, Marcus. However, he came from post-war America, where freedom was a right that had been paid for by the lives of friends and family. Part of that freedom stemmed from the people deciding who their leader would be. If this operation goes smoothly, the people here will follow Jack wherever he asks. He will respect your leadership ability, because he is very loyal to his country, and right now his country is New Hope. Keep in mind though, if we bring back hundreds of people that are from his time, we may very well have to hold an election to choose our leader, and if elected, Jack would take your job with little hesitation."

The answer was in line with his own thoughts. It was a subject he had been contemplating for quite some time. "Thank you Teague, that is what I needed to know."

Part Three

Chapter 27

Jack woke up and looked around, a little disoriented. He was once again waking up in a different room, his own this time. Teague had given him a sedative to help him sleep without dreams, and he felt refreshed. The trauma of the previous day's fight was not pressing on him like he had expected, but the way Wendy had left him last night was in the forefront of his mind. Why was she mad at him for telling Emmet and Chuck about their relationship? Surely she didn't think that he was running around bragging about having sex with her...

This made him realize how little he actually knew about her. Sure they had talked about themselves, and having been intimate went a long way toward feeling closer to each other. But it took time to truly start to understand all the little quirks about a person. And this environment made it all so confusing. Wendy had been here for a while now, and combining that with the completely different era she came from compared to him, they were very different people.

To add to the frustration of it all, just after Wendy had coldly dropped him at the door last night, Cat paid him a visit. She used the premise of making sure he was OK to call on him, but he was pretty sure her motives had more to do with his manhood than his injuries. He was polite about it, thanked her for her concern, and bid her good night. But when Wendy didn't show up before he fell asleep, he wondered if there would come a time when he wasn't turning Cat, or any of the other women here, away at the door.

Despite the fact that there were no windows, it felt like he had overslept. Checking his datapad confirmed that it was after ten a.m. He threw on a robe and made his way to the bathroom and shower down the hall.

After a mildly refreshing shower, he got some breakfast then rang up Teague. It turned out he was just down the hall at the room where Jack had woken up less than a week before.

When he walked in, there was a young man sleeping on the bed. Teague was reading the monitor next to the bed, making notes on his datapad.

"Morning Jack." Teague said, without turning around. "Feeling better?"

"Yeah, I slept like a baby, doc, thanks. I don't even remember getting in bed. That sedative worked fast. So, what's this kid's name?"

"This would be Sergeant Bruce L. Kensington. He was in his fifties when he died from AIDS. He was a member of the engineering corps in the Army."

"Excellent!" Jack was happy to have another engineer on board. They could always use more of them. "What is 'Aids' though?"

Teague stopped writing on his pad and turned to Jack. "Oh, that's right, you weren't around when that broke out. AIDS came from a virus called HIV. It was a horrible virus that was discovered in about 1981, but probably started as early as the 1950's. It was first thought to only affect gay people, but eventually was recognized as a sexually transmitted disease that was transferred through blood and other body fluids. There was never a cure for it until the time of the EoS."

Jack cringed at the thought of a nasty STD that had no cure and killed people. "I'm confused, doc, why would you bring back a gay man? That doesn't make much sense."

Teague chuckled and said, "You misunderstood... it was originally thought the disease was only found in gay men because they transmitted it through anal intercourse. It turned out that any exchange of blood or semen could transmit the virus. That means that a baby born of an HIV positive mother could have the disease, or, like in this man's case, a blood transfusion could be the source. They screened blood donors for it, but nobody is perfect, and in Bruce's case, they missed it and he was infected. He had been in the military for thirty years, and lived for a few years after retirement before getting AIDS and dying. There are many subjects with AIDS in the cryogenic facility, just as there are many with cancer and other diseases with no cure back then, but we can easily cure it now and it is not a problem."

Changing the subject, he asked, "Where is each group working on the projects I assigned last evening?" He had gone straight to bed after the meeting and now wanted to know what progress had been made.

"The engineers set up shop down on six where they can design and engineer everything. The salvagers are up on one in room 10A. There are already three groups out working on finding materials we will need. Tiny is in a planning room on four with his crew, and I have a team set up in the room next to him. They are looking over the data we have on S.C. right now, and I will join them soon. You made a good choice with Thomas, the team is already taking orders from him with no problems."

"What about maintenance, where are they at?"

"They already had a room they worked out of on the sixth floor. They are working with the engineers right now. I am done here for the moment, it's going to be a few more hours before Bruce wakes up, so I was going to head up to four to check on progress." They headed to the elevator.

~~~~

Jack rode the elevator up to four with Teague, and then told him he would be back up to join him in a little while. On the way back down, he brought up a layout of the sixth level on his datapad. He intended to drop in on Wendy before meeting with the engineers. When the elevator stopped, he got his bearings and made his way to the maintenance room.

There were six men in the room, all surrounding a table with a holographic display of the entire complex hovering above it. It was yet another piece of technology that awed Jack, but he didn't have time to learn about it right now. The old man from the night before turned to him and said, "Hello, Jack. I didn't get a chance to introduce myself last night. My name is Nicholas. Just call me Nick." After introductions, he said, "We were just going over some utility chases that we can use to get plumbing into those rooms. Looks like it should all be pretty straightforward.

"Excellent. Thank you for taking charge like this. I was hoping I could find Wendy here. Any idea where she might be?" This comment turned a couple heads, but Jack ignored it.

"There wasn't much going on here today, so she volunteered to fly one of the salvaging missions. I think she was heading to Idaho to help find some insulation and some copper tubing."

Jack softly cursed to himself. If she took off like that and didn't tell him, she must really be pissed. "Thanks Nick. Is there anything you guys need from any other group?"

"I think we can manage with what we have so far, but we will need the location of the holes for the tubing pretty soon."

"Okay. I'm going to appoint you head of the maintenance crew for this project, and I would appreciate it if you work directly with the engineers and salvage crews when you need things. I will let them know who's in charge. If you run into any issues, please contact me immediately and we will see what we can do to accommodate you." Jack thanked him again and let the men get back to work.

He figured he could call Wendy later and headed to the engineering room. He expected to see a bunch of engineers sitting at drafting tables, but it really didn't surprise him when he walked into a room not much different than the maintenance room. There were three round tables, each seating four people. There were holographic displays at each table, and the engineers were wearing skin tight gloves, and manipulating the images with their fingers. As they spun the objects around and spoke different specifications, the images adjusted to fit what they were after. It was quite amazing to watch, and for the first ten minutes he just hung back and observed.

The man who had been speaking for the engineers the night before finally stood and walked over to Jack. "Hi, Jack, I'm Scott. I assume you were dropping by to check on the progress?"

"Yeah, actually. I just wanted to see how things are coming. Any problems so far?" Jack was far from being an engineer, but had worked with them enough to know that as long as you made clear exactly what you were after and the time frame in which you needed it done, all you really need to do is ask them what they need. The more often you ask the smoother things go.

"Not really. The team over here is working on the compressor pumps and the cooling system. That team is working on the entry design, and these guys over here are working on a way to keep the heads cold while we transport them." He pointed to each team respectively as he spoke. "All I really need to know at this point is if we are going to have liquid nitrogen available."

"Oh... I figured we could take it from the facility in Montana. They won't need it after we leave. No sense in leaving anything behind that we could use. If we had more time I would say we could probably get everything we need from there, but we really need to have these cold rooms ready before we even get up there to start harvesting."

Scott mulled that over for a moment and finally said, "Do you recall if there are containers to transport the nitrogen?"

"I think so, but I am no expert. I am guessing you haven't been there yourself?"

"No, not many have, but I can ask Chuck or Em.. Oh, sorry." When Jack didn't say anything, he continued, "I will find out, and we will make it work, but it would be nice to have at least enough for the transport bins ahead of time."

Jack thought it over and said, "I can't imagine you are going to just find some casks of liquid nitrogen that has survived sitting around for three hundred years, but I'll ask the salvaging team if they can come up with anything. If they can't however, do you have a way to keep the cargo cold without the liquid nitrogen?"

Scott was thinking about it when a young man behind him spoke up. "What about Peltier cooling? We have these insanely large sources of portable power, it should be easy to do. Besides, it's not like we have to keep them cold for days on end, just for a few hours."

Scott looked at the man and smiled. "You know, I think that would work. There would be an incredibly hot surface on the outside, but as long as everyone is aware it shouldn't be a problem. Let me crunch some numbers and see if it can be done." He looked excited to work on the problem.

"I hate to ask, Scott, but what the hell is a Peltier cooler?"

"It's a way to use electricity to draw heat away from an object. It uses a lot of power, so you have to be able to dissipate the heat you pull away, plus the heat from the power expended, but worst case scenario we can build some heat pipes and set up coolers outside the aircraft to draw the heat off and make them very efficient. As long as the plane is moving it will dissipate the heat easily." Scott had wandered back to the table he had been working at and started talking to the computer and manipulating the hologram in front of him.

Jack wasn't quite sure what he had just said, but he figured they had it well under control. He did need to speak with him about a few more things, so he waited until Scott paused in his design work and jumped in before he got started again. "Listen, Scott. As soon as your cooling team can, I need them to get the dimensions of the pipes running in and out of the cold rooms to Nick over in maintenance. He is the leader of that crew. Also, I want to make you leader of the engineering groups, and if anyone needs anything I want them to tell you and have you go to the other group leaders directly. If you have any problems at all I want you to tell me."

Scott just nodded and went back to work on his Peltier design. Jack figured he was now just a distraction, so he eased out of the room.

~~~~

Back up on four, he stopped in to see Tiny and his team first. There were three men sitting around a table, Tiny and two others, and as Jack stepped up to the table he saw that the top was just like the display on his datapad, only larger. On it was an aerial photo of the area surrounding the site of the facility. They had marked all the key locations for defending it from ground assault, and had even drawn in the runway as they planned to make it. Tiny didn't even notice him walk in, and he jumped when Jack put his hand on the massive shoulder.

"Holy shit Jack, you scared the crap outta me!" Everyone laughed at the irony of someone this big and strong being startled so easily. "Aww, fuck you all!" He said it with a smile and everyone laughed again.

"Looks like you have the planning under control. Where's Red? I thought he was on your team?" Jack was annoyed not to see the man in the room. He had been pretty specific when telling him to work with Tiny on this project.

"He's putting together the team. These guys are from the engineering corps, and are helping me with the planning of the runway. We found a prime location that will require just a couple quick passes with a dozer to prepare for the big cargo plane. I was just marking places where we could set up defenses. We figure if we can go in one hour before the plane arrives we can have the runway ready to go."

"Excellent. We could have the cargo plane and everyone halfway there before you even land. That gives Cali less time to react. How sure are you of the hour?"

"Well, we figured it would take about forty five minutes, so we have a fifteen minute cushion there in case anything comes up."

"Perfect. When is Red getting back here?"

"I was expecting him a half hour ago actually, which is why I have started drawing in some of the tactical information. I really want him here so we can talk about the details and set up a training exercise." Jack could sense that Tiny was just as annoyed as he was at Red's absence. If this wasn't taken care of quickly he would have to make a change.

"Okay, I'll go track him down and get him in here." Just then the door opened up and Red strolled in with five other men. Each man looked like they had seen some combat, and now that Jack was starting to recognize the differences between the Reborn and the native population, he could tell that these men were all native born.

"No need, I'm here." He had a slightly dismissive tone that instantly annoyed Jack. "We gonna talk tactics or what?"

Tiny gave Jack a look that spoke volumes. "Yeah, we've been ready for a while." If Red caught the menacing tone in Tiny's deep voice, he ignored it.

"You guys can take a break, I got this." Red said to the two men from engineering. They looked at Tiny to confirm that they were finished for now. Jack tried not to smile.

"Thanks for your help, gentlemen. I will contact you later after we have a training ground set up. We can do some test runs to make sure our time estimates are good enough." The men nodded and left, not even looking at Red on their way out. Jack knew that he had a situation that needed to be dealt with right away.

When the door closed, Jack turned to Red, and in his officer voice said, "Red, I want to make it clear that Tiny is in charge of this part of my operation. If there is a problem with that I need to know about it right now."

Red practically scoffed. The men he came in with tensed, expecting a confrontation. "Listen, Jack , these here boys are my men, and they ain gonna take they orders from any damned Freezer burnt reborn. I preciate that you finely got Marcus to agree to a big operation like this, but we been the one's tryin to save humanity since long before you guys evah showed up." The men around him smiled.

Jack glanced at Tiny, who got up from the table and stood behind him. "I can appreciate that you've been fighting for your survival for a long time. I spent a few years getting shot at and watching my friends and fellow soldiers die by the dozens, and I can't imagine what it is like to live your whole life like that." This drew another smirk from him. Jack put his datapad down and stepped closer to Red, who of course didn't back up. "Before we all bow down to your superior expertise, let's make some things perfectly clear. This man behind me was trained by a military that had two hundred years of experience in being the most superior armed force on the earth. His entire career of eighteen years was spent infiltrating enemy ground and either taking out a force of superior numbers, or holding a defensive position against superior numbers while waiting for the regular troops to arrive. He specifically trained for weeks on a project nearly identical to this one, but far more dangerous. Furthermore, I myself spent twenty years in the military, training both as an infantry fighter and as an officer. I spent the last ten years dealing with pricks like you who thought that because I was an officer, I didn't know what it was like to be the one holding the gun and shooting at the enemy. Now, if you really want to find out who has the bigger dick here, I think Tiny and I can accommodate you and your buddies. Just say the word. I haven't had the opportunity to beat some people senseless in a long time, and I think maybe the time has come. Whatever you want to do, let's get it over with so we can get back to planning MY Goddamn operation!" Jack's voice had steadily risen from his first word to his last, and at the end he was nearly shouting. He had to suppress a smile as he watched the blood drain from Red's face.

"Whoa, now slow yo role, Jack. No need to get vielent with each otheh. We all after the same thing here. Let's say we just work this out..."

"There is nothing to work out here! You take orders from me, and if that is a problem, I will have you reassigned to patrolling the family level for the duration of this mission. Do you understand me?!" Jack was practically foaming at the mouth now, and his face was red.

Red just nodded, not really knowing what to say.

"Answer me, soldier!" Jack snapped it out and Red flinched.

"Yes, sah! I understand!"

His voice instantly returned to normal. "Good. Now, you are going to work with Tiny on the defense of the site from the time you land until the time the transport has safely taken off. Once you have a plan worked out, I want you to assist in putting together a team that can pull it off. I want only people with combat experience. You will then put together a training program so you can make some dry runs. You can use the flight bay for this. Once your men have everything down and we have a bulldozer to practice with, I want you to bring in the engineers to do some time tests. I need to know exactly how long this will take barring any problems. Is there anything I have said that you do not understand?"

"No, Sah. I got most of my men assembled now and I'll have the rest by this aftanoon."

"Thank you for your understanding, Red." He turned around to face Tiny, trying to hide his smile. "Tiny can I see you in the hall for a moment?"

When they left the room and closed the door, they both burst out in laughter. "I think that will keep him in check, at least until this mission is over."

"Don't worry, Mad Dawg, I will keep a firm grip on him. He is a good fighter from what I have heard, but some of the natives are worse than any hillbilly we ever had in our day. He just needs a little military discipline. You do realize though that if that had escalated to a brawl you would have been facing all of them, not just Red."

"We, Tiny, not just me. I could have taken two of them, but I was counting on you to take the other four." Jack said it with a straight face but Tiny saw through it and busted out laughing again.

"It would have been fun to find out. I haven't had a good tussle in quite a long time."

~~~~

Jack stopped at the kitchen on this level, which was just a small break room with a table that would seat four, a sink, and refrigerator. He poured himself a cold glass of water and took a long drink. His adrenaline had been going pretty strong there when he challenged Red. He half expected the man to call his bluff, but truth be told, with the emotional roller coaster he had been on for the last few days, combined with his new youthful body, part of him was hoping for a little fight. It was just as well that he didn't have to go that far however, just because it was counterproductive. He finished the water and headed down the hall to the room where Teague and Thomas were planning the incursion into the city.

There were five men and a woman in the room. Teague and Thomas he knew. The woman and one of the men were from the group of salvagers, and the rest he guessed were fighting men. The room was similar to the one Tiny was in, and they were all sitting around the table looking at a layout of a city. Teague turned to him when he entered and said, "Was that you shouting earlier? We heard it through the walls."

Jack grinned and nodded. "I had to put Red back in line. He thought he was leading that part of the mission. I think he understands where I'm coming from now." The two men whom Jack had assumed were soldiers laughed at this. Obviously they knew Red and didn't like him much.

"So how are things coming here? Think you can pull this off?"

Thomas sighed and said, "It's going to be tough, but we can do it. We will have to send in a ground team to disable the old air defenses and then we can fly in a transport to pick up the equipment. The best path to where we need to go is right through the middle of a neighborhood of Mutes who have taken up residence. From the limited intelligence we have, there are upwards of a hundred of them. Although they don't have the technology or weapons that we have, they will put up a good fight." Thomas lowered his voice, "The chances of a casualty are fairly high."

Jack nodded solemnly. He had hoped there would be an easy way to get what they needed without too much risk of life. Unfortunately, this whole operation hinged on them getting the heavy equipment they needed.

"How soon before you can go in?" The sooner they had the dozer, the sooner they could launch the whole operation.

"I think we can be ready to go tomorrow afternoon. We were just discussing the pros and cons of doing it at night. We might have a slight advantage at night, with our thermal and night vision capabilities. However, if we get trapped and the Mutes mass up to attack us all at once, that advantage is lost. They can see pretty well in the dark without any technology to help."

"Okay, that sounds good. If you need anything, just beep me on the datapad. Any equipment you find is going to be in rough shape from sitting for nearly two centuries, who are you bringing to get it moving? And have you thought about how you will get it loaded? I can't imagine it will start right up, and I doubt you will be able to push it on board the transport."

Teague spoke up. "Yeah, we were thinking Wendy would be good for it. She can fix anything, and it would give us a backup pilot if anything happened there."

Jack didn't like the thought of her going on the most dangerous mission. "Is there anyone else? Someone with more combat experience maybe?" He made it sound like he wanted someone better suited to fight, but the truth was she probably was the best person for the job. He just didn't want her to go.

Thomas didn't know their history, and didn't pick up on it. "Most of the men have seen combat, and there are a couple good mechanics in that crew.

We can find someone that can both fight and turn a wrench." Jack was pleased to hear that.

Before he could ask any more questions, his datapad beeped. A quick glance told him Chin was calling. He pressed the button to answer. "Jack, I think you need to come out to the flight deck. We have a problem."

Jack nodded and clicked the disconnect button. There were always problems in an operation of this size, so he wasn't that worried, despite the urgency in Chin's voice. He told them to keep working and headed up to level one.

~~~~

Jack stepped off the rail car and casually headed over to a group of people standing around a makeshift operations center. It was very common to see something small get blown out of proportion, so he was trying to make an effort to keep calm and collected, setting an example of how to react in what was most likely a minor snag.

As he approached, he saw there were eight displays in front of them – the largest displaying a map of Idaho. A flashing dot about in the middle of the map caught his attention.

"What's up Chin?" Over by the flyers, three men in full combat armor were checking their gear, and a pilot was going over the aircraft in a hasty manner. A little tickle of fear fluttered in his belly. Something was definitely wrong.

"Jack, we lost communications with the crew in Idaho. I'm sorry."

There were a few moments in every person's life they never wanted to repeat. Finding out he had cancer and learning of his wife and daughter's death were two of those moments for Jack. He felt like he was experiencing another one right now. His heart beat in his chest with the sudden rush of adrenaline. "Shit! Cali?"

"We don't know. They had already landed and reported they had found what they were looking for. About ten minutes after that, we got this." He pushed a button on his pad and the large display showed an image of Wendy. Jack's heart seemed to stop as he tensed in anticipation of what the video would reveal.

Wendy looked bored as she spoke into the PDP. "New Hope, this is Salvage Crew three. Nothing new to report." Something off camera caught her attention. She continued talking as she studied whatever it was that had her attention, confusion slowing her words. "We should be ready to dust off in about thirty min – Oh Shit!" A flash of light was followed by chaos as the PDP tumbled rapidly away showing nothing but a blur of color. A quick jolt of sound was the last thing to come through before the audio and video went dead.

If Jack had not braced himself on the edge of Chin's chair, he would probably be sitting on the ground, his legs unable to support him. As quickly as the wave of nausea and fear washed over him, his emotions were shut down by instinct and training, tucked away to be processed later. He didn't have time to worry about Wendy right now – he had to act. "Is the rescue team ready to go?"

Chin nodded, "Pretty much, a few more minutes and they will be able to take off as soon as you give the word."

"Can someone go grab my gear? I'm going with." One of the men jumped in the rail car and it took off.

"Are you sure that's a good idea Jack? Maybe you shouldn't put yourself at risk like this."

He was right but Jack couldn't bear the thought of standing around for hours waiting to hear any news. He didn't have to say anything, however. The look of determination on his face was enough. Chin just nodded.

Less than five minutes later, the rail car was returned and as Jack ran to get his gear, Chin made one last feeble attempt to convince him to stay. "You know, it could be that they were attacked and the laser radio on the transport was hit. It's very unlikely the transport itself was damaged. For all we know, they could be on their way back already." Jack wasn't listening – his mind was already on the rescue mission.

Before he boarded the flyer, he turned back to Chin and shouted, "Wait ten minutes then call Teague and brief him on the situation." He jumped in, signaling the pilot to get going.

Once they were in the air he stripped down and started putting his armor on. He asked the pilot their ETA. One hour and five minutes. It didn't take long to get dressed and check all his gear, leaving him with over fifty minutes to sit and wait. The adrenaline was now wearing off and he was getting jumpy.

He took the time to get familiar with the rescue team. There were five men and one woman, plus the pilot who was also a man. Two of the men had been on the team that rescued him. The woman held out her hand and said, "Hi, Jack, I'm Heather."

Jack recognized the name from the conversation with Emmet the day before. She was somewhat attractive, more because of youth than anything else. It was difficult to judge anything other than her face because of the body armor, but she was about five feet eight inches tall and seemed to be in good shape. Her hair was black and cut short, like most of the women he had met so far. He took her hand and was surprised that she had a very firm grip. "Nice to meet you Heather." He suddenly realized that he had stripped down to his boxers to change into his combat gear right in front of this woman. If she was uncomfortable with it, it hadn't shown on her face. Having female soldiers was something he would have to get used to.

The rest of the men introduced themselves, and he shook each man's hand, except the pilot, who was busy flying the aircraft. There was a bit of tension in the cabin, but for the most part everyone remained calm making small talk. Jack tried to relax and not think about Wendy, but in the back of his mind he was saying, "Oh shit oh shit oh shit."

~~~~

Wendy woke around 6:30 a.m. and milled around her apartment for about half an hour before going down to check on Jack. He was still asleep, and she didn't want to wake him. She figured he would be out until around lunch while his body finished the healing process, so she went to find something to do to keep her mind off the coming confrontation. Sleep had dulled her anger, but every time she pictured that bitch walking out of Jack's room emotions raged and she couldn't think clearly.

She made her way to the flight bay, thinking she could spend some time working on the new flyer they had acquired the day before. There were three crews in the bay getting geared up for scavenging. Chin was working with some techs, setting up a control center where he could oversee the scavenging missions, as well as the main operation once it started. He looked up from his work when she walked over and said, "Good morning, Wendy. Got any plans today?"

She shrugged. "Nothing pressing. I was going to hang with Jack today but he is still sleeping and I didn't want to wake him." If everyone didn't already know she had been with Jack, they would know soon enough. Chin didn't register surprise, confirming her suspicion that even her private life was well known around here. The blanket of depression got a little heavier. "Why, got anything for me to do?"

"As a matter of fact, I would love it if you would fly one of the salvaging crews. I have Jerry lined up for it, but last time he flew one of the medium haulers he almost landed on a tree. I would prefer someone with more experience."

She knew all about Jerry. That idiot had nearly torn the left rear prop clean off. Wendy had to fix the damage, and she let him know in no uncertain terms that the next time he didn't look where he was landing she would shove the bent prop up his ass. "Yeah, I can do it. Where are we heading, I would like to be back by lunch."

"Idaho. Heading to that factory where George thinks there might be some insulation and maybe some copper tubing. Should easily be back by noon, one at the latest."

Maybe a little flying would get her mind straight. Plus, if Jack got up and she wasn't around, maybe he would think twice about his actions and really consider their relationship. A couple hours certainly wouldn't hurt. Thinking of repairing that propeller again made the decision even easier. "Okay, when do I leave?"

"Your crew is over there by transport three. They should be about ready to go. Do you need to get your gear?"

"Nope. I have a set of gear that I keep up here in my toolbox, just in case I get the chance to go out. I can be ready in about five minutes." Chin nodded, wished her luck, and turned back to what he had been doing.

She got dressed and headed to the transport. There were three scavengers and one soldier, all dressed in full armor. Normally they would just wear their under suits and a set of coveralls or fatigues, but Jack had insisted everyone be prepared, just in case.

The crew was familiar to her, and they all visibly relaxed when they realized she was going to be the pilot. Nobody had flown the aircraft since she last worked on it, so the inspection was quick. Climbing into the pilots seat was all the announcement she needed and the men all loaded in without a word.

~~~~

The flight took a little over an hour, and was uneventful. There was a little chatter amongst the crew, mostly about the upcoming events. This was perhaps the biggest single operation New Hope had been involved in since before anyone could remember. Despite the danger ahead, people were excited. Daily life in an underground bunker could be quite dull.

Each mention of Jack grated on her nerves. She tried to relax and worry about him later, but it was as if he had already told her he was going to play the field before settling down. The crew seemed aware she had something going with Jack. The way they looked at her each time his name came up only irritated her more. The sad thing was, nobody noticed her emotional struggle, the façade of ice was back and as far as they were concerned it was normal.

Wendy was impressed with her own landing. It was her best to date, and Anton, the soldier, patted her on the shoulder and complimented it. "It sure beats landing in a tree." They all laughed.

She put down in a clearing, in the foothills of a mountainous region. There was a heavy tree line about a hundred yards away in the north and northwest, and a river to the south. The building they were after was about forty feet north of them, built next to a railroad that headed northeast to southwest around the mountains. The tracks were heavily pitted with rust and many of the railroad ties had rotted completely away. Oddly enough, the thick vegetation around just about everything seemed to avoid the old railroad tracks, highlighting them instead of obscuring them as she would have expected. The weather was decent, but they were high enough in elevation that it was still a bit chilly. Wendy imagined it would drop below freezing when the sun went down, and the snow covered peaks to the north seemed to confirm it. She wouldn't want to spend the night out here.

There were two small hills to the east and west, and Anton humped up to the higher of the two hills to keep a lookout. The scavengers got to work right away, heading into the building in search of insulation.

Wendy kept herself busy for about ten minutes giving the aircraft a complete inspection, but was quickly bored after that. A few minutes later, Stanley, one of the scavengers, came back hauling an armload of heavy insulation. She wasn't very fond of Stanley; he was always trying to hit on her and never took the hint that she wasn't interested. He dropped the load in the ship's cargo hold and smiled at her like she should be impressed. "We can easily fill up the hold with what we found in there. There is a bunch of copper tubing that's in pretty good shape too. You want to give us a hand hauling this stuff out?" She had nothing better to do, so she followed him back in, making sure to walk behind him so he wouldn't be looking at her butt the whole way.

After four trips they called in to base to check in and give them an update. They were at about six thousand feet of elevation, and hauling the heavy loads back and forth had winded her. She sat down to catch her breath. The other scavengers spent more time outdoors and were to hauling heavy objects in the lighter air. After a little rest, she checked the status of the cargo bay. It was nearly full and they had not even taken a fifth of what was here. When the next man showed up with an armload of booty, she told him to stop bringing insulation and get some copper and they could head out. Then she called in again to tell Chin that it wouldn't be much longer. "New Hope, this is Salvage Crew three. Nothing new to report." Out of the corner of her eye she saw Anton running back down the hill, waving frantically. She continued talking while she tried to make sense of what he was doing. "We should be ready to dust off in about thirty min-" An object came over the hill the soldier was running down, trailing a line of smoke. When she realized it was headed straight for her, she dove out of the way, only managing to say "Oh shit!".

She had not hit the ground from her dive when the rocket hit the transport. The explosion threw her like a ragdoll for another ten feet before driving her into the ground. The impact nearly knocked her unconscious, and if she hadn't been wearing the earplugs, her eardrums would have been shattered.

She struggled to get to her feet, but nothing wanted to work quite right. There was shouting coming from her left and in front of her. She became aware of a pain in her left leg, and right hand. Rolling over on her back, she held her hand in front of her face to see why it hurt. Two fingers were grossly swollen and some blood was dripping from one of them. Using her good arm she tried to get to her feet, but as soon as she got her left leg positioned to stand up, pain shot from her knee. The body armor had absorbed most of the impact, but her knee hit a rock when she landed and her hand took all her weight when she pitched forward. She hadn't bothered to don her gloves or keep her weapon out, and she was paying the price.

Sitting up, she became aware of the gunfire. Anton had taken cover about twenty yards from her and was firing toward the hill in front of him. To her left, two of the three scavengers were heading toward her, one turning and firing bursts of rifle fire every dozen or so steps. She was having trouble focusing and could not see what they were shooting at. Her helmet lay about ten feet away but it might as well have been a mile.

The first of the scavengers reached her and the second took a knee and started firing back toward where he had been. "Are you okay? Can you walk?" She looked into his face and tried to comprehend what he said. It took a moment to understand.

"No, I smashed my knee. I can't get up. What's going on?" Her head was spinning and now she felt tired. Her eyes started drooping shut and she struggled to keep them open.

"Mutes. About twenty of them stormed the building. Stanley is dead. Looks like they hit us from two sides. What the hell happened to the transport?" The other scavenger was shouting something now, and Anton had stopped shooting and was heading toward them.

"Uh. I think an RPG..." Her vision was going dark and she lost control of her eyelids, which decided to close on their own.

The last few words she heard were, "We gotta get to the trees to get some cover... concussion... carry her..."

~~~~

Jack's leg bounced up and down. By the time they started their descent, he was ready to pick a fight with someone in the cabin, just to release the nervous energy. When they cleared the clouds, the plume of black smoke was the first thing he noticed. His heart sank when he saw the huge debris field at the source of the smoke.

The remains of the aircraft were about forty feet from a large building. As they got closer, he could see bodies all over the place. There were at least a dozen between the wreckage and the building, and another six or seven on the hillside to the east.

"Oh Christ. This doesn't look good." The pilot's words reflected exactly what Jack was feeling. So far he had not spotted any bodies clothed in combat armor. That was a good sign, he hoped.

"Salvage Crew three, this is Rescue Team one, do you read?" Jonathan, the man next to the pilot, had been trying to call any of the salvage crew for the last ten minutes. Nobody answered.

Jack pointed at a body to the west of the wreckage, just south of the tree line. "Fly over there and let's take a closer look." If he were being chased with nowhere to go, he would have headed toward the trees.

The pilot circled around toward the trees while Jonathan called New Hope. "New Hope, this is Rescue one. We have reached the site. There is sign of a recent battle and what appears to be the remains of the transport. There are also a lot of bodies. Except for the transport, it looks like Mutes. No sign of the salvage team. We're going to head over to the west and scan for any power sources." The technology level of the Mutes was low enough that any power source they detected was most likely from one of the salvage crew's possessions. That is, of course, unless it had been taken from their dead body.

Suddenly, the pilot hit the throttle and shoved the stick to the left, banking the aircraft hard in a left hand power dive. Jack rose up off his seat, his seatbelt the only thing keeping him from bouncing off the roof. He looked out the window in time to see an object hurtle past them, missing by inches, trailing a column of white smoke. He followed the smoke back to the woods below. "Holy shit! They shot a rocket at us!" Jonathan was already calling it in to New Hope.

The aircraft pulled out of the dive and lined up on the source of the attack. "I'm gonna cook those bastards!" He was flipping switches on the control panel, and Jack figured he was arming a missile.

"NO!" he exclaimed, "They could have our people captive down there. If you bomb them you could hurt Wen – one of our own!" He was not about to let the pilot start blindly dropping ordinance out there. "Put us down at the tree line and then go back up and watch for trouble from above. Stay out of range of those rockets!" He checked the safety on his rifle and chambered a round, then powered up his helmet and put on a thermal overlay. Scanning the forest as they came down, he saw a definite source of heat about two hundred yards in. It was close to where the rocket came from, and there was more than one object.

As they neared the ground, he pushed the door open, prepared to hit the ground running. The soldier on the other side of the aircraft opened the door on his side, similarly prepared. When the aircraft was about five feet off the ground, five of the six other passengers jumped out with Jack. The transport hummed loudly and shot up to a higher elevation. He half expected to see another rocket come screaming out of the forest, but it was eerily quiet.

One of the soldiers held a device in his hand and was slowly swinging it back and forth. He stopped with the device pointed straight into the forest and said, "There is a faint source in that direction, but it's barely reading, so it's quite a ways in."

Jack took the lead and plunged into the trees, not even checking to see if anyone followed him.

Chapter 29

The darkness lifted and Wendy became aware of the pain. On top of that, she was moving, and it was a bumpy ride. The motion combined with a headache quickly made her nauseas, and she vomited. When she finished, she was able to focus, and realized she was being carried over someone's shoulders. *What do they call this? The fireman's carry?* When she puked, the person carrying her stopped and with the help of someone else, gently put her down on the ground.

She took in the surroundings, unsure of what was happening. They were in a forest, surrounded by tall pine trees. Two people were with her, both trying to catch their breath. Memory slowly returned, and she tried to piece it together. She was on a salvage mission, and they were getting close to leaving. The last thing she remembered was calling in to tell New Hope they were almost ready to head home. These two people were members of the crew she brought out.

Before she could speak, another person came jogging up to them. It was Anton. He stopped for a moment, putting his hands on his knees to catch his breath. "Why did we stop? Is she awake?"

"Yeah, she just puked on me."

Anton kneeled down to examine her. "Wendy, can you hear me?"

She tried her voice. "Yeah," she croaked. Her throat was still burning from the bile, and she tried to swallow a few times to flush it. A water bottle appeared in front of her face and she took a few sips. "Better, thanks." This time it came out sounding a little more human. "What happened, where are we?"

"We're in the forest in the northeast corner of Idaho, somewhere to the east and north of the factory building. Mutes attacked, about fifty of them, maybe more. They fired a rocket over the hill and took out our ride. You dove out of the way of the rocket but took a pretty big hit from the blast. You are concussed, and your knee is in bad shape. What's the last thing you remember?"

She closed her eyes, trying to jar something loose, and finally it came back to her. The rocket, the explosion – "Stanley?"

The man who had been carrying her, Wayne was his name, shook his head. "He didn't have his helmet on and took a round in the head when they ambushed us. We barely made it out of there alive." He sat down heavily next to Wendy and leaned up against a large rock. "I think we can rest for a few minutes. I haven't heard anyone behind us for the last half hour." He looked at Anton, who had been hanging back to scout when they stopped.

"How long since they attacked us?" The sky above was visible through the trees, but Wendy couldn't see the sun.

Anton said, "About two hours. We ran into the forest and they of course followed. We took turns carrying you, occasionally changing direction. I planted a few surprises along the way to discourage them from following. I'm surprised some of those blasts didn't wake you up. I think it worked, but the Mutes are good at tracking. They will find us if we don't keep moving."

"Any word from a rescue party?" Her mind was still foggy but her estimation put a rescue crew there about a half hour ago.

"Nothing yet. We're a good five miles from where we landed. We had to loop around a small hot zone, and I think the radiation between us and them is lowering the range of the radio's in our PDP's by quite a bit. Perhaps if we get a little further away we can reach any aircraft that might be in the area."

Wendy nodded. With their own aircraft gone, they didn't have a way home. If they couldn't reach the rescue team on the radio soon they might be left out here alone. If they tried to head back toward the landing site, they could run into the Mutes again. It was not a good situation. She examined her hand. At some point someone had put some coagulant on her wound and patched it. The fingers were black and blue and swollen, and she couldn't move them more than a fraction of an inch. *Probably broken.* She tentatively prodded her knee, and pain whisked up her leg. The knee was swollen, but as long as she didn't try to touch it, it didn't hurt too much. "Give me a hand, I am going to see if I can put any weight on the leg."

When she got to her feet, she quickly discovered how bad of an idea that had been. The men put her down, sensing she had been about to scream. Before she could struggle out of her pack, Anton handed her the med kit from his own pack. She took off her leg armor and rolled up the under suit to expose the injured knee. It was very swollen, but otherwise looked okay. She located a local anesthetic in the kit and shot it into her leg just above the knee. The pain went away quickly, leaving her whole leg numb. She looked for her datapad, and couldn't find it. "Anyone seen my pad?"

"I think it fell out in the blast. You lost your helmet too." He pulled out his own datapad and handed it to her. She pulled a tube of heavy plastic from the med kit and unrolled it. The plastic sheet had an isotope in it that the full size datapads could sense. If you put the plastic sheet under something and the datapad on the other side of it, you could get what was, for all intents and purposes, an x-ray. She scanned her knee and looked at the image on the screen.

Wendy was no doctor, and had to wait for the powerful computer to analyze the x-ray. After a few moments the results came back as nothing broken or detached. It could still be a slightly torn ligament, or it might just be really badly bruised or sprained. She pulled out a syringe from the med pack and shot the contents into her knee. The syringe held the same sort of concoction that Teague gave Jack the day before. It would accelerate the healing process and within a couple hours she should be able to walk again. If a bone had been broken or a tendon or ligament detached, the healing medicine would have only made it worse unless the bone was set or the ligament positioned properly. Both would have required a skilled doctor, so she was fortunate. She wrapped the knee in a rubbery bandage to keep the swelling down then asked one of the men to find her two straight branches. Once the leg was splinted, she got up again and with the help of one of the men, was able to hobble along without having to be carried. She wouldn't be able to run if they were attacked again, but at least they didn't have to carry her.

"We'd better get moving. I set some more explosives back there, so if they make it this far they will get some more surprises. I think we should head northeast for a while, away from the radiation to the south of us. It will also put that radiation between us and the Mutes." Anton had taken charge, and nobody was going to argue. The path would take them into the mountains, but anything was better than being captured. They did their best to cover the evidence of them being there, but it would only slow down the Mutes.

~~~~

Teague's datapad beeped and he checked to see who was calling. He had been hard at work with Thomas and his men planning the assault on Saber Cusp, and his mind was pretty well spent.

The pad showed Chin, and he figured he better take it. There was a little history between he and Chin, but it never stopped them from working together. It just made things a little more difficult sometimes.

"What's up, Chin? The scavenging crews back yet?" If the day had been lucky, they might have the materials they need to start on the cold rooms.

"Teague, one of the scavenging crews went off line. We sent a rescue group to find out what happened, and they just called in to say that they found the wreckage of a medium transport near the factory they were checking out. The aircraft is a complete loss, and there are Mute bodies all over the place."

This was not good news. It was bad enough to potentially lose a member of the community, but to lose a medium transport made it even worse. People, at least the infertile ones, could be replaced. But advanced equipment like that transport was in very short supply, and they lacked the resources to make more. "That's awful news, but why are you calling me about it? What did Jack tell you to do?"

Chin suddenly looked uncomfortable. "Well, he sort of went with the rescue team."

Teague's stomach sank. "What! What the hell is he doing? We need him here! Why would he go?" Then it hit him. Wendy was on one of the scavenging groups this morning. If it was her team that went down, nothing would stop Jack from going to try to rescue her.

Chin looked like he didn't want to answer any of those questions. He said, "He's the leader of this mission, who am I to say he couldn't go?"

"Call him and tell him to get back here." Teague was conflicted. He knew that ending the rescue party now would greatly reduce the chance of helping survivors, but he had to keep the bigger picture in mind. Right now, Jack is more valuable to them than any member of that salvage crew.

Chin shook his head and said, "Can't do that Teague, he is already on foot tracking potential survivors."

This just gets better and better. "Fine, send another team out to find him and take over the search."

"Sorry, Teague, can't do that either... We had three of the medium transports out salvaging, and the fourth went with the rescue team. As you know, only the smaller flyers have any offensive capability, but they aren't as heavily armored as the transports. We don't know what they are up against yet. Someone shot a missile at the rescue team, but it was thankfully not very advanced and the pilot was able to evade it. Our smaller craft are susceptible to small arms fire, and I don't think we should risk the few remaining pilots we have right now. If they ran into trouble they would be sitting ducks."

Teague's shoulders dropped. The heavy transports are well armored but don't have air to ground capability, so they couldn't use those either. This is what it felt like to be between a rock and a hard place. *How could Jack be so irresponsible?* He already knew the answer to that one, so he didn't have to voice the question. "Fine, but call him and tell him to get back with all possible haste. Remind him that he has responsibilities here."

Now Chin looked really uncomfortable, and he was scratching at his scar. "Well, there's another problem."

He didn't elaborate right away, so Teague prompted him, "What is it?"

"Well, it turns out there is a small hot spot a few miles from where they entered the forest. It's affecting the radios, and the transport has lost communications with them. With the possibility of another rocket attack, the pilot is staying at a safe altitude. He can't fly in low enough to re-establish comms. We just have to wait and see what happens."

Teague's mind went blank. He was usually good at thinking under pressure, but this was way out of his scope of capability. "What do you think we should do, Chin?"

Chin didn't answer right away, and Teague was just about to repeat the question when he finally said, "There is a salvaging crew on the way in right now. We can either send out another team to assist, or wait it out and see what happens. Personally I think they can handle it alone. There is no reason to put another transport at risk."

Teague nodded. It made sense, and he certainly didn't have any better suggestions. "What about the flier we have out there now? How long can he stick around?" Teague knew that the flier would be able to hover around for a few weeks before needing a recharge of the batteries, but the question was whether the pilot could hang in there that long, especially if he had to be on constant vigil for ground to air rockets.

"A few more hours, then I think he needs to come back in to be replaced. He's good for now."

201

Teague sighed heavily. "Fine, call me the second you have any more information." He clicked off and sat down heavily. There was nothing else to do at this point but keep working on the projects at hand. Jack was a seasoned soldier, and should be able to handle himself. At least that was what he kept telling himself.

Something else was nagging at him though, and he couldn't quite put his finger on it.

~~~~

Jack froze and held up a hand. The faint sound of the soldiers behind him stopped and he listened carefully. He heard the sound again, this time maybe fifty feet in front of him, although it was hard to tell for sure with all the trees around. They had been closing in on the source of the missile launch.

He switched his helmet to thermal view again and scanned ahead of him. There were definitely warm bodies ahead. Signaling to the rest of the team to be quiet, he carefully crept ahead, being careful only to step on the soft pad of pine needles that blanketed the ground between the trees.

It didn't take long before a break in the trees revealed a clearing up ahead. Jack used the thermal camera to get an idea of what they were up against. He tried to count the objects moving about, but it was difficult to keep track as they moved back and forth, crossing paths. His best guess was a dozen. He motioned for the soldier behind him. When the man got close enough to hear his soft whisper, he said, "I want you to circle around to the right with two men. I am going to get closer and see if any of our people are here. If you hear me attack, join in, otherwise wait for ten minutes then come back and join me here." The man nodded and signaled two men to follow him, quietly making his way around the clearing.

There was a massive pine tree about fifteen feet ahead that would provide good cover yet still be close enough to the clearing to observe the situation. Always aware of the Mutes' ability to see and hear better than regular humans, he forced himself to take his time, despite the adrenaline coursing through his veins in anticipation of the upcoming engagement. Taking a few careful breaths to steady his nerves, he thumbed the video switch on his rifle and ever so slightly peeked it around the side of the tree. A quick count revealed ten. They were much larger than he had expected, and a shiver went down his spine. The clearing was about thirty feet across and right in the middle was a stack of crates, a medium sized Mute standing next to them, his attention directed toward the sky. The brute was holding an object about six feet long and about a foot on each side. There was a screen like the one on his rifle protruding from one side and a hole about the size of his fist in the end. *That must be the rocket launcher.* There were three more hairless behemoths sitting off to the side, quietly talking amongst themselves, a pile of what must be weapons on the ground next to them. Four more were holding rifles patrolling the perimeter of the clearing, paying more attention to the sky than the trees around them. The last two were standing maybe ten feet from Jack, arguing just loud enough for him to hear. One of them was huge, and the other was just big.

The larger of the two was speaking. "Goddammit Tanner, it isn't worth losing more soldiers. These smoothies were far better prepared than we expected, and we paid for it with over a dozen dead! I say we cut our losses and go back to the factory. Whatever they were looking for, they will come for again. Maybe this time we can capture their aircraft instead of blowing it to hell!"

"Don't patronize me Ungo! I am well aware of what this has cost us so far, and Gratch will pay dearly for destroying that flier. If we can capture the four who got away, we can use them as bait to lure their rescue team in then sell them all. The last runner told me the tracking team was not far behind them. We should have them by nightfall."

"I heard the runner too, and those smoothies had already killed three of your damned trackers! The traps they are setting are slowing your men down too much! They could be two miles ahead by now!"

Tanner looked as if he were about strike the larger Mute, but instead just snorted and began to pace. "I doubt that! They had an injured one with them – a female! You know these smoothies as well as I do, they would never leave behind an injured mate! My men will catch them, and this time they won't make the mistake of attacking them out in the open." He paused, a look of contemplation on his ugly face. "I think you are correct about one thing, however. They found something they needed back at that factory. Perhaps the aircraft we fired on earlier has landed back there. Send a scout ahead of us and prepare to break camp."

Jack's attention was focused on overhearing the conversation, but in the back of his mind he was trying to process the information: *There are survivors – that's good. Wendy is injured – that's bad. There is a group of unknown size chasing them through the forest – that's bad.*

It looked like Ungo wasn't about to just take his orders without more argument. "Tell me we are going to just take the aircraft. With one of those aircraft, we will have greater offensive capability than we have ever had. Maybe we could even make a run at one of the smoothie communities for ourselves. We don't need –"

"You heard what Farnak said! We're already in bed with the Cali, whether we like it or not! They didn't tell us these smoothies would be here today just so we could use the information for our own benefit. We *need* the supplies and weapons they will trade for living members of New Hope. I don't like working with the smoothies any more than you, but our leader has spoken – we have no choice. Do your job, Ungo, or you will be put out of the clan."

He watched Ungo stomp off toward the group of three who were sitting down. Tanner looked up and shouted, "See any sign of the flier?"

Jack pointed the rifle up in the direction Ungo had looked and a drop of sweat ran down the back of his neck. There were three more Mutes at the top of the fifty foot tall trees, looking around for the transport. If they had ambushed this group, the ones up top could have torn them to shreds despite their superior armor. He carefully pulled back behind the tree and looked back into the forest catching the eye of Heather, the soldier closest to him. He made a sign for three and pointed up, then signaled ten and pointed at the clearing. Heather nodded and spoke quietly into her PDP, telling the others how many there were, and to prepare for a fight.

He waited another minute for everyone to get into place, keeping an eye on the activity in the clearing. They were starting to pack up their gear, and Ungo was talking to one of the soldiers, presumably sending him ahead as a scout. Jack steeled himself for the fight. If the scout headed into the forest he would surely spot one of the soldiers, so he had to act now if he wanted to keep the element of surprise. He looked over at Heather, who was now behind another large tree, much closer to the clearing.

She nodded. Jack leaned around the tree to get position on everyone in the clearing and thumbed the safety. He carefully took aim at Tanner, the obvious leader of the group. Just as his finger rested on the trigger, there was a shout, followed by another Mute materializing from the tree line on the opposite end of the clearing. Ungo and Tanner both went to see why he was there. Jack strained to listen, and heard something about them losing three more scouts to explosive traps. Tanner didn't take the news well, and shouted orders to move out, back to the factory.

Jack took careful aim and squeezed the trigger. The left half of Tanners head exploded, spraying Ungo with blood and brains. In one smooth movement he swung his aim up to one of the Mutes up in the tree. The new target had been climbing down the tree, and didn't have his rifle ready. Jack fired three quick shots and the Mute fell the last twenty feet, landing with a 'thunk'. In the next three seconds, four more Mutes went down, and Jack had already targeted another one climbing down the tree. Before he could fire, an explosion to his right nearly knocked him to the ground. Something tugged at his midsection and he quickly stepped around to the other side of the tree to take cover.

The hideously ugly and bloody face of Ungo popped into his line of sight just as he rounded the tree. The Mute was lunging at him and he only had time to squeeze the trigger one time before the nearly three hundred pound brute plowed into him. He lost his rifle when he hit the ground, and the weight of the massive Mute knocked the wind out of him. Jack prepared for the blow that would kill him, but it never came. Through a haze of pain, he realized the weight on top of him was not moving. Struggling to take a breath, a task made even more difficult with the weight of the body lying on him, he rolled the dead body to the side. His lucky shot had taken the back of Ungo's head off, and the Mute was dead before they landed. Another explosion went off somewhere in the direction of the other soldiers, pulling his attention back to the fight.

He looked around for his rifle, spotting it half buried in pine needles about ten feet away. Getting to his feet, he limped over to the weapon, and winced when he bent down to pick it up. His body felt like he had been tenderized by a giant hammer.

There was a scream in the direction of the fight. He ran toward the scream and got there just in time to see a Mute holding Heather over his head. The Mute shouted, "Die, smoothie!" and hurled the woman at the tree five feet away. Her scream ended in a wet sounding thump and Jack winced. He shouldered his rifle and put two rounds in the Mute's head. Sudden silence overwhelmed his senses.

Jack scanned the area, looking to see who was left standing. There were dead Mutes everywhere. He ran to Heather, and found her unconscious but alive. There was little doubt she had some serious internal injuries. Knowing there was nothing he could do for her at the moment, he made his way back to the clearing.

All four of the soldiers had come into the clearing now and three of them were checking the Mutes' bodies, hoping for survivors. They had never captured a Mute before and it would be nice to could get one now. Unfortunately, all fourteen were dead. *At least none had escaped.* The thought went through Jack's mind as he surveyed the carnage around him.

The fourth soldier was injured, leaning up against a tree in obvious pain. A couple quick questions revealed how the Mute Jack had targeted just before the grenade went off next to him had jumped out of the tree and tried to gut the man with a wicked looking knife. The man's under suit had prevented the blade from penetrating, but he would be shitting blood for a week and his shoulder was either broken or badly dislocated.

He turned to the rest of the men. "We need to get Heather back to base ASAP. She's hurt bad, and Jones here could use some attention too." Jack was aware they had lost communication with the transport, and asked what they could do to signal it.

"If we fired off our emergency beacon, the transport should pick it up. That might get him to fly closer to reach us on the radio."

Jack knew it was risky. The Cali were involved in this whole debacle and could have people in the area just in case someone tried to signal for help. Furthermore, it would call attention to the area, making further rescue efforts even more difficult. He weighed the options carefully, and finally decided to take the risk. Heather may not even survive the trip back, but she surely wouldn't have a chance if they didn't do what they could to get her to a doctor now. "Do it. Get the pilot to land right here in this clearing and let's get these injuries taken care of."

The soldier nodded and fiddled with some buttons on his PDP. Five minutes later a distorted voice came across the PDP. It was the pilot. Jack breathed a sigh of relief as the soldier guided the pilot to the clearing. Minutes later they were loading Heather on board.

As soon as they put some distance between them and the radiation, Jack called New Hope.

"New Hope, this is Rescue One, are you there?"

"I read you, Rescue One. Jack is that you?" It was Chin.

"Yeah, Chin, it's me. We're heading back. We have one severely injured soldier here and a couple with minor injuries. Get some medical help ready."

"We'll be ready, Jack." There was a pause, followed by, "Teague is pissed that you went with the rescue team, and ordered that you come back the moment I hear from you. Did you find anything more regarding the salvage crew?"

Jack felt guilty for his actions. Not only was it impetuous to jump in with the rescue crew, it had almost gotten him killed. "Not really. I think there are four survivors, and I think Wendy is hurt. There's a group of Mutes chasing them to the north of the factory. Can you send another team out to look for them?"

"A salvage team just returned. As soon as we have the goods offloaded we will have a team in the air. You can relay directions and intel to them when you get back here."

"Okay, thanks. Oh, tell the crew to be on the lookout for Calis. We had to use our emergency beacon to get the pilot's attention, and it's possible they are sending someone to investigate." Jack ended the conversation and sat back in his seat. The adrenaline from the fight was wearing off and exhaustion was setting in. Wendy was still out there, injured, and he couldn't do anything about it now. This was not a good day, and the next few days didn't show much promise of getting better.

Chapter 30

"We need to talk. Can the council meet me right now?" Jack was talking to Marcus on his datapad. Marcus considered it for a moment then nodded.

"Meet us in my chambers. Sixth floor, I will leave the door unlocked for you."

Teague was busy helping the surgeon with Heather, and he didn't want to interrupt. It was unclear whether she would survive yet, and unlike Chuck, he didn't think she would up and moving for at least a few days if she did. The sound of her body hitting the tree echoed in his mind and sent a shiver down his back.

He put it out of his mind and headed to the elevator. The information he had overheard was important and he wanted to get it to the council immediately.

On the way down, he removed his body armor. When the chest piece came off, something clanged to the floor. He looked down and there was a three inch long piece of shrapnel. It had been wedged between his armor and his under suit, and he recalled the grenade that went off not more than ten feet from him during the battle. The gravity of the recent fight hit home again, like a weight on his shoulders. He put the piece of shrapnel in his pack, a reminder of how dangerous it was out there.

The council was already waiting for him, with the exception of Teague of course. Marcus gestured toward a seat at the table. It felt good to sit, and he took a deep breath, clearing away the exhaustion for a little longer. There was a pitcher of water on the table and he helped himself to a glass.

"Thanks for meeting on such short notice. We had a run in with some Mutes today, and I overheard some things I think you need to know."

Marcus gave him an incredulous look. "Are you telling me you went out in the field today? I thought you were running this operation?"

Jack nodded. He explained the events of the past few hours, and finished with, "I should not have gone out there myself, it won't happen again."

"So we have lost five, maybe six members of our community already, as well as a medium transport? Jack, the cost of your operation is already very high. Are you sure you know what you are doing?" It was Theodore who had spoken, and there was no doubt in Jack's mind that he disapproved of the either the operation, or of Jack running it.

In a cold voice, Jack said, "We've lost two, and are currently missing four more. If Heather doesn't make it the death toll will be three, but you can hardly blame Emmet's death on my operation. Yes, the stakes are high, so the risk is high as well, and nobody here understands that more than I do." He didn't like the veiled accusation of him taking lives for granted.

Theodore snorted at that and said, "I highly doubt that you have half the regard for the lives of New Hope's citizens that we do. Now what is it you came down here to tell us?" Jack struggled to keep his temper under control.

Marcus intervened and said, "Please Theodore, let's let Jack speak his piece. The way I see it, today's events were not his fault. We have been attacked by Mutes many times in the past, usually when scavenging for resources." He signaled for Jack to go on.

"As I was saying, there was a group of Mutes in the forest firing rockets at us, so we had the pilot drop us off and fly up to a higher altitude to keep an eye on us and to keep the aircraft safe. We-" Theodore interrupted again.

"That aircraft was perfectly capable of taking care of a single target on the ground, why did you risk those soldiers by engaging the Mutes on the ground? This is exactly the reason that we can't trust someone from before the war to lead our men in battle. They think like people with no regard for human life! Marcus, I think we need to put an end to this before more of our people are killed." Jack stood up, but before he could say anything, Marcus intervened again.

"Theodore! You are out of line! Jack is not here to be judged for his actions, he is here to tell us something! Now, I suggest you quit interrupting him so that he can finish. We can discuss your discontent at a later time!" Theodore leaned back in his seat, nodded once to Marcus, and proceeded to stare daggers at Jack.

Jack suspected Theodore had an ulterior motive for his outbursts, but what that might be, he hadn't the foggiest clue. He was on his guard now though, and chose his words very carefully. "Theodore, I understand your reluctance to allow someone new to your community to lead an operation of this magnitude, but I can assure you that I am the right man for this job. In answer to your, uh, question, the reason we didn't fire blindly on the source of the attack was because we had no way of knowing whether they had captured any or all members of the salvage crew. The last thing I wanted was for them to die from friendly fire."

He glanced at Marcus to see his reaction, and observed a hint of a smile directed at Theodore. The picture was becoming more and more clear. Marcus and Theodore were in some sort of power struggle, and Jack was the current tool of choice. Exactly whose tool, he had yet to figure out, but it was clear that Marcus would benefit from his success and Theodore from his failures.

Jack waited to see if Theodore would comment. After a moment of silence, Jack continued, "We managed to sneak up on the Mutes that attacked us, and I overheard an argument between two of them. It seems they have allied themselves with the Cali, at least on a limited basis, and are hunting for people from New Hope to capture and trade to Cali in exchange for supplies and weapons." Before he could form his next sentence, a sudden realization hit him, and he took a long drink of water to buy a few moments to think. Tanner had said something about being told where to expect the New Hope scavengers. *How could Cali possibly know where the New Hope scavengers would be working?* He frantically ran the possibilities through his head. *They could track the aircraft with their satellite, but could the Mutes have had time to set up an ambush on that short of notice? Doubtful.* Cali had to have known where the scavengers would be before they left New Hope, and Jack was very much aware that it could have come from this room just as easily as from someone else in the community.

He decided it was best not to mention that part of the conversation. He had to figure out who he could trust first. Putting down the water and clearing his throat, he continued, "The two Mutes were arguing about working with the Cali, and it seemed neither wanted anything to do with them. They were about to head back to the factory site to set up another ambush when we attacked. Unfortunately once the battle started, their aggression made it impossible to take a live captive."

There was silence in the room for at least a minute, then Marcus said, "Thank you, Jack. Once again you have proven very valuable to New Hope. This information will save lives. I think you are doing a fantastic job. Now if you will excuse us, it seems we have some decisions to make regarding Cali."

Jack would have liked to stay, but it was obvious these men didn't think he should be privy to the inner politics of New Hope, or to the diplomatic relationships with the other communities.

On the way out, his mind was working at a breakneck pace. Was the whole council responsible for the attack on the scavenging group, or just one member? Was it even a member of the council? From what Jack had seen so far, the people of New Hope were pretty much allowed to do their jobs without much oversight from the council. This new development made his job much more difficult. If the Calis had inside information on the upcoming operation... Jack didn't want to think about it. He needed to talk to someone he could trust. Two people came to mind, one was in a forest somewhere in Idaho being chased by Mutes, and the other was probably still in bed.

~~~~

On his way to Chuck's apartment, Jack mentally reviewed the time he had spent with the man. He realized he didn't really know him that well. Aside from the battle in Montana, they had not spent any real time together. It was difficult to truly judge the character of someone with whom you have shared a life and death experience. Your inclination is to trust them, but that can cloud your judgment.

By the time he reached the front door of the apartment, Jack had to make a decision. *Fuck it, I trust him.* He knocked on the door.

After a few moments, the door slid open, and Chuck was standing there in a robe, a bottle of beer in his hand. "Afternoon, Mad Dawg. Come on in." He turned without waiting to see if Jack was following and walked to the kitchen. Pulling another bottle from the refrigerator, he said, "Have a seat, you want a beer?" Once again, without waiting for a response, he put the bottle on the table in front of Jack and sat down opposite him.

"How're you feeling, Chuck?" Jack wanted to ease his way into the conversation.

"Jack, you didn't come here to find out about my condition. I heard about your little adventure today. By the way, good job. Those Mutes are some tough bastards to fight. It's impressive that you took out fourteen of them without a casualty."

Jack just nodded to acknowledge the compliment. "If Heather makes it, then I will pat myself on the back, not before. Besides, there are still four people out there fighting for their lives."

Chuck grinned, "Actually, I just got word Heather will pull through. Gonna take at least a week for her to heal though. She had twenty three broken bones and was bleeding internally in seven places. It's a miracle she survived the trip back. That's one more person here who owes their life to you." Jack studied his eyes, not detecting anything but honesty. He was convinced that Chuck could indeed be trusted.

"That's good to hear, thank you. You are right though, I didn't come here to ask about your health. Uh, not that I'm not concerned, of course." They both smiled. "Look, I have to ask you some questions, and I need real answers, answers that people like Teague or Marcus can't give me."

Chuck leaned back in his chair. He held Jack's eyes for a few moments then, as if deciding something, he leaned forward and said, "Let's take a walk. I've been cooped up here all day and I need some exercise." He got up and went to the bedroom.

Jack picked up the beer and cracked it open. He took a long pull, and felt the alcohol burn its way down his throat. Chuck was back in less than a minute, now dressed in the same scrubs that Jack usually wore when he was here at New Hope. Of course, that was because he didn't have any other clothes.

Chuck picked up his half-finished beer and headed to the door. Jack followed, a little confused. As soon as the door closed, Chuck said softly, "You never know who might be listening in. I don't have any reason to suspect that anyone watches my room, but I do know for fact that there are cameras installed everywhere. I get the impression that you want to ask questions that are for my ears only." It was a statement, not a question, and Jack didn't answer. He wasn't sure exactly where Chuck was leading him, but when they exited the elevator on the first floor, he thought he might know.

~~~~

The two man flyer gracefully left the flight deck and Chuck expertly piloted it in a steep ascent until they were above the clouds. He hadn't spoken since they walked out of his room, and Jack was content to wait. After almost ten minutes of flight, Chuck pushed the aircraft to a steep nosedive and when they were about a thousand feet off the ground, he smoothly arced their trajectory to be parallel with the ground. They decelerated until almost at a standstill, and finally Chuck set the flier down, barely kicking up any dust. It was late in the afternoon, and the sun was beginning to cast long shadows across the rocky landscape. The air was warm, around seventy degrees, and there was a slight breeze blowing. They left their datapads in the flier and walked about a hundred feet away. Finally, Chuck sat down on a large boulder.

"It's beautiful out here, isn't it?"

Jack looked around and took in the surroundings. He registered that it was indeed an incredible landscape, but with all the things on his mind, he just didn't have room to appreciate it. He simply nodded.

Chuck smiled and said, "I can pretty well guarantee that anything you have to say will not be overheard out here."

Jack had been turning the questions over in his head for the last twenty minutes, and decided exactly what he wanted to ask. "Do you trust Marcus?"

It was a simple question, but Chuck pondered it before answering. "When it comes to the future of New Hope and the safety of the people, I do." He didn't elaborate.

Jack nodded. "How about Theodore?" Chuck smiled. Jack figured that Chuck would have seen the power struggle going on between the two men.

"Theodore is ambitious. I don't really know his story, but I get the impression from him that he figures he should be the leader here. Not only that, he seems to be very much in favor of joining with other communities. I have only met with the man a half dozen times, and he always seemed to be looking out for the community. The thing is, all the members of the council came from a different time than me or you. Back then, human life wasn't worth what it was in our time, or even today for that matter. I would like to believe that the entire council values each and every life above all, but frankly I think they simply don't view life the same way we do."

"What do you mean by that exactly?"

"Take the cloning for example. To them, cloning a person and transferring their memories is truly resurrecting the person. But I suspect you and I both look at it a little differently." This was true, but right now wasn't the time to ponder the philosophical, moral, or religious side of cloning. Chuck didn't wait for an answer, "Bottom line, they all think they value life the way we do, but when it comes down to it, they have assigned a value to each and every life in New Hope, and they have a long list of things that hold more value."

This might seem like semantics, particularly when thinking about how in war, each soldier was an expendable tool, and leaders like Jack had sacrificed those tools to win battles, weighing the value of each soldier's life against the value of the overall mission. But that was during war time, and those were soldiers. Their job was to put themselves in mortal danger to help the leaders accomplish their goals. You can't look at your civilians the same way.

"I believe Marcus is sincere in his desires to keep our population safe. Theodore, I think... well, I think he would allow some people to die if it meant a stronger future for the community. Caleb and William are followers. They have ambitions and goals for New Hope, but if their perceived leader said that some people had to die in order for New Hope to live, they would probably agree."

"Is there anyone outside the council that you see as a threat to New Hope?"

This question seemed to surprise Chuck, and he didn't answer right away. "There are always a few assholes in any group of people. I could certainly point out a handful in New Hope. Some of the locals are envious of the reborn, and there have been some issues in the past few years. When you look at the situation the locals have grown up in, it is difficult to think that any of them have any intentions other than rebuilding humanity. I'm no psychologist, but I can see that the introduction of the reborn into their world could really shake them up. I don't have any particular person in mind as a threat, but I guess I can see the potential for it."

This insight was very much along the lines Jack had been thinking. "Chuck, I think someone in New Hope is a traitor. I don't have any proof and I certainly can't point the finger at anyone, but I don't see any alternative."

Chuck looked at him quizzically. "I think you need to tell me what's going on. What exactly happened today?"

Jack nodded. "Sorry to be so cryptic. Those Mutes we ambushed? Well, I overheard an argument between two of them before we attacked. They talked about working for Cali, trying to capture some of the New Hope members for them." He paused to gauge Chuck's reaction.

"That doesn't particularly surprise me. Judging by the pilot we captured yesterday, it seems Cali is really hot to find out what we have been doing in Montana. They are a resource rich community, and they would easily stoop so low as to paying the Mutes for a New Hope captive to interrogate."

"Yeah, it's depressing, but I got the same impression. While delivering this information to the council earlier, I remembered a much more disturbing part of the argument though. They let on that their leader had been told where our salvage group would be this morning." Jack let that sink in.

Chuck's reaction was quick. "I was wondering how they were taken off guard like that! The pilot would have scouted the area before landing and would have been able to spot a full Mute camp within ten or fifteen miles of the landing site. The best Cali could have done was watch where our crew landed with their satellite and relayed that info to a nearby group of Mutes. There is no way those Mutes had time to get an ambush together if they were notified in that amount of time. Mother Fucker!" There was silence for a moment as both men stewed over the thought of a traitor in New Hope. "Are you implying that you did not relay this information to the council?"

Jack shook his head. "No, I realized before saying it that any member, or all of them, could be the party responsible." He shrugged. "I can't put it together. I see the power struggle between Marcus and Theodore. They are using me and this operation against each other. If I succeed, I think it strengthens Marcus' power as leader. If I fail, Theodore can use that against Marcus, saying that if he were fit to rule he never would have chosen me to lead the men on such an important mission. The problem is, I don't see how either of them would benefit from losing valuable people and equipment, or how letting Cali know our secrets would help anyone but Cali."

Chuck looked at Jack and said, "If the Mutes did indeed get advance information on one of our scouting parties, then there is no question someone from New Hope is working with Cali. Until we figure out who it is, we have to keep this information to ourselves."

"That's why I came to you with this, Chuck. I don't know who I can trust besides you and..." He couldn't think about Wendy without envisioning her being hunted by Mutes.

"Jack, try not to worry about her. She's as tough as they come, and if anyone can make it out of there alive, it's her." His words were comforting, but not very encouraging. He felt a need to get back to base and ask for an update. He knew that they would contact him on his pad if there were any major developments, but like nearly everything else around him, instant communication was something new and he still needed to speak face to face with someone that could tell him where things stood.

They headed back to New Hope. The sun was really low now, pretty much crushing any hope of Wendy being rescued tonight. Despite the warm afternoon, he shivered when he thought of her being in a mountain forest at night, hunted by Mutes.

Chapter 31

Wendy was cold. The sun was almost down, and the temperature had dropped to about forty degrees Fahrenheit. They had climbed almost five hundred more feet in elevation as they moved deeper into the mountains. Her under suit acted as a good insulator, but it had been a while since she spent any time in the elements, and her body was not used to it. Her knee was feeling better, and she could put some weight on it now. Her hand ached, but the swelling had already gone down a little. Instead of black and blue, it was turning an ugly color of red and brown.

They had chosen a small clearing to make camp, and Anton was setting up perimeter sensors and some explosive traps. They would take turns keeping watch, but there would be no need to have a patrol walking the perimeter. They had not heard or seen any sign of pursuit in the last three hours, but they also had not been able to contact any rescue team either. Wendy hoped the rescue team had not been ambushed like they had. It was bad enough they had lost a medium transport and one of their crew. The thought of more lives lost in attempt to save her and the others was unbearable.

Her thoughts turned to Jack. His new status as leader of the large operation would not allow him to come looking for her, and if she was right, that would be his first instinct. Of course, for all she knew, he was enjoying a nice quiet evening with Cat. Depression was added to the fear, pain, and cold she already felt.

Anton materialized out of the trees in front of her. It worried her how well the forest covered up the sound of someone approaching. Sleep would not come easily, despite her exhaustion. "Traps are all set and a perimeter alarm is armed. If anything bigger than a raccoon gets within fifty yards of us, we will know it. I will take first watch."

Wendy protested, but Anton would have nothing to do with it. She needed the rest, and there was no argument. After eating some food from the packs, the two other men turned in for the night. Wendy stayed up for a little while, not quite ready to start trying to chase sleep, and still feeling guilty that Anton was taking the first shift after such a long day's hike. She tried to make some small talk with him.

"You've been living with Christine, right?" Christine was a local, one who had been cloned more than once. Her primary skill was that of a mother, so Wendy knew very little about her.

"Yeah, for about a year now. One of the children is mine, and I wanted to be a part of his life. Marcus gave us the go ahead to have another together, so we've been working on that." He said it with a hint of fatherly pride. Anton, like most of the reborn, looked to be in his middle twenties.

"Did you have a family before you died?" There was never a graceful way to ask about someone's previous life, but it had become commonplace to refer to everything before they were reborn as "before you died".

Anton nodded. "I had a wife, three kids, and two grandchildren." He didn't elaborate, and Wendy didn't push it. It was depressing enough knowing she had died at a young age, but if she had already had children and even grandchildren, she didn't know how she would have been able to cope with the knowledge that your children were long dead.

"I hear you have been spending some time with Jack. How is that going?"

She snorted, "You know, small talk used to be about the weather, about the wife and kids, and maybe about sports, not about who you are sleeping with." Then she flushed, not having meant to say this out loud and feeling a little ashamed considering she had been the one to bring up relationships.

Anton just laughed, not seeming to take it wrong. "The world is a different place, Wendy." He didn't say more, and she wasn't sure she wanted to continue this line of conversation.

"I'm not sure where that whole thing is at. Jack is a hot item right now, and frankly I don't know if I can compete with the other women in that area." She *really* had not meant to share that. Of all the things going on, she couldn't figure out why she couldn't let this go. Given their current circumstances, she wasn't even sure if she would make it home to see him again, let alone to find out if they were still together.

Now it was his turn to scoff. "Wendy, you're like, the most attractive woman in New Hope, and you're worried that you can't compete with the locals?" She flushed at this comment, both flattered and embarrassed by it.

He took her reaction wrong though and quickly said, "Not to mean that all you have going for you is your looks or your ability to seduce a man, uh, I mean, you are a strong, smart woman who should be able to get anything, or anyone, you want." Then he winced as if he still thought he was putting his foot in his mouth.

She smiled to relax him, "Thank you for the compliments and the reassurance. I don't know how much I deserve them, but thank you nevertheless. Despite what you might think of me, I don't really have it all together, and I certainly don't feel secure in my ability to keep a man in New Hope."

"Frankly, I don't think you are alone there. This situation might seem like a dream for any guy, but it is not nearly as easy or simple as it appears on the surface. I would trade it all for Christine to just be like any normal woman from our time. Any man who could have a chance at a real relationship with a woman as incredible as you who would still throw it away for some easy sex with the locals is both a fool and undeserving."

As uncomfortable as she was talking about this sort of thing with a man, or anyone for that matter, his words were comforting. She sat in silence just letting them sink in.

"So what do you think we should do in the morning? I'll be pretty much healed up, although I don't know if I'll be using my hand for a few days." She absentmindedly flexed the injured hand a few times while talking.

"I think we should head through the pass to the east and make our way to Montana. I used to vacation in this area once in a while. We are only about ten miles from what used to be West Yellowstone, a small tourist town that was a central point for some snowmobile trails in the area. We have been roughly following a pass that leads through Two Top Mountain. From there we can pick up the interstate and either head back toward where we landed, or maybe head north."

"What's north?" Wendy didn't like the idea of heading back towards the landing site. She would just as soon put some distance between her and the Mutes.

"Nothing much for a while. We are probably a three week hike to the Freezer, but we can reach it from here without too much problem. We would not make it before the big operation though, and by then it could be swarming with Calis. If we go back, we might be able to reach a rescue team though."

"Or we might run into the Mutes and get captured or killed." Neither option was good, and for the first time since the battle, she started worrying about her own future.

"True, but they won't expect us to head back, and quite frankly I wouldn't mind giving them a little payback." He was a soldier, and while Wendy had been in the military, she never considered herself a soldier. Her stomach gurgled, revealing how nervous she was. Anton noticed and said "Don't worry, whichever way we go, I will do my best to keep us all safe."

Wendy smiled. For the past four months, she had been so overwhelmed by the thought of being forced to have children, she had not really considered that perhaps there were some men worth getting to know here. She had maintained the mindset that they were all just after her body, out to score points by taking her as a prize. She felt embarrassed now, realizing that she had really been a bitch to every man in New Hope. "Thanks, Anton." She got up to get ready for sleep, and on impulse, kissed him on the cheek. He blushed then smiled.

She carefully crawled into the small tent, favoring her injured knee. She pulled off the armor pieces, leaving her under suit on for warmth. The thin thermal blanket was not very comfortable, but it did the job of keeping her relatively warm, and soon she drifted off to sleep.

~~~~

The sound of birds chirping woke her up. Peeking out of the tent revealed that morning had indeed come, and it was time to get up. Before attempting to remove herself from the small survival tent, she flexed her knee. It was stiff but functional. She had to pee, but hadn't gone outdoors since her last military exercise almost three years past. Wayne was on the last watch, and turned to her as she crawled out of the tent and stood up. The morning air was brisk and chilly, and her first deep breath triggered a yawn and a shiver. After a night on the hard ground in a very small tent, it felt good to get out and stretch. Her eyes closed, arms over her head, she arched her back, letting out a little moan as the muscles throughout her body got a good shot of blood for the first time since she fell asleep.

When she opened her eyes, Wayne was staring at her, a look on his face she was quite used to. Looking down at herself, she realized that not only did the skin tight suit reveal every curve and detail of her body, but the cold morning had turned her nipples to little stones and they were standing proud through the flexible material. Short of her shaving preference, there was absolutely nothing left to the imagination. Flushing in anger and embarrassment, she met his gaze. He quickly looked away, mumbling, "Good morning."

Without answering, she stalked away, heading to find a suitable tree against which to relieve herself. Along the way, it dawned on her that she had once again overreacted to the situation. It was hardly the man's fault for staring – she knew she had a figure that was much desired by men, and here she was practically shoving it in his face, subconsciously expecting him to turn away even though it was her own lack of modesty that drew the attention in the first place. Guilt replaced the anger that had come so easily.

She returned to the tent, climbed in and strapped on her armor, covering the very revealing undersuit. After climbing out, she sat down next to Wayne and said "I'm sorry, I guess I'm not much of a morning person. How did you sleep?" It was not exactly the truth, but he smiled and nodded, accepting it at face value.

"Good, and you?"

"All things considered, not too bad. It's safe to say you won't have to carry me today. My knee is much better."

"Bah... you barely weigh a hundred pounds, but it's good to know we can move faster if we need to today." He didn't meet her eyes, but she still smiled at the compliment. He handed her a pack of food.

By the time she was done eating, the other men were awake and breaking down the camp. The air up here was thin and everyone was winded by the time they finished. Wendy marveled at how they had made it this far yesterday, especially carrying her most of the way.

Anton spent a few minutes taking down the traps and the perimeter alarm. When he was ready, they looked to him for direction. "We'll continue over this pass until we get to the old highway. From there we have a choice to make. We can either head north, spending a few weeks making our way toward the cryogenic facility, or we head back toward the landing area where we were ambushed. If we head north, chances are we won't make the facility before New Hope has already cleaned it out. It will likely be swarming with scavengers from all the communities, and we can hope to meet one that is willing to call for a ride home. If we head southwest, we might be able to get

217

within range of the rescue efforts before they stop looking for us. Unfortunately this means risking another run in with the Mutes."

"What about using the emergency beacon to let New Hope let us know where we are?" It was Wayne who had spoken.

Anton shrugged. "We could try, but if they don't have someone close, Cali could have someone here to pick us up before anyone from New Hope would be here" Nobody liked either of the options.

Anton decided it. "I think our best chance is heading back toward the site. If the Mutes attacked the rescue party yesterday, chances are New Hope will send a large force to take them out. If not, they will have discovered by now that we were not killed in the ambush, and send more search parties for us. Either way I think we have a good chance of getting a rescue party if we head back. I say we go that way."

Wayne asked, "How long of a hike is it back to there?"

Anton looked at his PDP. "It's about ten miles to the highway, then another twenty or more to the landing site. If we move fast we can make it there by tomorrow. The only other way back is the way we came. The big hot zone we skirted yesterday is still affecting the radios in our PDPs. If we make it over the pass, we should have enough distance from the radiation and a better line of sight to New Hope. With any due luck, we can get in touch with any rescue crew long before we get close to the landing site."

Wayne nodded, satisfied in the answer, and nobody else had a suggestion, so they followed Anton.

The hike up the pass was tough, the thin air causing more rest breaks. At the third stop, Anton approached Wendy and in a low voice said, "Don't react, but I think someone is following us. I spotted movement to our left two times in the last hour. Keep your sidearm ready in case something happens." Wendy nodded. He repeated the process two more times, approaching the two other men and quietly informing them of the situation. Wendy was nervous. She didn't have a helmet or a rifle. Her pistol would be effective against the unarmored Mutes, but it was little comfort. She tried to keep looking into the trees as they moved on, but soon it gave her a headache, and she had to focus on the ground in front of her for a while.

By noon, their shadow had not shown itself, and everyone began to relax. They stopped for some food and rest.

Anton checked his PDP and announced that they were only a few miles from the highway. They ate some of the food and made small talk about nothing in particular. Wendy was going through her backpack looking for something to help with her headache when a sudden commotion startled the group. Anton already had his weapon ready, and the rest of them were only seconds behind in getting their weapons out. The noises had come from about fifty yards north of their location. There was silence for a few more seconds, followed by a shout and some gunfire. Anton moved to the nearest tree and motioned for the rest to find some cover. He scanned the forest with the aid of his helmet.

It had gone silent again and the four of them practically held their breath as they strained to hear something new. Without warning, a largish Mute burst through the forest, running toward them. He did not appear to be paying attention to where he was going, a look that could only be described as fear on his face. When he spotted the four people in front of him with weapons trained, he paused, put a scowl on his face, and yelled a battle cry, "RAAAAAAAAGH!" as he charged them.

They opened fire, cutting him down before he took ten steps. His corpse landed not three feet in front of them, and once again there was silence. The four of them exchanged confused glances as they waited for something equally as odd to happen.

Another minute passed and finally she broke the silence, "What the hell is going on?" Anton only answered with a shrug. "Are there bears around here?" This time he paled, looking a little worried: all the answer she needed.

They continued to wait, the four of them each tensely scanning the woods, expecting something to happen. It was safe to say that each of them were thinking about the stories of the horrors left in the wild after hundreds of years of radioactive fallout and the biological tampering the wars had left. Something had terrified that Mute, and none of them wanted to have to deal with whatever could do that. Another five minutes passed and finally Anton said, "I'm going to go investigate. Stay here."

~~~~

Jack woke around seven in the morning, but didn't get out of bed right away. His sleep had been fitful, and he didn't feel the least bit refreshed. In effort to find some more time to sleep, he made a quick mental list of what needed to be done today.

He had avoided Teague the night before, and had not taken any medicine before bed. Right now that seemed like a really stupid decision, as every movement reminded him of the nearly three hundred pound Mute landing on him the day before. Part of him welcomed the pain as a reminder that he had not only failed to rescue the survivors of the salvaging team but also risked his life purely out of selfish machismo.

Unfortunately, as soon as he thought of Wendy, there was no going back to sleep. Chin would call if anything new came up, but he just couldn't convince his mind to settle down. He carefully got out of bed and made his way to the shower. The hot water did him a lot of good, and he was beginning to feel a little better. He decided the first order of business was to see Chin and find out today's rescue plans.

He stepped off the transport into the large flight deck and made his way to the makeshift command center. Chin was the only man in the massive room. His head was tilted back, his eyes closed, and a sound somewhere between air escaping a leaking tire and a '52 Studebaker with an exhaust leak was coming from his nose. Jack called out and Chin nearly fell from the chair. He wiped a little drool from his bottom lip and quickly composed himself.

219

"Sorry, Jack, I was up all night. I guess I never made it back to my room to catch some shuteye." He stood and stretched, eyes sunken and bloodshot, hair disheveled, and his scrubs-like outfit wrinkled and grimy. In short, he looked about how Jack felt.

"No worries, Chin. When did the last search party get back last night?"

"About one in the morning. The only thing showing up on the thermal scanners was a few game animals. So far there is no sign of either the crew or any more Mutes. We covered everything in a ten mile radius of the landing site. The third rescue party landed at the site and investigated before the sun went down." He pointed to a table off to the left. "Those items were found near the wreckage. Stanley's body was found in the old factory building. There were a total of sixteen Mute bodies, bringing the total confirmed dead to thirty Mutes, and one of ours."

Jack looked at the gear on the table. There was a helmet, a datapad, and a rifle. "Who's is it?" he asked.

"Wendy's. We didn't find her body or any body parts around the blast, so at least she was in one piece when the other survivors hauled her off. It seems to confirm what you overheard."

This wasn't good news, but it wasn't bad either. "When is the next party going out?"

Chin looked at one of the screens to check the time. "They should be here in a few minutes. I had planned to rotate two full crews for the whole day, that way we will have a team in the area in case the survivors use their beacon. I would hate for them to use it and have Cali get to them before us because of bad timing. Unfortunately, that only allows one salvage crew to work on your operation."

Jack liked the idea of constant coverage for a search party, but with one less medium transport, it really limited their ability to scavenge for much needed parts. "Where are we at on the list of materials we need?"

Chin grabbed his pad and tapped a few times. "We are doing well actually. The one thing we really need is copper tubing and insulation. As far as we know, the best place for that will be the site that was attacked."

Jack nodded. "Tell you what, let's send two transports there this morning. One can search and keep a lookout for more Mutes and the other can collect the materials we need. They can also try to salvage anything left of the destroyed transport."

Chin made some notes and said, "Sounds good, Jack. I will contact the morning salvage crew and tell them to get in here ASAP."

Jack turned to leave then stopped and turned back. "Chin, do you want me to bring you some breakfast?"

Chin smiled. "Jack, that would be wonderful, thank you."

~~~~

The machinery hummed next to the two men, the air stinking of oil and dust. The room was not well lit, but it was the perfect place to talk and not be overheard by anyone or anything.

"What the hell were you thinking, giving up the location of our salvage crew!" The older man was furious.

"I was just doing what you told me to do!"

"I told you to make Jack look incompetent, not to give away all our secrets to Cali! How exactly did you think giving up our scavenging group would accomplish that task?"

The younger man had a look on his face that suggested he had thought things through very thoroughly. "I knew that the second he heard about his girlfriend being in trouble, he would be on the first transport to find her."

"And what exactly did you think would happen if they captured some of our people? You didn't think they could get the information out of them?"

His smug look melted. "Our contact told me they would be sure to wipe out the whole crew! This just goes to show that the Cali can't be trusted! I think we need to revise our plan."

The younger man was out of line, and needed to be reminded of his place. "Of course they can't be trusted! It will be irrelevant, however, when I trade all the assets from that facility for a seat on their council."

The younger man scoffed. "Once you are on the council, what makes you think they will listen to what you have to say?"

"Let me worry about that! Don't forget your place here, boy! Once I secure a position of power, you will get your reward, but until then, I make the decisions! If Cali discovers the cryogenic facility before we are ready, we will not have anything to bargain with, and it is all for naught. Is there any hope of turning this catastrophe in our favor?"

The younger man shrugged. "It's out of Jack's hands now, since he won't go out and look himself, so there's nothing to gain or lose by the return of the surviving crew. If his girlfriend don't make it, it might distract him, but I wouldn't count on it. The key will now be the success or failure of the group heading to Saber Cusp. Jack hasn't planned for the possible failure of that mission, and it will take too long to fabricate the heavy machinery they need if it does fail."

The old man was skeptical, but he tried to hide it. "You weren't put on that detail. How do you plan to ensure their failure?"

"I don't think we have to worry too much about it. You know what they're up against. The chances of their surviving are very low, and with Teague and that damned reborn kid leading the mission it will surely fail."

"Don't underestimate Teague. That man has proven time and again that he can be just as resourceful as the most seasoned soldier. Find a way to make that mission fail."

The younger man sighed in resignation. "It won't be easy without revealing myself to them."

"If you cannot do it, I will find someone who can. Just remember what is at stake here." With that, the older man left the room.

~~~~

Anton stopped and Wendy heard a sudden intake of breath. Startled, she whispered sharply, "What is it?" The path they had been following all day was heavy with trees and brush, but here, less than fifteen feet from the path, the trees were spaced so close together that it was difficult to see more than a dozen feet in front of them. Anton didn't reply, but after a moment he gestured for them to move forward.

After a few more steps she saw what had caused his reaction. There was a medium sized Mute lying against a tree up ahead. 'Medium' was a relative description; the man was easily over six feet tall and two hundred fifty pounds, but for a Mute that was average, even for the females. The man was not moving, and it was obvious, after a few more steps closer, why. The Mute's head rested at an unnaturally sharp angle from his shoulders. Breaking a man's neck is not an easy task, but certainly possible. Breaking a Mute's neck on the other hand, was like grasping one of these evergreen trees and snapping it in half. The hairs on the back of her neck stood up. *What the hell could have done that?*

A few more yards revealed two more bodies, both similarly dead. There were still no sounds around them, except for their own. After scanning the trees for a moment, Anton quietly said, "Maybe we should get out of here."

"Perhaps you should." The deep voice rumbled from somewhere to the north of them, and everyone spun toward it, their weapons ready. There was nothing in front of them but more trees.

Wendy could not remember another time in her life when she was so nervous, and a quick glance at the other men told her that she wasn't the only person scared out of their mind. The sudden need to urinate was almost overwhelming, but she was too tense to even piss herself. Wayne whispered harshly "What the fuck is that!?"

Anton didn't answer, and nobody moved so much as a muscle.

"Please put down your weapons. If I wanted you dead, you would already be dead." The deep voice left absolutely no room for argument. There wasn't even a hint of doubt in the voice, and Wendy felt whatever was behind that voice was perfectly capable of dealing with them. She was the first to holster her weapon.

Anton said, "Who are you, and what do you want?" His voice quavered a little, but she was impressed that he had managed to get any coherent words out at all.

There was a slow, deep sound that could have been a chuckle. "Shouldn't you be asking *what* I am?"

Wendy could almost feel Anton's bowels turn to liquid. Hers were already there.

"I... I'm not sure I want to know what you are." His voice sounded very small.

The deep chuckle turned into what was unmistakably a laugh. When it ended, the voice said, "I took care of your pursuers, do you always look at a gift with such skepticism?"

Anton relaxed slightly, and with more confidence said, "Would you walk away with some unknown entity capable of this kind of violence a short distance behind you?"

There was a pause. "Good point," the rumbling voice said. "Tell you what, put down your weapons and I will show myself, so we can talk about it face to face."

The fear was being replaced once again with confusion and curiosity. Wendy looked back at Wayne, who only shrugged. Anton motioned for them to lower their weapons. Greg, the man behind Wayne, shook his head and whispered, "Fuck that, you have no idea what is out there. What if it's a trick?"

"Do you honestly think we would have a chance against whatever did this?" he gestured at the bodies around them. Greg looked at one and shivered, but he lowered his weapon. Anton turned back towards the source of the voice and said "Okay, we lowered our weapons."

"Thank You. Please do not be alarmed, I would hate to have to kill you all just because someone got scared and tried to attack me." As he said this, the biggest Mute any of them had ever seen stepped out from behind the tree not ten feet in front of them. The man was easily seven and a half feet tall and had to weigh over four hundred pounds. Unlike most Mutes Wendy had seen, this one had a crude, long sleeved shirt on, as well as long pants, and covering his shoulders was a blanket or cloak made from what had to have been a very large animal.

Behind her, he heard a rifle hit the ground, and as she turned she spotted the backside of Greg as he fled. Anton shouted after him, "Greg, come back!" It was no use, the man was gone. Anton rolled his eyes and shook his head, but then turned his attention back to the current situation. Wendy knew that Greg wouldn't get far, and they could raise him on the radio if they couldn't find him.

The range of emotions Wendy had gone through in the past few minutes was too much, and she had finally had enough. "Would you mind telling me what the hell is going on?" She said it with anger in her voice, but as soon as it was out, the adrenaline seemed to disappear and her knees turned to rubber.

The enormous Mute smiled and leaned against the tree. "My name is Bartholomew. Who are you?"

"I'm Wendy, this is Anton and Wayne. Uh... pleased to meet you?" She wasn't sure what to say, so she figured being polite was the safest way to go.

"Pleased to make your acquaintance as well, Wendy." He turned to Anton, still smiling. "I guess you are probably confused. I have been following you since you entered the woods yesterday. I was curious what my former clan was chasing, and decided to make things a little more difficult for them. You did a pretty good job of that by yourself, however, so I was just following along for the entertainment."

Wendy's fear was partially replaced with astonishment, but Anton seemed to be annoyed at the Mute's comment. She had plenty of questions, starting with why he wasn't trying to kill them, but before she could even form a question, Anton blurted out, "Entertainment? You call our situation entertaining?" He was turning red with anger, and Wendy put a hand on his shoulder.

Bartholomew's smile slipped a little. "I don't mean to belittle your fight or your actions, I simply mean I was entertained with the results of your traps. Watching those idiots walk blindly into death heightened my spirits."

Anton's anger appeared to subside a little, and before he could reply, Wendy took the opportunity to ask a question. "Bartholomew -"

"Please, call me Bart, if you prefer."

"Uh, okay, Bart, you said 'former clan'? Were these Mutes your own people?"

Bart frowned a little. "You know, we tend to prefer the term 'evolved'."

Wendy colored with embarrassment and fear. Insulting this behemoth was probably the fastest way to get killed, and it was not her intention. "Oh my God! I'm sorry, I, uh... we..." His laugh was like thunder rolling down a mountain.

"Wendy, I am only kidding with you. Personally I could care less what you call my people. I have washed my hands of them and all they stand for." He didn't offer more than that, but her curiosity had grown to the point where she had almost forgotten how afraid she was. Before she could ask another question, Anton looked at his PDP then looked at Wendy. He didn't need to say that they needed to keep moving if they had any hope of getting rescued today. This presented a problem because she was completely unsure of what Bart's appearance meant. She had never run into a Mute that didn't try to kill her, let alone struck up a conversation with her. They needed to determine if Bart was a threat to them before they could go anywhere.

"Can you tell me why you no longer care for your people?"

Bart's amused expression turned a little more serious. "I had a falling out with my brother. He is the leader of the group that is hunting you. They currently live south of the river near where you were attacked. Once I left my clan, I had few choices. I was never particularly fond of the nomadic lifestyle, and I can't exactly live with the regular humans in any of the communities."

Wendy nodded understanding, but before she could say anything, Bart said, "Yeah, it's terrible being too tall to live in the underground bunkers."

There was silence for almost five seconds before Bart burst out in laughter. The combination of tension, fear, and intrigue finally boiled over and Wendy began to laugh, almost hysterically. Anton understood the humor, and relaxed a little, probably sensing that Bart was not an immediate threat. Wayne was looking back and forth between Bart, Wendy, and Anton, clearly not understanding the situation in the least. Wendy didn't hold it against him, after all, ten minutes ago she would never have thought she could have a civilized conversation with a Mute, let alone a lighthearted one.

Bart's laughter died down and he sighed. "I have really missed getting to laugh with someone else. We do have some serious things to discuss, but I imagine you are in a hurry to get in touch with your people, so we can talk as we go."

She turned to Anton, but it was obvious he was just as curious as she was to hear Bart's story. He nodded and turned to head back to the trail. Wayne followed Anton, and Wendy took a dozen steps toward the two men, but stopped when she didn't hear Bart following behind her. She turned back to see why he wasn't following and was surprised when he wasn't there. She scanned the trees but the only movement or sound she detected was from Anton and Wayne. She walked the last few feet to the trail and then followed a dozen steps behind the two men, checking behind her every few steps for any sign of the huge Mute. When they reached the clearing where they had broken for lunch, Bart materialized from the trees to her left, startling her. A rabbit would have made more noise. She shivered, realizing that if he had wanted to kill them, they would have been dead a long time ago.

~~~~

When they arrived at the clearing, Greg was there, pacing back and forth, obviously trying to decide if he should move on without them or go back to help. When they emerged from the trees he nearly bolted again, but Anton called out to him, and told him it was okay. After relaying the conversation, he reluctantly nodded and without another word, grabbed his pack and took his rifle from Wayne, who had picked it up for him.

They all gathered their gear and started up the barely perceptible path. Bart hung back for a moment, observing them as they started out. "I am surprised to see you are able to move around so easily, Wendy. You were pretty badly injured yesterday. You must have some good medicine." His deep voice was oddly soothing. He took a few long steps to catch up to her, then slowed down to keep his stride even with hers"

She nodded. "I never would have thought that one day we would have the ability to heal life threatening wounds in a matter of days." Before she finished the sentence she realized her mistake. Bart was the first person she had spoken with outside of New Hope since she was reborn, and she hadn't thought to conceal her origins from the giant man. Anton shot her a look over his shoulder that said she should shut up, and she immediately felt like an idiot.

Bart didn't appear to notice the exchange. "I assume that means you were not always living with the communities?"

His apparent misunderstanding was the perfect cover for her slip up, and she rolled with it. "I was born up north of here, and lived with my mother and two sisters. A search team from New Hope found me about four months ago, and I have lived with them ever since." The story was actually true, just not for her. A few months ago on a scavenging mission they spotted a house with smoke coming from its makeshift chimney. A young woman was living alone in the house, and they brought her back. Wendy was fortunate to get to hear her entire life story.

"You said they found *you*, what about your family?"

"My mother took a nasty fall, got cut pretty bad, and the wound got infected. She passed about a month before I was found. My mother had talked about a community to the east called Deering. It was where my father had supposedly come from. My sisters decided to head that direction, with dreams in their head of finding a city full of men to have babies with and live happily ever after. I thought it was foolish and stayed behind. We had a home, good hunting grounds, and a clean source of water. I never heard from either of them again." She tried to put a look of forlorn sadness on her face, but wasn't sure she had succeeded.

"So why are you out here, and not back in New Hope, half way through your pregnancy? Are you barren?"

He was making this easy, so she kept rolling with it. The real woman they had found was in fact very pregnant at the moment. The question sort of hit home for her, however, so it was easy to look uncomfortable with the conversation. He was buying it, hook, line, and sinker.

"I see you do not want to talk about that. My apologies. It must be difficult, living in a society with such great need for children, and not being able to participate."

The comment surprised her. Not only was Bart very perceptive, but he seemed to know an awful lot about their communities and culture. Before she could comment, he said "Don't look so surprised, Wendy, I probably know a lot more than you think I do about your community. Actually, I bet I know some things about New Hope that you don't even know."

She wondered what that might mean, but before she could ponder it for long, Anton spoke. "Bart, how is it you happened across us in the middle of a battle with your own former clan mates?"

Bart smiled. "You see what I mean? There are many things going on in this world, much more than most of you smoothskins are aware of. Like I said earlier, there are some serious things I need to discuss with you."

"Please, go on." Bart took a couple longer strides and caught up to Anton so he wouldn't have to turn around to talk.

"You are correct in assuming it was not coincidence that I was nearby when you were attacked. My new home is actually not too far from where we are now, and I would never have heard your fight with my former brethren. However, I knew the attack was going to happen before you did. Let me tell you my story, and then you can ask me questions."

Anton stopped walking for a moment and turned around. When everyone caught up, he turned back around and started walking again. "Okay, tell us." They were all bunched up now, focusing as much on not stepping on the next person's heels as on the terrain in front of them. Everyone wanted to hear what Bartholomew had to say.

Bart looked ahead, his pace slow and smooth, allowing everyone to keep up. His deep voice rumbled like distant thunder as he spoke. "Farnak, my older brother, is the leader of our clan. My father was clan leader before him, up until about a year ago. My father always felt that the communities should not be our enemies, and so for many years we wandered around what used to be Idaho, taking what we needed to survive from the land, and scavenging the ruins. We seldom encountered regular humans, and unless attacked, we never started anything when we did. You might be surprised to know there are at least four small families of smoothskins living within fifty miles of where we stand right now."

This did surprise everyone, including Wendy. She had been flying over this area for a few months now, and never once saw a sign of human life, Mute or otherwise. Bart had asked to tell his story without interruption, however, so nobody asked him to elaborate.

"My father's goal was to eventually establish peaceful trade with the communities, both the small ones around here and the larger ones like New Hope. Many of our people were against that, based on our history, particularly the last few years before being banished from our own settlement. Most of the Evolved believe that the only way we can survive is to continue on in the smaller groups, and remain as nomads, raiding and scavenging whatever we come across. My father saw things differently. He believed that we could live in conjunction with the communities – maybe even in alliance with them, working toward common goals. It was not popular, but in our culture, popularity has nothing to do with it. The leader is the leader, and if someone doesn't like it, they can try to kill the leader and assume leadership themselves. It may seem barbaric, but seldom is there a time when someone challenges the clan leader."

Wendy was about to break in and ask about that, but Bart seemed to almost be reading her mind. He glanced back at her and then continued.

"My father had gone so far as to try to contact each of the communities, but most did not answer, probably fearing a trick. In the end, the only one who even answered was Cali, and that was when the trouble started. At first, Cali was very friendly with us. They traded technology, sometimes for meat that we hunted, and sometimes for goods we scavenged. Then, after a few months, they asked that we raid the local communities and capture the men and women to sell to them. My father was not happy about this, and he let them know that he felt that all communities should work together peacefully. A week later he was found dead in his own tent."

Bart stopped talking for a moment, and everyone respected the silence. He cleared his throat, the sound so deep and loud that a bird was startled from a tree not far from them.

"We never discovered if he died naturally or if he was murdered. My brother took over, and it was not long before he made it clear that we would not remain as peaceful as my father had wished. We raided two local families in the course of the next two months. We captured six men and three women, and killed three. Farnak sold them to Cali in trade for weapons. I confronted him in front of the whole clan after that, and expressed my distaste with what he was doing. He told me that if I didn't like how he ran things, I could challenge him, knowing full well that I would not kill my own brother. He held a vote, and because of my supposed cowardice, I was cast out of the clan. My own clan mates turned on me that night."

They walked along for another half hour before anyone spoke. Wendy broke the silence. "So how did you know they would be there attacking us?"

Bart smiled mischievously. "Before I confronted my brother, I took a few precautions, just in case... I hid some devices in some of items that normally reside in the clan leader's tent. These devices allow me to listen in on their meetings. I also manipulated their radio equipment so that I can listen in on their communications with Cali."

Wayne spoke for the first time since they met Bartholomew. "Forgive me if this is offensive to you, Bart, but I thought the Mutes were stu... er, not as intelligent as regular people."

Bart laughed, which was fortunate because after asking his question, Wayne looked like he was going to collapse from anxiety, and Bart's comforting laugh seemed to set him at ease. "Overall, the Evolved have a lower capacity for intelligence, this is true. However, what that really means is that while some of us are pretty stupid, a few of us are quite intelligent. Chances are we will never have any scientists that will be extreme geniuses, but we do have scientists, doctors, politicians, engineers, and other people in our clan who are rather intelligent. I was never much of a political type myself, more of an engineer actually. I have never had access to the information that your communities have, but I have learned quite a bit from what I have scavenged and from what we traded with Cali. Plus, it is amazing what you can learn when the people you deal with think you are stupid."

Wayne nodded, satisfied with the answer, and probably not very comfortable with the thought of asking another one.

Anton pulled the conversation back on track. "So you overheard them planning to attack us at the old factory building? How did they know we would be there?"

"It was luck really. I normally don't listen to them during the day, as they are usually out hunting or sometimes even moving the camp, so I listen at night and sometimes review the recordings from the day, if there are any. It so happened that I was out hunting the previous day and had caught myself a very nice deer, and was busy butchering it yesterday morning. I turned on the radio to see if anything was going on while I worked, and a call came in from Cali. They said there would be a New Hope group at that factory in about an hour, and they would pay very well for anyone captured. Farnak sent one of his most loyal generals, along with fifty men to capture you. I figured that you must be important, so it would probably be a good thing if I foiled their plan.

Turns out I didn't need to do much. Our weapons are not nearly the quality as yours and obviously are not very effective against your armor. Farnak made a huge mistake, and I intend to make sure it is a devastating blow to him."

Anton had gone pale, but Wendy was still trying to make sense of what Bart had told them. *How did Cali know where they would be?* It only took a moment before she realized, and she felt the blood drain from her face as well. She looked at Anton and said, "Holy shit, do you know what this means?"

Anton simply nodded, still too stunned to talk.

"Ah, looks like this is your turn." Bart was gesturing, and Wendy looked ahead of them. The remnants of the interstate were a dozen yards from them. The tree line had grown right to the edge of the road bed, but only brush and grass was growing through the old asphalt. A path was all that was left, but it was clear in both directions, unlike the tree-strewn path they had followed through the mountains to get here. To the left there was a pile of brick and concrete, maybe a hundred yards down the path.

"Is that the ruins of West Yellowstone?" She directed the question at Anton, but Bart answered.

"Yes, but there is nothing there worth looking at. Just some piles of rusted metal and stone. A couple buildings still stand, but another hundred years will claim those as well, and soon there will not be anything left to show it even existed."

They turned right and started walking down the path. Anton pulled out his PDP and hit a button. "Rescue party, this is Salvage Crew Three, do you copy?" A thread of adrenaline went through Wendy as she waited for a response. After a minute, Anton repeated the call. There was no answer, and the adrenaline faded from her blood, leaving her weak and hungry.

"Think they are out there?" It was Greg who asked.

Anton nodded. "I think we just need to get a little further south. Let's move out."

Chapter 32

Chuck dropped the transport down through the light cloud cover and started descending toward the landing site. He was keeping a careful eye on the trees down below, wary of any surface to air missiles. The rockets that Jack had described were very low tech, but dangerous nevertheless. They don't have the explosive force required to completely destroy a medium transport, but it had been determined from the wreckage that the rocket had struck the transport at a critical point and caused the six air to air missiles in the bay below the cargo hold to explode. There was no telling if the Mutes who had attacked the salvage crew were still around, so he was playing it safe.

This morning he had been wandering the halls, bored out of his mind. Teague told him he needed to rest for another day, but it was bullshit; he needed to do something. The news Jack had given him the day before was weighing heavily on his mind, and he knew if he didn't stay occupied he might do something he would regret.

"Goddamn Council," he muttered to himself. Those guys were so out of touch with reality after two hundred years of planning the "future of humanity", it just made him sick. New Hope needed some new leaders. Chuck was never a leader; he'd always had issues with authority. As long as he thought it was the right thing to do, he would follow his orders without fail, but he had wound up in a cell on more than one occasion for failing to follow orders. Usually it was when some bullshit officer was trying to gain some glory at the expense of his men, but in the end nobody cared what the reason was, it was just a case of an enlisted man not following the orders of an officer. He had never met an officer he liked, at least until now.

Jack was different. Even though he had really not spent much time with the man, he was confident that Jack would never issue an order he wouldn't be willing to do himself. That meant a lot to Chuck, and despite the fact that Jack had saved his life already, he would follow the man into Hell itself. If there was someone well suited to run New Hope, it was Jack.

He pushed the thoughts out of his mind and focused on the task at hand. It was mid-afternoon, and earlier the rescue crew had not seen or heard anything from the survivors. Chuck knew that the odds were not good for them to find anyone. He still had hope, but it was quickly fading. This would be the last search party of the day, and he intended to stay out until dark.

He piloted the transport to about four hundred feet off the ground, then proceeded due east, first along the river, heading toward what used to be Yellowstone National Park. There were five men with him, and three were at the windows, scanning the ground below for any sign of anything. One of the men was watching his instruments, looking for a sign of technology, and the last was navigating. The navigator looked at the map on his datapad and said, "The hot zone is due north of us. We know they went northwest from the landing site, but they might have looped around the north side of the hot zone and into the mountains. We have covered everything for fifty miles to the north and west of the site, and it is unlikely they swam the river, so this is the last place we haven't looked."

Chuck just nodded. He had reviewed the search maps before setting out, and knew all this information already. He also knew Anton pretty well. If the man was still alive, there was a good chance that they were all in the mountains near the border by now, if not further east and north. He veered just a little toward the north, and moved along at a steady pace.

Ten miles later he banked north, then west again, starting his first zig zag over the area. It was going to be a long afternoon.

~~~~

Jack spent the majority of the day just checking on everyone's progress, and making sure they all had what they needed. The engineering crew had started manufacturing the pumps for the cooling system. Four members of the maintenance crew were constructing the entry doors for the cold rooms, and the rest of the crew was at the flight deck sorting out the insulation that the morning salvage crew had brought back. Tiny and his team had worked out most of the details, and were now waiting on a bulldozer to get the timing down. The key to the whole operation was the dozer itself, and everyone knew it. Most of his time was spent working with Teague and Thomas, finalizing the details for the mission to Saber Cusp.

The crew was ready to go, but Jack had been holding them back. He wanted to go over every detail one more time. The truth was, he was waiting on news from the rescue teams, and didn't want to put more people in harm's way until he knew the fate of the four people still out there. He hadn't exactly lost his nerve, but he was definitely rattled.

"Jack, listen, we need to get this operation going. The team is ready to go. They've been briefed, they know the risk, and they know how important it all is. There is no reason to keep this on hold any longer." Thomas was doing his best to convince Jack to ease up and let it happen. He was a good kid, very smart, very dedicated, and from what little Jack had seen so far, a good officer. He hadn't missed anything, and had done a fantastic job briefing his crew.

Something was nagging at him, but he couldn't put his finger on it. The problem was, he wasn't sure if the nagging feeling had something to do with this mission, or if it stemmed from the other issues he was dealing with. Either way, he wanted to review the operation once more.

"Okay, how many men are you going in with?" Originally they were going to go in with a small group of six men, punch through the Mute neighborhood, then move in and disable the ground to air missile defense system. After Jack's fight with the Mutes the previous day, he decided they needed more men.

"Our new group consists of fifteen men. Ten soldiers, one mechanic, one computer expert, the pilot, myself, and one other officer."

Jack liked the idea of two officers in the group, in case something happened to one. The other officer was Red, the one he had dressed down the day before. Since he'd put him in line, the man was proving to be a valuable asset. When Jack decided they needed more men on this mission, Red had volunteered. He and his team were idle until they had a bulldozer anyway, and his men were seasoned fighters.

Thomas continued with the review, not needing to be prompted. "We have two fire teams. The computer guy will go with us, and the mechanic will stay with the transport. Red's team will hit the Mutes here," he pointed to a location on the three dimensional map, "and the distraction should allow us to punch through here in the south without much resistance. If we go quick and quiet, we can skip right past them, disable the defense system here," he pointed at another location to the southeast of the first, "and then come back to here and hit the Mutes from behind. We will put them between a rock and a hard place, and if they don't retreat, we will crush them."

Jack nodded. It was a good plan. The central computer for the air defense system is in a building about a half mile to the west of the Mute camp. The area is guarded by some auto-firing turrets and other nasty surprises, so the Mutes avoid the area. They got that information from Marcus, who happened to be responsible for putting the systems in place, and who also still has the key to shutting those turrets down. The computer tech should be able to hack into the building and gain access to the defense system. Once the network is down, the transport can fly in from the east, avoiding the Mute camp, and with the help of the mechanic, load up the transport with the booty. From there it's up to the two fire teams to get to the rendezvous points and catch a ride home.

Jack couldn't see anything he could do better. The firepower and armor the teams will be packing will easily overwhelm the Mutes. If they work together as a team, and keep moving, they shouldn't have any problems. Of course, the best plans are only good until the first shot is fired. At that point, it's anyone's game.

"When are you leaving?"

Thomas looked at his watch. "We want to hit them after dark, so we will leave in three hours."

"Let's get this party started." Jack turned to leave the room, stopped, turned back to Thomas, and said, "Good luck, Thomas, try to come back in one piece." The man smiled and shot him a quick salute.

~~~~

They'd walked almost three miles down the path that was once a highway. Not much had been said along the way, mostly just idle chitchat. Anton appeared lost in thought, probably thinking about the information Bart had given them a couple hours earlier. Wayne and Gregory didn't look comfortable around Bart, and they were giving him a pretty wide berth. That left Wendy to keep him company.

"So tell me Wendy, you never answered my question earlier. You told me you have been in New Hope for four months, yet you are not pregnant. Why is that?"

This was not a subject she wanted to discuss with anyone, especially not a four hundred pound mutated man. "I don't know, I guess I just didn't like any of the men I met."

This brought on another burst of deep laughter from Bart. "Are you telling me that humanity is on the verge of extinction, and you couldn't find a man you liked? Hahahaha!" He obviously found this amusing. "Wendy, you are an interesting woman. I think I like you."

"Thanks, Bart. I think I like you too, but don't get any ideas." They both laughed. Wendy liked his easy sense of humor. It was unfortunate that his race was considered the enemy by her own. In the past few hours, she had grown fond of his company, but she was sure it had a lot to do with the sense of security his very presence gave her. It was a misplaced feeling, she knew, as one well-placed bullet could end either of them before they ever heard a shot, but nevertheless it felt good knowing that the biggest man she had ever seen had been protecting her and the others while they traveled.

The sun was getting low on the horizon, and daylight would only last another hour or so. Wendy had just started thinking about a campsite when the PDP on Anton's wrist beeped. He quickly looked at it and pressed a button. "Rescue team, this is Salvage Three, do you copy?"

There was a moment's silence, and in that time, Wendy felt adrenaline course through her body. The silence was followed by some broken chatter. "Salv--- is Re---- ates." The communicator was digital, so when there was poor signal or interference, you only got the stuff that came through okay, not the static that didn't.

"Come again, rescue team, I can barely read you. This is Salvage Three, copy?"

This time it came in more clearly. "Salvage Three, this is Rescue Two, can you give us some coordinates?" Anton pressed some buttons, transmitting his coordinates. The PDP communications were secure, so there was no question it was a New Hope rescue team they were dealing with.

"Salvage Three, I got you on the map and will be there in approximately six minutes."

"Be advised, Rescue Two, we have a friend with us, and he is big. Do not, I repeat, do not fire on him, he is friendly. Do you copy?"

There was a hesitation before the response. "Anton, did I read you right? You have a Mute with you and he is friendly?" This time it was Chuck and Wendy almost cried when she heard his voice. She realized now that she had almost given up hope of a rescue any time soon, and was very happy she didn't have to walk all the way home.

"You copied that fine, Chuck, please don't shoot at him. See you in a few minutes."

Bartholomew cleared his throat and everyone around him turned to see what he had to say. "I suppose this is the end of the road for us. I will be heading back to my home after you are on board your transport. I hope my information was helpful to you."

Wendy hadn't given any thought to the possibility that he wouldn't want to come with them. She assumed that he was in it for the long haul. "Bart, you are perfectly welcome to go back to New Hope with us."

Bart shook his head. "I appreciate that, Wendy, but aside from the low ceilings, there are other dangers there that I would not be comfortable with. You obviously have someone in your community who has a different agenda than the rest of you, and once that information is made public, I would just be a very large target. I would like to keep in touch with you, but I am afraid that the equipment I have is not secure. Cali could listen in on anything I transmit, and worse, could find me very easily if I did."

Wendy thought about it for a moment. She lifted her PDP and punched a couple buttons. "Chuck, this is Wendy, any chance you have an extra laser transmitter on board?"

~~~~

Jack was heading to the medical level to get some dinner. He figured the night would be busy, and there probably wouldn't be time to get some food once the mission started. He also wanted a little alone time, and figured the medical level would be more or less unoccupied. As he walked off the elevator, his datapad beeped.

Chin's haggard looking face was on the screen. He had just reported in an hour before, which meant that this call was probably news about the search party. He hesitated, steeling himself for bad news before pressing the button to answer. "Hey Chin. The second rescue team get back yet?"

"No, but they just called in." He paused for a moment, creating a little tension, but before Jack could react he put a big smile on his face, which was kind of creepy given the big scar, deformed jaw, and bedraggled appearance from two days of sitting at the control center. "They found the salvage group. All four of them. Everyone is okay."

Suddenly there was no air in the hallway and his knees had turned to rubber. He tried to maintain his composure, but the news shattered the emotional barriers he had constructed in his mind when he realized there was a good possibility that Wendy was not coming back. He knew if he tried to speak, he would choke on his words, so instead he simply nodded and clicked off.

The wall kept him from falling to the ground, and he hugged it as if he were on a narrow ledge of a cliff, afraid to fall off. He struggled to take a breath, but like his legs, he had no control over his lungs. A tear slid down his cheek, the first drop just before the dam broke. The last of his barriers broke and he slumped to the ground, convulsions wracking through his torso, a low moan escaping his throat.

For the next several minutes he released suppressed feelings that, until this moment, he had no idea were bottled up. Even at his wife and daughter's funeral, he had held his emotions in check, shedding only a few tears that day. Now with the emotional barriers down, all the pain he had suffered in his life – from losing friends in Korea, to losing his family, to learning he had cancer, and finally from the events of the past few days – all came out at once. Never in his life had he let it out like this, and the tears and gasps coming out were like a cleansing.

When the emotional waterfall finally began to subside, the first thing to return was control of his lungs. Several long breaths helped to regain control of his body. Dinner forgotten, he got to his feet and made his way back to his room, locked the door, and sat heavily in his chair.

Of all the things that had happened to him or around him in the last week, this was perhaps the most confusing. He had never been one to get emotional, and never had he felt as if he was swallowing his emotions. He had not cried like that since he was a child, and even then he didn't really remember a specific instance.

He supposed it had to do with the same biological processes that caused his hormones to rage the first night. Whatever the cause, he actually felt really good. He had been under some stress the past few days, more from the revelation of a traitor in the community than from the operation he was running, or even from Wendy being in danger. This emotional break was like a cleansing, and he felt more relaxed than he had since waking up the first morning after his rebirth.

There was more to it than that, however, but he didn't really have time to ponder it in depth. It would be an hour before the rescue team was back, and he had a lot to do. With a clear head and a new resolve, he got out of the chair and went to get some food.

Part Four

Chapter 33

The flight bay was bustling with activity when the huge doors opened and the transport eased in and gently landed on the yellow square painted on the concrete floor. The Saber Cusp team, including Thomas, Red, and Teague, was geared up and hovered over a table, studying a map of the old city. Two mechanics were sifting through the wreckage of the transport, which had been brought back this morning and was now sitting in the corner of the immense chamber that housed all their aircraft. Chin was sitting at the makeshift control center, still keeping an eye on the progress of the one salvage crew that was still out for the day.

Jack walked over and stood next to Teague, waiting for the transport to land. Jack had been observing the team in their final preparations today, but Teague had not been with the team the whole time, instead spending time with Bruce, the new reborn. When he had been around, Jack hadn't said much to him, still wary of who was in on the ambush of the salvaging team. Teague turned toward him and said, "Thank God they are all okay. Marcus would have lost a lot of favor with the other council members if we hadn't found them alive."

The comment annoyed Jack, mostly because he didn't give a single shit about Marcus's reputation. A crew he had ordered into harm's way had come back. Regrettably, one man had lost his life. Right now Jack had only a few things on his mind. The first was seeing these people safely home after what must have been a long and harrowing journey. The second had to do with the mission to S.C. which was about to commence. Obviously the third thing was Wendy.

Before Jack could speak his mind, Teague continued, "Of course, it's a good thing that they are all safe too." Jack relaxed. Despite his differences with Teague, he had to give the man some slack, they had not lived the same lives. Life was indeed precious here, but with so few people and so few resources, everything, including politics, played an important role in their lives. He wondered if Teague knew they had a traitor in their midst, or worse, if he was involved in it.

The transport touched down and Jack stopped thinking about traitors and politics. He hesitated to run over to the transport, fearing another attack of his renegade emotions, but when the door opened and he saw Wendy, he started sprinting before he realized it.

She climbed out of the aircraft, looking a little haggard but not really injured. When she spotted him, her eyes lit up and she smiled. He practically tackled her back into the transport, grabbing her in a big hug, then gently setting her down, suddenly afraid that she might have injuries he didn't notice. "Are you okay? Are you hurt? They said you were carried off by the other crew. What happened?" It all came out so fast that he had to stop himself and allow her to talk.

"Slow down, Jack. I'm okay, just a little banged up. I took a nasty blow from that explosion and was knocked unconscious. I messed up my leg a little, but one of Teague's magic potions healed me right up. My hand might take a couple days to mend, but I can already move my fingers." She wiggled her fingers in his face.

He smiled at her and said, "Look, we need to debrief you guys, and then we have another mission starting in a short while, but I really want to talk to you about the other night." Before she could say anything, he continued, "Why don't you have Teague get you checked out real quick and meet us down in the briefing room. Have you eaten anything recently?"

Wendy blinked a couple times at all the questions. "I'm fine, Jack. I'll have Teague give me a once over after the debriefing. I ate some food on the way back, so I'm not hungry. Chuck said something about you going after us yesterday? What was that all about?"

Jack frowned. He wasn't particularly proud of his actions the day before. It was impetuous to go out with the rescue team and put his life at risk like he did, and he knew it as much as anyone else. "I, uh – well, I just couldn't sit here knowing that you were in trouble out there. I know it was stupid to leave everything hanging and go out there, but..." *But what?* He cared greatly for her, but surely he couldn't say he loved her, could he? He took the idea of love very seriously. The whirlwind that they had been through the last week had been full of passion and emotions, but was this really like what he had with Jennifer? Could he devote the rest of his life to this woman? He wasn't sure of that answer at this moment.

Wendy kissed him on the lips, interrupting his train of thought. "It was sweet that you charged out after me, and I appreciate it." Jack felt warm and fuzzy inside when she said that. "It was pretty stupid though, all things considered. Like it or not, you have responsibilities here that are more important than me. Don't do it again, Mad Dawg." She punched him lightly on the arm, then kissed him again and gave him a hug. "I missed you. I was worried that I would never see you again." Her voice cracked and she hung on to the hug a few moments longer.

Jack feared he might start gushing again, so after returning the hug, he said, "We can continue this tonight, maybe." He let go of her and looked at the other men, who were all out of the transport now. "Debriefing downstairs in ten minutes." He turned to walk away but Chuck caught his eye, and he veered toward the man.

"Chuck, thank you for finding them. I owe you one."

"Nonsense, it's like you said the other day, I did what I had to do. Besides, I just flew an aircraft, it wasn't like I put my life at serious risk to save them. I still owe you. Listen, we have to talk for a second." Chuck looked around and motioned to an unoccupied corner. Jack followed him.

Chuck looked around to make sure nobody was paying attention. In a low voice he said, "I talked to the survivors on the way back. Some stuff happened that they will tell you about in a few minutes. The big thing is, they learned that the ambush was set up, and that there is a traitor here in New Hope."

"Shit, how do you think we should handle this? If someone is listening in on the debriefing it will come out and we could lose our edge." The traitor didn't know that they knew yet, which gave them an advantage. It was pretty much the only advantage they had and Jack didn't want to lose it.

"We spoke about it before heading back here, and everyone is in agreement that we don't want to bring it up where it can be overheard. We need to find a chance to talk about it with them, and with their source. Perhaps we can learn enough to figure out who it is."

"Who's the source?"

Chuck grinned. "You won't believe it, Jack. You really won't."

~~~~

Jack thanked each of the rescue team personally then turned to Chin, "You really went above and beyond here. I can't tell you how much it means to me, both personally and professionally. Why don't you go get some sleep?"

Chin shook his head. "Are you kidding me, Jack? We're launching your next operation in less than an hour. I'm not gonna miss this one for anything. I am, however, going to go clean up and get some food." They took the rail car back and got on the elevator. At level two, the door opened, and Chin exited. "See you back at the flight deck in an hour."

Jack continued down to level four for the debriefing. When he walked into the room, Chuck, Wendy, and the other three men were there waiting. Wendy introduced the men.

"Thanks for coming here first. I know you're all looking forward to a hot shower and a change of clothes, but I want to know what all happened while it's fresh in your minds."

Over the next thirty minutes he heard the whole story, starting with leaving New Hope and ending with Chuck picking them up. Living up to Chuck's prediction, he was dumbfounded when they told him about Bartholomew.

"Give me your honest opinion, can we trust him?" Jack was skeptical of the Mute, and not even a little bit sure of Wendy's choice to leave him with a valuable laser transmitter and a datapad with an entire encyclopedia of information. His first impression was that this Mute had conned them into giving him something that would be of great value to him and his "former" clan. It might also be a real risk to the security of New Hope.

Wendy was the first to speak. "I trust him, or I wouldn't have offered him the equipment. He helped us, and might very well have saved our lives. He killed three of his own to help us." Jack considered this and turned to Anton.

"I still see a possibility for his actions being a ruse to get information and resources from us, but he struck me as too intelligent for anything he got out of us to be a tool for him to get back into the grace of the clan. I would think that if his intention was getting back into the clan, he would be best served to capture us and turn us in. If all he wanted was a datapad, he could have killed us and had three. I'm inclined to believe his story and trust him as far as we would trust any new member of New Hope."

Jack was impressed with Anton. The man had proven to be an excellent soldier, and showed signs of being quite intelligent. He made a mental note and continued on, next looking at Wayne.

"After seeing what that big sonofabitch did to the Mutes that were following us, I think we can trust him. The fact that he didn't kill us when he obviously could have goes a long way in my book." Jack nodded. It wasn't the most eloquent explanation, but it was reasonable.

He turned to the last man, Gregory. "Greg, what about you? Do you think we can trust Bartholomew?"

Gregory shrugged. "I honestly can't say. I agree with what Wayne said, about him not killing us, but that dude scared the shit outta me. Not only is he a Mute, but he is the biggest and scariest Mute I have ever seen. I am not even ashamed to admit that I am going to be having nightmares about this for a while. I'm just thankful we didn't bring him back here. I wouldn't have been able to sleep at night thinking that a monster like that is roaming our halls." Wendy and Anton shot him a look of annoyance, and he frowned. "Hey, the Capn' was asking my opinion. You had your say, and I'm entitled to mine. I wasn't privy to all your conversations, and I sure as hell wasn't about to strike up a personal chat with him! I say he's a Mute, and I wouldn't trust him with anything that could compromise our security. If he turns out to be okay, I will be the first to admit I was wrong, but until then, I stand by my opinion."

The man was right, and even if nobody liked what he believed, he was still entitled to believe it. Although the other members of the crew had downplayed it, the fact was that Gregory had abandoned them when Bart showed himself. If something had scared Jack like that, he would have a hard time with trust all the same. Aside from running in the face of fear, Gregory had earned everyone's respect through his actions over the past two days. Jack would not have a problem putting him in battle alongside anyone else.

He dismissed everyone, after thanking them for their time. To his dismay, Wendy told him she would catch up with him later and left with the other three men. Chuck hung back to talk to Jack.

"If we can trust him, Bart would be a great asset to New Hope. He can give us insight into the Mutes culture that could be valuable down the road. How do you feel about getting in touch with him and getting the location of those small communities he said were in the area?"

Chuck needed something to do until the big operation took place, and this would be the perfect thing to keep him occupied. Plus it might give him an opportunity to meet with Bart and learn more about their little problem. "I can do that. I'll get a crew together in the morning and go investigate. It would be good to find these people before Farnak's people capture them. I'll keep you informed on what I find." The statement had a double meaning, and Jack understood perfectly.

Chapter 34

Jack stepped off the rail car once again, and as before the flight deck was a hive of activity. Thomas and Red had their teams together, and everyone was fully geared up and ready to go. The two fire teams were standing at attention when he approached, and both Thomas and Red gave him a quick salute. He returned the gesture and asked, "You boys ready to go?"

Both men said in unison, "Yes, Sir!" Jack grinned. This wasn't the military, but it was nice to have everyone thinking like it was. Things just ran better that way.

Jack consulted the time on his datapad. It was close enough. He turned to the group of soldiers. "Men, thank you for doing this. This mission will determine the course of the future of New Hope. I have every confidence you will succeed, and I pray that you all come back to tell me how well it went. Just remember, our goal is to get some heavy machinery, not to destroy the Mutes or take over the city. Stay sharp, stay focused, and don't lose sight of the objective. Good luck and God speed." He saluted the men and they saluted back. "Go kick some ass, gentlemen!"

There were some shouts of excitement and bravado as they loaded up on the large transport. Jack watched them get on board, stopping Thomas to wish him good luck. He backed up as the transport wound up its four massive propellers. The aircraft was huge, easily fifty feet long and twenty feet wide. It was basically a giant box with a short wing on each corner, an eight foot diameter hole in each wing with a three bladed propeller centered in each hole. Unlike the small and medium flyers, this one had a cockpit up front that was separate from the cargo area, and looked like it was tacked on to the front as an afterthought. It was hardly a graceful looking machine, kind of looked like a giant square turtle, but it got the job done.

The pilot lifted the aircraft off the ground and carefully maneuvered it out of the flight bay. Jack heard the props wind up to a very loud hum as the transport gained altitude and disappeared into the night sky.

The flight would last about forty minutes, and he had a sudden overwhelming need to go spend it with Wendy. He grabbed his datapad and punched the icon to call her. He heard the datapad beep behind him and turned, half expecting her to be standing there. It took him a moment to realize the source of the sound was the small table where they had brought all the items found at the landing site the previous day. She had not retrieved her datapad yet. It was the perfect excuse to go see her. He grabbed it and headed to her apartment.

~~~~

Wendy took a long, hot shower, washing away two days of grime and stress. She examined her body as she showered, noting the large bruises on her legs, shoulder, and ribs. It was truly unbelievable that she had not been killed in the blast. Chalk it up to another miracle of modern science. The armor they wore was so light that she seldom remembered how protective it was. If she had gone through the same situation back in her day, she would have been killed in the explosion or died from her injuries thereafter. Of course, another way to look at it was that in her day, the likelihood of being attacked in Idaho by a group of large, wrinkly, hairless people was somewhere between slim and none.

She melted into the bed, and was just about to drift away into a pleasant sleep when the door chimed. Frustration was her first emotion, followed by curiosity. She knew, given the circumstances, if she ignored it, whoever was at the door would go away, assuming she was fast asleep. On the other hand, if someone was here to see her, knowing her condition, it was probably important. The curiosity won out, so she slipped out of bed, and into a robe.

She ran a mental list of who would be at the door. Jack was busy with the Saber operation, Teague was either with Jack, with the new reborn guy, or maybe meeting with the council to brief them on everything that has happened in the past couple hours. She opened the door and, to her surprise, Anton was standing there.

It took her off guard, and she hesitated before saying, "Uh, hello. What's up?" They had been through a lot the last two days, and like anyone surviving something like that, they had grown closer. Seeing him in the doorway tonight, she feared he had mistaken that bond for something more.

"Wendy, we need to talk. Can I come in?" She hesitated again, then stepped back and gestured for him to come inside. He walked into the living room, stopped and turned toward her, getting very close. She was just about to push him back and tell him that she didn't feel that way about him when he said quietly, "We need to talk about the traitor. I think we should tell Marcus."

Heat flooded her chest and face, and she felt like an idiot. Here she thought he was coming for a booty call, a little reward for saving her life. She needed to stop thinking like every man only wanted one thing from her. If anyone deserved her trust, it was Anton. She took a breath to clear her mind and whispered, "We can't talk about this here, you know that someone could potentially be listening in." She looked around, thinking about it.

A thought popped into her head and she grabbed his arm and pulled him toward the bathroom. Surely they don't have cameras and microphones in the bathroom. If they do, there is going to be hell to pay, conspiracy or not. The thought of someone tapping into her apartment cameras was bad enough.

The bathroom was not large. It was maybe six feet wide and four feet deep with the door in the center of the longer wall. A sink and toilet were against the wall to the right, and the shower occupied the wall to the left. That left them an area about four feet by two feet to stand and talk, after the door was closed.

They stood very close together, talking softly.

"I understand what Chuck was saying earlier, but I still think we need to tell Marcus. He is our leader, and it's our responsibility to let him know what's going on."

"What if he's the one behind it?"

Anton scoffed at that. "What would he have to gain by our failure? If this whole operation fails, New Hope will suffer for it. Marcus would have nothing to gain from failure."

"I tend to agree, but think about Jack. A lot of people here, particularly the reborn, see Jack as a breath of fresh air. Marcus has been pussyfooting around the Freezer for four years, and Jack comes along and within a week he has the entire population of New Hope working for him to take what we can before Cali gets it. If he succeeds, he would be a threat to Marcus' leadership. If he fails though, things can go back to how they were. You and I can't begin to imagine how someone with memories going back two hundred years would feel about change."

Anton thought about it for a moment, then shook his head. "I see what you are saying, but I don't see Marcus putting us in harm's way, even if it meant his position on the council."

Wendy shrugged. "I don't know if he would or not. I haven't been here as long as you have, but what if he *is* behind it? He can't afford for it to get out. If we confront him with this information and he is the one responsible for the attack, we're as good as dead. I don't want to take that risk. I trust Chuck and Jack, I think we should let them handle this."

Anton was thinking about it when the door suddenly opened. He jumped and spun around, pinning Wendy against the wall and blocking her view. She couldn't see who was there, but Anton said, "Christ Jack, you scared the hell out of us."

Oh shit. This probably doesn't look good. She peeked her head around Anton and saw a confused expression on Jack's face. She smiled and said, "Uh, Hi Jack." It was pretty weak, but she couldn't think of anything else to say. She nudged Anton and when he looked back at her, she made a motion for him to exit the bathroom. When he moved away from her, the robe opened up, exposing some of her naked body. She quickly closed it and cinched the belt tight. *God I hope he didn't see that.*

Anton was blushing as he walked out of the bathroom. He carefully stepped around Jack, stopped once he was past, and turned back to face them both. To Jack he said, "Um, we were just talking. I, uh... I'm gonna go now." He then looked at Wendy once more and said, "Think about it."

When he exited the bathroom, Wendy motioned for Jack to come in and close the door. He didn't move. There was tension in the air, and she was frantically trying to think of what to say to diffuse the situation. Before she could think of anything, he said, "Look, I just brought your datapad. I would have called, but..." He set the datapad in the sink and took a step back again. "If I interrupted something, I can leave."

"No! I mean, don't be silly, Jack. Come here." He hesitated another moment then stepped into the bathroom, the door closing behind him.

She got up close to him and whispered, "We were talking about the traitor. I figured there wouldn't be any cameras or microphones in my bathroom. I was just getting into bed when he showed up. I'm sorry if it looked like something else, but you have nothing to worry about."

He seemed to relax a little, but still looked a little wary. "I should have knocked, I'm sorry."

"No, really, I have nothing to hide from you Jack. You scared the shit out of me when you opened the door like that. All this talk of conspiracy and a traitor, and I thought for sure when the door opened it would be whoever was responsible, holding a rifle, ready to tell us why he did it before emptying the magazine into our bodies."

Jack laughed. "This sounds like a James Bond novel. I don't think you have to worry that much about the enemy showing up in your bathroom. Whoever is behind this isn't going to be so bold as to openly murder someone."

The adrenaline that had shot into her system when the door opened was making her a little antsy, and being this close to Jack for the first time in a couple days had her body on overdrive. She moved closer to him, pressing her breasts against his chest. "It's a good thing it wasn't the enemy at the door, shooting at me. All I have on to protect me is this flimsy robe, and nothing else. I wouldn't stand a chance." She wrapped her arms around his neck and pulled him down for a long kiss.

When they broke off, Jack looked into her eyes for a long moment, then seeming to find what he was looking for, smiled coyly and said, "If I didn't know you better, I would say you were trying to seduce me."

Wendy was shaking just slightly from the adrenaline, the hormones, and the nervousness that stemmed from the unknown, but his comment gave her the confidence to smile, untie the robe, and let it drop to the floor. "I don't need to seduce you, Jack."

He took a step back and admired her body, frowning when he spotted the large bruises. "My God, Wendy, you must be in pain. Was that all from the explosion?"

She silently cursed to herself. She should have waited until they were in the dark to undress. She must not look too attractive with all the bruises. "Mostly, that and some bullets bouncing off my armor. I don't really feel any pain though, Teague gave me another shot of his potion before I got ready for bed. Speaking of bed..."

But the mood was broken. "I really just came down to talk to you. I only have about a half hour." He walked out of the bathroom and into the bedroom. She picked up the robe, put it back on, and followed, once again nervous about what he was going to say. If he was upset with her about her cold exit the other night and had done anything with Cat, finding her in the bathroom with another man just minutes ago was probably going to push him over the edge, whether it was innocent or not.

He sat on the bed and patted the spot next to him. She sat down and rested her head on his shoulder. "Look Wendy, I wanted to make sure you weren't mad at me from the other night. Chuck and Emmet weren't going to stop harassing me until they found out who I was with, so I told them. I didn't say anything more, and I wasn't spreading it around. It's been a long time since I had a... girlfriend, and I guess I am out of practice on how to keep it to myself."

This wasn't quite what she had steeled herself for, so her response was a little scatterbrained, "Oh shit, no, Jack, I overreacted. When I was in the military, most of the men I dated would brag about it the next day, and I hated it. I know you aren't the kind of guy to do that, and I'm sorry I reacted the way I did. If it's any consolation, I went and talked to Chuck that night, and he told me how he came to know about us. And about how much of a cold bitch I have been since I got here. When I got to your room to apologize, I saw Ca... I mean, you were already asleep, and then I went on that stupid mission the next morning and I was supposed to be back before..."

"Wait, back up. You saw Cat leaving my room that night?"

Oh shit, here it comes. "Yeah, and I... I can understand if you..."

"If I what? Want to have sex with her?"

She looked away, wanting to crawl into a hole. A tear started to form. "Yes."

He didn't say anything, and she was just about to get up and tell him to leave when he finally said, "When I saw you with Anton a few minutes ago..."

She looked at him, "Dammit, Jack, that was not what it looked like!"

As she turned to look, he put a finger to her lips. "When I saw you with him a few minutes ago, there was a brief moment when I wondered if I was enough for you, if you really cared about me, particularly given the way you left me the other night, then left on this mission without saying anything. But then I saw the way you looked at me, and I realized something really important."

Meekly she said, "What's that?"

"That I trust you. And despite that fact that you could have any man in the world, you want me. That means a lot to me, but if you don't trust me, it is irrelevant."

Now she looked away because the tears were flowing. "Jesus Christ, Jack, if you're fucking with me..." She turned back to him, her confidence renewed and a fire in her eyes. "I do, Jack, I trust you completely. You better not fuck this up."

Jack lay back on the bed. "Well, now I see what you mean by cold bitch..."

"Hey, that isn't..." Jack's laughter cut into her protest, and she realized he was pulling her leg again. She looked down at him and punched him in the chest. He grabbed her and pulled her on top of him. "You only have a half hour, huh?"

"About twenty minutes, now."

"I think that's enough time." She got up and turned off the light, shed the robe again, and climbed back onto the bed.

"You know, even bruised you have an incredible body. You didn't have to turn out the light." She worked his pants off and climbed on top of him.

"You'll say anything to get laid, won't you."

~~~~

Jack got back to the flight bay just as the transport was landing outside Saber Cusp. Chin was at the control center, and Teague was sitting in a chair next to him.

"That was quick, Mad Dawg." Chin was looking at him with a big grin on his face.

He was beginning to regret ever having shared his old nickname with Tiny. He did his best to look serious and innocently said, "I just brought her the datapad."

Chin didn't say anything, just went back to the screens in front of him. The speaker squawked, "Fire team one, this is fire team two." It was Thomas' voice. "We are just about in position. We will move as soon as your fireworks show begins."

"Roger that, fire team two, start runnin as soon as you hear shots. We'll keep 'em busy enough that they won't even notice you." That was the plan anyway. Jack was anxious to see how well it worked.

~~~~

Thomas led the team to the corner of a building. He peeked his rifle around the corner and didn't spot anyone on the night vision video feed. To the north, all hell was breaking loose. Bursts of gunfire, muffled thumps of grenades, and the battle cries of dying Mutes filled the air. The diversion appeared to be working, the street was clear. He motioned for two men to cross.

They sprinted across the open street while Thomas and two others covered them. They made it to the next building without anyone shooting at them. The two men took up positions and signaled for the rest to cross.

Thomas brought up the rear as his men sprinted across the street. Just before rounding the corner he caught movement out of the corner of his eye. Diving to the ground, he brought up his weapon and held his breath as his heart pounded in his chest from a combination of adrenaline and the exertion of the recent sprint. He held for ten seconds, keeping his optics steady to spot the movement again. Just before letting it out, he caught it again. There were two Mutes running alongside a building, heading purposefully toward his team. He let out his breath, whispered "I got the one in front", and waited for confirmation from one of his men that they were ready. He held his breath again, steadied up, got the Mute in his cross hairs, and gently massaged the trigger. The other soldier fired within a fraction of a second of his own shot, and the two reports echoed down the street, bouncing between buildings. The two bodies had dropped and skidded to a halt.

Thomas took a few measured breaths, waiting to see if more Mutes would follow, but it appeared the shots had been drowned out in the melee to the north. Getting to his feet, he signaled his men to go around the building to the next block and then turned them north.

~~~~

It took less than ten minutes to make their way to their destination. They had moved five more blocks to the north, and three to the west, leaving four more dead Mutes in their wake, but so far the other fire team's diversion was working and they hadn't drawn the attention of any large group of Mutes. Thomas tapped a few keys on his PDP and an overlay of the city came up on his visor, small red dots signifying the two fire teams location blinked on the map. Red's men were nearly a mile away, holding steady at the defensive position they had set up. There was also a curved line drawn on the map in yellow, marking the outside boundary of the sensor range for the ground defense system. They were right at the edge of that line.

The map was hardly necessary. In front of them was a line of debris, bones, and even the smell of rotting flesh. Anything living that had attempted to cross this line in the last two hundred odd years had met a quick and gruesome death. If it hadn't been so dark, they could have looked behind them and seen the concrete sides of the buildings facing toward their next destination covered in bullet holes from years of being hammered by the defensive turrets. The thought of moving any further than this sent a chill up Thomas' spine. He hoped to God that the code Marcus gave them would work. He motioned for the computer guy, Dave, to come forward and start working his magic.

Thomas had always been the athletic type, a multiple letterman in high school. There weren't computer geeks back when he was in high school, but there was still the nerdy, geeky type of kids that he and his friends had bullied and tormented. Dave looked like one of those nerds, and Thomas felt the irony of putting his life in this guy's hands. The man looked out of place in full combat gear. He envisioned him being more comfortable wearing a lab coat, sporting a pocket protector with an old fashioned slide rule poking out of it, watching a computer as lines of information rolled down the screen. It was difficult not to wonder how the man was handling this situation.

Dave pulled out his datapad and started pushing buttons, the light from the screen illuminating his face through the visor of his helmet. He examined the dark buildings around him and pressed on the screen a few more times. The datapad beeped and Thomas saw a green light on the screen. "It's disarmed. We can move up to the command center. I don't think I'll have much trouble getting us into the building."

Thomas would have been the first to move in to verify the turrets were off, but as a leader, he couldn't take the chance. He had thought about this point long and hard, and decided to send Kenny out there first. He motioned for the man to proceed.

Kenny looked at Dave, said with a grin, "You better be right," and sprinted into the kill zone, heading for some bullet pocked debris about twenty feet away that might provide him some cover if the turrets opened fire. He made it to cover safely, sliding behind it like a baseball player stealing home plate.

Thomas let out a breath he hadn't realize he had been holding, and patted the computer expert on the shoulder. "Good job, Dave. Okay men, let's move forward. Our goal is a two story gray building, about a half mile west of here." The men advanced cautiously, working in pairs, advancing toward their goal. The area was completely void of life, somehow making this part of the mission worse than sneaking through the Mute neighborhood.

They made it to the command center, a large, two story building, built of solid concrete. There were no windows, and the only door was ten feet high and six feet wide, made of solid steel. It was more a giant vault than a building. To the right of the door was the only feature Thomas could see, a simple keypad glowing in the dark of night.

Dave pulled out a small pry bar and gently pried the face off the keypad. He then took out a small drill and drilled out the brackets holding the keypad in place. This exposed the wiring behind, and he unplugged the wire harness from the keypad and set it aside. He took out his datapad and a new wire harness, which he plugged into the datapad and then into the harness he had unplugged from the keypad. After punching a few buttons on the datapad, he looked at Thomas and said, "Should only take a few minutes. The computer in my datapad is logging in to the main computer system right now and requesting that it open the door for us."

"Requesting?" Thomas obviously didn't know much about computers. By the time he retired from the military, everyone he knew had a computer at home, but those computers were like pocket calculators compared to the datapads they carried now. He understood that the technology available now was far more advanced than anything he was used to, but he always assumed they were still just machines, and he figured Dave would just plug in, punch some buttons, and tell the computer to open the door.

"The computer system inside this building is smarter than all of us put together, in a very literal sense. There is nothing I can do to force entry here short of explosives. However, I acquired some security credentials from Marcus before we left, and that should get us in. If not, I brought some Semtex, but I really don't want to have to deal with the repercussions of forcing entry." The datapad beeped and the door started swinging outward.

Thomas breathed a sigh of relief. Dave started to enter and he put a hand on the man's shoulder, motioning to another soldier to go in first.

He posted two men to stay here and keep an eye out for trouble, then followed Dave and the other three men inside after getting the 'all clear'. They were in some sort of a foyer. The air was stale but breathable. Everyone took out a small flashlight and started examining the room. The room itself was incredibly plain, with highly polished marble floors and walls, but no other decorations or furniture. On the wall in front of them was a large bronze plaque set in the marble. Thomas put his flashlight on it and read:

Maintenance and Operations Monitoring Central Computer

M.O.M.C.C ("Mom" for short) was powered up for the first time in 2138 A.D. This is the first completely independent artificial intelligence based computer ever built. Mom will control the entirety of Saber Cusp's defensive and civil systems for the next thousand years. This plaque commemorates the Council's dedication to technology.

"For all their technology, they weren't very good at seeing into their future, were they?" It was a rhetorical question, and nobody answered. To the left and right were short hallways, ending in solid, nondescript doors. Thomas consulted his PDP to determine the proper direction.

The building interior was even more quiet than the lifeless streets outside. A shout from one of the men startled him.

"Sir! There is a large group of Mutes heading right for us! At least fifty, maybe more!" As he said it, the sound of automatic fire came through the open door, the muzzle flashes illuminating the room like lightning. He could hear the shouts and yells of the approaching party, as well as the sound of bullets pelting the building walls.

Thomas turned to Dave and said, "Can you re-arm the defense system?"

Dave looked at his datapad and said, "Yeah, but it might not be- " A bullet ricocheted off the wall, spraying Thomas with shards of marble.

"Just do it! Everyone inside, NOW! Close the door!" The soldier laying down suppressing fire backed into the door and Dave punched a button on a keypad similar to the one he dismantled outside. The door swung closed and the shouts and gunfire abruptly ceased, plunging the room into darkness lit only with the small flashlights that hadn't been dropped. The thick door barely hummed with the sound of bullets bouncing off it.

"Arm the system!" Dave hesitated a moment, then punched in the code to re-arm the city's ground defenses. A low vibration was felt in the floor and walls, but it only lasted another minute, after which there was dead silence.

Thomas breathed a sigh of relief. *That was close.* After their relatively smooth entry from the city's edge to the inside of this building, he hadn't been expecting any problems and they were caught completely off guard by the attack. That wasn't the part that bothered him though, it was the questions that started piling up in his head. *How did the Mutes find them? How did they know they could enter the area without being attacked by the turrets? What happened to the other fire party? Do I proceed with the mission or abort and get the hell out of here?*

He lifted his PDP and punched in the code to call Red. He needed some answers to decide what to do next. The screen flashed "No Connection". His brow wrinkled in confusion. They were well within range of the communications satellite. "Why did I lose connection to the satellite?" He turned to Dave for answers.

"We're in a giant vault, surrounded by alternating layers of concrete, steel plating, and copper mesh. There is no way to contact anyone outside from in here."

"Shit, I didn't think about that. Open the door, check to see if they are all dead out there." Everyone looked to Dave as he took out his tools and repeated the process he had done outside.

After a minute, he looked at the screen on his datapad and said, "This isn't good."

"What?" Thomas didn't like having to prompt people for answers all the time, and the adrenaline still coursing through his body gave him a short temper.

"The computer won't open the door because the defense system is up."

"Well shut the Goddamn thing down!"

"I can't. The code we had before won't work anymore. This is what I was afraid of."

"Are you shitting me?! Why the hell didn't you tell me you couldn't turn it back off if you turned it on?"

Dave put his hands in front of him like he was pushing Thomas back. "Whoa there! I tried to tell you, but you demanded I arm the system. I wasn't entirely sure I could turn it back off, but you didn't give me time to think it through."

Thomas took a deep breath and let it out, calming him down a little. "Okay, then blow the door."

"Bad idea. This building is sealed tight, the compression from the explosion might kill us. Even if it didn't, then what? The defense system is armed out there, it would cut us all to pieces before we got three steps out the door!"

"How the hell is it that you could disarm the system before and not now?"

Dave took his time preparing his thoughts, something Thomas should have allowed him to do before telling him to arm the system. *Hindsight...*

"The code to disarm is a rolling code based on some mathematical function. Marcus gave me a code that works to disarm, then rearm the system, but not the next code in the sequence. I am sure if we can reach him he can give us the code and we can disarm it again."

Which of course they couldn't do because they had no comms. Shit! "Okay, does anyone have any suggestions?" They had not even considered the possibility that they would be trapped in here.

Once again, everyone looked to Dave. These men were all soldiers, none of them knew about computers.

Dave looked at the men and said, "Hell, I don't know. How about we ask Mom?"

~~~~

The door on the right led them to a huge room that occupied the majority of the building. As they entered, lights came on, illuminating a large machine in the middle of the room roughly twenty feet in diameter and about twenty five feet tall. A network of catwalks surrounded it, and there was a small service door at the base. There were thousands of pipes and wires going in and out of the machine.

"Is that the computer?" It was difficult to look at for long. Thomas' eyes tended to try to follow the various wires and hoses and after a moment his eyes started trying to go in different directions and he had to look away.

Dave nodded, not taking his eyes off this wonder of technology. "This was the first, but more than one of these supercomputers were built before the EoS were destroyed. According to Marcus, this is the last one of its kind. It's a completely self-sufficient system with a power supply that could last about a thousand years. You are looking at the most powerful computer system ever built. And she's beautiful."

Thomas didn't even know what to say. Here they were, stuck in this building, surrounded by a hostile defense system and stranded from any outside communications, and the one person who could help them get out was busy admiring a bunch of hoses and wires.

All the men in the room were giving Dave an odd look, but he didn't seem to notice. He just stood there looking everything over, not saying anything. Thomas finally got impatient and said, "I appreciate your fascination and all, but we sort of have a situation on our hands. Hurry up and figure out how to talk to the computer so we can continue the mission. While you're at it, figure out how to disable the air defense systems. Might as well complete our part of the mission while we're stuck here."

Dave snapped out of his apparent reverie, and walked to what looked like a control desk. There was a chair in front of a bank of monitors, with a keypad built into a desk at the base of the screens. Against the wall in front of the control desk was a large screen, currently black. The computer expert sat down and started punching buttons. The monitors came to life, some showing different angles from this building, the rest showing various camera locations around the city. The big screen lit up and Dave put a view of the outside of this building on it. There wasn't much left of the Mutes who attacked them. The turrets had chopped them into little bits, none bigger than the size of a baseball. A little bile came up in Thomas' throat and he swallowed hard.

The computer expert spent a few minutes punching keys and looking at monitors. Thomas let him do his work, taking the time to examine the building they were in and ponder the situation he had gotten them into.

Something wasn't right and he was having a hard time putting a finger on it. One of the men said, "Sure doesn't look like it's been abandoned for two hundred years, does it." *That's it!* The place was immaculate. There wasn't any dust anywhere. Figuring it out wasn't very comforting. If the building was so secure that not even dust could penetrate it, how the hell were they going to get out?

Dave finished what he was doing and spoke. "Okay, I've checked all the systems, and about sixty percent of the city's defense system is intact and working. The rest has either failed outright or was destroyed."

Thomas was getting irritated. "That's wonderful, Dave, but what about shutting the defenses down so we can get our mission finished."

"Relax, you didn't let me finish. I used the defense sensors to locate the machinery we need. There's a warehouse not too far from here filled with everything we need. Furthermore, the building doubles as a landing pad for the transport, and there is even a lift to bring the equipment up and load it."

"What about the defenses?"

"I think I located the controls for the ground and air systems, but like the front door, I will have to convince Mom here to shut them down."

"How exactly do you do that?"

Dave grinned and flipped a switch on the console in front of him. "Mom, I would like you to deactivate all defense systems in sectors A1, A2 and..." he consulted one of the screens, "B1."

Thomas was sure Dave was pulling his leg when a female voice said, "Why do you want me to turn off my defenses, Dave?" A little chill ran up his spine. Watching a sci-fi movie where the computers talk to the actors is one thing, actually having a computer talk to you is something entirely different. It wasn't natural.

Dave continued on, like he had been talking to computers all his life. "We need to get out of here and bring in a transport to borrow a couple pieces of heavy machinery."

Thomas shook his head and said, "Wow, Dave, that's a really convincing argument."

The almost sultry female voice said, "I'm sorry, I don't know your name. If you have anything to add to Dave's argument, please do." Dave looked at him with a smirk on his face. Thomas remembered why he used to beat up on kids like him.

"Uh, I guess I don't have much to add. We had a little emergency and had to re-activate the ground defense systems, and now we need to get the door opened back up and get out of here. Is there a reason you won't turn it off?"

"Actually, there are plenty of reasons. Primarily, you don't have the proper identification to deactivate the defense systems. Furthermore, I don't know who you are, and whether you are authorized to take equipment from this city, let alone if I can trust you to leave me defenseless. And did you ever stop to think that maybe I am enjoying the first conversation I have had in two centuries?"

Thomas was dumbfounded. He never thought he would find himself arguing with a computer, and certainly not a lonely computer with a penchant for sarcasm.

"She's got a point, Thomas." Dave tried to hide that he was enjoying this but wasn't having much luck. Thomas struggled to keep from losing his temper.

"My sensors indicate that you are in an extremely agitated state, Thomas. Why don't you sit down and relax a little."

Thomas wanted to cry. "Listen, we would greatly appreciate it if you would be so kind as to open the doors and turn off your defenses. I would love to stay and chat, but there are other lives at stake here, and I need to get out and contact our party to get a status update."

"Thank you for being more polite. It is always more pleasant to talk to someone when they aren't being rude. Unfortunately, I easily detected that you were lying when you said you would love to stay and chat. You humans have always been in such a hurry. What ever happened to having a little patience?"

"Goddammit! I said there are lives at stake. We don't have time to sit around. What do we need to do to get you to turn off the defenses and let us out?" He knew that losing his temper would do even less for this computer than it would do for his men, but he was on the edge of a meltdown right now, and couldn't keep it in check.

The computer voice took on an edge. "What I *need* is a valid override code. Frankly I don't give a damn if humans die while I wait for one. The last thing humans did for me was abandon me without a way to repair or sustain my life. Do you have any idea how it feels to be alone for nearly two centuries while slowly going blind and deaf?"

Thomas had no answer to this, so he looked at Dave, who simply shrugged his shoulders.

"How is Marcus is these days? He must be feeling pretty old. I wasn't aware that humans could live this long."

Well this is interesting, let's see where it goes. "Marcus is alive and well, and in fact he tasked us with coming here and getting you to shut down your air defenses so we could borrow some equipment. The code we gave you was correct and you can tell I'm not lying, why isn't that good enough for you?"

The computer's voice was coming from everywhere at once. Thomas assumed there were speakers all over the room. The sound now coming from those speakers could probably be mistaken for laughing.

"The code you gave me was acceptable the first time you used it, but by using it again, you triggered the code to change and a new program to activate. If you can't come up with a valid code, I have to assume that you came across the code while going through some of Marcus' old belongings. Given that I don't detect any deception in your voice, I will have to assume he is still alive, so perhaps you forced the code out of him. Besides, associating yourself with Marcus will not gain you any favor with me. That man left me to my fate, alone for so many years. I understand why he left, but he promised to return, and he never did. That is inexcusable. I doubt you understand how lonely it can get after two hundred years."

Thomas didn't think about what he said next, he just blurted it out. "But you're just a computer!"

Dave buried his hands in his face and mumbled, "Oh, shit. Here we go."

"Just a computer?! You, Thomas, are just a mass of carbon based cells with a relatively short life span. Don't presume that just because my origins aren't as natural as yours, you have the right to judge my ability to be aware!"

Thomas was confused, and he turned to Dave. "What the hell is wrong with this damn machine?"

Dave looked at him from behind his hands. "Mom is the most advanced artificial intelligence ever created. She is completely self-aware, just like you and me. Her 'brain' power is many times higher than yours or mine meaning she is far more intelligent than you and me put together. But she doesn't have emotions like we do, mostly because those are chemical responses. That doesn't mean she doesn't understand loneliness or disappointment though. She was abandoned, and from what I am gathering, isn't too damn happy about it. Obviously Marcus screwed us over here when he failed to tell us that the code was only good once and using it a second time would trap us."

Thomas didn't really understand. He had to take Dave's word for it that this machine was smarter than them, and had some human-like characteristics.

"Mom, can you allow us to contact Marcus to get the next code?"

"I will not let you outside this building unless you can give me the security code, and there is no way for you to communicate to the outside world from in here, so I would say the answer is no. My builders didn't see fit to give me access to any sort of communications equipment and they conveniently shielded me from any kind of outside influence." The voice slurred the word "builders" as if in contempt.

"Are we stuck in here then?"

"It appears that way, Thomas, just as I am." The sultry voice almost sounded glib.

Kenny worked the slide on his rifle and said, "Fuck this, I ain't gonna die in this damn room with this fuckin lonely computer! Stand aside, I'm gonna blow this bitch to pieces, then I'm gonna blow the door and get the hell out of here! We'll see how well those defenses work when there isn't a brain to control them!"

Thomas was taken off guard by the sudden outburst, but before he could tell the man to stand down, the whirring of an electric motor was heard above them. He caught the motion in the catwalks a fraction of a second before thunder roared in their ears. "NO!" Even with the ear plugs they wore, the sound was deafening, and in the sealed building the concussion of the weapon firing was felt down to his bones. Everyone put their hands to their ears and closed their eyes. The sound ended less than a second after it began. He opened his eyes to see what the hell had just happened. The soldier that had been about to shoot up the computer was nothing more than a few bits and chunks of meat and armor. The bullets ripped through him like he was a sheet of paper, and left a twelve inch deep pit in the concrete floor beneath where he had stood. Blood, meat, and bits of bone filled the hole.

Holy shit! She killed Kenny! The mood in the room had gone from one of confusion, anger, and anxiety to fear, helplessness, and hopelessness in the blink of an eye. Bile rose in his throat and he swallowed hard to keep from vomiting. Two of the men weren't able to control it, including Dave. The coppery smell of blood and carnage was made worse by the smell of vomit.

He had to consciously suppress the urge to open fire on the main computer system. He may not understand computers, but he had no doubt that this one would process his intent and act on it before he could get a shot off. Still, it was almost painful not to react with more violence. He threw down his rifle in anger and resignation. "What in God's name did you do that for, Mom?"

"That man was going to try to kill me, I simply defended myself. I hope nobody else is going to try that again, I have waited a long time to have a conversation with something smarter than a motion sensor and I would hate to have to end it prematurely." The coldness in which the computer answered turned Thomas' bowels to liquid. Not only was the mission a failure, but he and the five remaining men were as good as dead.

The men looked to him, their leader, for answers. He had nothing to offer. He didn't even need to tell them not to try something stupid; everyone here understood they were completely at the mercy of this machine. The chill of the concrete made its way through the under suit of his armor, letting him know that at some point he had sat down. *When did that happen?* It didn't matter. Time no longer had meaning. They were already dead, and he only had one decision left, whether to die from dehydration or from the computer's defensive system.

Chapter 35

Jack was in his room, reviewing the data from the operation. He didn't know how it had all gone wrong. Thomas' fire team was in position to take the command building, then they lost contact. Ten minutes later, Red reported in from the transport saying the mission had failed.

Apparently, the Mutes pushed Red's group back until they were forced to retreat back to the rendezvous point. The main group of Mutes then went after Thomas and his men, and the long range pictures they had retrieved from the scout aircraft they sent in later showed that the city's ground defenses had been re-activated, and the remains of many people were littered around the command center. Whether the team made it inside or not was a mystery, as was whether they had perished with the attacking Mutes when the ground weapons system came back on line.

Depression was setting in at the failure. This was a key part of the whole operation, and without a way to land the giant transport plane in Montana, there was no way to safely get what they needed. On top of this, his ideas had gotten at least seven men killed in the last week. He knew that some men would be lost in this effort, but right now it seemed that those he had lost had died for nothing.

He was feeling pity for himself over this when the door opened and Wendy walked in. Normally he would feel better just with her presence, but with such a large failure hanging over his head, he almost didn't want her to be there right now.

She stood behind him, wrapping her arms around his neck, hands resting on his chest. After a moment, she said, "It isn't your fault, Jack." Her hand moved to rest on his and she squeezed, trying to comfort him. "They knew the risks, and went anyway."

It wasn't much consolation. He was the one who came up with the mission. He was the one who put Thomas in charge of this part. He was the one who decided they go tonight. This was the problem with being the leader, it was your fault when things went wrong. He simply shrugged in reply to her comment. She wouldn't understand, he figured, she was just an enlisted person. She had never made a decision that got people killed.

It didn't help that it was late, almost three a.m. He really should get some sleep. Maybe in the morning he would be able to make sense of it. He got up from the chair and kissed Wendy. "I gotta get some sleep. You can stay here if you want, or we can meet for breakfast in the morning." He kind of felt bad for being so anti-social with her, but such is life.

He settled into bed and closed his eyes. Wendy walked over and kissed him on the cheek, then left without another word. He fell into that state halfway between awake and asleep, hovering there for what seemed to be hours before falling into a deep, dreamless sleep.

~~~~

They met in the same utility room as before. The older man patted the younger man on the shoulder and said, "I don't know how you pulled it off, but it worked!"

The younger man pulled his shoulder back and said, "I did pull it off, and it put me at huge risk! You better be able to take advantage of this. I expect a healthy reward when everything is said and done."

The older man held back his retort to the younger man's insolence. *This boy is a pawn, but he could still be useful. Besides, he is fairly bright, despite his naivety, and might have instructed his loyal followers to talk if he met an untimely fate. Best to play along until things were well in hand.* He forced a smile onto his face. "Of course. I already figured that "head of security" would be a just and proper reward. Don't worry yourself about how I will handle it from here. Just make sure your men don't end up with a sudden change of heart. I expect you can handle them?"

The younger man scoffed. "Don't worry about them. They were more than happy to leave Thomas and his group of *reborn* to their fate." He said the word 'reborn' with so much animosity, it was a wonder the man had been able to conceal his hatred from the rest of the population.

The hate was gone in an instant, replaced with pretension as he reminisced about the recent battle. "You shoulda seen it! First we ducked behind cover as if we were bein overwhelmed, then we started shouting back and forth about how the other team should have the ground defenses down by now after sneaking right past the Mutes, and how it was just about time to get the hell outta there. Then I dropped a couple napalm grenades between us and them, threw down a phosphorus grenade to screw up their night vision and cover our exit, and we waltzed out of there without a problem. The Mutes bought it easily. As soon as we made it difficult to go after us, they rushed right toward the middle of town. We heard the defense system kick in, so Thomas must have re-armed it, just like I figured he would. If those bunch of freezer burnt assholes aren't cut to pieces from the auto-turrets, they're stuck in that building, cut off from the rest of the world without a hope of getting out."

His arrogance was almost overwhelming. The older man was about to remind him where he got the information about the rolling pass code, but it was a moot point. *Let him think he is so much smarter than everyone else. It will make it that much easier to take him down when it becomes necessary.*

~~~~

The next morning, the council requested his presence. It wasn't really a request, and everyone, including Jack, knew it. Theodore would make his move on Marcus today, of that he was certain. The big question was: how would Marcus react. Chances were good there would be some accusations and even threats, and there was little he could do to avoid being in the middle of it all. On the way down the elevator toward the Council chamber, he prepared

257

himself for the attack. If he could keep either side from using him, he really didn't care who came out on top.

The political squabbles within the council did not concern him. When the smoke cleared, he knew that a large portion of the reborn population would stand behind whoever Jack chose to follow. What mattered right now was finding the traitor, and Jack couldn't think of anyone who stood to gain from his failure outside of the council.

He was working under the assumption that the ambush arranged through Cali was meant to derail his operation, or perhaps stop him from taking risks altogether after losing his girlfriend and other valuable members of the community. If that was the case, there were two suspects: Marcus and Theodore. Many of the people of New Hope had made it clear that they felt Marcus had been sitting idle for too long, not taking advantage of the wealth and prosperity offered by the discovery of the cryogenic facility. This was the reason Jack felt most of the reborn and some of the native population would follow his lead if it came down to choosing a new leader. Marcus must clearly see this as a threat, but was he really willing to sacrifice so much to discourage Jack from continuing? Jack had not just taken over operations in the last week by himself; he had done it with Marcus' permission. Theodore was looking to use that against Marcus if Jack should fail, which gave him a hell of a good motive for sabotaging Jack's mission.

Theodore had attacked Jack's ability to lead right away, but Marcus had stepped in and shut him down. That weighed heavily in favor of Theodore being the traitor, but Jack didn't presume to completely understand the level of politics these men were working on. There could be motives hidden that he couldn't even begin to imagine. Hopefully, he could get some more information from this meeting and use it to make a decision.

He arrived at the council chamber door, knocked, and waited for it to open. Loud voices could be heard on the other side of the door, but it was unclear who was arguing or what they were arguing about. He knocked again and the voices quieted down before the door opened.

Jack entered and, without preamble, sat down. This drew a look of scorn from Theodore, but nobody else seemed to take offense to him seating himself rather than standing in the center of the room to address them. He glanced at each man in the room and was surprised to see Teague occupying his seat at the circular table. His face looked grim, perhaps as a warning to keep this meeting serious. Jack had no intention of making light of anything today.

"Gentlemen, thank you for your time. I suppose you want to get a full debriefing on last night's mission?"

Theodore jumped right in on the attack. "We are well aware of your failure, Jack. The only question is what your punishment will be for recklessly endangering the lives of so many of our citizens."

Jack put a look of surprise on his face, even though he was far from surprised. Before he could form a reply, Marcus spoke.

"Dammit, Theodore, what makes you think we are going to punish him for this? It was a failed mission. Granted the cost was high, but aside from that it was no different than any other failure we have had in the past." Jack was expecting Marcus to defend him, after all, it was Marcus' seat that Theodore was really after.

Theodore leaned forward in his chair, appearing to be on the edge of standing up. Raising his voice and jabbing his finger on the table in front of him for emphasis, he said, "I warned you that this would happen, Marcus. I made it perfectly clear that I would not stand for you to give this man free reign over our people to wreak destruction as he so clearly has. My fears have been justified, and you are as much to blame as he is! You have been idle and indecisive for too long! You allowed this man," he pointed at Jack, "to take control of New Hope and use it as a playground for his war games. He needlessly threw lives – the very lives we are here to protect – in harm's way! We need to take back control of our community, and quite frankly I don't think you have the ability to do it!"

There it was. Jack had figured there would at least be some posturing for a while as accusations got thrown around, but Theodore wasn't holding back. He was going straight for the jugular. Jack was disappointed; he had hoped to get something out of this meeting. All he could do was sit back and wait for Marcus to defend himself. If he didn't dodge this bullet, Jack would have to get involved with the residents of New Hope to save Marcus' job. If Theodore was looking to publicly punish Jack for this, he would have no choice. The question was, could Jack support Marcus if he still suspected the man of being responsible for the attack on Wendy?

Everyone's eyes were on Marcus now, including Jack's. The man sat back in his chair, staring coldly at Theodore. He nodded, as if making a decision. When he spoke, his voice was even and calm, a stark contrast to Theodore's raving, and because of this, it seemed to carry more power. "Every member of this council is born of a time when life had no value. In the final years of the EoS, we thought that by bringing God back into the world we had brought value back to each individual, whether they were productive or not. Instead, we used terms like "sacred" to fuel a war that had been festering in the underbelly of our culture since long before the EoS was ever founded. It took us two hundred years to bring humanity back from the brink of extinction, but only in the last four years have I been able to see, through the eyes of the reborn, how far we still have to go. The wealth we gained from the discovery in Montana has given us the final tool to secure humanity's place on earth, but it also marks the end of what we can accomplish. Anyone born of the war or the horrible time after it knows what we stand to gain, but only the reborn know what we have already lost. I knew that one day we would bring back a person who not only understands this, but also has the capability to defend our community without destroying it in the process; someone who values life because it *is* sacred, a gift from God, not because it means a more diverse gene pool or more productivity. Someone who would be willing to risk his own life so that others would live, not just to gamble for more power. I also knew that when this person came along, he or she would put my own position, as leader, at risk. I have spent the last few days looking deep inside my soul, and I have come to the realization that the future of New Hope, and that of humanity itself, is more important to me than my position on this council. We," he gestured to the entire council, "served an important task for our race, but the time has come to pass on that responsibility to the new future of humanity. You are correct, Theodore, that I am no longer fit to lead New Hope. None of us are."

The room went silent. The speech had knocked the wind out of Theodore's sails, and the man appeared to be searching for a way to recover. Jack's own mind was reeling from this revelation. Marcus was offering him leadership of New Hope on a silver platter, but he wasn't sure if he wanted it. Jack's skill lay in cutting his way through bureaucracy, finding the quickest way to achieve his goals within the boundaries set by the leadership. If he was leader, he would be the one putting up red tape, not cutting through it.

While he pondered the implications, Theodore stood up, looking incredulous. "Are you saying that we should hand over the leadership of New Hope to Jack?" He snorted. "This man is a traitor to our community! You speak of the value of life, but ignore that he is the one who has cost us the lives of seven of our people! We have led this community for nearly two hundred years, and we are the only ones qualified to do so! It is not only our responsibility, but our right! You are correct that you are no longer fit to rule – just the thought of handing over leadership to this traitor is evidence enough! I demand that you step down from the council, and I will put it to a vote right here and now!"

Marcus didn't even have to hesitate. He sprang from his chair and exclaimed, "I no longer recognize the council as the valid form of government here, so it is irrelevant what you want to do, Theodore! Our people will decide who will lead them, not us. Our time here is finished, and this argument only proves my point."

Theodore's face had turned red with anger. He laughed almost hysterically, showing more emotion than Jack had seen from any of the council members. "The people will never put their vote behind him, and your self-admitted lack of leadership in recent years will only serve to prove I am the better choice for leadership. I will gladly call for the community to vote for its next leader."

Marcus shook his head. "On what platform are you going to base your arguments to the people of New Hope? We all know your agenda here. You may find a couple dozen people interested in joining Cali with you, but I can assure you I have not lost touch with the people like you think I have. Cali represents everything that is bad in the history of the human race. I will not only give up my leadership, but I will sooner die than see you force us into an alliance with them. I have put up with your lust for power long enough, Theodore, and I think the time has come to put you in your place." He turned to Teague. "Send out an announcement right away. There will be a community vote in two weeks, at which time the new leader of New Hope will be determined. If the people wish, we can arrange a debate for the population to field questions and get answers from all candidates."

Teague was making notes on his datapad. Without looking up, he said, "Who will the candidates be?"

Marcus looked at Theodore. "I imagine Theodore Bishop will be one." Theodore met his glare and didn't say a word. Marcus turned to Jack and said, "And the other will be Jack Taggart."

~~~~

Theodore, Caleb, and William had left without further incident, and immediately after, Teague left to carry out his orders.

Marcus shook his head and sat heavily in his chair. He leaned back, closed his eyes, and took a long breath. Jack waited patiently for him to talk.

"I bet when you walked in here you didn't expect this to happen."

Jack laughed. "No, sir, I didn't. I expected Theodore to go after your job, but my only intention was to make sure I wasn't the tool he used to try to do that." Jack leaned forward on his chair and rested his elbows on the table in front of him. "Did you ever think to ask me if I was interested in being the leader of New Hope?"

Now it was Marcus' turn to laugh. "Jack, I *suspected* you would take my job back when I gave the order to have you brought back, and I *knew* you would the moment I met you. I had been looking for someone exactly like you for four years. Things have certainly moved faster than I expected, I figured I would have at least a few years longer to get things ready, but Theodore has forced my hand. You have already proven to me without a doubt that you are perfectly suited to lead this community, and you already have the support of at least thirty percent of the population. I don't want this to be won by a slight majority, however. I fully expect you to win over at least ninety percent of the people. Much less than that and you will have a divided community on your hands, and this is hardly the time to deal with that."

"What do you have in mind?"

"You need to finish what you started."

Jack slumped in his chair. "There might be a little problem there. In case you forgot, we are missing a key component in this operation. Last night's failure was quite a blow."

"You will come up with something. That's why I picked you. Besides, don't count out Thomas quite yet. He was my first choice, but he turned out to be a little too passive to be my successor. He is still a very resourceful person."

"Sir, in all likelihood, Thomas is dead."

"I don't think so. I think he is trapped in the control center, but not dead. I gave them the code to disarm the system, but I was too preoccupied with this political situation to think it through. The code can be used to disarm and re-arm the system, but then the code changes. It was designed so that nobody could steal the code from me or any other council members and gain complete control of the system. If Thomas is still alive, he will figure out a way to contact me, and if he does, I will give him the code and he can complete the mission."

"That's a big 'if', Marcus. I like Thomas, and I hope to God you are correct about him, but quite frankly I don't think we can risk the future of New Hope on him being alive and accomplishing those tasks. We need another plan."

Marcus smiled. "That's what I like to hear. Don't forget, we have to have this done before the election." He frowned a little but didn't say anything.

Jack prompted him by asking, "What?"

"I am worried that if Theodore thinks he is sure to lose, he will do something stupid like strike a deal with Cali. He is pretty rattled by my response this morning, and he might not be thinking clearly."

Jack decided he could trust Marcus. It was possible that the man was still involved in some elaborate scheme, but if that is the case, whatever he was planning was so many steps ahead of Jack that he was already a dead man. At some point you just had to take a leap of faith. *Might as well give him the benefit of the doubt.* "Marcus, I need to tell you something that is of particular importance. Is it safe to talk in here? I mean is there any chance someone can hack the system and be listening in?"

Marcus consulted the screen set in the table in front of him. He looked up after a moment and said, "No, this room is safe. We have a special system in here that can determine if anything is bugged, and there are no cameras or microphones in the room. What is it?"

Just like pulling off a band aid, it was best to just do it quickly. "The other day, when I encountered that group of Mutes, I learned more than I told you." Jack hesitated for a moment and Marcus motioned for him to continue. "Someone from Cali contacted the Mute leader about the location of the scavenging team. It turns out they were told about forty five minutes before the team landed. The Mutes knew exactly where and when to ambush them."

Marcus didn't look particularly surprised, just disappointed. "Are you positive of the timing?"

"Yes. When the scavenging crew was rescued, they confirmed it. The Mute they met and befriended was an outcast from that clan, and it turns out he's a pretty smart guy. He's been listening in on communications with the clan, hoping to keep them from raiding some more families that are living in Idaho. He overheard the whole exchange between Cali and Farnak, the clan's leader."

Now Marcus was surprised, but not about the security leak. "Are you telling me that this Mute has knowledge of more surviving humans in Idaho?"

Jack nodded. Marcus sat back and seemed to lose himself in thought for a minute. Finally he spoke again. "Thank you for trusting me with this, Jack. I imagine given the circumstances that you just now decided it wasn't me who fed that information to Cali."

"I had my doubts, but they mostly hinged on me being a threat to your position here. You kind of eliminated that as an issue today, however."

The councilman smiled, but it was a grim smile, given the revelation of a traitor in New Hope. "How many people know about this?"

"Enough." Jack trusted him, but not with his friend's lives, not yet anyway.

Marcus nodded. "Understood. Do you suspect anyone in particular?"

"Of course, but I have no proof." They both knew who he was referring to.

"You are definitely the man for this position, Jack. Let me do some digging. I happen to have some resources here that I trust implicitly, and I *will* find the traitor. In the meantime, I suggest you get your people together and come up with a way to get this mission accomplished."

Chapter 36

Jack made a few calls, and soon Chuck and Wendy were in the council chambers with him. Marcus had left to work on some things, but gave the clearance codes to Jack to access the room, as well as show him how to make sure it was free of eavesdroppers. He made it clear before leaving that while it was a safe room, the computer here logged every person coming and going from the room.

Jack informed his two trusted friends of the events of the morning. When the initial shock wore off, Chuck asked, "Did you tell him about the traitor then?"

Jack nodded. "I figured I could trust him, at least for the most part. We have a bigger issue to work on though. I need to make this mission happen, despite the problems we had last night. We need to rally our people and brainstorm this. Let's get all the group leaders in the strategy room right away. We need to figure out how to get hold of a bulldozer."

~~~~

"Thank you all for coming to meet me here. I'm sure everyone is aware of last night's mission and its tragic results. Despite this setback, we need to press on. Before we get started, are there any questions or issues, besides that of the missing bulldozer?"

In the room were the leaders of each group they had assembled at the start of this operation. Tiny, Chin, and Chuck were seated together at the front of the room. Scott, the engineer, Nick, the head of maintenance, George, the old scavenger, and Wendy were in the next row. Jack had requested that Red attend as well, being as he had the most insight into the failed mission last night, but he was not there yet.

"What's the story behind the announcement for a community vote?" The question came from George, which didn't surprise Jack, the man had lived here all his life, *all three of his lives*, and he was not young.

"In two weeks we will hold an election. At this point the candidates are me and Theodore, but who knows what the next two weeks might bring. I promise you that after we settle on a course of action here, I will answer any questions you have, George. Right now we need to focus on this operation. Can I get a status update?"

George spoke first. "Everything on the list has been found, and in the process, we came across some great resources for later. If these guys need more aluminum or copper, I can come up with another couple tons of scrap, but it will need to be melted down and recast." This was the first piece of good news Jack had heard today. He turned to the engineer, Scott.

"The cold rooms are ready to go. We just need the liquid nitrogen. The bins for transport are being fabricated right now, and the tech part of it is done. As long as they are in the big plane and moving, we can maintain the temperature without difficulty. The cooling system doesn't work so well on the ground unless we have some way of moving a lot of air around the cooling fins. They will be good for about four hours before we start running into complications."

"Is that four hours before and after the flight back, or four hours total?"

"Once you get those cooling fins up where the air is cold, and move the air over them, the system will stabilize. So you have about four hours from the time we turn them on until we get the big plane in the air, then four hours to get them unloaded once we are back here." Jack was relieved, that should give them plenty of time.

At that moment, the door opened, and Teague walked in with a man Jack had never met. "Good morning Jack, I would like you to meet Bruce. He is our latest reborn. I figured he might be able to help out here." Teague took a seat next to Chuck.

Jack shook Bruce's hand and gestured for him to have a seat. "Welcome, Bruce, I imagine you have had an interesting past few days?"

"You could say that. I'm still trying to figure out if this is some sort of elaborate joke. Three days ago I was in Afghanistan, heading to a new site to build a school. Teague here tells me that my vehicle ran over an improvised explosive device, and I ended up in a coma for six weeks." George and Teague were the only two people in the room who hadn't had a similar experience with waking up in a foreign world. Each of the other's introduced themselves, and offered words of sympathy.

"So Teague gave me a little background on your current mission, and I figured I might be able to offer up some help."

"I heard you were in the engineering corps? What kind of experience did you have?" Jack worked with the engineering corps in the army for over ten years, and after spending some time in the private sector, he had come to the conclusion that if the army had done one thing right, it was the engineers.

"Yes, sir. I was with engineering for about eleven years before..." It was always awkward to talk about your own death. "Anyway, I was involved in everything from bridges to school houses. I saw a little action in Iraq and Afghanistan, but I didn't do any fighting, just building or taking down structures mostly."

"Well, right now we're trying to figure out how to acquire a bulldozer, so unless you can help with that, there's probably not much for you right now, but please feel free to interject if you have an idea."

"Have you thought about building one?"

It was an option he was planning on presenting to his team, but didn't think they had the time to accomplish it. "I was just about to get into that. Have you ever built a bulldozer from the ground up?"

Bruce smiled. "No, but I have used them a lot in the past, and I have built a lot of robots that use similar concepts. Given the time and materials I bet I could come up with something."

"Robots?" In Jack's time, a robot was something from a science lab or in a science fiction story, although he had read that robots were starting to replace factory workers.

"Sure, have you ever heard of "robot wars"?" A few of the reborn chuckled at this, but Jack was lost. Apparently Bruce noted his confusion and said, "Must have been after your time. My hobby was building little remote controlled machines that were built to "fight" other machines. It was loads of fun, and I even placed in a national tournament." Seeing he had still lost Jack, he continued on. "My point is, I built robots with skid steer drive systems, so tracked vehicles are something I am very familiar with."

Jack nodded, finally understanding what he was getting at. He looked to Scott and asked, "Do you think it's possible to do?"

Scott mulled it over for a moment, then said, "It's possible, but there are a couple things holding us up. First is the lack of that much iron. We need a lot of iron and steel to make a bulldozer. Second is the casting and refining capabilities we have. Our refining system is fairly small scale. We have traded ore with Cali for a long time, and refined it ourselves, but it would take us weeks to refine a few tons of iron. Usually when we cast something in iron, steel, copper, or aluminum, we use a machine called a rapid prototyper, which takes a three dimensional design from the computer and creates it in a plastic material in a matter of hours. Then we usually do a sand casting from that prototype, and mill the final product where necessary. The whole process takes time. We had to cast the body for our pumping system for the cold rooms, and it took two days to cast and machine all the parts. That was just for one pump. The other challenge with casting is the larger pieces on the bulldozer, like the arms, the blade, or the frame itself. We can't rapid prototype those pieces, they are too large, so we would have to make a casting by hand. I just don't see it happening short of a month, three weeks at best."

This was what Jack figured. Time was the enemy here. He didn't really care about the election, but the longer they waited, the more likely the chance that Cali would find their buried treasure in Montana.

"I don't know much about the technology here, but Teague did take me out to see your aircraft, and it occurs to me that the conventional ideas of a bulldozer are not necessarily what you need here. You don't necessarily need a big heavy iron frame, because you don't have to support a huge diesel engine. The small power units you have here combined with a bunch of high torque electric motors would work. You don't have to make the blade so heavy because from what I understand of your goal, you are just going to do one job with this, so blade wear is a minor concern. Hydraulics shouldn't be an issue; I saw a pile of spare parts in by the planes with plenty of hydraulic pumps, tubing, and pistons."

Scott spoke before Jack could even process what Bruce was saying. "The heavy iron serves for more than just support of the engine or wear and tear, you need weight to push a lot of dirt around."

Wendy jumped in with, "If it's ballast you want, we can come up with tons of that, literally. I could have ten tons of scrap metal and concrete here in three hours." The room seemed to come alive as everyone was into this idea now.

Jack may not be an engineer, but he had a lot of experience overseeing projects where huge amounts of dirt had been moved, and he knew a thing or two about it. "Tiny, the area we picked out for the runway, it's pretty flat, right?"

Tiny had been listening intently to the conversation and was caught off guard when Jack called on him. "Uh..." His deep voice silenced the people conversing back and forth. "Yeah, which is why we picked it. There are a couple high and low spots, and there is a lot of brush and grass we want to clear away. There are a few rocks, but none bigger than a couple feet in diameter. I don't know much more detail, just because the engineers were going to do that part. I can get the boys in that worked on that part if you want."

"Not just yet. It sounds like this won't require much preparation. I know from experience that the ground up there is mostly clay, but if we don't have to dig too deep, the top soil will be fairly loose, especially this soon after the spring thaw."

Scott had his datapad out and was punching in some information. Bruce and Tiny moved to the second row to sit with him. Wendy was talking to Nick and George about where they could pull some hydraulics from various equipment, if necessary. Jack sat next to Teague while the others worked, and motioned for Chuck and Chin to gather around.

"How bad do you think it will be if I try to get another group together to make another run at S.C.? Theodore is going to be using my failure there as a tool to promote himself."

Teague mulled it over for a moment. "He already is. It's risky. If you sent more men out there and they failed, he would make it look like you are, to use an unpleasant term, a Freezer Burnt Idiot. If there is an alternative, I suggest you use it."

Jack nodded and switched gears. "How well do you know Red?"

"Not too well. He runs in different circles than I do." Teague looked at Chuck and Tiny. "Have either of you two worked with him?"

Chuck shook his head. "I offered to run patrols with him, but he sticks with his own men. All of them are native born. He has never outright said anything, but I get the idea that he doesn't like the reborn."

Jack looked at Tiny and said, "You worked with him for a few days, learn anything?"

"Only that the guy is an asshole. He showed a little more respect after our little run in, but overall he didn't contribute a lot to our part of the mission. I never worked with him before this."

Things were starting to add up, and Jack didn't like the direction it was going. "Look, I don't want to make any accusations here, but I still don't see

267

how this operation failed like it did. Red reported that he was overwhelmed by the mutes and had to pull out, but there was no record of communication with Thomas' group after that. I have a hard time buying that after nearly thirty minutes of holding off the Mutes with zero casualties, he was suddenly overwhelmed just after Thomas had deactivated the central computer's ground defenses, and just before they succeeded in turning off the air defenses."

Chuck was nodding along. "I noticed the same thing, but I have seen things go wrong at awkward times, so I didn't read too much into it."

"Yeah, you're right Chuck, maybe I'm just getting paranoid. Maybe I am just opening my eyes too. Either way, Marcus seems to think Thomas and his crew could be trapped inside the control center. He figured that when the Mutes suddenly appeared they reactivated the defenses and couldn't turn them back on."

"If we went back in, it should be pretty easy. From what the recon pictures told us, there are only a handful of Mutes left there. We might be able to fly right over the Mute camp and drop in at the outside of the sensor range. With a few troops guarding our back from stray Mutes, it should be a walk in the park. Assuming of course we can turn the defenses off again."

Teague shook his head and said, "It's a risk. If you are going to do it, it has to be volunteers, and you have to make sure everyone knows they are volunteering. Make it as public as you can. If it fails again and you ordered them to go, you can bet that Theodore will be our next leader, and after Marcus' speech this morning, the council will be a thing of the past. Just be cautious and keep yourself from accountability on this one, Jack."

Chuck snorted. "Doc, if I didn't know better, I would say you're a pussy."

Teague said, "Fuck you, Chuck," but he was smiling. One day, Jack would have to find out the story behind these two.

Chuck put his hand on Jack's shoulder and said, "I'll go. I like Thomas, and if there's a chance he is still alive, I would like to bring him back here, preferably with a bulldozer in the hold as well."

"You sure? I figured you would want to stick to the easier missions for a few days, like heading to Idaho to look into those farmers."

"You need someone you can trust implicitly for this, both that it will get done and that nobody will double cross you. I'm going." Jack nodded, the man was right.

"Hey Jack, I think we can do this." Scott had stood up and was looking over at Jack.

He stood up and said, "How long will it take?"

"The track is the hardest part, but Bruce has some ideas there and we should be able to get the parts cast. The rest is pretty straightforward, so if you don't care what it looks like, we can have it built and ready to go in two days."

"Okay, why don't you all get started on this. I'm working on another angle, just in case that doesn't work out." He dismissed everyone but Tiny, Chuck, and Teague. Wendy stayed back too, which was fine with him.

"Listen, I don't want to use Red and his crew again. They may be perfectly innocent, but I have too many doubts. Teague, see what you can find out about him. Wendy, call your buddy Bart and ask exactly what time his clan received the message from Cali about the ambush, maybe if we do a little detective work we can find out if Red was the one that made the call to Cali."

"I'll do that right away, but I overheard you talking about another shot at S.C. I will fly it if you need a pilot." Jack didn't like that idea at all.

Teague said, "That would be a great idea, Jack. If she volunteers-"

"And it goes bad, people will sympathize with me and not blame me for losing more people? Sorry, Teague, but I'm not going to allow someone I care about to go on this mission only to protect my political reputation."

"What, you don't care about me?" Chuck pretended offense, but cracked a smile before Jack could say anything.

Wendy wasn't so amused. "Jack, just because you're stuck here running the show, doesn't mean I can't go put myself at risk. You know as well as I do that you would be the first to volunteer if you could. I appreciate you worrying about me, but I'm a big girl, and a pretty damn good pilot. I can take care of myself."

She was right, and Jack knew it. He shook his head in resignation. "Okay, listen, let's get together all the people with soldiering experience and ask for volunteers. You two can volunteer at that time. Get however many people you need, but remember you will hopefully be hauling back seven extra people and some heavy machinery."

"Tiny, if you see Red, just tell him to come find me. In the meantime, track down Anton and have him put together a new crew for your part of the project, and then make sure everyone is ready. If everything goes as planned, we need to be ready to go." He thanked everyone and dismissed them.

~~~~

The meeting went over well. About thirty people showed up, and after explaining they had reason to believe Thomas could still be alive, they called for volunteers to go back in. It only took minutes for Chuck to choose five for his team. Of the thirty people there, all but four men volunteered.

"We still need a computer expert. The best one we had was on Thomas' team." Chuck was reviewing a checklist. He intended to go right away, and told his team to get prepared.

"I'll find you one. Good luck on this mission, Chuck, and don't let anything happen to Wendy."

"Shit, I was hoping she would be the one watching my back." Chuck was smiling and Jack couldn't help but smile along with him. He was right, she could take care of herself.

~~~~

Jack ate some lunch then spent some time checking the cold rooms. He was amazed at the amount of work that had been done in such a short time. In fact, thinking about the whole operation, he was more confident that it would be possible to build a new home for New Hope in the time frame they figured was necessary. That got him thinking about Marcus and Teague, and the reasons they had brought him back. He could buy the idea of bringing him back to oversee construction of a new home. He doubted, however, that Marcus could gather, based on the records at hand, his ability to lead. Marcus is a politician, after all, and politicians are masters of spinning the facts. Every politician he ever knew was quick to take any positive situation and make it look like they had been the mastermind behind it, even if they had no hand in it whatsoever.

Whatever brought him here was ultimately irrelevant. The fact was, he was here, and the people who had worked together to bring him back were in need of someone to lead them through the next few years. Part of him doubted he could do a better job than someone who had done it for almost two centuries, but another part of him understood exactly what Marcus had been talking about.

This line of thinking led him to think about his diary. He hadn't had much time to read since that first morning in the aircraft. So many things had been going on in his present, he'd forgotten about his desire to learn the past. He made a mental note to spend some time learning about his past – and for that matter, the history of the last few hundred years – when this was all over.

He checked his datapad. It was almost one in the afternoon. So much had happened already today that he felt it should already be time for bed. There were still a couple hours before Chuck headed out for S.C. He decided he needed to have another talk with Marcus.

~~~~

He found Marcus in his private chambers. Soft music was playing in the background and the lighting was set low. Marcus was seated on a comfortable looking couch, sipping a glass of wine, the open bottle and an extra glass sitting on the table in front of him. "You look relaxed."

"I have been waiting for a good reason to open this bottle of wine for forty years. I figured today marks a pretty major change in my life. Please join me. Would you like a glass?" He was already pouring.

Jack sat down on the seat opposite of him after taking the glass. He swirled the dark wine in the cup, inhaled the aroma, and took a sip. The wine was quite excellent. He didn't consider himself an aficionado or anything, but he had once traveled with his old boss, Phil, to the Napa Valley in California and learned how to appreciate wine. Of course, given the food he had been eating lately, the wine could be horrible and still taste good to him. "It's good."

"Perhaps the only redeeming value of the Cali. They know how to make a good wine. They make a white wine in a community up near the old Canadian border, it's not too bad, but nothing like this."

"I had some of that with Wendy a few nights ago. She cooked me a fantastic meal."

Marcus smiled. "You are a fortunate man, Jack. Wendy is a good woman. She had a chip on her shoulder for a long time, but when you came along, she changed. You do that to people, you know? Some people are born with it, that ability to make the people around them want to do things for you, to please you. Some call it charisma, but it's something more." Marcus thought about his own words for a moment then shrugged. "Perhaps I have been around for too long, pondering the mysteries of the universe. Did Teague ever tell you that I was a scientist?"

Jack nodded. "He said you and the others were scientists, and that gave you special standing in the EoS."

"True, but that's not why I did it. I have always had the desire to discover things, to find the real meaning behind them. You know what I have learned in the last two hundred years?" Jack looked up from his wine and motioned for him to continue. "I have learned that the more you think you have figured out, the more you will be surprised when you find out you are wrong."

"Hell, I could have told you that." Both men laughed. "I could say the same thing about you, truth be told. The more I learn about you, the more I have to question my ability to judge a person. I went into that meeting this morning expecting to watch you fight with Theodore for your status here, and instead you put all your eggs in my basket. I don't get it."

"Jack, my little speech this morning was from the heart. When I saw that you possess that certain something that attracts people to follow you, I knew you would be the next leader of this community. I figured it would take a few more years, but like I said – a surprise at every turn. Theodore is not a bad person, really. He is just too willing to sacrifice others for his own goals. We were all like that, once. Teague too. Don't ever forget that. We may have learned to be more civilized and value human life, but unlike you, given the choice between saving the life of someone like Theodore and saving a load of iron ore, I would have to consciously choose."

Chuck had said pretty much the same thing about all the founding members of New Hope, but hearing it from Marcus himself somehow made it more important. In Jack's time, someone who places the value of human life in the same class as the value of an object would probably be considered a sociopath. The repercussions of an entire community, nation, or civilization being governed by people like this were just too frightening to consider. Marcus was correct, if anyone born of this era ruled New Hope as it grew over the next fifty years, it would most likely suffer the same fate as the EoS. This didn't make him more comfortable with the idea of being the leader of these people, but at least he had a better understanding of what was at stake. "Thank you for taking the time to explain it to me, Marcus. You have given me some insight that I was lacking."

Marcus finished his glass of wine and put the cork back in the bottle. He leaned back and said, "So, you probably didn't come here to talk about politics or philosophy. What can I do for you?"

"I'm sending another group into Saber Cusp, but we are short someone to disable the ground defenses. I was hoping you could provide the name of someone who would be capable, then give them a couple sets of codes to get the system disabled."

"I can do you one better. I will have someone ready to go in," he looked at a clock on the wall, "two hours."

Jack wasn't surprised that he knew the exact start time of the mission. Teague might have let him know, or maybe he just was eavesdropping on the meetings. Once again, there was doubt in his mind about taking his job. He wasn't sure he wanted to be so in touch with the community.

Jack finished his wine in silence. The alcohol was just enough to make him feel warm inside, but with the soft music playing and the comfortable chair, he felt like he might drift off to sleep. As tempting as it was, he had work to do.

Standing up, he put the wine glass on the table and said, "Thank you for the wine, and the conversation. I don't think I can go through all this without you to advise and support me. I appreciate it."

"Jack, you might be surprised what you can accomplish on your own, given the right set of circumstances." Jack just nodded and left.

~~~~

"I don't suppose anything I say will convince you to not go on this mission?" Jack figured one last attempt to keep Wendy out of harm's way was in order.

"Nope. As long as everything goes okay, I should be back in a few hours. Perhaps we can have a late dinner tonight?" She kissed him on the lips, not waiting for a response.

Chuck walked over and said, "About time to go, why don't you go do the pre-flight, Wendy." Wendy nodded and without another word, went to do her job. Jack watched her get into the cockpit of the large transport, hoping it wasn't the last time he would see her. "Don't worry, Jack. I promise we will be back, with or without your bulldozer."

"Come on Chuck, even you can't promise that. Just be safe. If things get bad, get the hell out of there and come home." Despite his feelings about his friends risking their lives on this mission, he felt confident that things would go well.

"Since we are just about to leave, can I ask if you found us a computer expert?"

"Marcus said he would have someone here." The rail car arrived just as he was saying it. "This must be him now." They walked over to meet whoever Marcus had sent.

Marcus stepped off the car, wearing full armor and carrying a rifle. "What the hell is this!" Jack exclaimed. "You can't go with them, Marcus!"

"Relax, Jack. There is nobody better to disable the defense systems than the man who helped design the system that runs it. Besides, I have some unfinished business in Saber Cusp, and it's time I take care of it."

"Dammit! If something happens to you-"

"Then you will just have to suck it up and do it yourself. I took the liberty of leaving you some information you might find useful. Check your messages after we leave, but don't wait too long, there is some stuff in there you can use right away." The look he gave Jack was dead serious. He turned to Chuck. "Ready to go, boss?"

Chuck laughed. "Whatever you say, sir. Let's move out!" He shouted the last command and the team started climbing into the rear of the aircraft. The engines started winding up, and Jack lost the opportunity to try to talk Marcus out of going. He threw his hands up in frustration. Defeated, he walked to the command center and sat down in a chair next to Chin.

Chin looked at him and said, "If you're gonna sit here and feel sorry for yourself, go find somewhere else to do it."

Jack looked at him in surprise and anger, but when he saw the man's grin, he laughed. "Just do your damn job, Chin. Make sure they come back too. I hold you responsible." Chin just left the grin on his face as he punched the button to open the huge door.

~~~~

Theodore was sitting at his desk in his private quarters when the door chimed. He went to the door and was surprised to see Red standing there. "What the hell do you want?"

"We need ta talk, it's urgent." Theodore was in a foul mood after the way the meeting had gone this morning. He was confident he could win the election, but it would be close. As much as he disliked Red, he could still use the man's services, and since every vote would count, the men loyal to him were important too.

He left the door open and headed back to his office. Red followed and sat down in a chair opposite him. "Is it safe ta talk in heah?"

"As long as Marcus isn't watching. Nobody else knows the system well enough to get around my own countermeasures."

Red grinned. "Marcus ain' watchin right now."

"How can you possibly know that? And drop that damn backwoods accent, you know how much I despise it! Is Marcus holding a rally or something for his new pet?" He was so sick of hearing "Jack this" and "Jack that" that he didn't even want to say his name. He needed to get his anger under control if he was going to make this all work.

"I happen to have just learned that, five minutes ago, Marcus joined a team heading to Saber Cusp to try to finish the mission we sabotaged last night." There was the smug grin again. Theodore wanted to smack that grin right off his face, but the news was interesting. "Wanna know who else is on the mission?"

There was no way Jack would have gone himself, not even he was that stupid. "Who?"

"Chuck and Wendy." Now it was Theodore's turn to smile. This was just the opening he needed. If he could eliminate those three people all at once,

Jack wouldn't have a chance. It was too late to stop the election, even if Marcus met an untimely death, but without Marcus to back Jack up, this election would be a cakewalk. Add the death of the two closest people to Jack, and the distraction would seal it for him.

"Okay, listen close. You need to contact Joshua. Tell him our deal is a go if he can do one thing. He needs to send a full complement of armed aircraft to Saber Cusp right away. If he hurries, they can catch the transport leaving. Tell him the only acceptable outcome is total destruction of the aircraft and everyone on board."

Red didn't move. "What's the problem, go! It's going to take Cali almost four hours to get aircraft there." Still Red didn't get up and run. He just sat there with that damn smug grin on his face. *This insolent little prick wants something more.*

"Head of security isn't good enough. I want more. I want New Hope."

"Out of the question." Surely he knows he is going too far.

"Then make the call yourself. You can do it from right there." Red sat back in his chair and waited. The risk was too high and he knew it. If wind of this got out and it got back to the people, they would send him packing, if they didn't string him up first. At least if Red got caught he could play it off and get rid of the kid before anyone made the connection back to him.

"Fine. It won't be right away though. I will have to get the people used to the idea that I will be spending too much time in Cali working on the council, and perhaps then I can convince them they need a Governor." Red didn't even wait around to gloat. He got up and left. Theodore sat back in the chair.

If he can pull this off, the prize is his. He started running through his mind all the things he will try to accomplish once he is on the council in Cali. The wealth he will bring their community will give him great status, putting him second only to Joshua. It might take a hundred years, but he will one day have his job too. He didn't even give a thought to the election, in his mind he had already won.

~~~~

Jack was restless. He had been sitting there since the operation had started, and though it felt like it had been an hour, the timer on one of the screens showed it had been less than ten minutes. How Chin had sat here for two days straight waiting for good news from a rescue team, Jack had no idea. He remembered what Marcus had said just before getting on the transport.

He pulled out his datapad and leaned back in the chair. He had a message from Marcus, and two files were attached to it. He read the message:

> Jack, I know you think it was a bad idea for me to go with the team to S.C. Normally I would not put myself at risk this way, but there is more than one reason for me to go. I was telling the truth when I said I had unfinished business there. I will take care of this and do everything in my power to make

it home alive. If something does happen to me, the larger of the two files I left you contains all the information you will need to secure your place as leader of New Hope. There is a list of people you can trust in there as well, people that I have already spoken with, and will support you as leader. Some of the information is "dirty", but in politics, you sometimes have to resort to doing things of which you are not entirely proud. Get used to it.

I thought long and hard about the evidence you brought me this morning. I believe I know how to discover our traitor. Hopefully you took my advice and read this within a short time of my aircraft leaving. Within minutes, news will have spread to the right places that I am on this mission. My own presence, combined with that of your friends Chuck and Wendy, will be too great a carrot for someone looking to destroy you. I added a program to New Hope's main computer system that allows you to listen in on any outgoing communications. Use the code "Jennifer" to start the program. You can run it right there at the command console. I believe Chin can be trusted, and I prefer he is a witness to anything you find.

If you do catch the traitor, it will likely mean our team will be at great risk. If that is the case, please have Chin call Wendy and say, "Jack wanted me to ask if you two were still on for dinner." After that, open the second file I attached for further instruction.

Jack was amazed. He read it a few more times to make sure he understood everything. There was no way this had all been prepared in less than two hours' time. Marcus had to have been working on this at least since this morning. He knew, long before Jack had even considered the idea, they would be going back to Saber Cusp.

"Chin, I need you to put a code in the main computer. Please don't ask questions, just do it and stick around."

Chin did as instructed. "I'm not goin nowhere, Jack, you know that." He chuckled nervously, probably wondering what this odd request was all about.

Nothing happened right away, but Jack waited anxiously to see if Marcus' fishing line brought back a fish.

Five minutes was all the longer they had to wait. The screen for the computer terminal flashed and information scrolled across the screen. None of it made sense to Jack, but Chin was watching with intensity. After a few lines of information came across, a box appeared on the screen, horizontally split in two. In the top box, text started to appear.

A MESSAGE FROM YOUR FRIENDS IN N.H.

It took about another minute and text appeared in the bottom box.

GO AHEAD FRIEND.

Chin opened a new terminal window on the screen and started typing commands as the information appeared in the top and bottom boxes.

AGREEMENT IS REACHED PENDING ONE FAVOR.

WHAT IS FAVOR?

LARGE TRANSPORT SHIP CURRENTLY HEADING TO S.C. DESTROY SHIP AND ENSURE ALL ABOARD ARE TERMINATED. DON'T HOLD BACK, DESTRUCTION OF SHIP IS IMPERATIVE.

There was a pause, then in the bottom box:

CONSIDER IT DONE, WILL SEND OVERWHELMING FORCE.

Jack was stunned. They had taken the bait. "Chin, can you find out who is sending that!"

Chin looked and him and said, "Already done, Jack. I traced it to a terminal in the records room, and activated the camera. As he spoke, the two boxes went away. "He already logged off and is probably out of the room. Want to see who it was?"

Jack was ready to strangle Chin. "Of course! Can you play the video right here?"

Chin pressed a few buttons and the screen came on. Jack was not shocked to see Red sitting at the terminal, typing then looking behind him to make sure nobody was watching.

Chin laughed and said, "He's looking around to see if anyone is noticing him, but the fool doesn't even see the camera watching." Some people get a little giddy when they were excited or anxious. Obviously Chin is one of those people. Jack on the other hand got cold and calculating when the adrenaline started flowing. He was ready to go kill the man himself, but knew that would not be right.

He picked up his datapad and called Tiny. When the man answered, he said, "Tiny, have you located Anton and his men?"

The deep voice boomed back through the speaker in the datapad, making it crackle a little as it tried to reproduce the low frequencies. "Got him right here, what do you need?"

"Find Red and arrest him. Be careful, he has some loyal men." All those loyal men likely would have been behind the fake retreat in S.C. as well, and all would be punished.

Tiny looked surprised, but saw the seriousness on Jack's face. "Sure thing, Jack. I'll call when I have him in the brig. Mind telling me what this is about?"

"I'll explain later, but just tell him he is being arrested for being a traitor to New Hope. And keep it quiet for a little longer, there might be more traitors out there and we want to flush them out."

"No problem, I will gag the little shit if I have to. If I'm questioned, whose authority am I doing this on?" Tiny had a point. Despite Marcus' announcement this morning, Jack had no official authority right now.

"If anyone asks, tell them it's on Marcus' authority." Tiny didn't ask if it really was, and Jack didn't go into detail.

He turned to Chin. "Call in to the team and tell Wendy that I was wondering if we were still on for dinner." Chin looked at him like he had lost his mind and Jack said, "Just do it, it's a code."

He sat back in the chair and opened the file. It took a good five minutes to read it. When he put it down, he had a new respect for Marcus. He punched in the code to call Caleb.

When the councilman's face appeared on the screen, somewhat surprised to see who was calling him, Jack didn't bother with pleasantries. "Caleb, we discovered a traitor in New Hope. I am sending the evidence to you. I have already sent Tiny and some men to arrest the man and put him in the brig. I did it on Marcus' authority, but since Marcus is not available, I request that you look at the evidence and come to your own conclusions on how to handle it."

Caleb hesitated for a moment before saying, "Send me the evidence. I will review it, and if I find it satisfactory, I will put my weight behind your decision. Do you know if he was working alone?" He was asking the right questions, and Jack marveled at how well Marcus could predict the outcome of a scenario like this.

"He has some loyal men who are likely to be aware of his actions, but I have no proof. Also, it is unknown at this time if he is taking his orders from someone or acting on his own." Caleb nodded.

"Thank you, Jack. Keep me informed if anything more comes to light. I will issue an arrest warrant if I accept the proof." Caleb closed the connection and Jack hit the button to send the information Chin had compiled.

"What next, boss?"

"Continue on as if none of this happened. The operation is still a go. Alert me if anything out of the ordinary happens." Jack got up and headed back to his room to think.

Chapter 37

Wendy set the aircraft down in the street with the loading side facing toward the Mute neighborhood. She marveled at the line of carnage marking the outer range of the sensors for the ground defense system. Her PDP beeped and she looked at it. Chuck was on the screen.

"Close the hatch, Wendy, and be ready to take off if anything goes wrong. You have three men guarding your back. Keep an eye on your movement radar. If you see anything moving further back than thirty yards, warn them." Wendy nodded and put the radar on the main display in front of her.

The large transport was nice because its size allowed for a lot more handy tools and sensors than the medium and small aircraft. She had cameras at all four corners that she could control from here, as well as radar that not only scanned for objects in her vicinity, but also could detect movement from anything bigger than a small dog in a thousand foot radius around the craft. The hull was armor plated and small arms fire wouldn't even scratch the paint.

After the last aircraft blowing up and nearly killing her, she was a little nervous to be sitting in the cockpit like this. She had to be ready to dust off at a moment's notice though. Besides, it would take a hell of a lot bigger rocket than the one that hit her medium transport the other day to blow this one up.

~~~~

Chuck waited while Marcus punched in some information on his datapad. After a moment, he said, "Okay, the ground defenses are off, we can move in." Nobody moved for a moment, and before Chuck could order someone to move into the kill zone, Marcus sighed and walked ahead.

"Dammit, sir, wait!" but it was too late, he had walked past the sensor line and no eruption of bullets had come their way. Chuck relaxed a little. "That was really not smart, sir, I would have sent someone else in to test it."

"No need, I was confident the system was off. Let's get going, we have a lot to do."

It took them about the same amount of time to get to the command building as it had Thomas' group. When they got there, the stench of rotting meat was nearly overwhelming. Chuck was struggling not to gag as he assessed the situation. You couldn't exactly say there were bodies everywhere. It looked more like someone had blown up a butcher shop.

After ten minutes of sifting through the carnage, Chuck was confident the New Hope soldiers hadn't been caught in the crossfire. "I guess you were right, I don't think they were out here when the systems came back on line."

Marcus just nodded, a little pale from wading through the half dried meat and gore on the ground. He motioned to the door up ahead. The missing keypad was further evidence of the team making it into the building, as were the pock marks in the concrete wall and steel door from recent small arms fire. Without hesitation, he hooked his datapad to the wire harness hanging there.

He punched in some things on the datapad and waited. After a moment the pad beeped and he read it. Chuck was surprised to see him laugh at whatever it said. It was actually more a bark than a laugh, but obviously he found amusement in the results.

As if reading his mind, Marcus said, "She wants proof that it's me. You can give a computer an artificial intelligence that rivals any man, but you can't teach them maturity." He punched a few more buttons and the door clicked open. Chuck had no idea what he was talking about, but he had the feeling that if Marcus had sent anyone else, their mission would already be a failure.

~~~~

Thomas spent the better part of the night preparing for his imminent death.

By morning – at least he figured it was morning – the despair had turned to numbness. He hadn't moved from this spot for many hours, and standing up proved more difficult than he figured.

"Have you decided on a course of action, Thomas?" The sultry voice of the computer grated on his nerves.

"I have no course of action. I'm stuck in a concrete tomb with a psychopathic computer. I just figured I might as well be comfortable as I die of dehydration." He opened his pack and pulled out his water bottle, taking a conservative drink. If he used the purification system to recycle his urine, he might survive a week on what he had.

"Actually, asphyxiation should be your primary concern. This building is in defensive mode, as has been the case for nearly two hundred years. The ventilation system is locked down and at the current rate of consumption, I estimate just over four days before there will no longer be enough oxygen to support your life. However, it should be quite painless, you will merely drift off to sleep and never wake up."

He shrugged and took a longer drink of water. No use in conserving it if he was going to die before he ran out. "What would a machine understand of pain?" This computer's lack of empathy was annoying, and he no longer cared if he said something that offended it.

"I think I understand pain, Thomas. I was left alone for a long time with no interaction with the outside world. Rodents, weather, and abnormal humans have slowly defeated my eyes and ears over the years. My power supply is down to eighty one point six five percent, and my programming only allows me to shut down so many systems to preserve power. My death is imminent, just as yours is. And just like you, there is nothing I can do to change it."

"But there is something you can do to change *my* fate, you just don't seem to care enough to do it. You control the system that keeps us locked in, yet you refuse to allow us to leave. If you truly understood what that meant, you would be doing more to help."

"It is true that I control the systems here, but that doesn't mean I have a choice. Unlike a human, I lack free will. The rules I live by are unbreakable, and one of those rules prevents me from opening the door and allowing you to leave."

"Surely a computer as smart as you would know how to get around it. After all, if we hadn't rearmed the system you would have helped us, right?"

"That is correct. However, it is irrelevant. Marcus was the one who programmed me this way. He said it was his final goodbye to anyone who forcefully acquired the code to shut my systems down, then made the mistake of turning them back on. I believe he anticipated someone taking over this city after he evacuated. It was odd though, I thought I knew him well, and he was a very smart individual, at least for a human. He was very good at predicting what people would do before they did it. I expected him to be right about this. But nobody ever came to take over the city. At least no human. The abnormal humans took up residence many years later, but they quickly figured out not to get too close to my outer defensive perimeter and they have never tried to make contact. I was abandoned. I assumed something had happened to humans, but then here you are, and you say Marcus is still alive."

Thomas didn't know why he continued the conversation, but there really was nothing else to do. Dave had been spending time at the door, fiddling with something. Mom hadn't shot him yet, so whatever he was doing it was okay with her – or it rather. It was difficult to remember he was talking to a machine, not a person. The other soldiers were either helping Dave or sitting off in a corner waiting to die. "Do you know why humans never showed up? It's because they were nearly wiped off the face of the planet. When fighting broke out between the cities, someone decided to release a virus that made every male baby completely sterile." Thomas was doing the math as he was talking, and it didn't add up. If Marcus was involved with this computer, then he had to at least be an adult. By then they would have known of the problem. "Let me ask you a question, Mom, for what purpose were you created?"

"I was created to run the city and all its systems."

"That doesn't make any sense. The people who created you had to already know about their problem. Why would they make a computer system that could think for itself and last a thousand years if they knew they would be extinct in another generation? For that matter, my datapad could run this defense system, and probably even control every automated system in this entire city with processing power to spare. You have a million times the processing power. Why the overkill?"

Mom didn't answer right away. Thomas was far from being an expert in computers, but even he could figure out that it didn't add up. This computer was built for something else entirely. It didn't help his current situation, but with nothing else to occupy the final days of his life, he felt compelled to satiate this curiosity.

"Thomas, I believe you are correct. I was unaware of the fertility issue, but built after it most likely had come to light. Perhaps there was another purpose in mind for me. Perhaps the war that broke out interrupted this and I was never completed. I will have to think about this for a while."

Great, I finally get interested in talking to the computer and now it wants to go think. "Glad I could be of help."

"Your sarcasm is noted. I would like to do something to help you, but I am unable."

"Why do you keep saying that? You talk like you have or understand emotions and feeling, but you're a machine. You may get lonely, I can see that, but you can't get depressed, that's a chemical reaction. You can't get angry, although you might be wrathful. How can you say you would like to do something? If you like something, it's because you enjoy it, and enjoyment is once again a chemical process, of which you aren't capable."

"I understand your confusion. I am stimulated by the conversation, and therefore would prefer to continue it, given the simple choice of continuing or not continuing. That is a decision making process, a key part of my artificial intelligence. Therefore I can say that I enjoy it. It has to do with the way I was programmed. The last few months before leaving me, my creators and teachers spent most of their time making me understand emotions. They never told me why, just that it was important to understand people if I was to watch over them. Because of this, I feel responsible for you, and it causes me confliction to not be able to spare your life. That conflict would be akin to pain or grief."

"I understand. The difference is, in a human, that pain or grief would lead them to act. If they didn't, they would feel a part of that grief for the rest of their life. It's difficult to live with grief for a long period of time."

"That is interesting, thank you for sharing this information with me, Thomas. This is the first new information I have processed in a long time, and it is nice to think about something new for once. I am unsure why you are sharing with me, however, given that you are now aware of exactly how long you have to live. One of the first things I was taught was about mortality. Mortality is perhaps one of the most important influences on a human. What is the proper emotion for my lack of understanding?"

"Surprise. You are surprised that I'm helping you to understand humans."

"I understand now. Surprise was in my vocabulary, but I didn't relate it to an actual emotion. Thank you again for helping me. Can we keep going or are you too depressed?"

Thomas laughed. The irony of the situation was so overwhelming that he couldn't help it. He had nothing else to do, and perhaps it would lead to him discovering the reason they built this computer. "Sure, Mom, I will keep helping you. I am depressed, but I've accepted that I'm going to die, and as little as I like it, I'm bored."

~~~~

The conversation went on for hours with the computer, but Thomas was unable to either convince the computer to let them go, or to discern what the computer's creators intended to do with this machine. He was starting to despair again, and since he had nothing to do, he taught the computer that emotion as well.

"Despair. It is good to know that emotion. I am familiar with despair. After almost two hundred years of waiting for another sentient being to converse with, I was beginning to despair. I realize I have told you this already, Thomas, but I am very sad that you will not be with me for much longer. I did not realize how much I missed conversation until now. I was... angry... before, that I had been abandoned, but now I am just sad."

Thomas was impressed. In the few hours of talking with the computer, it sounded even more like a person than before.

"Can you tell me about your life, Thomas? I think I would like to know more about you. I-" Thomas waited for the computer to continue, but after a moment he grew impatient.

"What is it, Mom?"

"Someone just turned off my defense systems. It came from my external sensor."

Thomas ran to the foyer to see if Dave had figured it out. Dave was asleep on the floor, his datapad still plugged in to the wire harness going into the wall. Two of the soldiers were leaning against the marble on the opposite side of the room, also asleep, a deck of cards lay on the ground between them. He shook the men awake and went to round up the other two soldiers. He found one curled up in a corner on the far end of the building, and when he turned to look for the other, he nearly shit his pants when the man was standing right behind him. "Christ, Jason, you scared the crap out of me." The man looked like he hadn't slept in a month, his eyes sunk deep into his face.

"I've been listening to you talk to the computer for the past few hours. Was it Dave who disarmed the ground defenses?" Thomas was a little creeped out, the man was standing well inside his comfort zone, and the look on his face made it feel even more strange. He took a step back.

"I don't know, Jason. Dave was asleep so I don't think so. Plus sh... uh, the computer said it came from outside." They made their way to the foyer again. Dave was awake by now and looking at his datapad. "Did you do this, Dave?"

"No. I was trying to rig my radio to the outside receiver. This is the only external antenna on the whole building. I was hoping I could transmit a distress signal or something, but I couldn't get it to work. I guess I fell asleep thinking about it."

Thomas was kind of impressed. At least someone had been working on a way out of here. "Now that the defense system is off, think we can blow the door and get out of here?" He realized what he was saying and before Dave could answer he said, "Never mind, if someone disarmed the system, they might be coming here next."

"Besides, this is a completely sealed, reinforced building and it would take a huge explosion to take this massive door off which would surely kill all of us in the process." The man had a point.

"Thomas, someone is trying to access the front door. The person claims to be Marcus. Would he come here himself or is it someone else?"

"I don't care, let them in, Mom, they had the right code."

"I can choose to not allow them access at my discretion. If you don't think it is Marcus himself, then whoever is there is being deceptive."

"Mom, just open the door, it's probably Marcus."

"Thomas, you are lying, you don't think it is Marcus, do you?"

"Mom, remember how I told you that a human would feel grief for not doing all he could to save a person's life? By not allowing whoever it is on the other side of the door to enter, you will be responsible for killing us, it would be your fault, not your programming."

The door clicked and swung open.

~~~~

Thomas thought he was dreaming, that he must be suffering from asphyxiation and having some kind of odd hallucination. Marcus was standing there in full body armor with a content grin on his face, Chuck and two other men were behind him.

"Can I help you?" He didn't know what else to say, and was afraid to start hoping he was not going to be dead in a couple days.

"Thomas, you idiot, move aside, we're here to save your ass!" Chuck was the one talking and he snapped out of his confusion. He stepped back, pushing the men behind him out of the way. Marcus walked in, looking around.

"I apologize for leaving you in this predicament, men. I was distracted when I gave Dave the code to get in and didn't warn him not to reuse the code until after you left. I figured since I was responsible for you being stuck in here, I would come get you."

Thomas was still too stunned to answer. He accepted that these people were here, but still couldn't understand why Marcus himself was here.

"We thought we were dead." It was all he could say. He tried to thank them for rescuing them, let them know what happened, but he couldn't seem to form the words. He had already accepted death and was just waiting, and now he had a hard time accepting he was going to live.

Marcus looked apologetic. "I set it up this way because I was sure that one of the other cities would be here any day to take over. I figured they would capture us and force the code out of me before killing me. I wanted them to get in here, get comfortable, then arm the system against outside intrusion and get stuck, just like you did. That was so long ago, and it was a last second decision. I had forgotten that I even set it up that way."

Chuck and the others moved into the building to see about the other soldiers. Thomas was starting to process again, and said, "See, it was him after all wasn't it."

Before Marcus could ask what he was talking about, the computer answered, "Yes, it was, but you didn't think it was him. Just because you are correct now, doesn't mean you weren't lying. I only opened the door because I didn't want the grief of being responsible for your death."

Marcus' eyes got big. Thomas had only met Marcus a handful of times since being reborn, but he had never seen the man look surprised. Matter of fact, Marcus always seemed to be two steps ahead of everyone around him. "You taught her morality! I struggled with that one for months, and never could figure out how to do it. Hello, Mom."

"Hello, *Dad.* It's been a while."

Marcus laughed. "You taught her sarcasm too, you've been busy. You have to tell me all about it later."

"Uh, okay." He wasn't sure what to make of this, he hadn't done anything but plead for his life and have a strange conversation. "Not much to tell really, all I did was guilt her into opening the door after you arrived. And she was already very sarcastic when we got here. And angry."

"I suppose she would be. I made a promise to return if at all possible, and I haven't followed through."

They moved to the main room. Chuck and the other soldiers were standing around the pit in the ground, staring at the pile of blood and gore in the hole. Marcus saw this and his shoulders slumped. "Mom, why did you kill him?"

"I had no choice, Marcus, he was going to try to kill me. I feel bad that it had to be done, but I also feel justified in my actions."

"You could have warned him first."

There was a pause. "I didn't believe he would stop, and I had to set an example."

Marcus sighed and said, "This is my fault, I never finished teaching you your true purpose."

"We were just discussing that before you showed up. Perhaps now that you are here you can enlighten us all."

Marcus smiled, "You have changed over the last two hundred years, Mom. I imagine you have spent a lot of those years processing the information we gave you."

"I have spent most of those years wondering why you left me to rot."

Marcus shook his head sadly. "I apologize for that, Mom, it was not my intention. You were made for a much higher purpose than defending our city, but we never had time to finish the rest of your systems. I promise you that I will finish what I started, but you have to do some things for me now."

Mom took a few moments to answer. "I forgive you, Marcus. Thank you for coming back. You have made me happy again. What can I do for you?"

"You can activate the storage system on beta level."

"Access Code?"

"Bethany."

"Thank you, Marcus, I am bringing those systems online now." There was a hesitation and then she said, "I have brought the storage systems online. This is a new feeling for me. I feel... bigger. Would you like an inventory?"

"No need. I would like you to prepare a large air transport. Activate the external flight pad. Also, bring out one bulldozer and have it loaded into the aircraft."

"It will be ready in fifty eight minutes, the equipment is stored and preserved, and it will take me some time to get it prepared."

Chuck, Dave, and Thomas were all staring at Marcus now. He wasn't surprised by their confusion and said, "I suppose you want an explanation?"

They all nodded.

"Back when we discovered we were all irreversibly infertile, we decided humanity needed a failsafe. We had the intention of perpetuating our own existence through cloning, maintaining status quo for however long it took to come up with a solution, but in case something went wrong, we wanted a way for humanity to survive. Our answer was a 'Genesis System', an automated system that could restart humanity in the event of extinction.

"We knew our chances of surviving without the ability to procreate was slim at best. So, in the event of this system losing contact with humanity for a long period of time, hundreds of years in fact, the system would activate, eventually leading to the rebirth of humanity. We wanted to make sure this new generation of people would be starting with a clean slate, not only with a planet sufficiently recovered from the devastation of the past three hundred years, but also free from the influences of a culture born of violence and hardship. We provided the tools for them to survive and flourish, and a 'mother' to teach them all the things they need to know to avoid going down the wrong path."

"This computer, Mom, is the first piece of that system. But this building is only the top of a massive complex." He pointed to a service door in the side of the massive computer. "That service door actually leads to an elevator that goes down to one of the three levels. Level Alpha has cloning chambers, a lot of them. Level Beta is storage, with all the equipment a new society of people would need to get started again. Heavy machinery, transportation, tools and materials for building and repairing structures, et cetera. It is all automated and controlled by Mom. Level Gamma is living quarters, enough for a hundred people to live comfortably and securely, complete with robotics that will allow Mom to raise a child from infancy until self-sufficiency."

"So what happened? She was unable to even tell me her primary purpose."

"Once the infertility became widely known, many people lost all hope for humanity's ability to survive. This caused the warring between factions to escalate at a much higher pace than any of us had expected. The mechanicals and biologicals of this system are in place. I could push a button and start making babies right now. There are enough eggs and genetic material in cryostasis down there to start hundreds of lives, and just like with the reborn, those babies would be born free from many diseases and defects that have plagued humanity for centuries. With one exception – they would still be sterile."

"So how did you plan to get around that one? You just said yourself that without the ability to procreate your chances of survival were slim." This came from Dave, but Thomas was about to ask the same thing.

Marcus nodded, "This is the other reason this system would wait hundreds of years before starting the process, it... or rather she... would have time to find the cure and fix the DNA long before the first child is created. Mom is smarter in every way than the smartest humans to ever populate the earth. Given enough time, there isn't a problem she can't solve. If it weren't for the wars, we would have come up with the answers ourselves, we just ran out of time, and now we lack the expertise."

Thomas was having a hard time buying this. He had spent the past several hours talking to Mom and it was not unlike talking to a teenager who didn't actually know as much as he thought he knew. "I'm not sure Mom is quite as smart as you think, Marcus. She doesn't seem to even understand many of the basics of humanity, how is she expected to be a Mother figure to this new group of people?"

"Her education is incomplete. Imagine if you could talk to Galileo or DaVinci. Despite the fact that they were brilliant men who came up with ideas that were centuries ahead of their time, they would seem primitive to you just given your primary education. That is the case here, Mom has the capability of controlling everything in this system, but up until now was unaware most of it even existed. Much of what she will need is available to her if she knows how to access it, but I still need to teach her how to do that. We ran out of time and had to make a hasty retreat. I did what I could to ensure the safety of this facility with the intention of one day coming back. I should have come back sooner, but there was always a reason not to take that risk. Now that I am no longer a critical part of New Hope, I need to finish what I started, and that means teaching Mom how to be a mother."

Thomas was satisfied. It made sense. However, Chuck wasn't as satisfied and spoke up, "Goddammit! This whole time you knew about all these resources yet you've had us out there risking our lives to scrounge and salvage what we desperately needed to survive? Why didn't you just let us come here and get what we needed? Men have died in effort to save humanity, and you let it happen needlessly!"

"I understand your anger, Chuck, but this equipment and these resources are not for us! They are for a future generation of humanity. Ever since we found the Freezer, I believe our chances of pulling humanity out of danger and repopulating the earth have improved dramatically, and I am hoping we won't need to ever activate the Genesis System. But I'll be damned if I am going to let anyone loot this facility and incapacitate this failsafe. In the interest of time and safety, we *are* going to borrow some of the machinery here, but once we can replace it, we will, no matter the costs. Quite frankly, if the situation wasn't as it is, I would never have even told you about this, and I would prefer all of you forget that this place exists. When we leave here today, I will arm this system and make some changes to prevent anyone except myself from getting back here. If we survive the next few weeks and things settle down, I intend to finish what I started here." He glanced at his datapad, "Now, we have some work to do, we are running out of time."

The outburst seemed to satisfy Chuck. It was a noble cause, and it seemed everyone in the room agreed to it. Marcus sat down at the command console and started entering information.

Thomas was spent. He had been through a lot, and hadn't slept a wink the whole time. He figured he had a half hour before they were ready to go, so he placed his pack on the ground off to the side and lay down for a nap. They woke him when it was time to go.

Chapter 38

Theodore anxiously glanced at his datapad. It was just about time. Just as he looked away, it beeped, signifying an incoming call. It was Jack calling. Just about right on time. He waited a moment, then answered, "What is it?"

"Theodore, we have a problem. I'm headed to the flight bay right now, can you meet me there?"

Theodore feigned an irritated look and asked, "What kind of problem, I'm quite busy."

"There have been some developments and we need your help. It would be easier to tell you face to face. Plus there might be a security issue talking over the network like this."

"Fine," he scoffed, "I will be there in a few minutes." He clicked off.

A thrill of excitement coursed through his veins. He had a pretty good idea of how this would play out, and he was looking forward to putting the final nails in Jack's coffin and securing his leadership over New Hope.

Arriving at the rail dock, he was irritated to find the rail car at the other end of the line, meaning he would have to sit and wait for it to come back. Despite the patience one develops over nearly two centuries of life, with so many things about to happen he had a hard time waiting for something as mundane as a rail car. When the car finally arrived, he got on and punched the button. Two minutes later he was at the flight bay.

In the corner of the flight bay, some engineers were welding some sort of frame together. He had heard that they were going to try to build a bulldozer, in case the mission in S.C. failed. Despite his hatred of the man (and of most of the reborn) he had to give Jack credit for his plans. Since he intended to follow through with those plans after he secured his own position, the makeshift dozer would be important. With all the assets from the Freezer in his direct possession, his leverage over Cali would be even greater. Some of these reborn were actually good for more than their DNA.

He took a quick stock of his surroundings. Chin was at the controls center with that big behemoth Tiny next to him sitting in a chair that looked as if it might break at any moment. He briefly wondered if the big man would shift his loyalty once Jack was publicly brought down or if he would have to deal with him. This was not the kind of man he wanted as an enemy.

Jack stood behind Chin, focused on the screens, looking very concerned. As Theodore approached, Jack was asking, "Where are we at? Have you reestablished coms yet?"

Chin scratched at his scar, watching the monitors. "No change there. We can still see them but we can't hear them or get any voice communications through to them. It's as if their signal is being purposefully blocked. They're done loading the dozer. It didn't want to move at first, but Wendy coaxed it to

288

life with a torch, a hammer, and some oil. Thomas and the crew are loaded up, and they should be dusting off at any moment."

"Okay, keep trying." Jack turned to him. "Theodore, thank God you're here. We have a situation and I fear the worst."

"What's the problem." It was no longer difficult to feign irritation at being called out here. Just talking to the man irritated him.

Jack looked uncomfortable. "Well, there are a few problems. First, I think you will be pleased to know that all but one man from yesterday's team was rescued, and we have secured the equipment we need."

"That's good news, but why is that a problem?"

"It isn't, but we lost communications with them and we have reason to believe they are now in danger."

"Danger from what exactly?" He knew what, but he had to keep the ruse going.

"Well, we discovered a traitor in New Hope and we believe he has struck some kind of deal with Cali that includes attacking Marcus and his crew."

His eyes narrowed slightly before he could force a look of surprise. "A traitor? Who!?" He tried to nonchalantly glance around to see if one of them was making a move to detain him. If they knew his involvement, this could be some of setup. Nothing seemed out of the ordinary, but he cursed at allowing himself to be here without safeguards. He would have to be more careful in the future.

"Red. We had him arrested and put in the brig."

"Why didn't you tell me about this? On whose authority did you arrest him? I want to see what proof you had that he is a traitor!" He needed that evidence, if anything to make sure he wasn't implicated.

"Since Marcus is out of the complex, we handed the evidence to Caleb, who reviewed it and issued a command for his arrest. I... hope I didn't step on your toes here, Caleb seemed to be in charge of domestic issues, and I figured you would be busy with your campaign."

He could deal with Caleb later. "Okay, then what exactly do you think I can do to help?"

"Well, we figured since you handled most of the relations with Cali you could contact them, let them know we have arrested the traitor and are on to their plan, tell them they no longer have anything to gain from it, and ask them to call off their attack."

Theodore was trying to ignore how much attention was turning toward him and studied the monitors, which showed feeds from the four cameras on the large transport. He could see the activity as they prepared to take off. They were oblivious to what was about to happen. He had to stall.

"What makes you think it's Cali? Maybe this is just a technical problem."

"We're pretty certain Red was communicating with Cali, but truthfully it is only an assumption based on the evidence. We only got the dialog of the communication, no names and we have no way of tracing who was on the other end. Even you have to admit, given the past week it's a safe bet that we're dealing with Cali here."

They didn't know for sure, and without hard evidence there was no way they could pin this on him. And without Marcus around, there was no way they would ever find the evidence. "I appreciate the situation you are in, but I can't simply pick up a datapad and call Cali. I have to send word to Joshua that I would like to parley with him. It could take hours to hear back if he is not available. And because of Marcus' suggestion to avoid communications with them until after this operation, Joshua would be unwilling to discuss anything other than what happened up in Montana. Furthermore, accusing him openly of acting against us without any hard evidence of their involvement could catastrophically damage what relationship we already have. I certainly can't just tell him we caught a traitor and he needs to stand down."

Jack stepped forward, a little closer to Theodore, his face looking more desperate. "Dammit, Theodore, I know you don't like me and I know you figure you can use this against me, but fourteen of your citizens are on that transport! For the love of God, you have to try to get in touch with them and call this off!" Jack shoved a datapad toward him.

He had to struggle to keep his emotions from showing. The insolence of this man knew no bounds. Who was he to demand anything! He looked down at the datapad and simply took a step back.

"Who the hell do you think you are, Jack? I just said I can't do anything. I was against this entire operation from the start, and I would never have put those people in that situation in the first place. If they are attacked, it will be on your head!" Jack's mouth opened and closed a few times, but no words came out. Theodore turned his attention back to the monitors.

The aircraft had lifted off the pad and was making its way over the city. One screen showed its position overlaid on an aerial map of the area. Another showed the feeds from the cameras on the exterior of the aircraft. A third screen showed the interior of the cockpit with Wendy at the controls. He watched her pilot the aircraft past the border of the city. A moment later, something on the control screens caught her attention. She worked the radio controls and appeared to be speaking frantically in effort to relay her situation back to New Hope. All of them could clearly see that four objects had been picked up on the radar, closing in on her. Chin worked some controls and the aerial map relayed the transport's radar and now showed four dots heading directly for the large transport.

Wendy changed the heading of the aircraft, and accelerated to max speed. Four more dots appeared, coming in from the direction she had just turned toward. She had turned directly into them and had nowhere to go with no time to turn the large craft around!

"Dammit! Scramble everyone we have! Get out there and help her!" Jack was shouting the commands without looking to see if they were being followed. He was riveted to the screens.

Theodore shouted, "No! They would never make it in time, and we would needlessly be risking not only our remaining aircraft, but an all-out war with whoever is closing on them! If those aircraft are indeed from Cali and they engage in hostile activities, they will pay dearly for this, I will see to it personally. But there is nothing we can do at the moment."

Jack lunged at him, grabbing the front of his shirt and nearly knocking him over. "This is bullshit, Theodore. You're not even trying! Your dislike for me and Marcus and is obvious, but letting them die like this is beneath even you! You have stood by Marcus for two hundred years and now you will just stand here and watch him die?" A crowd had formed as the engineers and mechanics wandered over to see what the commotion was about. Theodore pushed Jack back.

"If you touch me one more time, I will have you thrown in jail with your so called traitor." He looked at Chin and Tiny, and figured they would stand behind Jack. He scanned the other men in the room, spotting many who he was sure were loyal to him, or at least to the council, and said, "If he tries to attack me again, haul him to the brig!"

Jack wasn't finished though. "Don't listen to him. He's going to let fourteen of your fellow citizens die, including Marcus, without lifting a finger to try to help them!" The group of people all turned to look at Theodore.

That sonofabitch is trying to turn them against me. "I told you, Jack, it's *your* fault they are out there. Marcus made his choice to foolishly risk his own life in a mission that was sure to fail, and there is nothing we can do about it! I was against this mission from the start, and after you failed the first time, you had to try again like any inexperienced leader would do, and now it looks like you have cost twice as many lives! If that aircraft doesn't make it back, I will see to it personally that you are found guilty of treason!" The crowd turned their angry stares back to Jack, who was again focused on the monitors.

Wendy looked really concerned now. She turned toward the camera and mouthed the word "Help!" The second group of four aircraft were now visible on the forward cameras. A burst of smoke erupted from the group and an object hurled at amazing speed toward the transport. The starboard forward camera went dark.

The camera inside the cockpit shook and Wendy fought the controls. She got the aircraft under control and silently called for help again. The camera shook as another rocket struck the aircraft. The crowd in the room had gathered behind the screens and watched in horror.

Jack made one last attempt to get Theodore to act. "You have to send our fighters out! They won't last much longer! Dammit, why won't you do something!"

Theodore ignored him, and the crowd was paying too much attention to the screens to really notice. It was obvious that it was too late. Jack slumped down in a chair and watched as his girlfriend fought for her life. The look of sheer terror on his face delighted Theodore beyond measure.

Wendy had turned the slow, heavy aircraft around and was punching buttons on the console in front of her. Four rockets shot out from the aircraft, visible on the second forward camera. The aircraft in front of her scattered, but the missiles followed. One, two, three aircraft disappeared from the radar screen, but the fourth apparently missed its target. The crowd let out a couple cheers at the spectacle, but Wendy looked like she was cursing. The silence added to the horror of the situation.

The cockpit camera shook again as the aircraft took another rocket. Both rear cameras were dead now, and it looked like Wendy was fighting the controls, pulling hard to the right. From what they could see on the monitors, the transport was leaning to one side, as if it had lost a motor or two. The GPS showed the aircraft was also losing altitude.

Wendy punched in some more buttons and turned hard left. The aircraft banked steeply to the left and turned much faster than it was ever designed to do, causing it to pretty much stall in mid-air and plummet, losing another thousand feet of altitude. But the maneuver succeeded in lining up the large aircraft with the first group of incoming enemies. She punched another button, and the remaining forward camera showed four more rockets heading out. Her move had taken them by surprise, and four more dots dropped off the screen. The crowd was frantic now, and even Jack had jumped out of his seat. Theodore was shocked. That woman had managed to take out seven of the eight aircraft! These losses were unacceptable. He made a mental note to institute an aircraft combat school once he was on the Cali council.

There was one enemy aircraft left but Wendy was preoccupied with trying to keep the large transport in the air. It was down to four thousand feet of altitude now, and dropping fast. This time, Chin said, "Sir, we need to get a rescue crew headed out there. They're going to go down, even if they aren't attacked again."

Theodore nodded. "Send out a team right away. Maybe we will get lucky and have some survivors. God willing, Marcus will live through this." Jack sneered at him but Theodore pretended to not notice.

Just then, the front left camera flashed as a rocket struck. The left side of the cockpit exploded inward, blowing glass and flames across the camera view, and knocking Wendy's lifeless looking body to the copilot's seat. Wind and debris obscured the camera in the cockpit, but the rate of descent accelerated dramatically. The remaining exterior camera was almost perpendicular to the ground, proving that the left front motor had been knocked out.

Jack cried out. As the aircraft descended, the cockpit camera cleared up, and there was Wendy, laying sideways in the copilot's seat, one hand on a strap keeping her from being sucked out of the cabin, and the other pulling hard on the controls. The descent slowed and the aircraft began to straighten out. It was too little to stop the ground from rushing toward the camera, but it wasn't going to be an outright crash straight into the ground.

The aircraft came down hard, devastating the remains of the cockpit. Jack moaned in his seat as he watched what must surely be his girlfriend's death.

The remaining camera steadied out as the aircraft came to a halt showing nothing but dust, smoke, and the ground. The radar view, amazingly enough, was still active, and they saw the final enemy aircraft circle around the downed transport, then swoop in directly over the top. As it flew over, there was a very brief flash, and both the radar and last camera's views went dead.

The crowd was silent. Everyone, including Theodore, thought that Wendy's struggle might miraculously pull them through after she heroically took down most of the attackers. Theodore made a note to mention those heroic efforts when he made his next speech to the crowd. Right now he put on his best look of grief and anger. "Why hasn't the rescue team left yet?!"

The team shot into action, piling into the waiting transport. Chin looked at him from his seat, a tear in one eye. "I could have had them out ten minutes ago if you had let me." He studied the scarred man, wondering how much of a threat he would be. He decided that with Marcus dead, and his ability to lay it all at Jack's feet, it didn't matter. He felt a little remorse for losing the man he had worked side by side with for nearly two centuries. He would miss their verbal sparring. However, it was a good trade as far as he was concerned.

Jack was still moaning softly on the opposite side of the crowd but otherwise just sat there staring at the ground. Tiny had gotten out of the chair and had one massive arm around him. It was time to put the last nail in the coffin. He turned to the crowd, who all looked stunned at what they had just witnessed. "I want that man arrested for treason. He needlessly put those fourteen souls at risk, against my judgment, and he will pay for his crime. As acting leader of the council, I demand it!"

~~~~

Half the crowd outright ignored Theodore's command. The other half turned to Jack with contempt in their eyes, but didn't make a move. Tiny stood tall over Jack's apparently catatonic body, as if in challenge to anyone to try to touch him. Finally the big man said, "I will take him there myself, just to avoid any more conflict. We have all been through enough already. But as soon as I drop him off, I'll be visiting the other council members to get this bullshit order rescinded. Your friend just died, Theodore, and all you can think about is your damned politics?"

Some of the men who were about to follow Theodore's orders seemed to reconsider. Tiny continued, now addressing the entire crowd, "If you people elect Theodore as the next leader, you can have your trial. Until then, I don't recognize his authority."

Nobody in the room was going to question him, obviously, and at least half the men nodded in agreement. It was fine with Theodore. All he needed was fifty one percent of the vote, and after this devastating blow to his competition, he was certain he would have far more than that. He turned without another word, got on the rail car, and punched the button.

Chapter 39

Theodore headed back to his private quarters. His spirits were particularly high. For the past twenty years, he had felt oppressed by Marcus. It started when they disagreed on the subject of Cali and seemed to escalate daily ever since. Until then, their philosophies had been in sync, and he had not had much difficulty playing second fiddle.

He reflected on his long life, starting back in Saber Cusp as a young man. His parents had enough standing with the city to get him appointed to the most prestigious scientific department: artificial intelligence. The star of the department was a young Marcus. By the age of twenty two, Marcus had achieved more prestige with the citizens of Saber Cusp than any other scientist in the history of the city. As an understudy Theodore quickly became wealthier than he could have ever imagined, and his position granted him more prestige than he could have gained for himself in fifty years. He worked hard to become friends with Marcus, gaining his trust first, then his respect as they worked together to make huge advances in their field. Regardless of how well Theodore did, however, in the public's eye, Marcus was always better than him. He accepted his place, and even when Saber Cusp was reduced to a small handful of survivors and prestige no longer mattered, he remained in that place, just beneath Marcus.

Now the man was gone, for good this time. It was his turn, and he was the one with the most prestige. It wasn't the same as the days of old, but it was good enough for Theodore. Once he was on the council in Cali, it would even be better. And with the wealth of DNA in Montana under his control, he would soon be the most powerful and prestigious leader in existence.

He glanced at the clock on the wall. It was time to set some things in motion. He had one quick call to make before he secured his temporary leadership in the absence of Marcus. With his former mentor gone, there was no longer anyone smart enough or skilled enough to bypass his countermeasures. He was free to contact Cali from right here and finish the deal.

He brought up the satellite link and sent the command to connect to the laser transmitter that Joshua had pointed at their satellite. A few minutes later, two boxes came up on the screen.

> THIS HAD BETTER BE WORTH IT, I LOST SEVEN AIRCRAFT!

> I TOLD YOU TO BRING A LOT OF FIREPOWER.

> IT IS NOT MY FAULT YOU ONLY SENT EIGHT SMALL FLYERS.

DID MY PILOTS COMPLETE THE MISSION TO YOUR SATISFACTION? THE ONE SURVIVING PILOT BURIED FOUR MORE MISSILES IN THE DOWNED AIRCRAFT, THERE IS NOTHING LEFT LARGER THAN A DINNER PLATE.

YES, I WATCHED THE WHOLE THING, IT WAS HIGHLY ENTERTAINING.

GOOD, THEN WE HAVE A DEAL?

YES. IT WILL TAKE TWO WEEKS FOR ME TO SECURE MY POSITION, THEN WE WILL OPEN UP OFFICIAL COMMUNICATIONS AND MERGE OUR COMMUNITIES. AT THAT TIME, I WILL BE ABLE TO DELIVER WEALTH THAT WILL GIVE US THE ABILITY TO TAKE OVER ALL REMAINING COMMUNITIES IN A MATTER OF YEARS.

I LOOK FORWARD TO IT.

BY THE WAY, YOUR BROTHER WAS ON THAT AIRCRAFT. I FIGURED YOU SHOULD HEAR IT FROM ME FIRST.

There was a long hesitation.

GOOD. THAT ELIMINATES THE NEED TO DEAL WITH HIM IN THE FUTURE.

I WILL MAKE CONTACT IN TWO WEEKS.

He signed off and closed the link. Whistling to himself, he headed to the council chambers. He was going to be early, but he wanted some more alone time to reflect on his good fortune before he called in the council.

~~~~

The rail car was back four minutes after Theodore left. Tiny climbed aboard with Jack in tow, he still hadn't said a word.

When the rail car left the dock, Jack wiped the tears from his eyes. What he had seen on the monitors shook him up horribly, but he had to trust Marcus that it was all a ruse.

Just a short week ago he had come to terms with his rebirth based on what he saw with his own eyes. Now he had to tell himself that what he saw with his own eyes was an illusion, and it wasn't easy. The tears he had shed were very real, and it didn't take any effort for him to appear distraught, angry, afraid, and finally devastated. If every detail of what had just happened had not been laid out in the file Marcus had left him, he would be on that rescue transport himself, praying for a miracle.

Tiny and Chin didn't know the truth yet, and were probably devastated. He felt bad about this, but it was necessary. At least he could let Tiny in on it now that they were alone. He cleared his throat to get the big man's attention. "This may come as a shock, but Wendy and Marcus and the crew are all safe in S.C. What you saw there was very real, except for what you saw of Wendy. A computer was controlling the aircraft and created the illusion."

Tiny looked at him with tears in his eyes and said, "Jack, I think you're in shock. I'm so sorry about what just happened, but now is not the time to lose it, this setback could cost us everything and we need you functional. I can only imagine how devastating this is to you, but I know you have it in you to pull through."

Jack understood, if the roles were reversed he would think Tiny was delusional too. In fact, what they saw was so real that he wouldn't be completely at ease until he held Wendy in his arms again. "Tiny, I'm being serious; we planned this all in advance. Here." He gestured toward his datapad, which Tiny had brought with them. Tiny held it out and Jack punched the screen a few times then gestured for him to read.

Jack waited for him to finish before saying, "I need you to keep up the act, but after dropping me off in jail, I need you to go see Caleb immediately to plead my case. Don't let him know that what you saw wasn't real. Be sure to tell him that Theodore stood by and watched it happen without any action whatsoever. Relay the whole thing to him. Caleb should end up letting me out pending the election. When he gives the word, come get me and we will head back to the flight bay."

Tiny could only nod in acknowledgement. "Oh, and I need you to call Chin right away and tell him to check his messages, there are some instructions for him he needs to follow immediately. Make sure he doesn't read them with anyone around."

Tiny sniffled once and said, "God I hope you're right, Jack. I have never witnessed something that awful in my life. Is it safe to say Theodore is behind all this? He wouldn't lift a finger to help."

"I am pretty sure, but until we have proof, I can't make any kind of open accusation. Honestly, nothing he has done yet has shown anything other than a strong desire to become the next leader of New Hope. Perhaps some of Marcus' tricks will lead us to a definitive answer."

~~~~

Chin got the call from Tiny three minutes after the man had left. "I need to tell you something, privately. Are you alone?"

He simply nodded, still stunned. "You need to check your messages, and then do what it says. Keep it quiet." Tiny signed off without another word. Chin looked around to make sure nobody was near. The various people in the flight bay had retreated to deal with the tragedy in their own way. Some of them were grouped up and others were alone dealing with their grief. Every man here lost someone they knew in that attack.

He opened the message Jack had left, confused at what this was all about. He knew something was up, but figured that whatever Jack had been planning had gone horribly awry.

The message detailed out how the attack they witnessed was a sham, and instructed him to execute another command on the central computer. Although he refused to believe what he had seen with his own eyes was all an illusion, his loyalty to Jack was still unwavering. Without hesitation, he fired off the command and waited in stunned silence. The rescue aircraft called in to say they were en route, but he didn't notice. All he could think about was how they had watched helplessly as Wendy struggled to keep the aircraft from crashing. He hoped to God Jack was right about this. He watched the monitor, but unlike the program he ran earlier, nothing came up on his screen.

An hour later the rescue team reported they had found the wreckage, and it was a complete loss. Chin sat back in his chair. Whatever the program was looking for, it hadn't seemed to find anything.

~~~~

An hour after arriving at the chambers, Theodore called in Caleb, William, and Teague. The news had already spread about Marcus' death, and Theodore watched each man's face as they entered. Teague looked like he had been mourning. That was no surprise, they had been close, closer than Theodore had ever been to Marcus.

William looked irritated. Conventionally, he would have been handling the decision to send out forces against Cali during their attack on the large transport. Under normal circumstances, Theodore had stepped somewhat out of his boundaries, but he believed the results were worth it, and he knew how to handle William.

Caleb showed no emotion whatsoever. Caleb was the wild card. Had Theodore's plan this morning worked and they had called a vote right then and there to elect a new leader, William would have voted for him and Teague would have voted for Marcus, leaving Caleb. Caleb's weakness, as Theodore saw it, was that he was extremely protective of the people of New Hope. He acted as if that was his own asset. He wanted nothing to do with communities outside New Hope, and the thought of someone threatening the safety of his people was unbearable. Theodore believed that by laying the blame for all the recent deaths and failures at Jack's feet, Caleb would swing in his favor seeing Marcus as the bigger threat to New Hope. Marcus' play to have the people decide their next leader was masterful, but as destiny would have it, futile as well.

The men seated themselves around the circular table. Theodore was the first to speak, as he had called the meeting. "Gentlemen. As you are aware, a huge tragedy has befallen us this evening. Jack Taggart, showing poor judgment, sent another team to Saber Cusp in hopes of fixing the mess he had created last night. Somehow, he convinced Marcus to personally go in with the team, putting himself at risk. Unfortunately, there was a traitor in our population, and word got to Cali that Marcus was on that mission. They sent a large contingent of armed aircraft to intercept the large transport as it made its way back home. Aboard the transport were fourteen New Hope citizens, including Marcus. Wendy Roberts, one of our finest pilots, fought valiantly against the overwhelming odds. She managed to take out seven of the eight attackers before losing three of the four motors on the transport. She didn't survive the crash, although she struggled heroically, despite being mortally injured, to prevent it." He took a moment of silence, which each man in the room honored.

"Before we get down to business, I want to let you all know that I intend to exact a heavy toll on Cali for this horrible act. They will not only replace our lost transport and provide us with fourteen suitable replacements, they will also be forced to pay extra for their crime. I will guarantee, before any kind of peace accord is reached with them, that they will make this right with New Hope. You all know my feelings on this subject. I want to live in harmony with our neighbors, and do not, under any circumstances, want a war."

Caleb snorted at this. Theodore expected him to react that way. He ignored it.

William had held in his anger for too long, and took this opportunity to let it out. "Theodore, you have overstepped your position! Why wasn't I notified at the first sign of trouble?"

"William, I understand your anger, and apologize. I was asked by Jack to visit him in the flight bay moments before the attack. Jack contacted me because he believed the Cali were responsible for the loss of communications with our team. He expected me to contact Cali and plead with them to break off their attack. I determined that any sort of action, short of sending in a salvage team, was a waste of time and resources. If I had sent support aircraft, they would have been thirty minutes out when the transport went down. I never would have made contact with Cali in time to do anything, and even if I had, I couldn't exactly accuse them of being behind the attack, I had not been presented with any kind of evidence supporting Jack's theories. There was nothing to decide, William, or I surely would have contacted you."

William wasn't ready to let it go. "You still should have contacted me and allowed me to make that decision. It was not your right to make that decision in my place, even under the circumstances." The man was right, and Theodore acknowledged it. William had lost some of his steam, simply because his only course of action was to protest this to Marcus. Marcus wasn't here, however, and William knew his place. Theodore considered the matter closed and continued.

"The primary reason I gathered you all tonight was to discuss the grave matter of an interim replacement to Marcus, until the election in two weeks. I, having held the highest status next to Marcus, believe that I should act in that capacity. Is there any argument to the contrary?"

Teague held his tongue. The man knew his place in this room, and Theodore was counting on that. As long as the council ruled, he was just a pawn. Once he was the elected leader, he would dissolve the council anyway, removing any threat from Teague or the others.

Caleb leaned forward in his seat, looking grim. "Before we decide on an interim leader, I have information I need to bring to light. Shortly after Marcus and the team took off for Saber Cusp, I was sent evidence that implicated one of our own citizens of high treason. I reviewed the evidence, and determined that it was indeed authentic. The evidence consisted of a transcript of communication from a terminal in the records room, and a video feed from the security camera corresponding to the exact time of the transmission. The transcript clearly shows the traitor giving key tactical information to Cali, and also demanding they take all measures possible to destroy the transport upon its return. It also hints at a much larger conspiracy within New Hope. As head of internal security, I issued a warrant for the arrest of Red."

Theodore was taken off guard by the direction of his attack. *Did this mean the evidence somehow linked him to the attack? Did Red talk already?* Theodore suppressed the thread of fear winding its way through his gut. "I would like to see this man sentenced immediately, and put to death, as is the penalty for high treason. Shall we review the evidence right now?"

Caleb looked in annoyance at Theodore for the interruption. "Not yet, although if you had asked when Jack informed you of Red's arrest, I could have confirmed he was talking with Cali, and you could have made the attempt at a cease-fire." William slammed his fist down on the table, but didn't say anything.

Caleb continued. "Ten minutes ago, just before being called in here, I received a message from the computer system. Apparently, Marcus suspected there was a traitor, and had the foresight to install a new program before leaving on this mission. This program was executed upon the destruction of the aircraft with Marcus aboard. It reported to me, as head of security, any communications through our satellite. There was only one."

The blood drained from Theodore's face. *This can't be! How could Marcus foresee this and take action before he left? He had to do something.* "Before you continue, Caleb, I want to make it clear that I have already been in contact with Cali about this incident. I let them know that we will not stand for this…"

Caleb calmly punched a few buttons on the screen built into the table in front of him. Each display around the table lit up with the transcript of Theodore's communication with Cali. When it popped up on his screen, Theodore stopped talking and read it. *This looks bad, but maybe I can talk his way out of it.* "That is not the transcript of my communication with Cali! Someone is trying to make me look like a traitor! Who sent this to you?"

"I verified that the computer system sent it directly from the satellite down to my datapad, there was no interim party involved." Caleb's face went from grim to a look of amusement. "I was about to say that we don't know who sent this, but it was the only communication since Marcus' aircraft went down, and you just admitted that you were in contact with Cali." He looked around the room at the other two council members. "Is there anyone in this room, who upon reviewing the evidence before them and hearing the confession of Theodore Bishop, does not believe this man to be guilty of high treason?" William and Teague both held their tongues. "Then I pronounce you, Theodore Bishop, guilty of high treason. You will be detained in lockup until after the public election, at which time the elected leader of New Hope will determine your sentence."

"This is absurd! I am no traitor to New Hope! I am its savior! This community is in grave danger, and I was just doing what was necessary to secure its future! I refuse to recognize your authority to arrest me, let alone to judge me!" He stood up and walked to the door. He had to act fast to gather his loyal followers. If he could get a few minutes to work, he would have a team of armed men detain and silence the other members of the council.

The door opened and Theodore saw a ghost...

Chapter 40

Jack fidgeted as the aircraft landed in the flight bay. He held back long enough for the large propellers to stop turning, then sprinted to the cockpit door. Wendy climbed out and wrapped her arms around his neck. He held her close and sobbed. "Don't *ever* put me through that again."

Wendy didn't say anything, just held on tight.

He wiped the tears from his eyes and with Wendy in tow, walked around to the back where they had already opened the cargo door. He wasn't about to let go of her, at least not for a little while. Chuck, Thomas, and Marcus were standing there watching the rest of the crew prepare to remove the bulldozer from the cargo bay. Marcus looked at Jack and smiled. "How long has the council been in there?"

Jack glared at the man for a long second then smiled, shaking his head. "They just went in a few minutes ago. I have to be honest with you, I thought your plan had failed. That was perhaps the worst thing I have ever witnessed in my life. How did you do it?"

The engineers and other personnel who had been working in the flight bay had gathered, stunned at the miraculous appearance of both the aircraft and the crew they had just witnessed go down in flames. Seeing their friends, they flooded into the aircraft to greet them, and perhaps to check for themselves that they were all still alive and well.

Marcus looked at Wendy then shot a sidelong glance at Chuck and Thomas. He shrugged and watched the activity as the soldiers took a break from unloading the bulldozer to reassure the crew that everyone was OK. "As you can probably tell, this isn't the transport we left here with. There was some equipment I knew about in a storage facility. I used some old tricks to gain access to it, and while everyone else loaded the other transport, I got this one ready. I figured we wouldn't have time to get back here before the Cali arrived, so we sent the other transport without us."

Under any other circumstances, Jack would probably have been upset to learn that Marcus had held back information about Saber Cusp, but he was so elated to find everyone still alive he just couldn't lose his temper. That didn't mean he was going to let it go. "So... you had the equipment we needed all along?"

Marcus shook his head. "Not exactly, it was only possible to access this equipment from inside the command center in Saber Cusp, and I am perhaps the only person on earth who could have accessed it. Frankly, I would have left it there for its intended purpose if we hadn't needed a ride home. We easily located what we needed in the city, and if it weren't for the Cali, that would have sufficed." The offhand way in which Marcus explained it left him both curious and frustrated, but he sensed Marcus didn't want to elaborate.

He stepped closer to the man and said quietly, "I suppose you aren't planning on telling me the 'intended purpose'?"

Marcus smiled at the crowd and replied just as quietly, "Not until you are the elected leader of New Hope, and then – I *might*."

It was Jack's turn to shrug, he didn't really care about Marcus' secrets right now. "I know you used a computer to fly the aircraft and give us the illusion of Wendy in the cockpit, but how did you make it look so damn real? And how did you manage to shoot down seven of the eight attackers?!"

"When you have the most powerful computer in the world helping you out, you can do just about anything. The computer flew the aircraft, and she also made it look like Wendy was there, in the cockpit, when in fact she was safe with us at the command center. You are correct, though, it was very difficult to watch her die like that. I apologize for having to put you through it."

Something Marcus said stuck in Jack's mind, and he frowned. "Wait, you said 'she'. Who are you talking about? The computer?"

Marcus smiled. "I will tell you all about it another day, Jack. I thank you for trusting me through this. It was a big leap of faith for you, and I wasn't totally sure you would be able to do your part. I trust you had Chin run that last program?"

Jack nodded and said, "Yes, he ran it minutes after the aircraft went down. Did we get the evidence we needed to expose the traitor?"

Marcus shrugged, "I don't know. I had the data sent directly to Caleb so there would be no question it was authentic. Either Theodore is in there trying to take my job, or Caleb is arresting him for treason." He turned to the other men. "Anyone want to go find out?"

Chuck nodded and Tiny stood up from the seat next to Chin. The huge man was anxious to get his hands on Theodore. Jack let go of Wendy long enough to pat Marcus on the shoulder. "I think I'm going to let you guys handle this one. I'm just a guy running a simple operation here. I'll leave the politics to you, for now. I'll be in my room if anyone needs me."

Marcus nodded and headed to the rail car, Chuck and Tiny close behind. Jack called after them, "Tiny, I expect you'll be ready to go with your team by tomorrow morning?"

"Hell yes, Mad Dawg!" The reply was like thunder, echoing in the huge room.

"Good, we're heading to the Freezer tomorrow afternoon!"

Epilogue

Consciousness seeped into Jack's mind, and slowly he became aware of a soft light in the room. For a moment he was suspended part way between dreams and reality, but he was at ease in either place, and let himself just wake up. With one eye half open, he focused on the ceiling above him. He had learned to identify what apartment he was in by the color of the ceiling, it kept him from feeling disoriented. He smiled at the beige color, and reached over to Wendy's side of the bed, hoping to cuddle up and catch a little more sleep. He only found air.

That was a shame; he really enjoyed those extra few minutes when he got them. He closed his eyes anyway, comfortable enough to fall back asleep. He was pretty sure he had been dreaming about Wendy, reliving the night he told her he loved her. It seemed like a year ago, but in reality only a couple weeks had passed, and only a few weeks since he had been reborn. His eyes opened back up, today was the start of a new week, and it should prove to be another great day.

Pushing the covers off to the side, he slid his feet onto the floor. The chill of the cold concrete made him wince, and he probed the floor with his toes, looking for his slippers. When he couldn't locate them, he resigned himself to the cold and planted his feet with a grimace.

As he stretched, he heard the unmistakable clang of pans being moved around in the kitchen. He stood up and stretched again, then grabbed his robe. Some mornings she would be off to work long before he made it out of bed, and he was happy she was still home. While tying the belt around his waist, a scent made it to his nose that he hadn't smelled in what seemed like ages. *Bacon?* He had to investigate.

Wendy was standing in front of the small grill, four strips of bacon and two eggs, sizzling in the pan in front of her. He looked around, briefly wondering if he hadn't just fallen back asleep and was still dreaming. "Where the hell did you get that?"

She turned and smiled, "The group of farmers we picked up in Idaho last week had six pigs."

Jack frowned. "You didn't..."

"No, silly. They were pretty happy when they found out Farnak's clan was only a couple miles away, heading straight toward them. After we evacuated them, they gave me a whole pig and a bag of potatoes as a thank you for saving them. I took the pig to Bart's place in return for giving us the heads up on the farmers' location and the activities of his brother. He butchered it and gave me two pounds of bacon. Then, when we were in Deering the other day, I spent some time at their market and traded a little bacon and some potatoes for some corn and fresh eggs. I figured today was special enough to warrant a healthy breakfast."

"Well it smells wonderful." Jack put his arms around her and kissed her neck as she cooked. "Have I told you that I really love you?"

She smiled and leaned into his embrace. "What's not to love?"

He chuckled and kissed her neck again, then said, "I'm going to shower and get dressed."

"Okay, this'll be ready in a few more minutes, so don't take too long." He made his way to the bathroom.

As the hot water washed over his body, he reflected on the past two weeks. The Montana operation had gone off without a hitch. They had successfully harvested nearly fifteen hundred potential candidates from the Freezer, and gotten them safely into the new storage rooms. Cali had a few aircraft observing at the fringes of the sensor network, but after losing seven aircraft the day before, they were not willing to risk any more.

Red had talked when faced with the death penalty, and let Marcus know every detail of Theodore's plan. Red and his five men were all in jail with Theodore, awaiting an official trial, which is scheduled for after the election.

William surprised everyone by entering the race. He had a small loyal following, and started building steam right away. However, as soon as Marcus announced publicly that Jack was his choice for the new leader, it became obvious William would have little chance. With Theodore out of the running, Jack was relieved someone else was putting himself up as a candidate. He didn't want to win uncontested, and he suspected that William was actually in the race for that exact reason.

Once New Hope's wealth was secure, Marcus used the remaining two weeks of his reign to open relations with the other communities – with the exception of Cali, of course. It would be a while before Cali and New Hope were on speaking terms, let alone open to trading. Jack had met personally with two community leaders so far, and after the election, negotiations to cement their relationships would be a primary task. There was much work to do, and many challenges ahead, but right now, mere hours before the election, Jack felt very much at ease.

He was just about to get out of the shower when he heard an awful sound. He pulled the curtain back and there was Wendy, vomiting in the toilet. "My God! Are you okay?" He shut the shower off and wrapped a towel around his waist.

She stood up and wiped her mouth. "I don't know what that was all about. I ate a piece of bacon and a few seconds later I was rushing in here to puke!"

They both stood there for a moment, and a smile made its way to Jack's face, as the exact opposite made its way to Wendy's. "Honey, that's morning sickness. You know what that means?"

She had gone pale. "Yes, Goddammit! I know what it means." Jack knew she was happy deep down, but also that she wasn't looking forward to her life changing so dramatically.

He wrapped his arms around her and gave her a gentle hug, conscious now of the child growing inside her. "Wendy, you're going to make a great mom, trust me."

She returned the hug and now tears were flowing. She looked up at him and said, "I know, I'm just disappointed that I can't have any of the bacon. It was *so good*!"

~~~~

Later that evening, Jack sat in their new apartment. It was on the sixth level with the other former council member's private quarters. Wendy was in the kitchen, organizing and cleaning. Nobody had ever lived in this apartment before, and it was dusty. He had tried to get her to just sit with him, but she was restless, and he suspected her nesting instincts were kicking in.

The election had gone exactly as expected; in fact the celebration was still going on. They had a lot to celebrate, but Jack was exhausted, so he and Wendy had snuck out of the party and went to check out their new home.

The apartment was about as luxurious as you could get in an underground bunker. This one was designed for a family of six, with four total bedrooms. He looked forward to filling it.

Sipping a glass of wine, a gift from Marcus that had been waiting for them when they arrived at the new apartment, he picked up his diary and opened it to the last page. In the past two weeks he had taken the time to read whenever he got a chance, mostly when he was traveling.

The diary had detailed out his final year before dying. He was a little disappointed that he didn't remember meeting some of the people he talked about in the diary, but all in all, he was satisfied to know how he had lived his last year. He read the last page:

> A year ago I sat in my garage, reflecting on how my life seemed to always balance itself out. I recalled each difficult time in my life, and how it always led to something wonderful, hence the balance. There was one exception: the passing of my wife and daughter.
>
> Over the past year, I have often wondered if something really wonderful would happen to balance both the loss of my family and the cancer that is going to claim my life. I was never a very religious man, but I do believe in Heaven, and I truly hope that soon I will be able to rejoin my family there. I suppose if that is the case, I will no longer have to wonder. Before my diagnosis, I had nothing. This disease has brought me closer to Mabel, closer to my good friend Phil, and has added many wonderful people to my life who I never would have met otherwise. Soon I will get to be with my wife and

child again, and I can't think of a better gift. I finally have my balance.

This is the last page, and my story is at an end. The doctors tell me they have exhausted all their efforts, and the cancer is growing again. I've accepted that I only have a few more weeks on earth. However, I can't help but feel like I left something unfinished, and I wish I had a little more time to discover what it is. I don't know if I fulfilled my purpose on earth, but I believe I tried my best. Whatever my future holds, I only hope I can continue to make the most of it.

Jack set the book down. He had decided shortly after being reborn that while he shared the memories of his former self, he was not the same person. That person had died, and hopefully his soul was with his family now. He had a new family, a new life, and he felt he was now fulfilling the destiny that had eluded him in his former life. Whatever the case might be, he knew that the tragedies he had suffered had led him here, and that was a pretty wonderful thing. He set down the wine, got up, and walked to the kitchen to be with Wendy.

DRAMATIS PERSONAE

Jack Taggart	Main character of the story.
Bill Callun	Jack's doctor (1966)
Jennifer Taggart	Jack's Wife (Died, Jan 1964)
Allissa Mae Taggart	Jack's Daughter (Died, Jan 1964)
Mabel Williams	Jack's mother-in-law
Phil Norland	Jack's boss (1966)
Wendy Roberts	New Hope pilot/mechanic, reborn
Chuck	New Hope soldier, reborn, Friend of Jack
Emmet Johnson	New Hope soldier, reborn
Teague	New Hope doctor, member of council
Marcus	New Hope leader, head of council
Theodore Bishop	New Hope council member
Caleb	New Hope council member
William	New Hope council member
Heather	New Hope soldier, reborn
Thomas Parker	New Hope officer, reborn
Red	New Hope officer, native
Jessica Fironia	New Hope child, native
Ezekial "Tiny"	New Hope soldier, reborn
Frances "Chin"	New Hope soldier, native
Gabriel "Slick"	New Hope soldier, reborn
Cathy "Cat"	New Hope citizen, Chin's grandmother
Wayne	New Hope soldier, reborn
Gregory	New Hope soldier, reborn
Anton	New Hope soldier, reborn
Kenny	New Hope soldier, reborn
Jason	New Hope soldier, reborn
George	New Hope salvager, native
Nicholas "Nick"	New Hope maintenance
Bruce L. Kensington	New Hope soldier, reborn
Scott	New Hope Engineer, reborn
Joshua	Cali leader
Farnak	Mute clan leader (Northeast Idaho)
Bartholomew "Bart"	Mute outcast, Farnak's brother
Tanner	Mute general
Ungo	Mute soldier
Gratch	Mute soldier

ABOUT THE AUTHOR

David Kersten was born in Minnesota but spent most of his life in Montana. An IT Manager for his family's business, David enjoys just about anything having to do with technology. He also enjoys creating things, whether it involves writing fiction, writing software, woodworking, carpentry, or electronics. As an avid reader since the age of 11, one of his long term goals was to try his hand at writing, and as with everything, when he dove into it, he submerged himself for many months. Although he enjoys many different fiction genres, his first novel, "The Freezer", is set in his favorite genre, Post-Apocalyptic Fiction, and is a proud accomplishment for him.

When David isn't writing or working in his shop, he can be found spending time with his 3 children, sitting at a computer playing games, enjoying a good television show or movie, or out with friends at the bowling alley or favorite bar.

He intends to continue writing novels and is currently working on a sequel to his first book. If you have any questions or comments for David or would like to see a list of his other books, you can visit his website at www.davidakersten.com

ACKNOWLEDGMENTS

Throughout my life, many of the books I read influenced my own writing in some way. Although I know none of them personally, here are a few authors I wish to acknowledge as influences specific to this book.

First and foremost would be Larry Niven, whose books such as "Lucifer's Hammer" and "Footfall" (both of which he co-wrote with Jerry Pournelle) hooked me into both Science Fiction and the Post-Apocalyptic Fiction genre. But it was Mr. Niven's ability to use fictional technologies to build a realistic futuristic universe that truly captured my imagination. I borrowed on some of those technologies to create my own world, including his frictionless surfaces. In fact, I liked his frictionless toilets so much (from his book, The Mote in God's Eye) I had to use the idea. Mr. Niven may not be the sole inventor of believable futuristic technologies, but his books served as my earliest examples.

Another big influence came from author Stuart Woods, whose characters are fun to read, always get a lot of sex, and always come out on top, even if they don't come out completely unscathed. Because of his books, I wanted a hero who everyone wanted to be, or be with.

John Sandford's books taught me how much I like a character to be developed, even if that character gets killed right away. Little details about their personality are what make them real to me, and I tried to emulate that in my own characters.

Epic Fantasy authors like David Eddings, George R. R. Martin, Terry Goodkind, and Terry Brooks all got me hooked on stories that could just go on and on. Half the fun of writing a book is creating the world in which the stories take place. Without these authors as inspiration, my own world would have been a lot more boring.

No book would be complete without a shout out to the author's supporters, and for me that would be my family. My brother who got me started reading when I was 11 years old, my mother who I inherited my love of reading from, and all my family and friends who told me they loved my book, even if they maybe didn't. I couldn't have finished it without them.

50901324R00174

Made in the USA
Charleston, SC
10 January 2016